ENCHANTED
HILL

ENCHANTED HILL

EMILY BAIN MURPHY

UNION
SQUARE
& CO.

NEW YORK

UNION SQUARE & CO.

NEW YORK

UNION SQUARE & CO. and the distinctive Union Square & Co. logo are trademarks of Sterling Publishing Co., Inc.

Union Square & Co., LLC, is a subsidiary of Sterling Publishing Co., Inc.

© 2023 Emily Bain Murphy

ISBN 978-1-4549-4981-7 (print)
ISBN 978-1-4549-4982-4 (e-book)

Library of Congress Cataloging-in-Publication Data

Names: Murphy, Emily Bain, author.
Title: Enchanted hill / by Emily Bain Murphy.
Description: New York, New York : Union Square and Co., [2023] | Summary: "Two young people with an entangled history collide while both working undercover at a Hollywood tycoon's lush California estate"—Provided by publisher.
Identifiers: LCCN 2022060434 (print) | LCCN 2022060435 (ebook) | ISBN 9781454949817 (trade paperback) | ISBN 9781454949824 (epub)
Subjects: LCGFT: Novels.
Classification: LCC PS3613.U7285 E63 2023 (print) | LCC PS3613.U7285 (ebook) | DDC 813/.6—dc23/eng/20230105
LC record available at https://lccn.loc.gov/2022060434
LC ebook record available at https://lccn.loc.gov/2022060435

For information about custom editions, special sales, and premium purchases, please contact specialsales@unionsquareandco.com.

Printed in Canada

2 4 6 8 10 9 7 5 3

unionsquareandco.com

Cover design by Studio Gearbox
Cover photos by Miguel Sobreira/Trevillion and Roman Becker/Shutterstock.com
Interior design by Rich Hazelton

"Until the day when God shall deign to reveal the future to man, all human wisdom is summed up in these two words—'wait and hope.'"

–Alexandre Dumas,
The Count of Monte Cristo

For my parents

PROLOGUE

*T*he first time Cora McCavanagh saw the zebras grazing at the base of Byrd Castle, she told herself that they were a trick of the light, or perhaps her own eyes.

She had paused on the terrace of a mansion set atop the sloping Santa Lucia mountains and second-guessed herself. But there they were: a dazzle of black-and-white zebras, ambling free and uncaged in the lush mountain grass while the Pacific Ocean glittered behind them.

And unlike almost everything else at Byrd Castle, the zebras were exactly what they appeared to be.

Truman Byrd's famous guests often stood on the Castle's balconies, getting drunk on salt air and the scent of star jasmine as the sun caught in mosaics of cut-glass tiles beneath their feet. A visiting statesman once watched the horizon carve into the sunset like a knife and declared it paradise found—an enchanted hill.

But seeing those black-and-white stripes roaming amongst the waves reminded Cora less of paradise and more of the most infamous prison in America, Pelican Island. It was a thought that held no fear or revulsion in it. Instead, it sent an echo of longing through her.

It reminded her of home.

CHAPTER ONE

SUNDAY, APRIL 27, 1930
~ Day One ~

Long before Cora ever stepped foot onto Enchanted Hill, she knew it like the back of her hand. She had pored over the blueprints of Byrd Castle in her small, leaking New York City apartment six months earlier, the light flickering above her head, the winter draft slicing through the soft rotting wood of the windowsill. She had pulled her sweater around her shoulders and committed to memory the intricate honeycomb of passages, gardens, citrus orchards, glass-tiled pools, and guest houses—eighty-five rooms in the main house alone, set among mazes of boxed hedges and fountains hewn from white marble. The estate was designed by a woman architect, who took newspaper magnate Truman Byrd's ideas and spilled them first onto paper and then raised them to life. The realized dream perched on top of the cliffs, disappearing and reappearing in the ivory fog. The gardens smelled like hyacinth and orange blossoms during the spring months, and the parties built in size and clout as the days rolled toward May.

Cora had arrived on the Hill last November, and she had long since stopped sparing a glance for the zebras. Now she hurried along the hallways of the servant cottage, tying on her apron, donning a stark black-and-white uniform of her own. She loved the first morning light that spilled through the corridors, and the way the air was chilled with mist and ocean salt. A breeze rustled the palm fronds while the sky turned as orange and red as the insides of a pulped peach. She was tempted to stop and breathe it in. There were things about the Hill that she would miss. But Cora couldn't risk losing the one position she'd worked months to finally slide into.

Cora quickened her pace across the esplanade. The red Spanish tiles were laid out underfoot like checker pieces, spattered with the shadows of palm trees and the looming bell towers. The glass remnants of last night's party glittered in the sunlight beside discarded curls of lemon rind, and, just beyond, something dark fluttered in the bougainvillea. Cora paused to pull it free and examine it in the morning light.

It was a man's necktie.

"I control the guest list on Enchanted Hill," Truman Byrd always declared on the first nights of his parties, crooking a wide smile, "and Prohibition wasn't invited." He would stand, towering and formidable, at his customary spot next to the eight-foot fireplace, as Cora and the other maids distributed cocktails of elderflower sprigs and gin, or decanters of heady red wine pressed from his own grapevines—and just like that, the rules from the outside world simply evaporated. From the looks of it, the previous night's party had been no exception.

Cora tucked the necktie deep into her apron. She had gained a reputation for her uncanny knack of finding the owners of lost things.

"Cutting it close, Miss Duluth," Mrs. Macready barked when Cora stepped into the kitchen a minute later. She was buxom and meticulous, and she often reminded Cora of the warden's wife on Pelican Island, who kept a switch over every doorframe in her house so that she could easily take one to a wanton child's backside. As a girl, Cora had once told her to shut her clackbox, and when her father got wind of it, she had spent a week moving rocks from one side of the island to the other. Cora briefly wondered what Macready would do if she repeated that sentiment now. Instead, she kept her mouth shut and moved deeper into the bustling kitchen.

Dorothy, the cook, stood over two copper pots billowing white steam. Almost all the food at Byrd Castle was sourced fresh from the grounds—citrus plucked from branches just beyond the kitchen's windowpanes, breakfast eggs gathered when they were still warm. The poultry came from the ranch nestled at the bottom of the hill; the fresh, frothy milk from speckled dairy cows grazing among the zebras. Cora took her spot next to Dorothy, setting an herb omelet beside sourdough toast, two pats of fresh butter, and apricot jam, all served on a silver tray engraved with nightingales. Next went a sterling silver dome, a pot of coffee, and a glass of fresh orange juice choking in pulp, all topped with the morning's Byrd newspaper. Cora sneaked a glance at the front page.

CLEMENTINE GARVER STUNS IN NEW FILM, the headline said. The image next to it was of a striking woman, her dainty lips parted as if in surprise, her hair set in waves that swept along her cheekbones. The film *Perfume of Dusk*—bankrolled by Mr. Byrd's own production company—was due out the next month. Cora noted the date and felt a heaviness settle deep within her as she lifted the tray. Only a week remained for her to secure what she had come for.

Because her real employer was getting antsy.

Cora carried the tray out of the kitchen, across the marble foyer, and then up the grand front staircase. The hallways were dim, with unlit sconces dipped in bronze, and tapestries depicting musty scenes of archery and owls and unicorns with long, golden horns. Cora took pleasure in how the ice cubes barely grazed one another in the glass when she crested the third floor. She almost wished her father could see her, a thought she instantly banished as ridiculous. Did she really expect him to be impressed that she could hold a tray?

And why would it matter anyway, she asked herself. She wasn't six years old anymore, twirling and balancing on the rocky soil of Pelican Island, desperate for his attention. Perhaps she was still trying to make up for what happened all of those years ago, no matter how far she had tried to outrun it. She knew well the taste that regret left behind. Bitterness, without anything sweet to cut it. The dried track of salt down a cheek.

Cora paused just outside the Astral Bedroom and gathered herself. The faint scent of perfume wafted through the oak door, sweet like narcissus, with a note that lingered of biting spice. Cora knocked and pulled open the door.

Inside, the Astral Bedroom was a honeycomb box of teakwood and light. The sun carved through wooden panels that had been patterned after a Moroccan trellis. It shone through the walls in solid beams, turning the room inside a rich amber. A woman was lying in bed, draped in a silk crepe chemise the color of a robin's egg. She was lush and beautiful, with her pillowy lips and her hair honey in the sun.

The woman brushed her curls away from her face and looked at Cora expectantly. "Morning," she said breathily.

Of course her quarters were separate from Byrd's, for appearances' sake. He had a reputation to uphold, and an entire floor of the mansion to himself, stretching above their heads.

Cora glanced around the room for anything like a wayward tie or one of Byrd's monogrammed slippers, hearing her father in her ear all the while. *Weak evidence,* he'd huff in his strained voice. *And you know it.* His forehead would crease, his face settling into a pockmarked map. He seemed torn between his interest in the job Cora was doing and a concern for her safety.

He knew all too well what fits of jealousy, what sneaking around, what the hot fire of passion and rage could do, after working on a place like Pelican Island himself. He knew what dark and rustling things could be uncovered when you started turning over rocks—and what lengths people would go to in order to ensure they stayed hidden.

Cora cleared her throat. "Breakfast, miss?" she asked. She glanced up from the photograph of the starlet on the front page to see the woman in the flesh before her.

Clementine Garver.

Cora's mark, and the real reason she had come to Enchanted Hill.

CHAPTER TWO

Six months earlier, Cora had arrived at a penthouse in New York City on a day heavy with threatening snow. Gray sludge had settled along the street corners, sloshing up from the passing trolley wheels and streetcars; it clung to Cora's new leather pumps in wet grime.

High above the street, Mrs. Mabel Byrd blew delicate coils of smoke from the long end of her cigarette holder. Mabel Byrd was Truman Byrd's first, and current, wife.

At least on paper.

Cora rang the front bell wearing her smartest suit: charcoal tweed with a cinched waist, gloves, a cream flat-brimmed hat she had spent a week's salary on. Not that it mattered. Cora realized that it was like holding a candle to the sun as soon as she stepped into the massive foyer and was greeted by a doorman wearing shoes more expensive than hers. He pulled the golden elevator gate closed and they rode to the top floor. The moment he delivered her into the sitting room and announced her name, Cora noticed the remainder of someone else's chewing gum on the bottom of her pump.

"Miss McCavanagh." Mabel Byrd greeted Cora warmly, coming toward her as if welcoming an old friend for afternoon tea.

"Mrs. Byrd." Cora stole a sweeping glance around the room, her gaze a rake through silt, picking up details that she would clean off and examine later in the quiet of her room. She'd never seen such flagrant, unapologetic opulence before. The lush fabric of Mrs. Byrd's dress whispered its own language whenever she moved. There were clocks with bronzed swirls of Arabic; paintings thick with the texture of the original oils; tasseled curtains the width of a bound book.

Cora took a seat as the maid poured the tea, feeling a creeping sense of unease as Mabel made no pretense of examining her. Cora's dark auburn hair was pulled into a tight, imperfect chignon. Winter had made her skin pale, with shadows beneath her eyes and freckles that should have been masked by makeup.

As soon as the tea was poured and the maid left the room, Mabel Byrd's face sharpened. The warm welcome slid off like a second skin she could tuck into her pocket and wear as a mask.

"Everything we discuss here is to be kept in the strictest confidence," Mrs. Byrd said. Cora nodded.

The two women eyed one another from satin chairs patterned with chrysanthemums. Cora kept waiting for Mabel to reach for the minicakes set in tiers on a porcelain tray. She hadn't tasted a cake like that in years. They were smooth with pink fondant and dotted with immaculate little pearls, and they reminded Cora of ones from a bakery she used to visit with her mother. But Mabel didn't offer them, nor take one for herself.

Cora was tempted to break the silence, but she forced herself to wait. She sensed that the meeting would be a head game. She lived for those sorts of games.

And she almost always won them.

"I'd mind it less if it was a steady stream of them," Mabel eventually said. She nodded toward the paper, where Clementine Garver smiled coyly from the second page. "That tart is an open secret." Mabel took a long drag of her cigarillo, as if the smoke were filling an ache in her chest. Her eyes were cold and blue.

"But I need more than rumors and society gossip to grant me a divorce and ensure I retain the fair part of my fortune. I need proof. The sort I can bank on in court."

Cora took a sip of steaming tea and listened, watching as Mabel fought to keep her voice level, but her cheeks flushed with a telling spot of red. Cora had studied up on the Byrds before she came, taking crisp notes in her diary. Truman Byrd had married Mabel young, when she was some second-rate actress. She had been with him since the beginning, before the days when he launched the first Byrd paper. They watched it soar to heights unseen in the tabloid wars, with a few juicy, timely breaks at the beginning. Rumor had it that Truman Byrd wanted to one day enter politics himself. And having his pulse on the world, to sway thoughts like dams and change currents, could only help. They had wed twenty-five years ago. Now Mabel was nearing fifty, and Clementine appeared to be the understudy stepping into her role.

Cora reached into her handbag for a pen, hoping that Mabel wouldn't dangle the assignment in front of her and then leave it unoffered on the tray. Opportunities like the one she had hinted at on the telephone were rare. At least for a woman like Cora, trying to sow a name for herself in a field owned solely by men.

"Her birth name is something tacky and low class—*Judy Crump*. She came from a Florida swamp," Mabel said bitterly.

"So you are looking for . . . ?" Cora had asked, pen poised.

Mabel blew out a plume of smoke. "Someone to pose as a maid at Byrd Castle. Truman tends to have as many connections among the sordid set as he does with the privileged, so I need someone fresh, with no track record in this sort of thing. But you'll have to convince me to take that chance on you. So, tell me. What was it like," she said throatily, "growing up on that godforsaken island?"

Cora froze, and Mabel let out a small, dry laugh. "You think I don't have private investigators to look into my private investigators?"

The thought sent a chill down Cora's neck. She hadn't spoken of Pelican in years. People always wanted to know what it was like to be a young girl growing up at the most infamous prison in the country. Their eyes went wide when they learned that Cora's father had been stationed as head guard on the rocky island in the middle of the Bay where the only way off was by ferry—a ferry that sometimes came to port only once a day. Cora was used to the look of hunger that would come across a person's face as they waited for Cora to answer, imagining the horror of growing up so near to cutthroat murderers and thieves. They wanted to know if she ever saw acts of brutal violence, if she had grown up in the constant shadow of fear.

The truth was, though Cora had never admitted it to anyone, that some of them had terrified her. Like Samuel Mason. Everyone called him The Gasper. His eyes were wild, as if there were something soulless peering out from behind them. He'd been sent to Pelican after he lost a game of craps and stuck two forks through someone's pupils.

"My background at Pelican Island gave me the training to be a perfect fit for this job," Cora answered. She fixed her bright, hazel eyes on Mabel and did not blink. "I'm not easily intimidated."

"It's unusual," Mabel agreed, sitting back, "to find a woman willing to do a job of this nature." The ash trembled in a long, porous strip from her cigarette.

It was much more than that for Cora, though, and she prayed that her feelings of desperation didn't show. She had worn guilt and shame like a suit of armor, living beneath its weight for so long that she had given up all hope of escaping. But then one day it came to her. She couldn't spend her life merely working as a secretary or a shopgirl. She needed to bring about some sort of justice. It wouldn't undo the things she had done, but perhaps she could tip the scales by making other wrong things right. Unfortunately, the police force had found the idea of a female detective absurd, so Cora had been forced to strike out on her own—and her choice of assignments had swung on a pendulum between laughably impossible and morally unacceptable.

Her money and her hopes had been drying up, until Mabel's inquiry had come in.

And finally—for the first time ever—being a woman PI would work to Cora's advantage.

"Living in the house," Cora said, "I'd be allowed and expected to go where others normally don't."

"You would need to be the most discreet," Mabel said, tapping the ash away. "My personal maid would train you here for two weeks, and then I would arrange for one of my moles at the Castle to recommend you for a job. He'll ask it as a favor. For you to be near your ailing father, or something of that nature."

Cora shifted in her seat. She hadn't seen her father in years, and the thought sent a deep pang through her.

"You will sign whatever binding contracts and nondisclosures that my personal lawyer wishes you to sign. You will tell no one the true nature of your employment. Not a lover, not your closest bosom buddy, not your own mother."

"Good thing I don't have any of those," Cora said briskly, and Mabel nodded cruelly. Because thanks to her private investigator, of course she already knew that.

"You will have six months to get the evidence. Photographic. Uncompromising. You are permitted to take any means necessary. And then you will bring it directly to me. No photographs, no payout. But if you deliver. . . ." Mabel scribbled down a figure—and when Cora glimpsed it, her knees went weak.

"And in return, you will pass my name on to anyone else in your circle who might be able to use a private investigator," Cora countered.

Mabel smiled coldly. "You'll have to prove yourself first," she said, stubbing out the cigarette. "And Miss McCavanagh—I don't take kindly to disappointment."

Cora didn't pause to think about it. She signed her name to the papers then and there, and finally reached for one of the tiny, pearled cakes. The frangipane melted in her mouth as she rode the golden elevator back down.

Now, almost six months later, the faint ticking of a second hand was starting to buzz like a gnat in Cora's ear. She stood in the Astral Suite of Byrd Castle, running out of the time she needed to prove herself.

"Cream, miss?" she asked, but Clementine Garver didn't answer. She barely spared Cora a glance, and it struck Cora anew just how invisible her life had always been. Growing up amidst society's lowest degenerates and now with its highest elites—a hidden cog, functioning at the periphery.

She supposed that was actually what made private investigators good at what they did. Until the moment the switch turned, and they suddenly became the wrench that changed everything.

She watched the zebras over Clementine's shoulder, and she wondered whether Pelican or Byrd Castle was actually the more dangerous, in the end: when people who had nothing to lose—or everything to—gathered in a single, isolated place.

*   *   *

It wasn't until two hours later, when Cora and her roommate Daisy were tidying the guest cottages down the hill, that Cora remembered the necktie in her pocket.

"Whose is that?" Daisy asked, smoothing her blond hair back as Cora pulled out the tie and examined it. While Cora set aside her earnings each month, watching the creased envelope grow satisfyingly plumper, Daisy tucked hers into letters addressed to her sister Anette and baby niece Esther in Bismarck. She talked incessantly and saved all her sister's letters in a hat box that she kept on her nightstand. She liked to stay up late eating black licorice and smoking cigars in her pajamas, telling Cora stories about her childhood pet rooster, Poppy Clarence.

Despite Cora's best intentions, she had grown quite fond of Daisy.

"I'm not sure yet," Cora said. The tie was fine satin, dyed a deep violet, with a clean, intricate diamond pattern overlaid on top. When she brought the tie to her nose and caught a whiff of cologne, her heart dropped. Peppercorn and black currant.

It was the scent Bobby had always worn.

Daisy gave out a short laugh, showing the slight chip in her bottom tooth. "What? Does it smell rotten?" she asked. Occasionally, and only when Daisy was relaxed and off-guard, Cora could hear the Polish lilt beneath her syllables. It was one of the things that gave Cora begrudging respect for

Truman Byrd—that he would hire Irish and Polish, and he paid good wages. Ninety dollars a month, plus room and board.

"No," Cora said, running her thumb over the soft fabric. "It just reminds me of someone I once knew."

She'd received the letter from a mutual friend the day before she left for California. Robert Connelly—Bobby, *her* Bobby—was marrying someone else. The thought of him made her feel suddenly faint with unexpected grief. She remembered the way she had smelled her clothes after coming home from their early dates, filling her nose with the scent of him so that her heart and her hopes took flight. They had spent summers walking the avenues to window-shop for things they couldn't afford, lying on blankets in Central Park, reading mysteries, and eating crisp, cold grapes that tasted like candy. She loved his quick laugh, the way he could flip between accents as easily as a mimic. She could still feel the grained texture of the letter, the blue ink of her friend Theresa's secretary script. *Bobby and Helen are to be married in April.*

Perhaps by now they already were.

She had given him up because it had been the right thing to do. But she couldn't escape the vision she'd had for half a moment of a bouquet trailing with myrtle and lily of the valley while her father walked her down the aisle. Of finally letting even one person in the world know every part of her, every last, ugly secret.

But she had turned Bobby away and kept hold of it instead.

With that, she suddenly remembered the flash of purple tied around a neck last night. "This belongs to Mr. Cobb," she said.

"The aviation pioneer?" Daisy asked.

Cora nodded. "Here, why don't you hurry and return it to him before he leaves the Hill," she said. "I bet there'll be some money in it for you."

"No, Ella," Daisy said. "That money's yours. You're the one who found it."

Cora tossed the necktie at her. "Didn't I tell you? I'm an heiress. I just clean the jacks for fun. He's staying in the West Oak suite. Go, before he departs at noon."

Daisy wrinkled her nose at Cora in a look of gratitude, and grabbed the tie.

Cora was glad that it was gone, and that she couldn't smell the memory of Bobby Connelly anymore. Her chest felt empty, because she had loved him. But what had happened on Pelican Island all those years ago was the insistent tap on glass, the shadow that passed over every happy moment. Sometimes when Cora looked into Bobby's eyes, she saw the convict she had once befriended staring back at her. Taunting her. And then the guilt would come, as sure as the fog sweeping across the Bay. No one knew her darkest secret but the two of them—the convict, and her.

And now it was only her.

Because he had drowned off the coast of Pelican Island when she was fifteen years old. But not before he had betrayed her, and killed again.

CHAPTER THREE.

A t a quarter past ten o'clock in the morning, Truman Byrd sat at his mahogany desk with a cup of black coffee, a cherry iced pastry, and the day's array of papers. Two men sat across from him, each dressed sharply in suit and tie: Dallas Winston, his head of security, and Ronald Rutherford, his long-time friend and future campaign manager.

Ronald was drinking his standard grapefruit tonic water. He was freshly shaven, his shoes gleaming with polish.

"Truman, they've put a hit out on you," Ronald said with his typical bluntness. "Don't you think we should reconsider the social events?"

Truman grunted irritably and leaned back in his oversized chair. The beginnings of tomorrow's papers were already spread out in neat rows along the expansive floor. He had circulations in New York, Atlanta, Chicago, Boston, San Francisco, Pittsburgh, and Seattle; magazine titles like *Home and Housekeeping; The Nation; Engines*. He had a production company that made moving pictures and radio programs. But advertisers were fleeing *en masse* with every new bank that shuttered. Soon, running his information empire might even become a losing endeavor. It made him feel irritated, harkening back to the days when he was both penniless and powerless. But he wasn't either anymore, and so it was easier to fight the sudden urge to do something cruel.

He picked up the unlit cigar that rested along his crystal ashtray. Light flooded in from the windows, and he watched the animals grazing amidst a green swath of land that dipped down to the sea. He had seen the view in his mind before Florence had ever built it for him. Florence Abrams was his right-hand woman—a diminutive firecracker in a man's suit and a man's profession, and he trusted her more than most people he'd ever met.

If he could delegate his security to her, too, he would.

"Don't be absurd," Truman said. "Why did I hire the best security money can buy if Dallas can't handle this?"

"I appreciate the vote of confidence, sir," Dallas said. He was a young man with the sort of hulking size one didn't quite realize until standing next to him. There was a revolver concealed on his hip. "However, I think given the circumstances we should take every precaution. You do have visiting dignitaries this week, sir."

"Truman, we're talking about one hundred and seventy thousand acres of property to cover here. I don't think it's unwarranted to be concerned," Ronald continued.

"We'll guard the periphery of the immediate grounds, surrounding the house and the guest cottages," Dallas said. "Increased patrols."

"And all the staff have undergone strict background checks?" Ronald pressed.

Truman waved his cigar vaguely. "Yes."

"What of the guests?"

"I can assure you that almost all of them would heartily fail any sort of moral screening, but they've passed my own scrutiny," Truman said. "Do you trust my judgment?"

Dallas Winston shifted. "Our utmost priority is to keep you safe, Truman."

"I've hired you so that I don't have to think much about that, Dallas. As long as you do your job, it shouldn't be a problem."

Ronald sighed.

"I'll take care of it, Mr. Byrd," Dallas said.

"I expect you will," Truman said. He waved the man off with his cigar. Dallas obediently left the room, closing the door with a click behind him, and Truman felt the studied attention of his oldest friend.

"What did you do to provoke them now?" Ronald asked. He almost sounded amused.

"Where to start?" Truman asked. He glowered. "First, I sank their judge."

It was well known among those in the underground that a network of New York mafia families ruled the city. They put the politicians in place who would either ignore or actively cooperate with their massive, corrupt system. The Conti family had also issued a veiled ultimatum to the members of the press—play along, or else. Other newspapers had capitulated, but Truman hadn't blinked. A threat didn't make him cower, it made his blood beat hot in his ears, a gift from years of listening silently to his father suggest he barely deserved to bear his own name. "I don't like your tone," Truman had countered, and had effectively given the entire New York mob the finger by printing two damning pieces about their candidate in succession, followed by a fawning fluff piece about the opponent. Predictably, his politician, not theirs, had won the election.

Ronald picked up his drink. "That was months ago."

"True. But then I took out their Senate candidate." Truman couldn't have that popular senator possibly interfering with his own envisioned presidential run. So he had aggressively tanked him with some well-placed smear articles. He owned the largest-circulating paper in New York City, and he put it to good use.

The Contis had responded by sending him an envelope full of bullets last month.

And that's when he had let them know what he *really* had on them.

It was yet to be seen whether they were going to slink back to their hole or stop at nothing to get rid of him.

But Truman had his own way of doing things, his own moral code, and he wasn't about to let a man whose nickname was Five-Fingers Fitz put a damper on the life and freedom Byrd had spent decades building.

He turned his attention to Ronald. "Who knows, an attempted assassination could be just the thing to kick off a burgeoning political career."

Ronald groaned. They had been friends for almost a quarter century. Ronald was cut from the same cloth—a gambler, a go-getter, a ball-buster, a man harsh with ambition. They had met at a campaign rally for Charles Evans Hughes, blown it off, and met in the back to smoke cigars and talk politics, architecture, and horse racing. They ended up at a billiards hall, where Mabel had kept up with their shots of cheap liquor and still beaten Ronald in three straight games of darts. The three of them had drunkenly walked home, singing "The Mermaid's Song" at the top of their lungs.

Ronald was one of the only people who could still say whatever he wanted to Truman's face, and though he never wanted Ronald to know it, Truman was glad for that.

"Let's wait on the sympathetic assassination vote as a last resort, shall we?" Ronald said, reaching across the desk to tear a piece from Truman's pastry. "So we're in agreement? After this last hurrah, no more partying with starlets?"

Truman held his cigar up to his nose—fragrant with cherry and coffee—and didn't answer.

"It's time to buckle down and get serious," Ronald said. "The press could ruin your bid for election before it even got off the ground."

"I *am* the press," Truman snapped. "I've made certain that the Hill is like being sealed inside a damned envelope."

Truman had fought tooth and nail to get there. He had done unspeakable things, destroyed his marriage, and had no family to speak of, but he had scaled the dual jeweled peaks of Hollywood and the press. He had built the Byrd media company and his namesake newspaper empire from the ground up, which now functioned like a well-oiled network of train lines, carrying information all over the nation. And what was more powerful than controlling raw information—than shaping the narrative, deciding what was known and not and how it was presented? The nation's perceptions were shifted day by day by his stories, depending on what quotes were used or omitted, which page number a story appeared on, what size font its headline was given. Truman Byrd was elbow-deep in crafting and manipulating reality itself, and that was just the way he wanted it.

Ronald shrugged. "It's your choice, Truman. But you have to choose. If you want a higher office someday, you must keep a lower profile. Especially with Clem."

If he wanted. Truman felt the itch then, the one that tickled like his father's hot drunk breath whispering cruelly in his ear. Maybe it could never truly go away, now that his father was half-senile and barely able to even recognize his only remaining son. But even that miserable old bastard would have to acknowledge how wrong he'd been in the face of the office of senator, of the presidency, wouldn't he? Hell, Truman was running out of things to achieve.

Ronald drained his grapefruit tonic and winced at the tartness. "You've captivated the attention of a nation. You entertain them in the cinema, you tell them what to think over their morning coffee. Isn't that enough? You could divorce Mabel tomorrow, even marry Clementine if you want. Truman— maybe this is already the pinnacle. Maybe you're already there."

Truman glanced away. He saw a herd of horned elk grazing down the hill.

He saw Clementine, slipping the negligee strap down her smooth shoulder.

But there was still a hot, cruel breath in his ear that whispered *"more."*

*　　*　　*

"I have to say, it mollifies me when the weather's bad on a day someone horrid arrives," Cora said. She moved past Daisy to look out the window and down the vista, to where fog was gathering like a cloak.

"I hope this doesn't mean someone particularly awful is coming today," Daisy said, violently scrubbing the grout clean between the tiles. Cora pulled the glass windowpanes closed against the gray clouds threatening rain.

The week's new spate of party guests weren't scheduled to reach Enchanted Hill until three o'clock. Most would fly in Byrd's chartered puddle-jumpers to the dirt airstrip that had been carved beside a mountain a mile down the coast, or be met off their train in San Luis Obispo. Byrd's chauffeured car, a Rolls-Royce polished to a gleaming onyx, would then wind along the coastal highway and bring them up the hill on a switchback road that took ten minutes to crest. Antelopes, zebras, peacocks, and red deer grazed at the base, and the castle would grow steadily larger, the vegetation becoming lusher and more verdant, the higher the car climbed. By the time they stepped into the vast quarters of the main house, reality would have completely receded.

Cora touched the worry stone she kept in her pocket and tried to ignore the trickle of sweat that was dampening her starched uniform. It had taken her two months of work on the Hill to secure a strategic position cleaning the third floor, where the Astral Bedroom was located. Since then, Cora and Daisy had thrown jacks each morning to see who had to clean the lavatories. Cora felt a twinge of guilt that she had pretended to be hopeless at the beginning, and now won a carefully curated 62 percent of the time.

After all, she had come there to unearth Byrd bushwa. Just not that sort of it.

"What's today's question?" she asked.

Daisy dunked her sponge into a bucket of water. "Favorite game growing up?"

"Mancala," Cora said. It was one of the days when she could answer truthfully. "I used to play it with my father." She remembered the birchwood board, the way the smooth glass pieces felt like colored water droplets in her hands.

"Were you close to him?" Daisy asked, squeezing out her sponge.

Not as close as I wanted.

"Sure," Cora said.

Most of the personal anecdotes she'd told Daisy over the last six months were either fabricated completely, or shaded with enough additional color to make them barely belong to her anymore. Cora had even added a file to her diary for herself—to keep track of the embellished facts and memories she had spun, and to stop them from seeping in to alter any of her real ones.

"Mancala, huh? I never played that one. I liked Old Maid, growing up," Daisy said. "I suppose it was prophetic."

Cora whipped her with her towel. "Bli-mey!" she said, laughing. "You're what? All of twenty?"

"Twenty-one."

"Still practically a baby," Cora said. When she had been twenty-one, she had moved across the country to New York in a desperate bid to reinvent herself. For the first year, she had fashioned stories about her life, trying on new identities. She worked at a department store for money and stayed in a boarding house. She went dancing and flirted with sailors. She laughed. She made girlfriends named Helen and Theresa, and she tried to forget all about the convict who had ruined her life.

She had managed to become someone else for a while, but only in part. She knew loneliness well—it was a tattered blanket, letting in every nip and chill.

"And how old are you, then?" Daisy asked. She wrung the sponge in the bucket and turned to look at Cora expectantly.

"Closer to thirty than I wish," Cora said evasively. She pulled the jacks from her pocket. "Should we play for the lavs?"

In New York, she had no longer been the strange girl from the prison island. She had told acquaintances that she was from San Benito. She ran so hard from herself that for a brief time, it was enough. But at night, she would dream of red alarms blazing, of her father reaching for his gun, and would wake up in a cold sweat.

HEAD GUARD TERMINATED AFTER BLOODY ESCAPE, the papers had crowed. Cora's father had been a year away from his dream job as warden.

Cora handed the ball to Daisy. Those were the stories that she had kept from Daisy and from everyone else she'd ever met. She caught her reflection in the immense brass mirror as Daisy threw for the jacks. Her father's eyes, sharp and hazel, looked back. He had taught her how to disarm a man twice her size, how to duck out of meaty hands attempting to close around her neck. But she didn't know how to fight off this pernicious feeling of desperation. Her time was running out. Byrd was leaving on a trip after the week's final party, and by the time he returned Clementine was off to shoot her new film. Cora could hear her father's gruff voice in her head:

The first rule in work of this nature is if a job starts to go south, then you get out.

But Cora had inherited her father's eyes and his stubborn inability to follow his own advice.

"Horsefeathers," Daisy muttered under her breath as she missed the final two jacks. "I'm hopeless."

"You're getting better," Cora lied. Daisy threw her a look and went in search of the vinegar.

But then she stopped and peered out the window. "Are we expecting someone early today?"

Cora came to stand at her shoulder. The arrival of a new guest always brought Cora back to when the Pelican ferry transported a prisoner to the island. She would gather with the other guards' children and wives at the fence, her fingers curled around the tendrilled steel, and watch as the boat cut through the gray waves toward them. The guards would line up in their sharp gray uniforms, their batons at their hips, their arms behind their backs. Her father at the head of them.

"No," Cora said. "Not for two more hours, at least."

Yet there it was, undeniably: amidst the grazing zebras and mounting fog, a black automobile, moving toward them.

Cora felt her curiosity awaken. Few people possessed reputations large enough to precede them. After all, a soul had to have a certain amount of cachet to wind up on either Pelican or Enchanted Hill—and in both places, new arrivals always brought a certain sense of fascination.

Daisy whistled next to her. "Macready is going to cast a full-on kitten," she said as the carillon bells rang out the hour. "Wonder who's inside?"

Cora felt a prickling sense of foreboding as the car took the final switchback and the first drops of rain spattered the window glass.

CHAPTER FOUR

"You're early," the chauffeur said to Jack, glancing in the rearview mirror. He was a young man, polished in his black suit and brimmed hat.

Jack straightened his cuff links.

"I caught an earlier train," he said, flashing a wide smile. "Do you think Mr. Byrd will mind?"

The chauffeur coughed. "This your first trip to the Hill?"

"Is it that obvious?"

"Mr. Byrd doesn't like early."

Too late now, Jack thought darkly. He could hear a faint Mexican accent just beneath the chauffeur's English. For a moment, it made Jack think of an old friend, now long dead. He leaned forward, banishing that thought. "Is that—?" Jack craned his head as the car passed something by the side of the road. "Did I just see an ostrich?"

The driver just laughed. He wore impeccable white gloves. The automobile smelled new, like varnish and fresh leather.

Jack kept an easy smile on his face, but his stomach lurched as the car rounded a bend and he caught his first glimpse of Byrd Castle. It was perched high on the hill, with tall, thin palm trees shooting upward around it like sparklers.

How long had he fought for this chance? Jack concentrated on relaxing the joints of his fingers, the knots in his shoulder. He tried to look like a man who was merely there to enjoy a week of parties at the most coveted invite in the country. But beneath his pressed suit, his heart beat slick and hard.

"Best get your papers ready," the chauffeur said. "You won't be admitted to the house without them."

"Of course," Jack said. He reached into his leather bag for his identity papers and the invitation, its thick paper raised with embossing. "I'd imagine the security Mr. Byrd has in place is first-rate," he said carefully. He studied the chauffeur's face in the mirror. "Is this road the only way on or off the Hill, then?"

The chauffeur caught his eye. "It is."

Jack looked away and straightened his tie as the wind rippled through the espaliered trees. With a storm coming, the pine cones would be silently shifting, their scales tucking into themselves to hide.

Jack kept his expression neutral and his eyes out the window, looking for guards. For boundary fences and foot paths. For escape routes.

The Hill must have been able to see him coming, even though he was arriving hours ahead of schedule. The thought made him uneasy. He could already see two butlers gathering at the top of the drive, holding trays of drinks and refreshments. Sweat beaded beneath his tie as the car came closer to the security guards, who stood armed and waiting. The house was even more like a fortress than he'd expected. He cracked the joints in his hands one more time.

A sudden rap on the window made him jump.

"State your name," the first security guard barked through the window glass. The second had a list ready to double-check his identity.

"Pleased as punch," Jack Yates lied. He smiled. "The name's Everett Conner."

The chauffeur passed Jack's papers to the security team. They examined them for a long moment. Jack watched the roses tremble in the wind as they snaked around the bases of the palm trees and he hardly breathed. There was no turning back now.

Then the chauffeur opened the door for him and said: "Welcome to Byrd Castle."

*   *   *

Cora and Daisy dropped their dust cloths and moved to a better vantage point to watch the black car crest the hill. They pushed open the door to the loggia and stood on the mosaic tiles between potted palms as the car curved around the arcing drive and came to a stop at the base of the boxwood maze.

Daisy took a step closer, and in her face Cora saw the same flash of curious excitement that she felt. On their nights off, Cora and Daisy stayed up late, drinking cheap bottles of liquor pilfered from Byrd's hidden cellar and playing cards with a butler named Liam who was sweet on Daisy. Sometimes the chauffeur, Matias Rojas, joined them. Over a glass of bourbon, Liam had once told them a story about a certain rising star named Oliver Luck. "He drank one too many gin and tonics and swiped an ancient ceremonial headpiece from Byrd's library," Liam said, doling out the story like a hard candy.

"No!" Cora had said deliciously. She took a swig of wine and leaned forward.

"And then he wore it streaking through the Venetian fountain."

"No!" Cora had crowed, covering her face with her hand.

"Byrd watched the whole thing coolly, smoking on a long cigarette, never saying a word," Daisy said, jumping in to finish the story while Liam lit a cigar. "But after that night, Mr. Luck was moved farther and farther from the main house." It was one of Byrd's nonverbal cues, his little games—if a guest displeased him, their accommodations were downgraded, their views gradually shifting from the endless vista of ocean to the ridged mountains and then to the gardens overlooking the servant quarters, until the message was painfully clear.

"Did Oliver leave then?" Cora had asked. She felt the alcohol bloom in a flush across her cheeks.

"Yes," Daisy had said, "and he hasn't appeared in Byrd's films or papers since."

Cora peered over the esplanade. This new guest was already starting off on the wrong foot, because Truman Byrd didn't take kindly to being surprised. He had an almost tyrannical need for control. The entire estate was built to maximize it, designed with hidden doors and passageways so that he could come and go throughout the house in whatever manner he pleased—slipping in unnoticed, or commanding a dramatic entrance. Perhaps if the staff decided they liked this guest, they would try to cover for him and hide his early arrival.

Cora shifted the palm vase for a better look, and she and Daisy took turns peeking between the balustrades. Though Daisy was afraid of heights, her curiosity got the better of her.

"Can you see who it is?" Cora asked.

Daisy stood and bravely leaned over the balcony. "It's a man," she whispered. "I don't recognize him. He's never been here before."

Cora thought back to the notes she had scrupulously recorded in her diary. Only two guests had never been to the Hill. "It must be that Everett Conner, then, who Mr. Byrd recently met gambling—or that rising star."

"Beau Remington," Daisy sighed, leaning forward. "Who isn't coming, last I heard. Which means I'll never meet him—one declined invitation to the Hill, and he's good as dead to us."

Cora's curiosity heightened. The man who was arriving was the one who, despite all her research, she knew the least about. Everett Conner: a self-made man, some sort of cattle tycoon flush with new money, from Nevada. His face was turned away from her, and all Cora could glimpse was the back of his dark head, the sloping curve of his shoulders, the smart cut of his suit as his baggage was unloaded. He accepted a lemonade and commented on the hazy humidity, the darkening glass of the ocean, with the barest hint of a drawl. She remembered then—humble Midwest beginnings—like Byrd and his father. She could almost feel the ridged paper of her notes beneath her fingers. Byrd had met Conner last winter at a "trade conference"—code for high-stakes gambling—in Reno.

And then the man stepped forward.

He turned in profile, and Cora let out an inadvertent sound. It was the handsome cut of his nose. The dark eyebrows, which used to be lighter. She froze, certain that just like the zebras on that first day, her eyes were playing tricks on her.

But then he laughed, and the color drained from Cora's face. It was the very same laugh she still sometimes caught as an echo in her nightmares.

She saw her own girlish fingers, passing him a piece of her mother's freshly baked bread through the whorls of a barbed-wire fence. How her skin had brushed the sleeve of his chambray prison uniform.

All the blood rushed to Cora's head.

"Jack," she gasped to herself.

And the convict looked up.

CHAPTER FIVE

"Are you all right?" Daisy asked. "You just went whiter than this rag." Cora swayed, feeling the contents of her stomach threatening to come back up.

"Sit down," Daisy said, forcing her to the floor. Cora drew several deep breaths and concentrated on the cut tiles of the mosaic beneath her legs. They were a wash of colors, sea-glass green, aqua, cream, like the mancala pieces she used to cup in her hands. Daisy ran to get Cora a glass of water, and Cora gulped it down.

"I don't know what happened," she said. "I just felt faint all of a sudden."

"Here, let's get you back to the room," Daisy said, helping Cora to her feet. "You should lie down."

"No! I'm fine." Cora's heart was beating a cacophony. She was hallucinating. She was mistaken. It couldn't possibly have been him. "I mean—yes, I'll lie down. But I'm quite sure I can make it myself. Cover for me, just this once?" she asked. "I'll do the lavatory shifts for a week."

"Of course," Daisy started to say, her brow knit, but Cora had barely waited to hear her answer. She hurried down the grand staircase and across the marble foyer, still feeling as though her legs might buckle beneath her at any moment. Her heart was in her throat as she scanned the esplanade for the convict.

But the black car was gone, the esplanade clear. The butlers had already taken Jack to his room somewhere on the Hill.

31

Cora's fingers were trembling as she inserted the key into the lock of her own room. To think, that very morning she had been brimming with self-congratulation over holding a bloody tray.

She should go to Dallas Winston immediately, or possibly even Truman Byrd himself. If Jack Yates had arrived under an alias, they likely didn't know who he really was. He'd been merely seventeen when his mug shot was taken, and the copy that ran in the newspaper had been dim and grainy. He was fifteen years older now, his hair dyed dark—all but unrecognizable to anyone who didn't know him as well as she had. To anyone who hadn't seen him daily for two years on Pelican Island, and then in their nightmares ever after that.

Cora should call the police.

But she didn't. Instead, she headed to the closet that smelled of rich cedar. There was a safe hidden within it, and a black lacquer box secreted within that.

Part of her had always wondered if he had really drowned like they said. But he had never once tried to contact her. A wave of anger flooded through her now like a riptide, strong enough to pull her out to dark places. She felt as though she had been duped all over again.

She opened the box, removed the hollow book holding her Leica 35mm camera, and lifted out her diary. Its lined pages were ridged with the texture of her handwriting. At the back, several yellowing, folded newspaper articles were tucked inside.

The first article was from a crime solve Cora had played a hand in. With a bit of self-initiated detective work she had managed to track down the thief who had stolen a case of perfume from the department store where she was working as a clerk—and it was that article which had led Mabel Byrd to contact her in the first place. Folded behind it was her mother's death notice. *Alice McCavanagh, died 1920, after an illness.*

Cora pulled out the final article and came to what she was looking for.

The paper was worn—as thin and brittle as insect wings pinned under glass—and so creased that its folds could dissolve in her hands. It was the only article about Pelican that Cora had kept from the long, endless onslaught that followed the escape. And she had kept it because of the picture that ran with it—Jack's mug shot.

She took a sharp breath. She had to be absolutely certain.

Those very same eyes, staring soulfully at the camera. It was the same nose, though his hair was now longer, sleek and dark. There was no scar on his lip in the picture—the only shot of him that all the papers ran. That scar wouldn't come until later.

INFAMOUS YATES BROTHERS ESCAPE PELICAN, the headline screamed.

Cora closed her eyes. If she went to Dallas Winston now, that's when the questions would start. Questions she had no intentions of answering. Her own careful alias might unravel.

And what if Jack talked?

Bitterness surged within her again. Hadn't he already cost her enough?

She had carried the shameful secret for years, as carefully as a blade beneath her ribs. She would do anything to prevent other people finding out about what she had done.

Especially her father.

*   *   *

Cora's father had taken a job as guard when she was five years old, and they had moved to the narrow ridge of slate-and-rust-colored rock that rose up out of the Bay. She could barely remember life before Pelican Island. To her, and perhaps no one else, Pelican was beautiful. Cora's family lived with the other guards in converted military barracks that were turned into stucco cottages the color of taupe. They were actually quite cozy, especially when it rained.

She had curtains, and tea time. Her mother played the piano. A portrait of her grandmother hung on the wall.

But when ships passed, they kept a wary distance away, and Cora would watch the starkly curious faces of the passengers as they craned their necks toward the island. She saw the way they took in the chain-link fences, the cell house painted blinding white; the guard towers dotting along the perimeter, the water tower pitching its distended belly on stilted legs high overhead. But they never saw what Cora saw: the six other young families that lived there, or the way the wildflowers grew out of the rock—delicate Queen Anne's lace and bright orange poppies bursting from the ridges. The steep cliffs and seawalls where the Bay bashed against their sides like a lace veil some mornings and others, a foaming mouth.

She shared the tiny island with two hundred inmates, some of the worst criminals on earth, but they were separated across the fence and locked up behind bars. Two thirds of the island were strictly off-limits—but she knew the side that was hers like the back of her hand, the clefts and crevices and the civilian commissary with its wooden crates of tobacco, salted caramels, and powdered milk. There was a handball court, a quarry, a playground, even a small two-lane bowling alley. It didn't strike Cora as particularly odd that she lived on an island penitentiary until the year she turned twelve and realized that no classmate had ever accepted an invitation to come to the island. None of them had seen the inside of her bedroom, because their parents wouldn't entertain the idea of it, even after Cora's father ventured with her into the city, his gun and badges and hulking form on display for reassurance. Cora had overheard her friends talking about it one overcast March day, congregating and giggling while they drank their bottles of Coca-Cola beneath the school's awning.

It was the first time Cora had ever realized there was a difference between being in the shade and the shadows.

*   *   *

Cora examined every groove and angle of Jack's face in his old mug shot. High cheekbones, a cut jaw, hair that sideswept into his eyes. Fifteen years, she thought. Fifteen years since the day they had met for the first time. Jack and his brother Leo had been pulling weeds in the spindly garden just beyond the barbed-wire fence. Cora could hear them talking to each other. She had recently discovered a certain hidden spot on the eastern side of the island near the fence, where she could tuck herself into the ridge of a rock. It smelled like rotting seaweed but was delightfully cool, and she could stretch out her feet and lean her back against the wall. It felt like her own secret place, a virtual impossibility on a tiny island crawling with criminals and guards.

And it gave her a chance to spy on the inmates who were on outdoor duty.

She had climbed inside to read a book—her mother thought it was *Rebecca of Sunnybrook Farm*, but really it was *The Hound of the Baskervilles*— when she heard their thick Dorchester accents begin.

She had stopped to listen. A guard was patrolling the far end of the pitch. The watch tower was a box of blank glass above their heads.

"You know what they call this place?" Jack asked. He squinted into the waves, at the place where the sun turned them brilliant white and searing.

"Stop it, Jackie," Leo had said, adjusting the button of his work gloves with a deep-set weariness. "I don't care."

Leo launched a pebble into the foaming waves and then promptly picked up his gloves to weed somewhere else.

Jack had stayed, squinting up to feel the sun on his face, and Cora peeked out from the rock as he peeled off his stained work gloves. The skin on his hands was smooth, and she stole a glimpse of his tanned skin, his long, thin fingers. Cora's father always made certain that no large rocks remained on the prisoner side of the fence—none capable of being wielded to bash in a skull. The job of sorting the rocks sometimes fell to Cora when she was earning pocket money or being punished. When all the prisoners were locked safely inside their cells, she often collected the heavier stones to bring to the civilian side of the island or—when she was younger—to heave them off the cliff as though she were feeding her pet, the sea.

"Do you know why they call it Ratite Rock?" Jack had said again quietly. Cora's heart took off in a gallop when he cocked his head and glanced in her direction. He knew that she was there. She had frozen for a moment, and then she had moved infinitesimally, sending out a shower of pebbles down the cliff face. She glanced up at the blank windows of the guard tower, trying to gauge if anyone was watching.

Then she emerged from her hiding place and shook her head.

"Ratites are birds that don't fly," he had explained, his voice still low. He shrugged. "Ratite Rock. I guess because no one's ever going to leave here."

He said it so matter-of-factly that it made something in Cora sad. Like he had wrestled it and accepted that his fate was tied to a millstone, only this one sat on the surface of the sea instead of sinking to the bottom. *Ratite Rock.* Cora knew how badly all the rest of them wanted off of it, but she would have lived on Pelican Island all her life, if she could.

"Oh," she said. "Ratite Rock. I get it." She had stolen a glance at his eyes. Gray and piercing, like silver. Jack was the youngest prisoner on the island, and she was drawn to him that day, with his hair the color of wet sand, tinting a little bit red in the sun. He was skinny, with high cheekbones and long arms that made him look gangly. He didn't have the haunted look in his eyes, like most of them, or the pulling, vapid presence that Gasper did. He looked hungry and young and alive.

She knew good and well the horror of what he had done. He and his brother Leo had stolen priceless art from a Boston museum to sell on the black market, Rembrandts and Vermeers—cut them right out of their frames with a razor blade, the papers said—and brutally murdered two guards who tried to get in their way.

BUTCHERY AT THE BASTION, the papers had shrieked. The papers covered the trial in every salacious, gory detail. Eyewitnesses testified that they had seen three masked men enter the museum. Two of those men were Jack and Leo Yates, who were apprehended inside, still standing over the guards as they lay dying. The guards' blood was found on their clothing, their skin. Beneath their fingernails.

But they must have had an accomplice, who managed to squirrel away the paintings in a large briefcase and—perhaps—even on his person, beneath a coat or cloak. The rain washed away his footprints, and he vanished, along with the art, like mist. None of the paintings was ever found.

So the Yates brothers came to Pelican—maybe for life.

And at that point, Jack Yates still had a lot of life left.

"What's your name?" he had asked.

She bit her lip. "Cora," she said, the wind blowing her hair into a ratty mess. The scent of flowers and brackish seaweed that carried on it were like smelling salts, strong enough to be a warning. To remind her of sense. She thought of this man killing a guard in cold blood. A guard who was just there, doing his job.

A guard like her father.

Over the years, Cora had wished a thousand times that she could go back to that day and erase it. The first pebble, starting a coming avalanche.

She folded the newspaper down its crease, cutting Jack's face in half.

CHAPTER SIX

J ack followed the butlers as they descended down a flight of tile stairs, opening their umbrellas over his head like flowering tulips. He looked around, gathering his bearings. A series of cream-colored guest houses with Spanish tiled roofs were scattered down the hillside, and the air around them smelled like rain and honeysuckle. The porter led Jack to one nestled in between a landscaped grove of cypress trees and palms, flush with a wall of creeping bougainvillea. Jack clutched the glass of mint lemonade in his hand as the porter deposited his luggage in a large room on the second floor with expansive views of the sea. With a grimace of apology, he gestured toward Jack's luggage.

"I'll need to perform a quick search, sir."

Jack took a long sip of his lemonade and drawled as casually as he could, "Go ahead."

The porter clicked open the luggage and felt through Jack's clothes with gloved hands, checking for weapons and secret compartments. Jack stood in the center of the room and turned. The room was well-appointed and flush with windows, and one wall led out onto a tiled loggia. There was an elaborately carved oak bed and matching wardrobe, and a worn Oriental rug over marbled floors. The ceiling was coffered in an interlaid pattern of hexagons, stars, and suns. He eyed the painting on the wall, a dark still life of fruit, then stepped into the private bath and ran his hand over the smooth skin of his jaw, examining himself in the mirror. He'd dyed his hair freshly dark again the day before, and it no longer caught him off-guard when he saw his reflection. He'd done it for so long that it was now a part of him. One more false element of who he had become.

"Thank you," the porter said, clicking the suitcase shut. "Please dress and join Mr. Byrd in the Assembly Room at 5 o'clock sharp."

Jack tried to slip him a tip, which the porter soundly refused. Jack shut the door behind him and exhaled.

He unlocked the glass doors and stepped out onto the loggia, breathing in the rain-tinged air. The overhang was a Venetian-style colonnade that protected him from the elements. He had heard from his source that there was a careful hierarchy to the rooms. The more Byrd liked a guest, the closer his or her quarters approached Byrd's in the main house. Each room had a nickname—the Sanctuary, the Venetian, the Meadow, based on the delicate masterpieces painted on each ceiling. Rumor had it that whenever the prime minister of Britain visited, Byrd set up oil tubes and an easel on his balcony so that he could paint landscapes and smoke cigars in his bathrobe. And the crown jewel, the Astral Room, was where Miss Garver always stayed.

Jack turned back to his room. He had grown up in the Catholic Church, and his gilded, formal suite reminded him a little of that. He had once loved the earthy, sweet smell of incense. The way his soul used to feel when the hymns started and human voices turned to bells. He used to picture it almost turning colors, like the sun shining through the stained-glass windows. Even as a child, he had loved being part of something that had gone on for thousands of years before him and would then continue on, cresting like a wave long after his own life was done.

He hadn't set foot in a church since being sent to Pelican, and he would hate to see what color his soul was now.

Jack methodically unpacked his clothes, then showered, shaved, and dressed. It had been thirteen years, and he still never took the private shower for granted, the ability to hold a razor blade. He had once lived in a nine-by-five cell, able to stretch and touch the span of both damp walls. He watched his hands now in the mirror as he tied his tie, then tied it again. Part of this wouldn't be hard. The part where he told the truth about where his fortune had come from. Luckily, no one ever cared about what you did or who you were before you had money. He had been able to avoid any outright lies when he met Byrd playing cards at a high-end gambling den in Reno. Their meeting there wasn't by happenstance, of course. Nothing was.

He split open a new deck of cards and shuffled them in a waterfall. He thought of his brother, Leo. His mother, Althea. The mosaic ceiling in the church of his youth, flashing gold with light. The way his mother used to quietly cry with joy over the music.

He thought of three different men as they had died in front of him, his hands covered in their blood.

Then he went over the blueprints of Enchanted Hill in his head one more time, and let the cards fall in an effortless arc.

∗   ∗   ∗

Clementine slid the party dress over her body, feeling the satin caress her skin like chilled water. The rain was lessening, the clouds clearing off. Through the carved wooden openings of the Astral bedroom, she watched the stream of new guests arriving.

"You look lovely," Truman said, leaning against the doorframe. He'd ordered the dress she was poured into, its satin the exact shade of the lemon rinds that would soon be curled around the rims of the party drink glasses. Clementine was glittering. Her earrings swung like miniature chandeliers.

She fit a bejeweled headpiece into her honeyed hair, a swollen jewel resting on her forehead, remembering as she often did how, when she'd first met Truman Byrd, she couldn't even afford a bottle of perfume. She had gone out and picked violets herself and crushed them against her wrists and her neck for her first film premiere. She was an up-and-coming actress, and, at the party afterward, Truman had sidled up to her and told her she was like lightning on the screen.

"I'm flying tonight," she'd admitted, soaked through with champagne and the feeling that she had caught a drift and nothing could stop her rise. "I suppose a Byrd must know what that feels like."

He'd smiled, and she hadn't known it, but she'd stumbled upon one of his favorite things—plays on words.

"That scent you're wearing," he'd said, sipping from the crystal tumbler in his hand. "It's alluring. What is it called?"

"Do you like it?" she'd said. She'd raised her wrist to her nose and breathed in. "I picked it myself." He had mistaken her refusal to give him a straight answer as a flirtation. She had picked up on that and leaned into it. She wasn't much for books, but she had a quick, sharp wit she'd inherited from her grandmother Tallulah, and she learned soon enough what an appetite Truman Byrd had for games.

The more complicated and higher the stakes, the better.

"Ronald is worried," he told her now, coming to stand next to her. He kissed her neck. Reached up to touch the pulse beneath the skin of her jaw, and she closed her eyes.

"So we have to be extra careful?" she asked throatily.

He nodded against her hair. "Which makes me want you even more."

She took a deep breath. "Truman. Aren't you nervous about the rumors of the mafia hit?"

"No," he said immediately. His voice was hard, but not afraid. He ran his hands down her shoulders, the dip of her clavicle. The hit was just another high-stakes game he expected to win.

Truman and his games. Sometimes she wondered if he wouldn't divorce his wife because he just wanted to keep both her and Clementine guessing and vulnerable. To play with Clem's mind, to keep the power balance in his favor. To see how much she would put up with, and for how long, before she would try to walk away.

She touched the jewel on her forehead and kissed him deeply, then turned and left him wanting more, always more, by walking to the bathroom vanity. Two years ago, he had cast her in a bit part in one of his films; and by the second one, when she had a more starring role, their affair had begun.

Now it felt like so long ago, but at first she hadn't been certain where the line was—was there any part of her that was attracted to the man Truman was, or was it entirely his fortune, his unquestionable power over her career? And if she ever wanted to succeed, did she even have a choice in the matter of attraction? She didn't waste much time thinking about that. She pushed down those sorts of questions and watched Truman in the mirror's reflection as she spread blush across the ridge of her cheekbones. Somewhere in the last two years, part of her had grown to care for him. He snored. He liked luxuriously soft cashmere socks and occasionally cooking himself a little snack in the kitchen. He liked music and art, and he was so much wiser and more cultured than she was. She wasn't very educated but she was quick enough, a little feisty, and she knew he liked that. It kept him on his toes.

So she kept herself sharp and witty, laughed easily, and measured her waist every morning. He could be like a little boy sometimes, with his love of train cars, and costumes, and animals. And he could be as cruel as a little boy, too. His words were like cut stones: glittering, small, and lethally precise.

They went right for the jugular when you least expected it. From the snippets she'd heard, he had inherited that gift from his father.

Yet she liked to feel the rise of his chest and the soft whistle of his breath when he fell asleep beside her, until she woke him and he traipsed up the back stairway to his own room. Sometimes she wondered if he had come to love her, the way she sometimes wondered if she had come to love him.

"You look delicious," he said from the doorway.

She blew him a kiss, and he disappeared, leaving a wafting scent of cedar behind him.

She examined herself one more time in the mirror. Three other starlets were arriving that night. She was excited to see Rita, whom she actually considered a friend. But she wished the others weren't coming, never quite sure if Truman was planning to wear her for a season like a coat. It was true that he seemed more interested in keeping up with the latest in politics and news rather than trying out the latest in fashions, or in women.

But perhaps his first wife thought the same thing.

For now—Clementine daintily applied a set of false lashes—he kept putting her in his pictures and the Astral suite where, under Truman's touch, even sunlight turned into bars of gold.

She smoothed the yellow satin of the dress against her body. At some point later that night, she and Byrd would make the party rounds together, ostensibly as a star and her producer. But for now she knew the rules. She would enter the party without his company. She would keep a distance, careful to never quite touch him, secretly wondering all along if the game Byrd was playing was her.

She had long left the violets behind her. She spritzed a cut-glass bottle of Guerlain Shalimar Eau de Parfum on her wrists and walked down the staircase alone.

CHAPTER SEVEN

When the carillon bells rang across the esplanade at five o'clock, the party was set to begin.

Cora's heartbeat was a quick, light thing, pulsing in her ears as she changed into her evening serving uniform and followed Daisy to the house for their last-minute briefing. They knew from their dossiers that rail tycoon William Morton liked ice-cold lime juice sweetened with honey and served in a chilled bottle with salt along the rim. When the President's press secretary came to visit, he enjoyed first editions of classic novels, particularly those by Jules Verne, and Byrd always made sure to stock the man's room with them before he arrived. Byrd was observant and meticulous when it came to his guests. He would make for a good PI, Cora thought. Which meant that she had to be an even better one.

Daisy slid closer to Cora. "What's he doing here?" she whispered under her breath.

They were gathered in the billiards room, adjacent to the Assembly Room. The time was generally used by Macready, the head housekeeper, and Mr. Rather, the head of staff, to remind them of specific guests' preferences. Instead, the man standing in front of them was the head of security, Dallas Winston. He was an imposing man dressed in a three-piece vested suit the color of smoke. He had close-cropped blond hair and eyes sharp enough to peel the skin from fruit.

"As I would suspect you are all aware by now, specific threats have been made with regard to the well-being of Mr. Byrd," Mr. Winston said. His gaze sifted through them, one by one. Cora's senses were unbearably heightened; otherwise, she might not have noticed the way that Liam took a step toward Daisy; the way her hand subtly found his in the shadows before dropping to her side again. "You are the eyes and ears of this estate," Winston continued, "and we are on higher alert than normal. You will report anything at all unusual. It is not your job to assess the danger or importance of a thing. No matter how small, you will find me directly and report it."

A trickle of sweat made its way down Cora's chest as she nodded her assent and began to circulate through the room with trays of aperitifs. She could stay on the fringes of the crowd in the Assembly Room and still follow the orchestrated schedule. Dinner would be held from seven to half past eight o'clock in the dining room, with films and a newsreel shown in the private theatre in the evenings, and alcohol flowing freely until the moon began to set and the guests were half-boiled from the gin. The party would begin without Byrd's presence; he would appear suddenly through the hidden door next to the fireplace like an apparition.

She stole a glance around the room, looking for Jack, but he hadn't yet arrived. This was a man who had gotten through life with skin under his fingernails. He was the only one who knew her true identity—the only one who could unveil her two biggest secrets, and in one fell swoop destroy her past and her future. She moved through the periphery of the room with her tray of appetizers and cocktails and thought of the alarms that had blared that night on Pelican. Of the sick feeling in the pit of her stomach. Of the look in her father's eyes—as if he knew what she had done.

"Drink, sir?" Cora asked the man to her right. It was Simon Leit, the tennis champion. The guests were beginning to gather in the Assembly

Room, mingling in their silk dresses and formal dinner jackets beneath vaulted ceilings. The walls, paneled in dark walnut, made the room's immensity still somehow feel intimate. Cora eyed the grand fireplace set at the room's center. It was seven feet wide and tall enough to stand inside of, its stonework pared into life-sized herons, lions, and birds of paradise. And to the right of it, invisible unless one knew just where to look, was a door. There was a symmetry carved into the mantel, and only the sharpest of eyes would notice that a space remained to the right where a heron should go. It was where Mr. Byrd himself liked to perch instead. It was a little visual puzzle, and a hint that a visit to Enchanted Hill entailed more than just a week of parties—it was an invitation into a game of luxury, loose rules, and wit.

Cora kept her face relaxed and smiling, but her eyes sharp. The room's outer windows were thrown open onto the loggia, and a breeze sent a tremor through the pink roses that cloaked the bases of the palm trees. It carried the scent of golden chickens roasting on the spit for dinner, hollandaise sauce, and buttery puff pastry. The energy on the hill had ticked steadily upward now that the guests had arrived, and Cora marked each guest off on a mental list as she passed by them with her tray.

Theodore Gilham, the portly governor of California.

William Morton, the railway tycoon, wearing a bow tie and holding his chilled bottle of lime juice.

Albert "Berty" Boyle, a diminutive man with a small mustache, was a behind-the-scenes producer, beloved in Hollywood for the three surprise hit musicals he'd bankrolled. He was rather less well known for his ties to the drug-trafficking ring that Cora's father investigated five years ago near Santa Barbara. The story, predictably, had been buried. And now that Cora had seen how close Berty and Byrd were, she no longer wondered at why.

Cora approached the cluster of starlets and offered them drinks. Each declined the food, except for Lola Iris, famous tragedienne, who reached for the heartiest scallop wrapped in bacon. Cora instantly took a liking to her.

"I'll have one of those, though," Rita Blanchard said, gesturing toward Cora's array of drinks. Rita was impossibly beautiful, the kind of woman one couldn't help stealing glances at. She had enormous blue eyes that turned down at the edges so that she would almost look melancholy, except for the thousand-watt smile that was quick on her lips. She was one of the highest paid actresses in the world. To the side of her was Kitty Ryan, perpetually cast on the silver screen as an ingénue. She slid a maraschino cherry into her mouth from the end of a toothpick. The three starlets swirled around Clementine in their silks, all glowing skin, white teeth, excitement, and sexuality. Clementine was lit up, laughing, the jewel gleaming amber on her forehead. The other three were beautiful, but Clementine had a charisma that was weighted with a mass all its own. Judy Crump or not, from a Florida swamp or not, the room was drawn to her, and she owned it. Cora could see why Truman had wanted her for his own.

And then a man stepped across the threshold into the Assembly Room dressed in a debonair suit; and when the light fell onto his face, Cora instantly stilled.

It was Jack.

He was still hauntingly familiar to her, even wearing more than a decade of extra years. He was clean-shaven, because any stubble would give away the fact that he dyed his hair. She could see the same soft indentation he had across his upper lip. The scar he'd gotten from the time he had faced off against Gasper.

But his eyes were darker than she remembered. She watched them sweep the room, turning his head in the direction of the card game. She saw the slightest tensing in his spine when someone hollered and threw their cards across the table.

The very way he moved was the same.

It was definitely him.

She could still remember the way he looked when the sun turned the rock face of Pelican golden, pulling the prickly strands of crabgrass and weeds from the scarps. The way he had turned to her, squinting through the fence, and asked: "Cora, do you have a favorite flower?"

She had traced the grit of the sandstone she was sitting on with her fingers, felt the craggy rock beneath the thin cotton of her dress.

"I like black-eyed Susans best," she said after thinking for a moment. "Because they attract dragonflies."

"Dragonflies?" he had asked. He'd given an almost comic shiver. "I don't like the whirring sound they make. Like a fly crossed with a bat."

"They are not!" she had said. "They look like flying rainbows."

He had laughed, and warmth had bloomed in her chest at the sound of it. He had been such a perfectionist, noticing every little weed, prattling on to the guards about fertilizer and deadheading, growing on terms that bordered on friendly with them. They let him be the official gardener into the late fall. Gave him kitchen scraps and even dirty bathwater for composting so the flowers practically burst from the rock.

Cora had seen, with her own eyes, how good he was at winning their trust.

Yet she hadn't realized until too late that he had been doing the same thing to her.

Her grip tightened on the tray. She stole through the shadows now, watching him with a growing dread.

The castle was on high alert for someone who could slip inside its defenses on behalf of the mob. Someone aiming to kill Truman Byrd. Cora's stomach turned.

Surely all the guests were thoroughly searched before they set foot on the property, she told herself. But her hands were shaking so much that she sloshed a bit of the pitcher's contents onto the floor. She wiped another trickle of sweat from her brow. She should turn Jack in right then and there, her own consequences be damned.

And yet she didn't.

She would do almost anything to prevent her secret from coming to light.

Even, she was discovering, if it meant risking another man's life just to save her own skin.

*   *   *

Jack was standing in the breeze of the opened window, eating a shrimp-and-cucumber canape, when a walnut panel in the wall next to the fireplace began to silently slide open. Jack stole a calculated look around him. He was the only one who seemed to notice when Truman stepped into the vast room, closed the door behind him, and clapped his hands.

The guests turned with delighted gasps.

"Welcome!" Truman said, raising a martini glass with a yellow curl of citrus rind. "I propose a toast—to all of you, and to a week of events that begins now, the likes of which none of us are soon to forget."

The room exploded in cheers and raucous applause.

Jack smiled and took a pretend sip of his drink. He gripped the tumbler in his hand. He had waited for this moment for so long.

Three of the male guests were playing cards on an oak table. Two women he recognized from the silver screen were draped over their chairs. The table top was scattered with cards that appeared to be from Byrd's custom deck. They were filigreed with gold leaf and featured different suits of birds. Quails for queens, peacocks for kings. Jack's fingers itched to hold those cards himself, but he waited. Took out a cigar and lit it, letting the smoke waft toward the opened window as he observed.

It was almost jarring, how removed the Hill felt from the rest of the world. It had risen above the clouds like a golden tower, absent the raw desperation that coated the people below it like grime. Over the years spent in back-room dens and high-stakes poker tables, Jack had learned to recognize the aura of money. The guests who came from old money had a cloying sense of assurance, of immovability, an iron horse with its hooves staked down through a marble pillar. As for those with new money—the rising starlets like Clementine, the freshly made oil barons—they had a dizzying sort of electric energy that rose like fumes from their skin. At first, Jack had mistaken it for charisma or luck. But he saw it now for what it was: someone walking a tightrope, giddy and on top of the world, knowing that any moment they could fall with the slightest misstep. Or the slightest push.

And with the economy collapsing, and the stain spreading out from Black Thursday so banks were folding faster than houses of cards, it was a longer way to fall than ever.

"Everett Conner!" Truman Byrd suddenly boomed. He moved toward Jack, but his face was devoid of humor. Jack watched him approach, the expression on his face inscrutable. He felt a surge of nerves.

"Truman," Jack said, extending his hand. "Good to see you again." As Truman's hand closed around his, he did not flinch. He kept his mind clear of what he had come there to do, so that not even a hint of it could be read on his face.

"You were early today," Truman said. He took a long drag of his cigar and fixed Jack with an intense gaze. "Took us all by a bit of surprise."

Jack smiled and felt the trickle of sweat down his back. "I guess my anticipation got the better of me," he said. He raised his hands in surrender. "Ever since our time in Reno, I've been itching for a rematch."

Truman studied him for a long moment.

"You're a damn good card player," he said gruffly. His face suddenly broke into a grin. "I've got some people for you to beat." He clapped Jack on the back, and Jack leaned forward to mask his relief.

"Please tell me one of these rooms has a roulette machine made from solid gold in it," he said conspiratorially.

"The real kick," Truman said, with a sharp wink, "is that you have to find it first. Now, let me introduce you around."

He started with Governor Gilham. "Gilly, this is Everett Conner. We met last year in Nevada. Best chap at craps I've ever seen. I brought him up on the Hill almost solely for your entertainment."

Jack nodded. "Nice to make your acquaintance, Governor."

"Call me Ted, here. Please. I like to be on a first-name basis with someone before I take their money." He laughed riotously, and Jack stole a quick glance at the paintings hanging on the wall behind the governor's head. He calculated their size and weight, almost as a compulsion.

He couldn't help himself.

"Everett, is it?" Clementine Garver's voice rang out like bells behind him. Jack recognized her instantly from the film *The Man from the Docks*. Beyond her was Lola Iris, a woman he had seen only in magazines. Part of him never truly believed they were real until they were there standing in front of him, close enough to touch. They smelled like narcissus and rainwater.

"Miss Garver," he said, giving her a slight bow. "I fear to find that somehow you're even more charming than I had imagined."

"I'm always delighted to best an imagination," she said with a lovely smile. It widened with a touch of wickedness. "A rather intimate accomplishment, I would think." She leaned forward almost imperceptibly. "Have you met my dear friend Rita?"

"I haven't had the pleasure," Jack said. He tried to keep his eyes from straying to the large jewel on Clementine's forehead.

"You're the card player who Truman keeps raving about," Rita said, studying him over the rim of her glass.

"Yes, he says you're unbeatable," Clementine said. "A master of your craft."

"Cards are little more than luck," Jack said, raising his own glass to his lips. "The deck's the real master. I'm just its obliging servant."

"I'm sure it's a mix of being dealt a good hand and bringing two of your own to the table," Rita said, tilting her head.

Kitty Ryan bit her lip. "Yes, I've often found that good hands have quite a lot to do with getting lucky."

Jack gave them a knowing grin. The starlets laughed in delight and sauntered away.

Ronald Rutherford, Byrd's long-time friend and adviser, puffed on a cigar. He made a singular round of the room, shaking hands with all the men, and then stepped back into the shadows alongside the head of security. The two of them stood together, making conversation—but really, Jack could tell, they were watching every move. Their eyes missed nothing. He would have to be exceedingly careful around those two.

Jack wondered what Leo would think if he could see this. He thought of his older brother squeezing his eyes tight, playing the violin. Then of the cold, black water of the Bay.

Of the guard, looking up at them in terror. Choking on his own blood. Jack turned away.

Out of the corner of his eye, one of the maids walked past him, her head down.

Something stirred in him when she passed. A flicker of something familiar, something buried from long ago. *It can't be*, he thought to himself.

It was just his conscience, rising up to play tricks on him at the most inconvenient times. The maid reminded him of that young girl, with the auburn hair and the bright, gold-ringed eyes. The picture of innocence somehow blooming right in the midst of Pelican. She used to venture out of the guard cottages with a ribbon in her hair, and she reminded him of his younger cousins—a deep breath of pure air. He would talk to her through the fence. It was the only true kindness he remembered from over the better part of two years.

"Did you sing at Christmas?" he had once asked the girl. It was tradition, on Christmas night, that the families of the guards would sing carols first at the warden's house, and then to the prisoners. She had given a shy nod with that sharp chin of hers, and he remembered how cold his fingers were as they twined around the wire fence. He had spoken so quietly, he wasn't even sure that she'd heard: "Thank you. Hearing those songs was the first time I have felt like myself again."

It had reminded him of church. Of the golden mosaics. Of his mother, singing next to him.

He would see a flash of the girl's face sometimes, in a store window. Someone walking down that dusty little street in Bakersfield. On a train in Albuquerque. The underground bar in Reno. It was never really her. Just a wisp, a figment, his own guilty conscience.

He raised his drink to his lips, pretended to drink it, and put that impossible thought out of his mind.

*   *   *

After dinner, Cora wound her way through the mild evening air. Shadows swept across the esplanade like silk, and the orbed lampposts were lit in a circle of white moons. Down on the lower veranda, a live band was tuning. For once, Cora was glad to see the night guardsmen strolling the grounds.

The moon hung low and bright in the sky, and Cora was careful to keep her face always turned away from the light. She glanced over suddenly at the sound of Clementine's delighted laugh. Jack was at her elbow. His face was cut with angles, a sharp jaw and cheekbones, and he looked debonair even among the film stars in his white-tie tailcoat evening wear. She still remembered the battle she had fought with herself the day after they had first met. She had gone back and forth between fear and curiosity, and curiosity won out. The first encounter had been an accident. A mistake. The second one was deliberate.

She had found a marigold that he had tied with a short, frayed piece of twine along the barbed-wire fence. As though it had been left for her. She had carefully unraveled it and taken it home. Tucked it into her copy of *The Hound of the Baskervilles*.

No one had ever given her a flower before. Not even her father.

How stupidly easy it had been.

"You ever had Moxie, Cora?" Jack asked the next day, when she went out to the fence. He said it as if they were already old friends.

She paused. "No," she said. "My mother doesn't buy it."

"Well. It tastes a bit like molasses and old cigarettes that have been doused together in kerosene."

"Can't wait to try it now."

He had laughed, as if she had surprised him. "It's god-awful. But it reminds me of home." He had been so disarming as he talked to her while he weeded—how he missed salted potato chips and his mother's lemon pie. "Tart enough to make your mouth pucker, with cream as cool as a cloud on top." He had closed his eyes and she still remembered the look of wistfulness and bliss on his face, the way he swallowed, as if his mouth was actually watering.

She wondered, looking back, if the seeds of his plan had already taken root in his mind by then.

Cora shivered now as a cold wind blew through the ivy wall behind her, raking it like fingers. Some of the guests had retired inside to sit by the large fireplace for dessert. Clementine and Rita moved to sit near the water's edge of the Neptune Pool, gossiping and dipping their feet in where the waves caught the light. The candles burned low until it was just Jack and Truman sitting together, playing cards with William Morton.

"Rich blood," Morton muttered good-naturedly, playfully throwing his chips on the table and pulling himself to his feet. The fountain burbled hypnotically beside the card table, and Jack leaned back in his chair, looking relaxed. The servants offered him a new glass of whiskey on the rocks with Welsh rarebit, one of Truman's favorite late-night snacks. Cora could smell the melted cheese soaked in cherry brandy, the nutty scent of the cigars. It mixed with the fragrant bougainvillea that carried through the wind. They were a long way from Moxie now.

She watched from the shadows as Jack dealt another hand. He had grown into his cheekbones and jaw, and his lashes were long. He still had the same whirl of cowlick behind his right ear that his fingers used to glance upon when he was troubled by something, but today he folded and flipped the cards like streams of water, quick and certain, and she didn't let her focus stray from his hands. Her nerves were on edge because he and Truman were together, alone. She thought of her gun, hidden in the wall of her room.

She knew all too well what Jack was capable of.

She just didn't know what she was.

*   *   *

Jack looked at Truman Byrd sitting across the table from him and casually reached for the deck of cards. He was acutely aware of Byrd's nearness. The scent of him, mingling with the cigars and the whiskey. The blue veins snaking at the man's temples.

"Another hand?" Jack asked.

Truman studied him, and Jack forced himself to look back.

"You remind me a little of someone," Byrd said.

Jack took out his lighter slowly and flicked it on. Leaned forward and lifted it to the end of Byrd's cigar. He watched the pulse beating in the artery in Byrd's neck.

"I get that a lot," Jack said. He lifted his glass nonchalantly and felt the whiskey hit the back of his throat for the first time. The night he'd approached Truman in Reno, he'd waited until Truman was three drinks in. He'd sweated through the shirt beneath his jacket when he pulled up a chair at the card table, wondering if Truman would recognize him. It was true, Truman Byrd had not been the one to toss him on Pelican and throw away the key. But he had played a part in Jack's downfall all the same.

Byrd breathed in the smell of the cigar, a smile crossing his face. "Ah," he said. "This is the good stuff." There were small burst blood vessels in his eyes, and Jack wondered if he ever slept.

Jack remembered the look of utter horror on his father's face when his two sons were sentenced to life on Pelican for murder. It was the last time Jack ever saw him.

Jack still dreamed some nights of the maniacal laughter that went through Pelican Cell Block D when the lights went out. He thought of the day he came up behind the Gasper, his rage building, hitting him in the face and how good it felt. He had once cut off a man's fingers and hardly flinched. He could feel the temptation of it rising up in him again now. A thirst. An almost-unstoppable desire.

"Sure," Truman said. "One more hand."

Jack took the two-dollar cigar that Byrd offered him between his fingers. "Thank you," he said, nodding, raising it in a half salute.

Jack drank another sip of his drink and then played the winning card. Byrd took one look at it and threw back his head to laugh, exposing his jugular. Jack's muscles tensed. He knew there were guards lurking close by. He had to bide his time, get the information he needed, or it would have all been for nothing. He forced himself to breathe. To think clearly. To wait.

Byrd settled back in his chair, at ease and seemingly delighted that Jack had bested him, and Jack wondered at a man who could laugh at his own losses.

"All right, one more," Truman said cheerily, waving at Jack to deal again. Sucking in his cigar. Oblivious to the temptations running through Jack's mind.

Jack broke into a cold sweat and dealt a final hand. He purposefully threw the game, gave the win to Truman Byrd. To keep Truman's spirits high and unsuspecting.

And just to prove that he could.

*   *   *

Cora wove down to the esplanade and sneaked bites of leftover food from the trays: puff pastry, figs with bacon. Caviar with crème fraiche. She let the butter and salt melt in her mouth, then took a swig of a drink for herself as she watched Jack from the shadows.

She had once believed with all her heart that he was innocent.

Cora's mother had forbidden her from knowing the details of the inmates' crimes, but of course Cora had researched all of them and discovered exactly what crimes they'd committed to get sent there. She never romanticized the grotesque things they had done. But even as a child, she was fascinated by human beings, their makeup and motives, their characters and the points where they boiled and broke. She wanted to understand why people did what they did—especially when they were grown up and should have known better.

Cora took another swig of a drink.

She still remembered the day she had invited her school friends to her house for birthday cake and to listen to records. She was turning fifteen; and for the first time, two of her girlfriends had been granted permission. Her father was to come to the mainland on the ferry and accompany them all there and back. Cora's mother was making a cake for them with flowers and candy buttons. And then Cora had made her fatal mistake.

She'd worn a new blouse to school, one that didn't keep her dog tag secured well enough. Its sleek, embossed silver slipped out from behind the fabric at her neck during recess.

"What's that?" Lira Sutton had asked, head cocking. Reaching to touch it.

"It's nothing," Cora said, fumbling to tuck it out of sight.

"It's a dog tag," Molly Wright said. Her eyes gleamed.

"A dog tag!" Lira had exclaimed. "Whatever for?"

"*All* the Pelican children have to wear them," Molly said, whose mother was the principal's secretary. "The school administrators said so."

"Why?"

Cora had shoved the chain down, her face heating. Molly's mother had made her decline the invitation.

"In case someone connected to an inmate tries to kidnap one of them, of course," Molly said, her voice lowering. "You know. For a hostage exchange."

"Oh," Lira had said uncertainly. She took a step back.

When Cora's father came to meet her on the ferry that afternoon, Cora was alone.

"Where are your friends?" he asked, looking behind her.

"Sick," she said curtly. And then she'd turned her face away from him and refused to say another word.

"Caught you," a female voice said behind her now.

Lola swayed, the sequins on her dress catching the light. She tittered a little. "Shh," she said, winking, "I won't tell. But I'll take one more of those, before you go." Lola raised a half-empty glass in her hand as if to "cheers" Cora. "What's in this, by the way?" she asked, with an almost astonished delight. "I'm absolutely zozzled."

Then she laughed and abruptly let go of her glass, as if she were suddenly too bothered to hold on to it any longer. Cora jumped when it exploded in glass fireworks at her feet.

Instinctively, without thinking, Cora did the one thing she should not.

She looked across the esplanade at the same moment Jack glanced toward her.

For one split second, their eyes met.

Cora swore and dropped down as quickly as she could, hiding behind her hair. She pulled a frond from a nearby palm and used it to protect her hand from the glass.

Jack's face had remained blank when their eyes met, not betraying even a flicker of surprise.

Cora forced herself to bide her time, waiting a full two minutes on her timepiece before she stole another look at Jack. He hadn't moved, and he wasn't looking in her direction anymore.

He hadn't recognized her.

It was dark, she told herself. And she had hidden her face in time.

She stood, the glass glinting in her hands, her heart pounding slick and hard.

She was almost completely certain.

*   *   *

On her fifteenth birthday, Cora had eaten cake with her parents alone, a record playing quietly in the background to fill in the silence. Then she had slipped out the back door and gone to the fence to see Jack.

"Happy birthday," Jack had said, and fallen silent when the tears had unexpectedly began to spill down her cheeks. He artfully ignored them and instead showed her the packets in his hands.

It took her a moment to realize what she was looking at: they were seeds.

For hundreds of black-eyed Susans.

"I persuaded the guards to let me plant them here, right along the fence," he said. He had smiled at her. "So the dragonflies would come."

CHAPTER EIGHT

PELICAN ISLAND, 1915

"They don't look like murderers," Cora said. She cocked her head, examining the front of the paper at Tito's corner store. She and Dina each had an ice cream—vanilla with nuts for Cora, peppermint for Dina—while they waited for the ferry to take them back to Pelican after school. They had recently become something close to friends. Before that, Dina had thought Cora was babyish and Cora thought Dina was stuck up. But Cora realized that she would never have to explain to Dina about the dog tags, or the way the city lights winked at Pelican through the morning fog as the Bay turned a hundred different shades of blue. So a tentative friendship had formed while they waited for the ferry, and on juicy news days, they ordered a single scoop of ice cream each and pooled their money for an additional bottle of pop and an illicit tabloid. The ice cream left a thin film of white on Cora's upper lip.

"Most murderers don't look like murderers," Dina said, licking melted ice cream from her fingers.

"The Gasper does."

"Gasper does," Dina agreed.

They sat down on the side stoop at Tito's and cracked open the bottle of pop before the ferry came to take them back to Pelican. They took turns sipping it and looking at the newspaper.

"Hurry up," Dina said, tapping her foot on the pavement. She bummed a cigarette from a passing teenage boy and lit it while Cora surveyed the pictures.

BUTCHERY AT THE BASTION!

EXCLUSIVE PHOTOGRAPHS! the page shouted.

The carbon image that accompanied the article was dark and gritty; but if Cora squinted, she could make out a wall where a painting had been carved clean out. She could see knife gashes in the satin damask wall behind the empty picture frame. In the bottom right of the photograph was a leg, splayed awkward and lifeless on the floor. The angle of it made Cora's ice cream taste too sweet.

> *Mar 24—BOSTON—A theft at the Dolores Williams Bastion Museum occurred just after ten o'clock last night. By 10:23 PM, blood ran red in the prestigious museum—and five pieces of priceless art had vanished.*
>
> *Early eyewitness reports place at least three masked thieves at the scene of the crime. The suspects used razor blades to butcher the art masterpieces straight from their frames, and then brutally dispatched two guards who got in their way.*
>
> *Two suspects were apprehended at the scene, but their accomplice—or accomplices—escaped!*

"'Five irreplaceable masterpieces in total are currently missing,'" Dina read breathlessly over Cora's shoulder. "'The Bastion reports that the pieces taken were two Vermeers, two Rembrandts, and a Renoir. Their joint value is estimated at close to a million dollars.'"

She whistled.

"Here," Cora said, handing over the paper. Cora waved her hand in front of her face and scooted away so that her father wouldn't smell the smoke on her.

"They're kind of handsome," Dina said, inhaling, studying the picture.

Cora wrinkled her nose. "They're *murderers*."

Dina shrugged. "Doesn't mean they're not handsome."

Cora studied the picture once more as the ferry whistle sounded. "They won't come to Pelican." She licked the last of her ice cream, pushing it down into the hollow cone with her tongue. "They're too young."

Dina stubbed out her cigarette. "Just because they're young doesn't mean they don't have to pay for what they did."

* * *

Three months later, Jack and Leo Yates arrived on the same ferry Cora rode to school each day, only it was outfitted with a black flag that meant prisoners were aboard. They were already dressed in chambray, their hands cuffed behind their backs. They looked different from their mug shots—even younger in the flesh. The older one looked sick, almost as if he were frightened. It was hard to imagine either of them being a murderer. But Dina was right. Murderers and monsters wore normal human masks. It wasn't what they looked like that made the difference.

It was what they did in the dark of the night, when they thought they could get away with it.

Cora and Dina watched through the fence. The crowd that gathered to watch them was a larger crew than usual, because the crime was so infamous, the boys so young, and there were two of them. Brothers. Cora stood next to the Johnson baby in a pram, who had almost no hair and crystal blue eyes that peered out from behind the fence. Even Cora's mother came. She usually never did. And her mother's silent, weighty presence suddenly made Cora feel as though she were watching something shameful that she shouldn't be.

It took seventy-five guards and personnel to run the prison, and a third of them lined up to meet the disembarking prisoners, including the island's chaplain who always smelled like peppermint. He came out to watch grimly. There were two new tattered souls in his care.

Cora's mother took her hand as the brothers stepped onto the island. The older Yates brother looked up to where they were standing and said something in surprise, and Guard Johnson swiftly rapped him on the wrist with his baton. Beside Cora, her mother flinched.

She dropped Cora's hand. "They aren't animals," she said softly. Then she turned away, as if she had seen enough.

Leo kept his head down after that, and Cora had shifted to watching his brother. Jack Yates had a slight cowlick. He followed behind his brother; but instead of shuffling with his head lowered, he turned and looked at all of them.

"That one's going to be trouble," Dina whispered next to her. "Mark my words."

Cora felt a strange, electric crackle inside her when she met Jack's gaze. She was struck most of all by the fiery look in his eyes, because it wasn't hateful, defeated, or full of fear like his brother's.

It was just defiant.

CHAPTER NINE

MONDAY, APRIL 28, 1930
~ Day Two ~

In the morning, Truman Byrd looked across the massive expanse of his desk and studied the woman sitting in front of him.

There were three women in Truman Byrd's life who he had ever truly loved. The first had been his mother, Rose Byrd. The second, before it turned ugly and warped, had been Mabel. And the third was the diminutive architect sitting in his office, Florence Abrams. She was smoking a cigarette and watching him with her odd little bemused look, the one she seemed to give him more often than not. Florence was the architect whose steel-reinforced buildings withstood earthquakes that otherwise flattened entire blocks, and therefore she was the one he awarded the contract for Enchanted Hill—female architect be damned, and a Jewish lesbian to boot. They argued about structures and materials and silhouettes, sometimes raising their voices at each other in a near-feverish pitch. He secretly loved the times when Florence got worked up enough to bring her petite frame up on her tiptoes, trying to shout in his face. They had created the Castle together—their minds coming together over many intimate sessions to conceive and birth it. The result was a brilliant partnership, in which Florence showed a steady, tolerant amusement of him and his whims.

She studied him now across the desk, wearing a smart navy pantsuit, her hair cut in a sharp bob. Florence took a drag off her cigarette and pushed aside her breakfast tea. "Am I here for a new project, or a revision?"

"Come, now, you know the Castle will never truly be finished. It's like a garden; an ongoing, living thing."

"So a revision, then."

"I want to talk about an expansion to the outdoor pool. It feels cramped at times."

She snorted. "*Cramped.* Truman, you're patently ridiculous."

They glared at each other over the desk. Florence had once argued with him about the materials for the Hill's cornices for the length of two months. She had not yelled. Instead, she had calmly taken her plans for teakwood and limestone and hammered them to his front door with a stake, then driven off without another word. The castle had ended up with teakwood cornices over-taking the white limestone below like a cresting wave, just like she wanted. And he'd be damned if they weren't the prettiest thing he ever saw.

She had designed, hand-painted, and glazed the tiles for the stairs of the esplanade herself. Overseen their implementation, setting them like jewels into the wet clay. The Castle was their shared love. It had become their own never-ending puzzle to solve. And despite the way her eyes rolled with each new project, they also lit with the challenge, and he knew how she secretly loved it.

She pulled out a graphite pencil and a piece of sketch paper just as the telephone on his desk rang. He gave her an apologetic look and she waved him off, already bending toward her drawing.

"Yes?" Truman asked.

"Mr. Byrd," Rather said, his head of staff. "There has been a change in plans that will alter the guest list for this week."

Truman's jaw tightened slightly. "What is it?"

"I've just received a telephone call that Beau Remington is now able to attend."

"I thought Beaumont couldn't make it," Truman said, his tone markedly clipped. He looked at the monogram embroidered on his sleeve. Beau Remington, the up-and-coming actor, was a nascent shooting star—just emerging, but his trajectory was destined to be both swift and brilliant, there was little doubt about it. Charisma in a man like that came about once a decade, with a face carved like a Roman god, and he was about to sign a contract for a movie starring alongside Clementine that could make both of their careers soar.

The timing was important. Truman's studio needed a hit, especially with the recession causing studios to fold. He just wasn't certain he liked how artfully Clementine was angling for this man to be her costar.

"Yes, fine. Put him in the Garland Suite on the second floor," Truman said, rubbing his temples. "And let me know the moment he steps onto the Hill."

"Certainly, Mr. Byrd."

He set down the receiver and watched the back of Florence's shorn hair along her neck as she bent her head and sketched. The tea in her cup darkened the water in whirls.

"Florence," Truman said, as if their conversation hadn't been interrupted, "while we're discussing revisions to the Hill, perhaps we might shore up its defenses." He picked up his cigar to examine it but didn't light it.

She paused in drawing to look up at him, her rose lips pursing.

"So the rumors are true," she said. "Is the mob coming after you?"

He shrugged. "You know I'm less concerned about the present and more about the future."

"You're considering it, then?" she asked quietly. Her sharp eyes watched him. "A run for higher office?"

He smiled cryptically and didn't answer, rubbing his jawline.

"Your inability to sit still is bloody exhausting," she said, but the words betrayed a begrudging fondness.

Her eyes were crystal-clear but held a hint of concern. "We'll shore up the defenses," she said with a short nod. She was rarely outrightly warm, instead preferring to show affection with subtle hints. She had only ever once verbalized her appreciation to him, when they had broken ground and the champagne had loosened her tongue, letting it slip that she was grateful he would hire a woman. Then she had rolled up her blueprints with a snap and said something unintelligible about the soil and the sightline.

"This place was built like a palace, not a fortress. We made it fit for a prince. A politician is another matter," Florence said.

Truman nodded. "Are you coming back for the party?"

"I'm not much for parties," she said.

"Oh, come."

"I'll think about it. I'll be in touch with ideas first."

She stood, and he followed her to the door, watching the way her fingers tapped against the fabric of her pantsuit like a Morse code of ideas. Florence fastened her hat and said "I'll see myself out, Truman; I think I can find the door I set on its own hinges," and he smirked and said "Until then."

He stood in the light-flooded hallway and looked out at the palm trees, the mountains that appeared as though they were a green wave sliding down into the sea. The Pacific beyond it was an open chest of diamonds, with endless facets glittering in almost every direction. He had come so far from the days when he was eating beans out of a can for months on end simply to survive. The scent of them still made him want to retch. He and Mabel had visited parks and movie theaters and museums on the days when they were half-price or free, and sneaked into them on the days when they weren't. Mabel had wanted pretty things, and how he had wanted to give them to her. They had talked about the future together, imagined what they could become. He had believed in the dream of it all so fiercely that he had even forced himself to grovel to his father for a loan to launch his first paper. He had bet on himself—and so Truman sat with beans in his stomach and listened to his father sneer about how it was money he knew he would never get back.

Truman walked out of his father's house with Franklin Byrd's money in his pocket and what felt like spit on his face, and he told himself he would never be humiliated like that again.

Truman glanced down at where Clementine liked to sit in the sun, slathering oil on her golden arms. He had done it. He had made a name for himself. He had built this fortune by leaving part of his soul behind, and he damn well sure wasn't going to be assassinated—or cuckolded—in his own castle.

He narrowed his eyes, thinking. Listening to his intuition. And then he picked up the telephone again.

$$* \quad * \quad *$$

After checking to make sure that Truman had retired safely to his own quarters the night before—unharmed by Jack, and not visiting Clementine—Cora's sleep had been hard and deep, without dreams. As she often did when she was overtired, she woke wondering if Bobby was sleeping somewhere next to his new bride, Helen—if Helen had moved into his tiny Brooklyn apartment next to the train line that rattled the walls and overlooked a bakery that always smelled like fresh challah. Cora wondered if they were happy.

"I've got the jacks today," she had said to Daisy, tying on her apron. "I remember."

"You mean you have the jacks all week, right?" Daisy asked with a sly grin. She had helped Cora pin up her hair and then went to work as the guests of Byrd Castle had begun to emerge from their rooms, dressed in silk dresses and day suits. Cora had done a half-hearted job on the toilets before stashing her cleaning supplies behind an urn. Her thoughts kept returning to the moment her eyes had met Jack's across the room. Had he recognized her, or not?

And did any part of her want him to?

She was scouring a bronze grate patterned with birds on the fourth floor when Florence Abrams left Truman Byrd's office. Cora had been peering through the quatrefoil arches to watch Jack, Clementine, and Governor Gilham on a walking tour led by the head gardener. Cora felt something curl inside her when Jack said something to make Clementine laugh. Clementine's silk dress billowed out behind her, surrounded by grazing peacocks, and then she and Jack disappeared behind a copse of cypress trees.

Cora turned toward the low sound of Truman's voice drifting from his office. Florence must not have closed the door all the way.

"Rather," Truman was saying into the telephone. "I've changed my mind about Beaumont's arrival. I don't want him in the main house. Put him in the Whitstone guest cottage down the hill."

There was a pause.

"And tell Macready—" Truman said. He lowered his voice even further, so that Cora had to strain her neck to hear. "If Miss Garver were to receive any . . . special attention from another guest, I want to know about it. And it isn't possible for me to be everywhere at once."

Cora felt a faint stirring of exhilaration. She had been looking for a wrench like this: a stress point to apply until something between Clementine and Byrd splintered. And nothing made people splinter as easily as jealousy. It dried out the marrow of relationships, making them so brittle that a mere twinge could cause them to snap.

She stood just as Truman hung up the phone. Quicker than she expected, he appeared at the door.

Cora smiled and curtsied, not quite meeting his eyes. On the wall just behind him, she glimpsed the framed copy of the very first edition of his paper, *The Post-Courant*, from 1913.

Once again she wondered—why would Jack take such a risk coming to Enchanted Hill, with its enhanced security and watchmen, its scrutinized, high-profile guests—to a *news tycoon's house*, no less—a news tycoon who had covered his crime, arrest, and trial?

She glanced at the place where Clem and Jack had disappeared into the trees together and let her curiosity win out.

It had been Truman's paper that broke the story of the Bastion theft and murders. *The Post-Courant* had been merely a rag at the time, but its readership hit it big after that lucky break. The paper ran incriminating photographs, salacious interviews that were either made up or embellished. They heavily insinuated the brothers' guilt, leaning on every sort of sensationalism to sell more papers and get the Byrd brand off the ground.

It convinced the public of the Yates' brothers' guilt long before the verdict came down.

The thought hit her with a chill: Was that why he had come?

She waited until Byrd had gone, and then she made her way to the main floor, across the esplanade, and down to the Pacific Suite.

After checking surreptitiously over her shoulder, Cora entered Jack's room. Then she closed the shutters for privacy and locked the door behind her.

$$* \quad * \quad *$$

Cora surveyed Jack's room. It was neat, the bed already made up and his leather shoes set in an even line. Several suits hung in the wardrobe. Three books were stacked on his nightstand, on subjects of bridge architecture, the Eiffel Tower, and desert botany. He had showered that morning; there were still beads of water on the tile, still the faintest hint of steam collected at the corner of the mirror. She saw his Pepsodent tube, neatly curled on the sink next to a silver tin of mints. He used to grow mint leaves on Pelican and chew them like cud, saying he wished for a pack of Lifesavers.

These were the things about him that were true, that Cora could trust. Inanimate objects couldn't lie. Because otherwise, the truth always seemed to have a twisting way about it, shimmering and impossible to grasp, the nearer Jack was to it.

Jack had only ever mentioned his crime once to her. Once. But it was like a seed that went deep into the soft parts of her and planted something there.

"I didn't do it, Cora," Jack had said. The sea had crashed against the rocks behind him, as if it were trying to break itself apart. He'd cleared his throat and held her eyes. "What they said I did. I swear to you that I didn't."

The breeze had gone cold on her skin, the cruel way the chill haunted San Francisco summers, and she had shivered. What she had noticed most of all was that he said "*I* didn't do it." Not "*we* didn't." An investigative detail she marked down in the pages of her notebook that night in her bedroom. Maybe Jack had had nothing to do with that horrible crime, just like he said. The idea began to curl inside her, vining, using Cora's mind as a trellis. Maybe he was innocent. Unjustly imprisoned, sent to Ratite Rock in place of someone else. Or maybe he had tried to cover for his brother. Maybe Jack had even been *willing* to come, so that his brother would not be alone.

Maybe what he had done was the opposite of wrong.

Maybe the real crime was that he was on Pelican at all.

She had believed him so desperately. Perhaps because she had wanted to. But there was no denying now that the Yates brothers were exactly what everyone had said they were.

Because as soon as they got the chance, they had killed again.

She rifled through his toiletries, his undergarments, and his personal effects, careful not to move them out of place, looking for any hint as to why he had come. His identification papers were folded neatly in the top drawer of the nightstand, next to a gold pocket watch, a deck of cards, and his wallet. She found two hundred dollars of crisp bills tucked inside his leather billfold, along with a matchbook for a place called The Silver Dunes in Nevada.

She palmed it while she stole a glance at his papers.

Everett Conner, born March 1, 1898, in Des Moines.

It was a fake birthdate, of course. She knew that he was born in Dorchester, that his real birthday was in November.

Cora squatted down to knock along the bottoms of his bureau drawers, looking for the echo of a hollow space, and instead got a whiff of his clothes. They smelled good, stirring something dark and yearning within her, which instantly made her irritated. She tried to keep herself detached from the intimacy of being in his room, of being among his private things. She continued to methodically knock along the drawers until she hit a dull sound unlike the rest and yanked up a false bottom.

Her heart quickened.

He did not appear to have brought any weapons with him—no pistols or knives, and no gold bars or velvet pouches of diamonds either. There were no bindles of white powders tucked inside, no glittering, illicit needles that were sometimes hidden in the quarters of the other guests. Instead, there was simply a small, flat book—some sort of diary or ledger.

Cora snatched it up and sifted through the pages. They were almost entirely blank, save for—

Cora froze at the sound of footsteps coming up the stairs.

She moved backward, tucking herself behind the bathroom door.

For a long moment, she waited. And then the footsteps continued on down the corridor.

She let out a long exhale and then riffled through the rest of the book's pages, which all appeared to be blank, except for the very last one.

There was a list of names and dates, written in tiny handwriting.

K. Abernathy, 1/2/25.

L. Movignon, 7/8/28.

A. White, 2/22/29.

There were more than fifty of them. She studied them, wondering what they could possibly mean, and why Jack would have brought them in a book that he had tried very hard to hide.

She wanted to stay and solve it, knowing those names and dates held some sort of clue to why Jack was there. She didn't have the time to copy them all down. But her eyes caught on something else. Small letters and numbers were written on the pages in the bottom corner, if she flipped the book the opposite way. There was one on every tenth page.

MU5275.

A set of initials followed by a date, like the others?

No—she realized. MU was a telephone exchange for east Manhattan.

It was a telephone number.

Cora found a pen in the nightstand and copied the number down on her thigh. She blew against the ink as it set.

Then she hid the book, opened the shutters, and swept out of the room as though she had never been there.

*   *   *

Cora made her way up to the esplanade, turning down the pathway toward the adjacent glass structure that Truman had made into a ballroom. She paused in the shadow of a limestone relief of Saint Peter, and the wind swept through her hair. Could Jack have come to the Hill to exact some sort of revenge? Or—she let her fingers trace along the cool white stone—was Jack like a moth to the flame, drawn there by the irresistible temptation of more priceless art and the seductive danger of lifting it?

At the sound of approaching footsteps she tightened her breath, until all she could hear was her own heartbeat. She listened.

"Daisy?" she called quietly.

There was nothing but the swaying of the palm fronds in the breeze.

She could laugh at herself. She was getting paranoid. Just like she had thought those footsteps were coming for her in Jack's room.

Not cut out for this job, her father's voice whispered in her ear.

She was barely going to hold on to this week by the skin of her teeth.

She turned.

And then Jack Yates emerged from the shadows and grabbed her roughly by the arm.

CHAPTER TEN

Cora was hit with the scent of him like a tidal wave, the old him that used to carry on the breeze. Her thoughts spun out. So many at once, fracturing and blinding.

"Cora," Jack said.

She choked back a scream as his grip on her arm tightened.

He hadn't forgotten.

He had recognized her. He still remembered her name.

"Let me go," she said, her voice low and gritty in her throat. His hand loosened on her arm, and in some distant part of her brain she had the thought that this was the first time they had ever really touched each other. The first time they had spoken without a fence between them.

She took in the swift, faint beat of his pulse at the base of his neck.

"I need to talk to you," he said in a low voice.

"I don't think so," she said. Heart racing, she glanced furtively at the walkways, at the places where the guards would pass by at any moment.

"How did you find me?" he demanded. He was dressed more casually than he had been the night before, wearing a three-piece day suit. He ran his hands through his hair, coolly, but he grazed the cowlick on the side of his head the way he always did when he was nervous.

He thought that she was there to catch him out.

"Wouldn't you like to know," she said. She glanced toward the ballroom door, keeping an eye on her escape route. Her blood quickened. She could hardly believe that after everything that had happened, they were breathing the same air again.

"Damn it all to hell," he said. He rubbed at his clean-shaven chin, and glanced behind her. "Should I be expecting an escort to appear any moment?"

Every nerve in Cora's body sparked. There were things she almost *needed* to know from him. Answers to long-held questions she'd never hoped to get. Wounds she had sheltered for so long. She tried to hide the slight tremble that went through her.

They stood in the shadows of the ballroom. Its doors were all glass, glinting behind them like a frozen waterfall.

And then Jack tensed, turning his head infinitesimally, like an animal. Cora heard it too: a guard approaching, his boots a soft click on the stone path. Even despite everything else, they weren't supposed to meet together— an esteemed guest and a maid, in dark corners. The rules had been drilled into Cora by Macready since day one. No dalliances with guests, or she would be out.

For one brief second, it felt just like their days on Pelican. Trying not to get caught by a guard. Their eyes met, and she was struck by the look in his. Haunted. Hunted. They both knew that with one scream, the rest of his days would be spent rotting in a tiny cell.

Cora opened her mouth.

Then against her better judgment, she hissed: "Come with me," and pulled open the door to the ballroom.

*   *   *

Bloody bout of endless bad luck, Jack thought. He tensed as he stepped inside the ballroom, half-expecting to be greeted by the entire San Luis Obispo police outfit with their weapons drawn—but instead he found a still, quiet indoor courtyard set beneath a glass skylight. A fountain burbled quietly in the center. He scanned the room, instinctively glancing up to the open-air balcony that overlooked them, but it too was empty. A veil of brilliant orange nasturtiums was draped over the second-floor terrace, and a massive chandelier hung above their heads. The light poured in through the glass, and—for a fleeting moment—he almost felt peace.

Cora led him to the side of the room, where they could talk in secret. He followed her warily, wondering what she was playing at. Why hadn't she turned him in yet? There was something he was missing, and it set his nerves on edge. He felt like the first time he'd sat down at a blackjack casino and realized he was playing with a rigged deck. He had to keep playing until he could get out without losing everything.

"What are you doing here, Jack?" she asked in a low voice. She glared at him, across air that held the lush scent of roses. She looked older to him, of course, but the same fire was still there. When she turned, he saw flashes of her as a young girl again. Her innocence on Pelican, the wind blowing her auburn hair.

He smiled at her ruefully. "You wouldn't believe me if I told you."

"Fair play to you," she shot back immediately. "I don't intend to believe a single thing you say."

She took a step nearer to him. The scent on her breath was lemon and sugar. He could see the fine hairs at her ear. The way her curves had filled out beneath her dress and her cheekbones had risen so that she was no longer a girl. "And yet I am admittedly quite curious," she said, turning to fix her bright eyes on him. "You were the first convict to ever escape Pelican and survive. Everyone thinks you're dead. Why would you risk all of that by coming here?"

He felt guilt like a sudden punch to his gut. The way she looked at him, with those eyes that looked suspicious rather than trusting. Once she had believed in his innocence.

Once, a very long time ago, he *had* been innocent.

He hesitated. Cora was the single thing he couldn't have prepared for.

"Did you finally burn through all the money from the Bastion heist and now you need more?" she continued, guessing at his silence. "And with Byrd as your target—maybe you saw a chance for a little extra . . . payback?"

He felt a jolt. All the inviting warmth of being near her instantly dissipated. Instead, her words felt like a branding iron. "If I wanted Truman dead," he said curtly, "I could have done it last night."

It was just a look, but he saw the flash of her acknowledgment. She knew that. She had already reached that conclusion herself. She must have been watching them.

He felt a flicker of irritation. This was going to be trickier than he thought.

But he had spent thirteen long, bitter years to get there. Done unspeakable things. Nothing, and no one, was going to stand in his way at this point. Not even her.

"Are you with the mob, then?" she asked.

He thought quickly. Calculating just how much he should reveal.

It had been a much more straightforward answer at first. After Pelican, he had done what he had needed to survive and stay hidden. He had started off working as security in card tables, listening for bits of information. Over the years, he had found people who deserved to be punished, and he punished them. He had formed his own moral system. He wouldn't take jobs that targeted debts or settled petty crimes. He went for the traffickers, the men who beat women behind closed doors. He had cut off the fingers of a pimp who kept his dolls too drugged to fight back; afterward, he wondered why it didn't make him feel better than it did.

He leaned toward Cora. "I know you have no reason at all to believe me," he said. "But I guarantee you that nothing here is what it seems."

Cora's hazel eyes widened. They both heard the sound of the glass door sliding open behind them.

A maid stood silhouetted in the daylight. She hesitated in the doorway as her eyes adjusted. She looked to the two of them, standing in the shadows, alone.

". . . Ella?" the maid asked tentatively. She took a step forward. And that's when Jack saw it. The last thing he had expected to see in Cora's eyes.

It was alarm.

Something bigger was going on there, something he couldn't quite put his finger on. The maid looked past Jack to Cora, and gave her a searching glance, as though it wasn't the first time a guest had cornered one of them in a dark, empty place. A guest who was used to getting whatever he wanted.

That thought made Jack flare with unexpected anger.

"I'm fine, Daisy," Cora reassured the maid. "Just helping Mr. Conner here with something. Can you come back in a few minutes and we'll finish cleaning then?"

Daisy hesitated. But at Cora's insistent nod, she turned and slowly let the glass door drift closed behind her.

Jack tilted his head at the faint flush that was spreading up Cora's neck, her cheeks.

"'Ella?'" he echoed. Realization was dawning, and his curiosity sharpened, followed by a slow smile.

When she turned toward him, her eyes were fire.

"Why are you here with a name other than your own?" Jack asked.

"I could ask you the same question," she retorted. "I'm wondering what the going reward might be for turning you in."

"So you haven't turned me in, then," he said, watching her face carefully.

"Yet," she said.

They stared at each other, breathless, and he had a sudden memory of the Western radio shows that Leo used to listen to when they were young. Two outlaws, facing off. He saw the rise and fall of her chest. Her hazel eyes were alert and dilated, framed by a fringe of lashes.

"You're working as a maid here, but you don't want anyone to know your real name," he said. "Interesting." He kept his eyes on her. "You wouldn't need to go to any of that trouble on my account. Unless . . ." He fiddled with the button on his cuffs, thinking. "You're actually not here for me after all."

His smile became easier when he rolled up his sleeves. More relaxed, like a fist loosening, and with a fierce, hot swell, Cora looked as though she hated him. It was fascinating to watch the planes of her face, the way she had grown from a girl into a woman. He had never seen her truly angry—scared or annoyed, sometimes, and sad, and so many other emotions that had played out across her face as a young girl, but this was something else entirely.

"It appears we both are different people than everyone else thinks we are," he said. He leaned forward, just a bit.

"And yet that's where the similarities between us end," she said, drawing away from him. "Because only one of us is a killer who should either be locked up or rotting away in the Bay."

He nodded agreeably, as if she had merely commented on the weather. The longer this went on, he was feeling more and more confident, even though he had no idea what she was playing at. He shrugged. "Then turn me in," he said. Almost as if he were daring her to.

She didn't react. She still had the faint groove in her forehead from when she had fallen as a child and needed a stitch. At her silence, he said:

"It seems that you have your reasons for being here. And I have mine. So perhaps we can keep it that way. For a few short days."

She laughed suddenly, the sound of it so bitter that it practically hit him in the face. "I'm not interested in making any more deals with the devil," she said. "I did that once already, and I learned my lesson."

He nodded and took a deep breath. "It's only right that you should be the one to turn me in. Seems like my luck just ran out."

"And surely you're about to follow it," Cora said.

"No," he said grimly. "I won't. I'm not leaving this house until I've gotten what I'm here for."

"And what is that?"

"I doubt I'll find it tonight." He shook his head. "But my lot starts and ends here. I've been on a path for so long, and it was always meant to end here, one way or the other." The sun was turning the skylight above their heads into a thousand colors, violet and gold and azure, as though they were inside a bubble. Cora's lip curled. She was no fool, he could tell. She never had been. But now she had a hardened shell, the sort that only comes from getting burned.

How many lives were ruined in the wake of the Bastion? All because of one single, fateful decision he would do anything to go back and change?

"I do believe that I owe you, Cora McCavanagh, and someday I would like to repay that debt," he said. "But I *will* give up your real identity if you give up mine. I came here for something and I'm not leaving without it— even if it means I have to blackmail you into holding your silence just a little bit longer."

"Ella?" Daisy asked again. She was standing in the shadows, waiting.

Cora turned to him. "Find me at the party tonight," she whispered. "I'll hold my tongue as long as you give me the answers I want. And you'd do well to remember something this time, Jack." She leaned toward him, her breath as soft as a kiss. "I'm not the naïve little girl I used to be."

She placed the Nevada Dunes matchbook she must have stolen from his own room into his palm, and closed his hand around it hard enough to hurt.

*   *   *

Two hours later, muscles aching, Cora scarfed down a cold lamb sandwich with weak tea for lunch. What she wanted was a hot shower, and she felt the muscles in her shoulders tighten as she wiped her mouth. She sensed Daisy's eyes on her. Daisy had kept quiet while they scrubbed the ballroom's floors, too loyal to say anything in front of the other maids—but she shot a look at Cora now that made her know she was going to have to answer for it later.

"I've got a call with my Da," Cora said, and abruptly stood up.

She made her way to the wooden telephone booth that was tucked beside the morning room and pulled the sliding door shut tight behind her. It smelled strongly of pine inside, and it always reminded her of the Pelican Island commissary. Lost in thought, Cora felt absently for the small metal dog tag she hadn't worn in years.

Cora picked up the receiver. Wrapped the telephone cord around her finger.

For the first time, she allowed herself to consider: What if she turned Jack in to her father? Her stomach roiled at the thought. Her father had settled in Bitterlake, a painfully tiny outfit nearly ninety miles from the Hill, where he took orders from a boss who shined his oversized gold belt buckle twice a day. Chief Bellanger was the sort of man who routinely missed the lettuce caught in his own front teeth but never passed up a chance to make cracks at

Cora's father's expense—especially concerning the escape at Pelican. "Don't let McCavanagh handcuff the suspect, he might give him the slip," he would joke in front of her father's colleagues—and, at his most disgusting, sometimes even in front of the perpetrators themselves. "Don't let him watch the snack drawer, something might go missing," he'd say with a smirk at Cora, just to humiliate him in front of his own daughter.

Cora had scheduled weekly check-ins with her father since taking the job for Mabel—a call that she always simultaneously dreaded and longed for. She had always hoped that her father's love was unconditional.

But she had never had enough courage to find out.

Before Jack's escape, there had been six other attempts in five years. The one Cora remembered most was on a November afternoon in 1916, when the alarm sounded through the misty drizzle. Normally she would have been at school, but that day she was home with a fever, and at first she wondered if she was having a hallucination. But then her mother had appeared at the door, her face pale, and Cora had known that one of the prisoners had gotten loose. Perhaps other people felt a similar fear when the sky warned of a storm front moving in. Then they, too, locked their doors and windows, praying that something dangerous wasn't heading right for them.

Cora stroked her worry stone ferociously as her mother ushered her into the closet and deadbolted the door from the inside. Cora nestled under a worn blanket that smelled faintly of mothballs. "We'll make it cozy," Cora's mother said, giving her a tight smile. She hummed "It is Well" under her breath and rooted out a candy bar wrapped in foil while sending up fervent prayers for Cora's father. Cora realized then that she didn't really believe if those Pelican prisoners managed to escape their cells, it was because they wanted to hurt her.

They just wanted to get out.

The convict who tried it was dumb as a post. Dobran had been sent to Pelican for counterfeiting money and he didn't make it very far that drizzly November day. He decked a guard—Smitty, a friend of Cora's father's who loved cigars and Dixieland jazz—and climbed over a fence, shredding his hands on the barbed wires and falling to the rocks below. The guards brought him back handcuffed to a stretcher, yelping about his broken vertebrae. First he was bound for the medical ward, then a long stint in solitary.

"The new hire isn't proving impressive," Cora's father said to her mother that night over beef stew. He didn't think Cora was listening, but she was, and she knew exactly where the new hire was stationed: to tower duty, as they always were when they first started out. "If Warden Thomas wants to keep up Pelican's reputation, he'll need to start sweetening salaries and attracting better stock," he had said. "And don't get me started on the damn fences. There's a whole section of it on the western side that you could practically crawl under when the rains turn everything to muck—."

Cora's knife had paused.

He seemed to notice, because he cut himself off and gave her a long look. Then he glanced down at his beef stew and said, "Cora-thorn, tell us what you've got on for homework, will you?"

*   *   *

Cora took a steeling breath and dialed the Bitterlake police department, GS-8300, studying the whorl in the wood panel that always looked like Edvard Munch's *The Scream*. The phone rang. For the first time, she hoped he wouldn't pick up. Her hope climbed as it rang twice, three times, with no answer.

"Bitterlake Police Department," her father said.

Her heart fell. "Da," she said softly. "It's me."

CHAPTER ELEVEN

"Cora-thorn," her father said gruffly.

She could hear the shift of him as he turned away from the office, probably shielding the receiver with his large, coarse hand. At the familiar sound of his voice, she felt swept away by a sudden gust of homesickness.

"How's it, Da?" she asked.

"Same as usual," he said wearily. "Chief Bellanger has been in a bit of a lather."

"Oh? What is it this time?"

"Somehow a bookie dumber than a box of rocks has managed to elude him."

"What's a step below a dumb bookie?" she asked, twisting the telephone cord round her finger. "Sentient algae?"

"I believe it's egg salad."

She felt her heart lightening. This was what she wanted, what she yearned for. He had grown distant in the years after Pelican, and she hadn't known why—because of what happened with his job? Because her mother died? Because she was growing up?

Or had he known what she did?

She smiled into the telephone, and then choked back a vague threat of tears. She thought of her father's head, downturned for weeks after Jack's escape, walking past the newspaper stands in the streets that screamed his failure. She thought of the endless months he had to send out resumes to jobs further and further from the work he wanted to do, while her mother lay dying. The empty silence of the telephone, and the mail slot that held only bills.

She cleared her throat.

"How's things over there? You pouring the champagne yet?" He kept his tone light, but they both knew what he was saying. Mabel's deadline was almost there, lurking in the shadows.

"Not quite." She paused. "But I might have found a wrench here, to get things moving," she said, lowering her voice into the telephone.

She could almost feel her father's interest heighten, and she relished it. When she had first taken the job from Mabel, the old hunger had risen in his blood, and he showed more interest in their conversations than he had in years. This job had brought them closer together than they had been since Pelican.

"Which one is it, then?" he asked. "Lust, jealousy, anger, greed?"

"Jealousy," she said.

He took a deep breath and lowered his voice. "You got your gun?"

"Mm," she said.

"Then twist the wrench until it cracks."

She could picture him as he was, tapping the right side of his face, where the skin had started to sag like a stone's throw of ripples. Home was something else Cora had lost in a moment at fifteen. Now the closest thing she had to it was a person.

And she couldn't give him up yet.

"Have you heard from that Bobby of yours at all, Cora-thorn?" he asked. She winced at the sound of hope in his voice.

"Actually, no." She cleared her throat. "I'm told that he was recently married to someone else," she said, closing her eyes.

She felt a pang at saying the words out loud. He had tried so hard to love her. But she had never fully allowed him in.

"I always feel like you're holding something back," he had told her one night when they'd both had too much to drink. They had been sitting in a booth at their favorite speakeasy, and her tongue was loose and slurring. She had almost told him then. Almost taken the key he had offered and gotten herself out of the cell. Shame was a lonely, barren place, a place she had lived for so long. For one brief second she thought: maybe he wouldn't think it was that horrible, what she had done.

But then, with a cold, dank fear, she thought: But what if he did?

She had looked into his eyes and hesitated. "There's nothing," she had said softly, and felt the key he had handed her slip from her hand. "You know everything about me."

He had kissed her then, hungrily. "And I love you," he said. "I would love you no matter what."

She had felt the first crack that night, one that would eventually splinter out and make it impossible for her to keep him. What he sensed was right; she was holding back the deepest parts of her that he could never know, not truly. Later that night, she had gone to throw her dog tag off the Brooklyn Bridge; but at the last moment, she pulled her arm back and saved it. The wind whipped at her hair, and she placed the dog tag back in her pocket. She had been wearing red lipstick and her dead mother's dress. At twenty-four, she was still the same gnarled, broken person inside who she had been ever since she first heard the Pelican guard alarms blaring and the black phone going off in her house. She remembered the way her father had reached for his rifle, the flare of spotlights, bright and sharp as cut glass; the guard dogs, bared teeth, barking. Then later, when Cora had to pack up their house, take her grandmother's picture off the wall, and get on the ferry for the last time, she'd seen the dragonflies, their wings reflecting like oil slicks in the sun.

"Well." Her father cleared his throat, and then the silence hung between them. They had never been very good at navigating emotional waters without her mother there as a sandbar, a place of safety and refuge between them.

"I'm okay, Da," she told him quietly. She traced the whorls of wood with her fingertip. They had one check-in left before the job was through.

"Cora," her father said brusquely. "The end is always the trickiest."

She knew it was the closest thing he would say to "I love you."

"I know," she said.

She hung up.

There was a brisk knock on the door. "Almost done in there?" a male voice asked from just outside the telephone booth. It was Matias, the chauffeur. The one who had helped Mabel get Cora this job.

"Just a minute," she called.

Cora rolled up her skirt and looked at the number she had written on her thigh.

MU-5275.

Her pulse rose as she turned back on the stool. She dialed the number and listened to it ring.

The ringing cut short.

A voice heavy with an Irish accent answered.

"Muddy Dahlia's."

She breathed, then set the telephone down carefully with a click. It was what she had feared.

The Muddy Dahlia was an Irish pub in New York that was little more than a front for a mob joint. Its symbol was the Irish pinwheel dahlia, a flower that was golden in color and striped with red from the inside out. Like it had been shot.

Her heart beat faster.

"All yours," she said to Matias, opening the door to let him in. Jack was in this up to his neck, and she had a sudden, choking feeling that she was treading water over something that was about to swallow her whole.

* * *

Truman finalized the evening dinner preparations with Rather, his head of staff, before walking the grounds. Drawn toward the distant sound of laughing, he leaned against the carved balcony overlooking the pool. He relished the way his guests waved at him and cheered, raising their glasses. He could smell the jasmine pooling off the blossoms, reaching toward the two cranes Florence had carved as the laddered entrances into the water.

zTruman felt the sudden presence of a man at his elbow—someone rather squat, who had a towel draped across his hips and a straw boater hat perched jauntily on his head. Truman wasn't a small man by any means, but he positively felt like a giant next to Albert Boyle.

"Berty," Truman said, acknowledging him with smug amusement. "It's an interesting look, to choose a hat over a shirt."

"I call it a topless hat," Berty said.

What Boyle lacked in size he made up for in antics. Across the veranda, Truman caught a slightly disapproving look from Rutherford. "People like Berty are fine enough company for the image of a Hollywood czar," Truman could almost hear Rutherford saying in a low voice in his ear, ashing his cigar. "Not as good for a high-ranking senator, or possibly the president of the United States." Truman caught Rutherford's eye and tipped his cap. He could almost read Rutherford's thoughts across the expanse of sky. But they both knew who called the final shots. Because, ultimately, he chose his own company.

Two maids appeared with freshly poured glasses of lemonade swimming in mint and vodka. Truman knew that, as per his instructions, Albert's would be watered down. Berty's antics ramped up considerably when alcohol was served, a disgraceful thing that Truman didn't tolerate or have much patience for. But Berty had sensed something in him early on, sniffed it out of the air like a dog, and he had been one of the first people willing to partner with Truman when he was coming up from nothing. Truman liked to consider himself loyal, at least where his business interests were concerned.

"It's been too damn long since we've worked together on a film," Berty said. He popped a handful of cashews in his mouth, some of the salt catching on his mustache. He drained his drink in one go and placed it on the edge of a fountain.

"Ah. Great minds. I was thinking the same," Truman said. It wasn't a lie, exactly. Being associated with a good film, the right kind of story beloved by audiences, would only help warm attitudes toward his political career, and give him a legitimate reason to appear in his own press besides. Albert's hands seemed to turn the films he touched to gold. "And I have someone in particular in mind for your next go."

They both turned toward the pool, and Albert's eyes came to rest on Clementine, her legs lifting into the air in a golden handstand. When she came back up, she was dripping in water and sunlight. Truman paused, watching her. He loved that she would get her hair wet, unlike the other starlets, who either laid out to bask in the sun or squealed when anyone came near to splashing them.

"Interesting," Berty said. He fished out the lime from his empty lemonade and squirted it into the glass. "I'm lined up to do another musical next. I know she's got stems." He gestured toward the water, his mouth parting beneath his salt-streaked mustache. "But what about pipes?"

Truman cleared his throat. Albert Boyle was crass, and his mother would have hated him. But Truman liked how gritty he was, another outlier who had clawed his way up into a society that he didn't quite fit into. They were under no illusions that the women who surrounded them now would have given them a second look if not for their bank accounts and their powerful sway behind the scenes. In that way, he felt a fondness toward Albert. He was scrappy. He was a fighter. And Truman still felt an affinity for the underdog; still remembered the scratching, searing hunger of what it felt like to be one.

"She can sing," Truman said with confidence. "She's got talents you can't imagine."

"Oh, I can imagine," Albert said, giving Truman a long look. And Truman gave an equally long thought about striking him; but instead, he let it rest. He knew Albert wouldn't dare touch Clementine.

The mafia wasn't the only one who could put out a hit.

Albert picked through the nuts, digging to the very bottom of the dish, and sucked the salt from his fingers. "How's Mabel? You keeping her happy and quiet?"

Truman snorted. "Come, now, you know she's never been either of those."

He had loved her once, back when everything was young and desperate. She had been an actress trying to make it on the stage. He liked to go and watch her, to see the rest of the crowd take her in with their eyes, and know that he was the one she was going home with. She could make the audience laugh, but they were children looking at a toy through an outside window, and he got the real thing. She pushed boundaries, had mad ideas like breaking into the Museum of Natural History at night to touch the stuffed grizzlies before the alarm caught them. She had a thrilling streak and a wicked sense of humor.

And if Truman's mother would have hated Albert Boyle, she would have rolled over in her grave and back again over Mabel.

"You've got a good thing going here," Albert said. "Lotte's fine with the occasional dalliance, but she would have gouged out my eyes if I had a regular piece on the side."

Truman grunted. He tried to remember Mabel on their wedding day. She'd worn a simple white muslin dress she'd sewn with shells to look like pearls, and a gardenia behind her ear. It had been early days, before he'd paid back his father's loan and the paper had taken off, before his shrewd investments in rail, steel, and tobacco had skyrocketed. She had been there when he made his first dollar; and when she wasn't scheming or hollering, she had looked at him like she believed in him. The way his mother used to.

And then one day along the way, she had started to hate him, and he her. He couldn't pinpoint when, any more than he could the exact moment he had fallen in love with her. A hundred moments, scattering seeds that they had each cultivated until they became something more.

Berty looked around for a maid to replenish his empty glass. "You ever consider cutting the cord?"

Truman knew he had put to words what everyone else was thinking, when they asked politely after Mabel—or, more tellingly, didn't ask after her at all. Why hadn't they divorced, when everyone knew the marriage was over?

"She wants too much," Truman said, and it was a version of the truth. A year ago, he'd visited her in New York. The marriage was long over, and he'd considered divorce, but Mabel was better controlled under his thumb, and it kept Clementine from angling for more. He'd slept in his separate bedroom in the penthouse suite. They'd gone together to the society dinners she treasured, and he had put on a tuxedo and taken her to the opera; and afterward, she'd thrown a porcelain dish at his head and tried to get half of his fortune.

"I've been with you since the beginning," she'd said, and if her words could have carved into his skin, they would have.

"Yes, but I've done all the work since then, my dear."

"I deserve half."

He'd choked on his drink. "Not on your life, Mabel," he'd said.

"I could ruin you," she said.

She couldn't. And he knew, without a doubt, she wouldn't. They were tied to one another, for better or worse. If she'd tried to divorce him on her own, a judge would side with him over the fortune, and the rest of polite society would side with him for all future social occasions. And then, when he was still considering how much of his fortune he was willing to part with, his priorities had changed. It was no longer about money and wooing Hollywood and dignitaries. He'd set his sights higher. He was dreaming of politics again. And he wouldn't accede to a divorce at all.

"You just mean to humiliate me and give me an allowance," she had said, her eyes flashing. "Like some sort of kept woman. Without freedom, or love."

For the briefest moment, he had pictured her that day on their wedding, with the flower tucked behind her ear, looking up at him with those lit green eyes. "You have always been able to walk away," he said. "Instead, I think fur stoles and lunches at L'Aiglon mean more to you than freedom, or love."

He had left that night and gotten a lift to his private plane, had his personal things shipped back later. When they came, they smelled like her perfume. And, in Mabel's way of giving him the figurative finger, she had slipped in a matchbook from L'Aiglon.

He watched Clementine swimming in the pool. Her delighted laughter, her long strokes cutting through the aquamarine water. He'd decided the sacrifice was worth it, to put up with Mabel for a little while longer to pursue this final dream. But would he give up Clementine, if push came to shove?

He leaned against the marble balcony. "Who are you thinking of for the male lead?" Truman asked Berty. He set his empty glass down, and another round of lemonades and spiced nuts instantly appeared, as if by magic.

"You," Berty said. He guffawed and popped a handful of the nuts into his mouth. "I'm not sure. Can Beau Remington sing? I've got my eye on him."

Truman raised his eyebrows. That made two of them.

Normally, Beaumont's decline of the invitation to Enchanted Hill would have irked Truman as an unforgivable slight. But instead, what he had felt was relief. He instantly zeroed in on that emotion, examining it, alone in his study, when he walked along the aisles of his newspapers. He didn't discount his gut feelings. They had led him the right way before, and he had learned not to ignore them.

Clementine splashed in the pool, catching sight of him. "Are you coming down?" she called. She was young, and happy, and she glittered in the water, as if she were a well of sunlight.

Meanwhile, the very sound of Mabel's voice had begun to grate against his nerves like the teeth of a metal comb. He saw the wrinkles in her skin, the hateful way her mouth twisted. And she saw all his failures and worst secrets, the ugliest sides of him he tried to forget. They had seen one another naked down to their cores, more rotten than they wanted to admit, and they were ashamed. It became easier, then, to simply wish she didn't exist. To stop seeing the mirror she held up to him, and instead find something more beautiful to look at.

CHAPTER TWELVE

Cora opened the door to the Gothic library on the second floor and stepped inside.

The cavernous room was kept dim. The shutters were always drawn, to protect the ancient texts and priceless first editions. It felt reverent, with its dark walnut panels and honeycombed ceiling hung with heavy lanterns. The library was the place where Byrd kept his old newspapers—a copy for every day of the past seventeen years, locked away in dated drawers to age like wine.

Cora grabbed a duster from the closet and quickly brushed it over two bookshelves. All the while, she soundlessly opened the drawers, gliding through the years and closing them again. Each day had once been a blank page, now inked with the choices and actions of life's grandest winners and losers. News was only given to those on either end of the spectrum, and Cora wondered what she had done to fill each of those days. She, like most people, was part of the in-betweens. Her quiet life had passed through the years like whispers, and never once warranted a drop of ink.

Except for one single, solitary day.

It had started the afternoon Cora had been sent to the commissary for milk. The Pelican Island commissary had been perched on the civilian side of the fence, near the pier where the ferry came in, sloshing the gray waves of the Bay onto the white wooden dock. Cora had loved that commissary, with its drawers of paper and stamps and tins of coffee; the way it smelled of musty pine and the dust swirled in sunbeams. The store windows were always brilliant and clean, the light sluicing through them to fall in shafts on the newspapers, taffy, tobacco, crates of powdered milk. Margaret, who worked the cash register, had fingers stained by tobacco and a laugh that sounded like hinges turning. Beneath the counter there was a warped wooden crate of saltwater taffies, each wrapped in a crisp white paper. Cora's favorites were the banana creams.

Cora saw a copy of *The Chronicle* with a photograph of Warden Thomas pacing in front of a tight line of guards. Her father was near the end on the left, standing at attention. IMPENETRABLE FORTRESS, the headline said. Pelican had been branded as the most secure prison in the United States—a golden charm winking in the light, urging criminals to even try to escape it.

Cora eyed the paper and then turned to the bottles of Moxie. She had bought a lukewarm bottle of it for the first time with Dina at Tito's, and she wanted to tell Jack that he was right, it tasted like rust and molasses. The prisoners weren't ever allowed to set foot in that store. She stood in the golden light of the commissary and reached into her pocket for an extra coin. She thought about getting him a lemon piece of taffy, like the pie of his mother's he liked so well, but she had tried them all and finally settled on the one she thought was best. She slid a pair of coins to Margaret across the counter for two banana creams and then walked past Warden Thomas's home, holding the milk and wearing an oversized sweater pulled tight around her shoulders, gravel crunching like shattered glass under her feet. Two pieces of soft, chewy taffy sat in her pocket.

She put the powdered milk away, thinking of what her father had said about the new hire, and waited until the tower guard was likely listening to the daily radio serial, his attention divided. Then she went to the barbed-wire fence, lacing her fingers through the iron links. A light, misty rain was falling, and the fog seemed to be eating through the sunlight. Jack had been crouched fifty yards away on his knees, mud splotching his trousers, a thin coat pulled around the collared blue chambray shirt all of the inmates wore. Cora smiled at him and held out the taffy, wordlessly.

He rose and slowly moseyed over to the fence, all lanky limbs. His face seemed to Cora to be growing sharper the longer he was on Pelican, his muscles growing more defined beneath his shirt, even though he was painfully thin. The day was cold, but his hair was slicked to his forehead, sweating. He saw the taffy she offered, and hesitated; Cora still remembered how deliberate and careful he was not to touch even her fingers when he took the small white package. He unpeeled the delicate wrapper as though it were the last present he might ever get. After a quick glance up at the guard tower, he bit into half of it. Chewed it slowly, savoring it. His lashes were long and dark when he closed his eyes.

Cora unpeeled hers and ate it alongside him. Silently, on the other side of the fence, jaw working. It was almost better to watch him savor it than eating it herself. He swallowed the first bite and examined the soft marks his teeth had left.

"Do you mind if I save the rest?" he asked quietly. "For my brother?"

Cora hesitated. She had bought it for him, to enjoy a small taste of freedom, and she knew they could both get in terrible trouble if the candy was found in a search. But it made her love him a little bit that day, that he would save his only present to share with his brother. And that was when she had noticed how bright his eyes were.

Feverish.

"Are you ill?" she asked.

He shrugged. "It's always cold in there," he said, and a sudden shiver racked his body like a seizure. The first floor of "D" block was kept clean enough, but the constant moisture made mold grow; made everything dank and cold and dim in the winter, in those small cells.

Cora watched him shake from within the warmth and softness of her knit sweater. She half wished she could take it off and pass it through the tiny openings in the fence. When she was sick, her mother placed a cool hand to Cora's forehead, made squash and apple soup, read to her from *Pilgrim's Progress*; and then hummed to the radio while she cleaned the dishes. Her presence did more than all the rest to comfort Cora.

With one more glance up at the guard tower, Cora had gingerly touched her fingertips to the fence. "What did your mother used to do?" she asked. "When you fell ill?"

He always seemed to relax when he talked about his mother. Like he was warming up from the inside, finding something that hadn't quite completely frozen yet. A look appeared on his face that was somehow both pained and grateful.

He cleared his throat. "She would sing." Under his breath he hummed a song Cora had never heard before. She pretended not to notice when his voice cracked a little, and he cleared his throat again. He had seemed so much older than her, but really he hadn't been. "She used to make eggs and hash," he said, almost embarrassed, "and she'd sprinkle salt and cheese on top and say 'Abracadabra.'"

"What is her name?" Cora had asked. "Your mother?"

"Althea." He had blinked, as though he had gone away and then returned to Pelican anew. "It's going to be a long winter," he said roughly. He tucked the unfinished taffy away.

"You probably won't be outdoors much, soon?" she had asked, and she heard the wistfulness in her own voice. He would be tucking himself into the darkness for the winter, just like the flowers.

"I wish it were spring. I have to believe it isn't always going to be this way," he said roughly. "Gotta believe there's something happening in the dark, that we just can't see yet. Something better coming."

"You should hang something in your cell to cheer you," Cora said. "Pictures of flowers, from a magazine, maybe. That's what Margaret does."

"Margaret?" he asked.

"The lady in the commissary. You know where that is?" she asked.

He nodded. "Yeah. But I've never been in there. It's on the civilian side of the fence. Right by where I planted those dahlias."

"Yeah," she said. "My da's worried about that part. He says the ground there washes out in a heavy rain."

Her face had flushed red. She could hardly believe she had said it.

"Enjoy the taffy," she had said, and then she had taken off in a run.

It had been an accident. She hadn't really meant to tell him and betray her father's confidence like that.

Cora grimaced.

Not that first time, anyway.

*　　*　　*

Cora opened her eyes and forced herself to find the newspaper front page that still haunted her. Her hand closed around the drawer handle, and she slid it open. August 14, 1917.

Rusty Weathers's familiar face looked back at her. She felt the familiar tightness clamp down in her chest. She looked into the halftone photograph of his face. He was wearing his Pelican uniform.

He used to come over to their house for dinner on the nights her mother made a roast. He liked clam chowder, and telling the same jokes over and over, and he had a chess set with pieces carved like forest animals. He gave out licorice ropes and a nickel each on Easter. Cora had known Rusty since she was five years old.

And then the Yates brothers had killed him.

GUARD SLAUGHTERED IN DARING PELICAN ESCAPE, the headline said.

Rusty's obituary ran beneath it.

Cora stood in the still, dim room with golden dust swirling around her. On the thirteenth of August every year, she sent Rusty's daughter a wad of cash. Anonymously. It was the one day of the year she went to church. She wasn't Catholic, but one year she considered going to confession, just to let the awful truth finally pass her lips. Instead, she stayed at the back of the sanctuary, soundlessly mouthing the words to the hymns, and lit a candle before leaving halfway through.

She stood in the dark-paneled room and gently touched the image of Rusty's face, remembering the way she had watched from the doorway on the day his body was recovered. It had washed up on shore. "Barely recognizable," Dina had told her grimly. "Those boys bashed his face clean in with a rock."

Dina had been caught off guard when Cora had turned her head and retched. She kept retching, and Dina had held back her hair. "Cora, golly. I didn't know you were so sensitive," she said.

But Cora's life had altered forever in that moment, tilting off its axis. She had tried to convince herself until then that maybe Rusty had been in on it somehow. That he had aided Jack and Leo off the island and then fled, as convinced of their innocence as she had been. But at Dina's words she felt the truth of it all settle deep into the hollows of herself. She had made a choice that had killed a man. It could just as easily have been her own father they had pulled from the Bay. That realization ricocheted through her, leaving a path in its wake as clear as a bullet, setting off dominoes that hadn't stopped falling to this day.

But how had Jack managed to find his way here? How had he gone from escaped fugitive to a guest of Truman Byrd? He'd arrived on Pelican still practically a kid. He'd spent two years as a prisoner, then escaped and lived as a fugitive. How had he constructed the vast empire of money, prestige, and influence required to breach the Hill when he'd started out with less than nothing—no assets, no viable background, no birth certificate, not even a real name? He had been little more than a wisp of smoke trailing a deep shadow, just like that stolen art that vanished and had never been recovered.

Where had all his money come from?

Cora felt in her pocket for the smoothness of stone, running her fingers over it. Even split three ways between Jack, Leo, and their unnamed accomplice—those paintings would have given them each the sort of power mortals long for: enough money to bury their sins and start over. To create an entirely new life from the ashes.

But the murders at the Bastion had been fifteen years ago, and the paintings had never resurfaced.

Jack's voice kept returning to whisper low and dark in Cora's ear.

Nothing here is what it seems.

She paused over the picture of him and Leo side by side in the ancient paper, struck by a new, troubling question. Jack Yates and his older brother Leo had been inseparable, from their childhood in Dorchester up until their imprisonment together at Pelican.

If Jack was on Enchanted Hill, then Leo couldn't be far behind.

So where was he?

* * *

Truman Byrd emerged onto the esplanade just as evening was descending. Electric white globes sat atop iron posts like moons between marble fountains and vast, swaying cypress trees. The evening air had coaxed more and more partygoers outside to lean over the balconies and take up residence at the card tables set on the terra-cotta tiles. Clementine was wearing a satin gown in the color of her namesake, a modest halter in the front that, when she turned, cut down the deep curve of her back and gathered in blush-colored panels at the base of her spine. Her lips were a deep maroon, her ears studded with art deco earrings, and she carried an enormous feather around with her, ushering guests to sample the trays of fig tarts and golden caramelized pears.

Truman surveyed his kingdom. Trumpets and the sound of Duke Ellington floated on the breeze. Fizzy laughter was quick on Clementine's lips, and she blew kisses and reached down from one terrace to another to tickle one of the other starlets with the tip of her maroon feather. Truman was pleased to see that his guests were beginning to settle into the week on Enchanted Hill. A day in the sun had tanned their faces and made their careful façades slide off like film from the surface of fresh milk.

As the sun began to dip toward the hills, Truman made his evening rounds, talking about politics with Gilly, dividends with the banker John Hanson, and horse racing with Simon Leit. Clem looked lovely, and he had her special drink sent over to her as a sign. Clem's eyes swept to him as the maid brought her the drink, and she fluttered her lashes, her red lips curving. He cocked his head in acknowledgment and then began to slip away as he always did, at the height of the party, to pace the white rows of tomorrow's news, red pen in hand.

But he stopped suddenly at the sound of an automobile door slamming. A ripple of his staff was gathering near where the boxwood maze spilled out onto the main terrace.

He turned, his interest growing.

"Nerts, is that Beau Remington?" Rita suddenly called out with delight. Lola looked up from the terrace, and Clementine set down her glass. Kitty Ryan smiled down into her drink, her dark lashes grazing her cheeks.

"Perhaps he'd like to join us for a midnight swim later?" she said.

Truman paused beneath the alcove, in the dusk. His guests stood and left their cards and half-eaten plates, moving toward the boxwoods in waves to greet Beau. The young man laughed in surprise at the reception as the starlets offered him cheeks to kiss and the men reached out with welcoming hands to shake.

Still, Truman bided his time. Waiting for the moment Clementine stepped forward to greet Beau.

"He's going to be bloody bigger than Gable," Albert Boyle said, suddenly appearing next to Truman. He drained his drink to the dregs.

"Yes. I think I'll prefer not to stand right next to him, for comparison's sake," Governor Gilham said. He gave a chortle. "But *you're* welcome to stay close, Berty."

Albert retorted with an expletive, and they moved forward to greet Beau together. Still Truman waited and watched. He remembered standing with Mabel the day another man had come up beside them. Flirted with her; tried to grope her right in front of him. It had been the same humiliating day Truman had realized that his fledgling paper wasn't going to make it. That he was going to have to return to his father and tell him that the money was gone.

And then he had been approached with an idea. A scheme that promised to change Truman Byrd's entire life. It had been the last day he had ever felt desperate—or powerless.

Yet he had caught the way Clem's face brightened upon seeing young Beau Remington. Like the flare of a match the moment it was struck: small, and definite.

*   *   *

Cora moved through the crowd. Always, she kept her senses trained on Jack. He was standing to the right of railroad tycoon William Morton, sending a casual waterfall of playing cards between his fingers. His navy suit was cut to a broad shoulder and followed the narrowing of his waist. It had been made to fit every angle of him, and it was the right color for him, too—a deep, lush blue. She was aware of every time he threw back his head and laughed, when his fingers massaged his wrists, when he brought a glass to his lips.

She was careful not to look when his eyes came to rest on her, and she knew he was keeping track of her, too.

"When I was younger," he had once told her, "I wanted to study the stars."

"An astrologer?" she'd asked.

He had laughed. "Astronomer." Then, seeing the flush on her face, he added "But I'd given that up long ago. I was working to become an engineer before . . . all this happened. I wanted to build bridges."

She had recovered quickly, her wit working to cover her embarrassment.

"You didn't want to be a gardener?" she had retorted; and when he smirked, a hot thrill had shot right down Cora's spine.

Now Cora scanned the crowd, picking up an abandoned glass of icy lime, mint, and gin. A breeze shivered through the espaliered mimosa trees.

"Is that Beau Remington?" one of the starlets cried from below, and Cora watched as the party turned toward a new magnetic center. Beau Remington had been in only two films, supporting roles that were both tragic enough to break hearts and set them racing. He had golden skin and broad shoulders, cut cheekbones, and blazing blue eyes. Cora watched as Daisy almost slid an entire army of cocktails off of her tray before righting it just in time.

In fact, Cora felt as though she were the only one to notice that Byrd had slipped to the periphery of his own party. The guests were moving past him to greet Beau, and Cora watched as Jack, amused, leaned against a marble banister, observing as he nursed a drink.

"So, he came after all," Daisy suddenly said behind her. Cora turned as Daisy lowered her tray. "You setting your eyes on a new guest now?" Daisy asked playfully.

Cora ignored her.

"Here," Daisy said, pushing a handful of crumpled bills toward Cora. "I forgot to tell you that Mr. Cobb tipped me for returning his tie. I thought you should have half."

Cora felt strangely touched. "No," she said. "You keep it." She gave Daisy a firm smile that ensured she wouldn't argue, and pushed the money down into Daisy's apron pocket.

"So, what was that I saw in the ballroom earlier?" Daisy asked, shooting Cora a mischievous grin. "With Mr. Conner?"

For the first time, Cora wondered whether she should ask Daisy for help. Confiding in her about Jack was out of the question. But she could use a hand with Truman and Clem. She couldn't be in two places at once.

Cora looked over at Jack.

The exchange with Daisy had been only a handful of seconds—but Beau's arrival had stirred up the party, sending the guests into an eddy to welcome him and then to ripple out again. One minute, Jack had been there, on the party's fringes.

And then he wasn't.

Cora pushed past Daisy.

"Cora," she heard her father's voice whisper low in her ear. "Do you know what happens when a dog tries to catch two rabbits?"

He gets none.

She had last seen Jack only a moment ago, on the esplanade, near the swan and pheon arrowheads carved into the main house.

Her heart sank. He must have seen an opportunity in Beau's entrance and used the moment to disappear.

As Truman stepped forward to greet Beau Remington, William Morton grabbed a glass from Cora's tray and raised it in the air. "Hear, hear!" he said.

And out of the corner of Cora's eye, she saw a shadow move.

She turned her head to see Jack slipping into the main house. The door closed silently behind him.

She set down her tray on the fountain and darted to the house, pulling open the immense door herself. It was heavy, plated with iron and gold; and by the time Cora had wrenched it open, the atrium was empty. She stopped to listen carefully. The entryway opened up into two stories of intricately carved marble and limestone, and the main staircase was carpeted to absorb footsteps; but Cora noticed that the pots of ferns that surrounded them remained still, their fronds undisturbed.

Cora's heart beat steady in her chest, strong and powerful, as though she were hitting her stride in a race she had been born to run.

Instead of panic, her thoughts felt clear and razor-sharp.

The sounds of the party grew distant, and she finally caught them: the faint echo of footsteps, disappearing down the east hallway.

She followed them. The east corridor was easily forty feet long, and she glimpsed Jack before he'd reached the end of it. He was stopping to try each door, peeking his head in to the morning room first, then one of the sitting rooms. He was just opening the door to the Billiards Room when Liam, the butler, intercepted him.

Cora pressed herself to the wall and hid behind a bronze statue.

"May I help you, sir?" she heard Liam ask.

"Just nipping back into the Assembly Room for something I left behind," Jack said.

"Certainly. Do let me know if you need help locating it," Liam said.

Liam began walking down the corridor again, and Cora waited until he had passed before allowing herself to peek out. She watched Jack pull open the door to the Assembly Room and duck inside.

Cora rose, knowing that she couldn't follow him through the doorway without giving away her advantage of surprise. She needed more answers than he had given her earlier in the day.

But she also wanted to know what he would do when he thought no one was watching.

She doubled back toward the foyer, stopping in front of a weathered bookcase. She searched the faded spines for the one called *Daedalus's Labyrinth*, then pulled it free and re-shelved it at the top right, fitting it into a carved indentation. The book slipped neatly into a lock apparatus, and Cora heard the faintest click. Then, using all her weight, she dragged open the bookcase and stepped inside.

Cora pulled the door closed behind her into almost complete darkness. She was standing in the entryway to Byrd's secret passage: the one that led to the right of the fireplace, where Truman liked to emerge and surprise his guests.

She heard the sound of her own breathing and suddenly wished for her gun. Her father had bought her a pistol when she was twenty. It had a silky silver barrel, a pearlish white handle. She had fought with him for months over wanting to become an investigator or a detective, or perhaps to join a police force somewhere—to follow a slightly different path from him that still bore traces of his footsteps. She had taken typing classes and would start off as a secretary somewhere, but she planned for that to be a stepping stone to something else. They'd had it out over dinner, lowered voices over onion soup and sourdough bread. And finally he had folded his napkin and said: "Your mother would have hated it." It was his trump card, and they both knew it, and for one day Cora almost changed her mind. Then it had steeled again, like fresh metal over a bear trap, and he had known the argument was over.

A week later, he had come home with a package. "If you're determined to be in dangerous work, then you'll have to become more dangerous than it is," he said.

He had presented Cora with the gun as his olive branch, and Cora thought it was so like her father that his peace offering was actually a weapon.

And then he had trained her to use it.

She felt along the corridor as she moved forward. She had expected it to feel stuffy and airless in the passage, but it was made from plain stone and the air inside it was cool. The walls were smooth beneath her hands, and were bare except for sconces kept so dim that she was only just able to see.

When she reached the end of the corridor, she met a door. She put an ear to it, listening, and then eased the panel open the barest crack. The room was fairly dark. The windows were closed, and light from the outside lamps was cast through golden panes of glass set into the wall like honeycombs.

She bent forward and peered through the crack to watch.

CHAPTER THIRTEEN

J ack was inside, moving along the walls and studying them as though taking some sort of inventory. Cora watched him, her suspicion mounting. He paused for a long moment in front of the southern wall, the only one in the room void of any oversized windows or fireplaces. He was carefully examining four heavy, gilded frames.

Frames that held priceless oil paintings in a straight, masterful line.

Cora's breath went ragged.

She pushed open the door and stepped out from the shadows.

"That's William Blake, is it?" she asked suddenly.

Jack swore, turning so fast that he bumped into a glass lamp. His hand struck out to catch it just before it fell.

Cora actually smiled. It felt delicious, for once, to be a step ahead of him, and she relished the taste of it.

Jack set the lamp aright and smoothed his tie. It was a lush pattern of fine, gray dots that mirrored his pocket square. His hair was slicked back with pomade.

"Yes," he said, then turned his back to her and examined the painting. "Blake," he continued. "It's called *Oberon, Titania, and Puck with Fairies Dancing.*"

Cora took another step toward him, keeping her focus on the fireplace poker.

"And another William?" she asked. She came to stand beside him and nodded toward the second painting. Cora admittedly knew very little about art, but she had stolen a glance at the Yeats signature in the corner and made a calculated guess. Jack gave her a side glance at that, as if amused; and when their eyes met, a jolt shot through Cora's veins.

"No. That's a Jack, actually," he said casually, crossing his arms, as if he had all the time in the world. As if he wanted nothing more than to be there standing with her, teaching her about art. "Jack Butler Yeats. Spelled differently than mine, and a good bit cleverer with a paintbrush. This one is entitled *The Liffey Swim*."

"You see something here you like?" she asked. "Your collection isn't quite complete yet?"

"Truman Byrd has good taste," Jack said, his tone cooling. He turned back to the art.

Could he really be planning to steal more from right under Byrd's nose? *What a brazen bastard*, Cora thought, practically marveling. They stood there together, Cora dressed in her maid's uniform, Jack in his crisp hundred-dollar suit, gazing at the wall with their elbows almost brushing. In an alternate universe, they could almost be on holiday together at a museum, looking at art for pleasure. Every nerve in Cora's body was awake and tingling as Jack examined the third painting closely—a portrait of Byrd. Surely he couldn't intend to steal a portrait of Byrd himself? She glanced nervously at the door.

"This is a Celeste Lourd," Jack said conversationally, as if reading her mind. "It's an interesting choice for a commissioned portrait. She's a real up-and-coming young artist."

"And you know your art better than anyone else here, I'm sure," Cora said. She wielded her voice like a delicate knife.

"It's been quite an informative decade since Pelican," Jack agreed, but there was a look in his eyes that Cora had never seen before. Almost as if he were holding back an ace he desperately wanted to play.

They circled each other in the dimness, the plush rug giving softly underfoot. Jack glanced slightly toward the fireplace, toward the panel Cora had shut behind her. Cora sensed that he already knew it was there. If Jack had studied the grounds of Enchanted Hill as well as Cora had, then he knew there were ways to smuggle art out of the Assembly Room without ever being seen. The fourth and final painting that hung behind them was a Degas. Even without any expertise in art, Cora could guess that the pieces that hung in that room were worth close to a hundred thousand dollars each. Maybe more.

"Just so you know," she said, "if I don't come back tonight, I've left your real identity hidden for one of my maid friends to find."

"Noted," he said.

Byrd's portrait loomed above them, his hand tucked into his vest, the chain of his pocket watch dangling in a golden arc from his pocket. Celeste Lourd had painted him with generosity, making him seem younger and more athletic than he truly was. But she had rightfully depicted his imposing glare.

Cora followed Jack's gaze toward it. "What are you doing in here, Jack?"

"I'm a connoisseur of the arts," he said. "I thought you knew that."

"Yes, your reputation precedes you in that regard. Yet you still expect me to believe that you aren't here to take Truman out or steal something?"

"I already told you," he said. "That's not why I came."

"For some sort of revenge, then? For the way Byrd took you down in his papers?"

"Not revenge, exactly, no," he countered. He touched his chin and looked at her with piercing eyes. "More like justice."

"What does that mean?"

"Ah. See, now: information will cost you information," Jack said. He was close enough that she could smell him, like pepper and leather.

"All right," Cora said warily. "What do you want to know, then?"

"I want to know why *you're* really here."

"Isn't it obvious?" she said, gesturing to her uniform. "I'm a maid."

"Bushwa." He folded his arms across his chest.

"Fine," she said. "I'm working undercover on something."

He cocked an eyebrow. "Who hired you?"

She hesitated. "I'm not at liberty to share that information."

"Who are you here to watch, then?"

"Clementine."

"Byrd hired you to watch Clementine?" Jack guessed. "So you're here acting as his own personal spy."

Cora gave the smallest nod and thought: *You have no idea.*

"Now," she said. "You have one more chance to answer my question." She turned toward a hidden panel in the wall and pulled it open, revealing a secret telephone. "Or I'm calling the police. Why did you come to Byrd Castle?"

*   *   *

Jack felt himself go cold. He could tell, looking at Cora's face, that she wasn't bluffing. With one finger, with a few potent words, she held the rest of his life in her hands. Whatever the fallout for her, it would be worse for him—she had the upper hand, and she knew it. But he had one play left—it wasn't a sure ace, but had that tingle of being the winning card anyway.

He took a deep breath and, like he always did, went for the gamble.

He turned and looked at her. Calmly, he said "I'm here to find out what really happened the night of the Bastion murders."

Color flooded into Cora's face. "Not this again, Jack," she snapped. "I stopped believing in your innocence about the time we found Rusty with his head bashed in."

Jack flinched. "Fine. But let me ask you this," he said. "The night of the Bastion theft. Where were the stolen paintings, Cora? Why weren't they found on Leo and me that night?"

She looked at him with suspicion. "You had an accomplice."

"Or we were *framed*." He could hear the anger in his voice, as fresh and raw as ever. Cora cocked her head and raised her eyebrow. She was going to be much harder to convince now than when she was fourteen, he could see that. "There was no third person that night. It was just me and my brother, at the wrong place at the wrong time. Trying to *help*, even." He shook his head in disgust. "Like a pair of rubes."

"The evidence against you was indisputable," Cora said, her voice rising. "The guards' blood was on your clothes,"

"We were trying to *help them*," Jack said, fighting to keep a hold on his frustration. It threatened to escape his grip. "We were trying to save their lives. We were passing by late that night when we heard a woman scream from inside the museum. We went running toward it, like fools, right into a trap."

"There were eyewitnesses who saw you," she insisted. "You were convicted before a judge and jury."

"They were paid off. There were no weapons on us, no art to be found. And yet we were thrown into Pelican to rot."

He took a step closer to her, both his anger and frustration and hers simmering just beneath the surface. The air practically crackled between them.

"Don't play me for a fool," Cora said quietly. Dangerously.

"When I told you I was innocent, I was telling the truth, Cora. I didn't kill those men and I've never touched that art. I've never even seen it with my own eyes. I've been trying to find it for years." He fought to keep his voice low, but he felt his desperation mounting. For some inexplicable reason, it suddenly felt like the most important thing in the world to make her believe him; like he was lifting a piece of his armor and waiting for her to strike the fatal blow. "I spent years honing my chops on cards and craps, making connections and infiltrating the underground so I could find out what really happened that night. That path led me here. Because Truman Byrd knows more about the Bastion murders than he is saying," Jack said. "And I want to know what that is."

Cora was spluttering. "And you expect this to come up over cocktails and canapes?"

"Of course not. I'm going to speak to Byrd in the language he understands."

"Which is what?" She glanced at the paintings. "Ransom?"

"No. Blackmail."

Cora paled. "I can't believe I'm hearing this."

"Let's just say that Byrd has come into possession of something that some very influential people are very eager to get back."

"And what would that be?" Cora asked suspiciously.

Jack looked over his shoulder, then took a step toward her. "Damning evidence that he's gathered on the mob and every single one of their high-ranking politicians in the state of New York. He's been holding it over them as collateral, and they want it back."

Her hazel eyes narrowed. "So you *are* working for the mob."

"I don't work for the mob," he said. "We've struck a temporary agreement based on mutual necessity. I work for myself."

"They're just paying you handsomely, then?"

"Yes. But not in money. In information." Jack took a step toward her and lowered his voice even further. A private confidence. "If I bring the damning evidence to them, they've agreed to tell me who sold those stolen Bastion paintings on the black market. You have to understand, giving up a player like that is not something they do lightly. The system only works if they can be trusted to keep sensitive dealings entirely confidential. So I have to bring them something in exchange."

She nodded, her eyes still narrowed.

"Or," he said, close enough to her now that he could see the lightened ends of her eyelashes, "alternatively, if Truman wants those files to stay in his possession badly enough, then perhaps *he'll* tell me who paid him off to frame us in his papers all those years ago."

Cora fished out a cigarette and lit it. Her fingers were long and slender as she held the flame near her mouth. They betrayed the slightest tremble, and he could tell she was trying to decide whether or not to believe him.

It was strange to think about being alone with her. How he hardly thought of her as a woman, but she was now. She would be twenty-seven—twenty-eight? It was unnerving, when all those years after Pelican he had pictured her as a girl, frozen forever in time.

The ember of the cigarette blazed and lit her face, casting a shadow that slid along her cheekbones, her mouth. "Believe me or not," he said, meeting her eyes, "but I've thought of you often over the years. You were the only kind thing I remember on Pelican."

She gave him a look that reached deep inside him and yanked. All the things he had tried to tell himself over the years—that he hadn't ruined her life; that she would find it in herself to understand—fell away like ash.

She shivered slightly and tried to hide it, but he saw.

She folded her arms across her chest as though unconvinced, but Jack sensed something deeper in the gesture. There was anguish behind it. It was self-protection from more of his lies, his subterfuge. She believed that their friendship on Pelican all those years ago had meant nothing to him—that she had simply been a means to an end.

And she had. Yet it wasn't that simple, and never had been. Whether she believed it or not, he had truly cared for her.

She had just opened her mouth to say something when the door behind them suddenly opened.

Cora took an instinctive step back.

"Ah, Conner! So here you are." Governor Gilham strode into the room, the skin on top of his head as polished as a cue ball. His grin grew when he saw Cora standing there, and he gave Jack a sly look. "Not interrupting anything here, I hope—mm, Everett?"

"Just stepped away for a self-guided tour," Jack said with a broad smile, gesturing vaguely toward the wall. "Are you much of a connoisseur, Gilham?"

Gilham barely spared the paintings a second glance. "They're swirling like vultures for a game of euchre out there." He waggled his finger at Jack. "What do you say?"

"I'm afraid I'm still nursing a bottle-ache from last night," Jack said. "Not sure how much of a partner I'll be."

"Come on, old chap," Gilham insisted. "Truman says you're the best. I won't be taking no for an answer."

He clapped Jack on the back and firmly ushered him toward the door.

Jack glanced back at Cora. She stepped out onto the loggia, the lit end of her cigarette glowing like a firefly in the dusk. Her expression was unreadable.

He had no idea whether she believed his story or not.

Under the watchful eyes of Byrd's portrait, he walked away.

CHAPTER FOURTEEN

TUESDAY, APRIL 29, 1930
~ Day Three ~

"Truman."

Byrd looked up from his mapled bacon and coffee. He'd been breakfasting with Ronald and Clem in the morning room when his head of security, Dallas Winston, entered with a pointed nod. Truman folded his crisp white napkin on the table, excusing himself, and led Dallas to his office. Rutherford followed.

"What's the news?" Truman asked, taking a seat behind his desk. He gestured to the chair in front of him, but Dallas preferred to stand. Rutherford leaned against the wall, nursing a coffee.

"There's some trouble," Dallas said. "My intelligence picked up chatter that the mob is going to try something soon."

Byrd remained silent, steepling his hands.

"How soon?" Rutherford asked.

"They might be planning to infiltrate the party itself."

Rutherford groaned. "So they would try to hit the Hill."

Byrd said "I'd like to see them try. It's like Masada up here."

"You do know what happened at Masada, don't you, Truman?" Rutherford asked.

"I hate to tell you this, Rutherford, but if I run for a higher office, this is only the tip of the iceberg," Byrd said. He felt the stubborn tightening in his throat. He refused to live in fear. He had secret bouts with paranoia, but that was much more about attacks from the inside. From his estranged wife, from being cuckolded, from being robbed. Not this.

"Still. Have you welcomed any new staff in recent weeks?" Dallas asked.

Byrd shook his head. "No new staff for at least three or four months."

"And the guests?"

"Most of them are long-time friends of mine, Dallas."

Rutherford said quietly: "But not all."

Byrd turned to Dallas. "Where exactly did this intelligence come from?"

"Our channels within the black market," Dallas said. Byrd nodded. Money was more than currency there: it was language, judge and jury, worth more than blood or loyalty. It wasn't the first time they'd gotten valuable information from their contacts inside, paid to keep track of and report on anything Byrd might be interested in.

Truman leaned back in his chair, feeling the give of the leather. Of course, plenty of his guests had dabbled in the black market. William Morton had from time to time; Truman knew that Albert Boyle was in deep with them, running his illicit drug ring. The black market and the mob were often tangled in the same webs, their threads overlapping. But surely none of those men would want to kill him. Why would they?

Still, he felt a hint of unease. Which he hated. He paid a lot of money to make sure he never had to feel worry. He desired, and purchased, the closest thing to complete control. Now he was seeing a threat in his guests and friends, his wife, his help, his own home. Annoyance flared in his gut.

He had dreamed of growing older and having money like this, particularly on the day his mother had wanted a simple pair of new gloves that his father had refused to buy for her. His father held the purse strings and the power. The first thing Truman had purchased with his paycheck was a pair of gloves for her, fine satin and lined with mink. He wanted money to take away the discomfort of want or worry, of depending on anyone outside himself. But no one ever talked about the way money brought so much additional weight to carry.

"Who is new to the scene, of your guests?" Dallas asked.

"Everett Conner," Truman said. "And Beau Remington."

Dallas raised a single eyebrow. If it were up to him, he would politely ask them to leave the grounds now.

"What do you know of them?" he asked.

"Beau is a rising star. There's no benefit to him wanting to do anything but kill me with kindness. I hold the keys to his career."

"And Everett Conner?"

Truman had met Everett gambling in Reno. They had sat next to each other at a high-stakes table, and something about the man had reminded Truman of his brother Elias. It was the way Everett kicked back his head when he laughed, and touched his cowlick, just like Elias used to. They didn't resemble each other much physically, but Truman had caught the movement from the corner of his eye and the familiarity of it had almost made him gasp.

From then on, Truman had liked having Everett near. He was a damn good card player. But more than that, sometimes Truman pretended he was playing with Elias.

"All right," Byrd relented. "We were meant to have the costume party in the ballroom tonight. But let's switch up the plans and flip the game. Keep people off balance, and guessing."

Dallas nodded.

"I highly doubt there's a threat present from any of the women. I'll have Clementine host them for a women's evening, and I'll keep the men close. And all of the security with me."

"Good," Rutherford said.

Truman waited until the men had left and then pulled out the small iron train on his desk. It was heavier than it looked, and the latches were a delicate clasp, securing the locomotive to the freight car. His father and Elias had built it together.

Truman had once tried to take an interest in the things his father loved—and the things that Franklin Byrd loved were fishing, hunting, and his first son, Elias. On his mother's insistence, one of the few fights she ever won, his father had taken them camping at Starved Rock. The air was thick with pine, the water as cool and clear as melted crystal, and Truman felt as though he were trying to pass some sort of test. They played cards; and when he beat his father in blackjack, his father looked at him for the first time the way he looked at Elias.

Truman had tasted that hit, and he wanted more of it. He wondered if that was why his mother liked her laudanum so much. But then he had tripped over a stray root when his father sent him to gather firewood and landed hard on his right wrist. He knew the bone had broken, but he kept it hidden, holding it gingerly through the night from the pain. His deception was discovered the next morning when Elias was trying to teach him to whittle, and his father wrenched his wrist so hard it made him yelp. Afterward, Truman's father had drunk deep from his flask and packed up their things in silence.

Franklin Byrd was a man of few words. But he taught Truman their power. Words were precise. Words could be wielded as a shield or a weapon. He knew that well. And sometimes the absence of words was the greatest weapon of all.

Truman ran his fingers over the metal of the train, feeling its crevices. Truman couldn't hope to beat his father or Elias when it came to anything with his hands, but he could beat them with mind games. Elias had once painted a bird on the side of the toy freight car, gold and black. Showed Truman the way the light hit the paint in the sun and flashed, so that it almost looked like it was taking flight. "We're brothers. We're Byrd men," he said, and gave Truman the train while his wrist was still healing. Elias had contracted pneumonia shortly after. He died at the age of seventeen, when Truman was twelve years old.

His father had gone on a bender that lasted for six months, and his construction business almost went under. Franklin told everyone at the bar how Elias understood wood and grains and the way beams should fit together, understood it like a doctor understood how bones fit together in a body. All of Franklin's hopes were pinned on a boy who went underground before he turned eighteen. And Truman spent the rest of his life trying to live up to a dead boy. A lifetime trying to earn favor with a man he didn't even like.

"I was going to name my company Byrd and Son," Franklin said a year after Elias was gone. He had come home wearing grief that had settled into deep grooves on his face, pooling in the hollows of his words, and Truman didn't realize how drunk Franklin was until it was too late.

"You still could," Truman had said softly.

His father gave a short, cruel laugh. "My name is wasted on you."

Truman ran his fingers over the old train, which had faded and chipped with age. The gold bird that his brother had painted looked dim in the fading light.

Whether it was to spite his father for stripping him of the name Byrd or to honor his brother for once wearing it, Truman still didn't know.

But he had grown up and put it on everything.

*　　*　　*

Cora's head swam.

She looked at herself in the mirror, her eyes bright with their haloes of gold, sleepless shadows gathering beneath them. She had needed to get away from Jack last night. She had felt the confusion starting to swell as Jack talked, the doubts planting themselves like seeds within her again. He had a way of tricking her into thinking that things sounded reasonable. Had she learned nothing from Pelican? The water ran in streams down her knuckles as she dunked her sponge deep into the bucket and scrubbed grit from the Astral Bedroom sink. Soap bubbles gathered in the sink drain like translucent pearls.

She had found a single black-eyed Susan tied to the fence in the days after Jack's escape. It had wilted; and when she came upon it, something inside her had ripped, the way it does when a person grows up too quickly. It happened in a violent instant, without the years to stretch and make room for passage.

She had loved Jack. Trusted him. Believed in him. And he had fled, and made her an accomplice to a crime she never could have imagined him capable of.

That wound had never healed. It was the most tender part of her, and she would never show it to anyone. When she moved to New York she had prayed raw, desperate prayers that her story could somehow be redeemed. But as the years went by, she didn't see how it was possible. So she decided she'd do it herself, somehow. She'd become an investigator. And giving up Bobby was probably the most selfless decision she ever made. She had forfeited the chance to be truly known, with the clear-eyed understanding that Bobby was her last good shot and she would likely end up alone. She hoped that he had found real intimacy with the woman he ended up with. But some nights, lying awake, she wondered if he ever still thought about her.

Daisy pushed open the bathroom door and closed it behind her. "Ella!" she said in surprise. "There you are."

"Where else would I be? I live in the lavatories now, remember?" Cora asked lightly. She squeezed the water from the sponge and set to scrubbing the grout.

"You look a bit tired," Daisy said, examining her carefully.

"Thanks," Cora said.

"No, I don't mean it like that. Just—are you still feeling badly?"

Cora looked up at her. Sweet Daisy. She felt the tug again, to ask for help. To tell the truth, for the first time in so long. To let someone in.

"I didn't sleep well last night," she admitted. She opened—then closed—her mouth before she could say more.

Daisy leaned against the marble wall. "Are you going to tell me what's going on with Mr. Conner now, then?" she wheedled with a knowing smile.

Cora raised an eyebrow. "Are you going to tell me what's going on with Liam?"

Daisy's eyes widened in surprise. But Cora had seen the way Liam looked at Daisy, and the way Daisy sidled off shortly after her shift was over. Cora drew toward her. "Mmhmm. I thought so," she teased. "Turn around. You missed a button."

"Fine," Daisy said, turning and holding up her hair. "Yes. Liam and I have been sneaking around a bit."

Cora nudged Daisy and made a sound. "I knew it!"

"If Macready found out. . . ."

Cora buttoned the notch on Daisy's uniform. "Better be worth it. Is he a good kisser, then?"

Daisy bit her lip at her reflection in the mirror. She pulled her uniform to the side and showed a mark on her neck.

"You little vixen!" Cora laughed in surprise and snapped her with the end of a towel.

"Your turn to spill, now," Daisy said. "You knew Everett Conner before this, didn't you? You got white as a sheet when he arrived, but I didn't put it together until I saw you talking."

The smile fell from Cora's face.

She swallowed.

"I knew him before, yes," she said carefully. "Years ago."

"In New York?"

Cora didn't answer. "When I was younger. We were both very different people."

"You didn't know he was coming?"

Cora shook her head. "I hadn't seen him in years." She knelt and began to collect her bucket and scrub brush.

"You weren't happy to see him."

"I thought we were friends once." Cora hesitated, not looking Daisy in the face. "He did something that hurt me."

"Well then, I'll kill him," Daisy said. She nudged Cora. "I could slip something in his tea that would give him the runs."

Cora laughed again.

"But really, Ella. Should I intervene if I see you together again?"

Cora thought for a moment. Wondering again how much she should believe Jack's story. She thought of the list of names and dates hidden away in his secret book. A list, perhaps, of the information he was meant to be looking for. And it would explain why he had the mob's telephone number.

"No," she said finally. "I can handle him myself."

"All right, then," Daisy said. "Just don't run off with him and leave me to clean the jacks. This whole week's yours, remember?"

"I remember," Cora said.

"Oh! I almost forgot. This came for you in the post." Daisy drew a crisp white rectangle out of her apron pocket.

It was a postcard.

Cora took it from her, examining it warily. The image on the front was an art deco print of a rose. It was dying, its head tilting downward, its petals shedding like black raindrops. It looked ominous, and Cora had a guess as to who it was from before she turned it over.

The back of it was blank, save for the name *Miss Ella Duluth* and the address of Byrd Castle.

The postmark was from New York City.

The meaning was clear, without Mabel having to write a word.

"Who is that from?" Daisy asked.

"Just a friend," Cora said.

"Come on," Daisy said. "If you're feeling tired, you can sneak a tea."

"Be there in a minute," Cora said. "I have one more thing to finish up here."

She waited until Daisy had closed the door before she took out a small pocketknife. She flipped open the blade and approached the door to the Astral Room balcony.

She crouched, examining the openings in the teakwood wall. She gauged the angle to the bed.

She would either have to hide out on the balcony until nightfall without being found, or scale the balcony from the outside—something she was actually considering. One night, one risk, to set her up for the rest of her life. Perhaps that was how Jack once felt. Cora took her pocketknife to the screen and cut out a flap just large enough to fit her camera, then replaced it so carefully that it was unnoticeable.

She reached for the worry stone in her pocket, then the chain around her neck bearing her mother's small, silver cross. Cora had sown her seeds of doubt about God the year that Jack escaped, then gave up on Him entirely when her mother died a year later. "God always plays the long game," her mother had whispered when it had been Cora's turn to brush the thinning hair from her mother's face. "Remember." She had clasped a frail hand around Cora's with a firmer grip than Cora had expected. "Even when it is longer than we want."

Cora returned her knife to her pocket. She thought the game had ended thirteen years ago.

But perhaps it had only lain dormant, and Jack's arrival meant it wasn't really over, after all.

*　　*　　*

Cora met Daisy in the kitchen, where they filled trays with silver bowls of ice and glasses of lime rickies, iced teas, and lemonades. The cook was scraping pieces of yesterday's tenderloin into the trash.

"What are you doing?" Daisy cried.

Dorothy threw her a look. "The starlets won't eat them," she said.

Daisy's face contorted, red flushing in patches along her neck.

"My niece would actually grow properly if she could eat what this house treats as garbage," Daisy bit out, her jaw grinding. "Esther is only two, and my sister is making her soup out of *Russian thistle*."

Tumbleweeds. Cora flinched. She touched Daisy lightly on the hand.

Daisy took a deep breath and smoothed her face back into a pleasant mask before she picked up her tray and stepped out into the sunshine. Across the esplanade, the guests were gathering on the clay tennis courts. Clementine was with Rita, the two of them dressed in jewel-toned, wide-legged trousers. They swiped playfully at each other with their racquets. They wore straw hats and silk scarves tied pertly around their necks, and small dogs frolicked around the edges of the court, yipping.

Cora flushed at the sight of Jack there, racquet in hand, loitering alongside Byrd and Beau Remington. They were all dressed smartly in tennis flannels and tailored suitcoats. She moved toward him in the shadows of the palm fronds. Her heart had quickened when she had leaned toward him last night, in the golden darkness of the Assembly Room. She had smelled his scent and was appalled that her body had responded just like it had when she was fifteen, wanting to be closer to him.

Governor Gilham leaned in to say something, and Jack threw back his head and laughed. He looked well rested and at ease, twirling his racquet in his hand, throwing an easy grin at the starlets. Cora felt a sudden urge to stab him with her pocketknife.

When she approached, she could practically feel the dull purple hollows beneath her eyes. Jack gave Daisy a wide smile, and didn't spare Cora a glance.

Something curled deep in Cora's belly. Watching Jack, one would never dream that anything was wrong, which made her trust him even less than she already did.

Cora took a little dried biscuit out of her pocket and slipped it to one of the dogs, a small schnauzer terrier. She straightened just as Rita Blanchard picked up the bowl of nuts and put a cashew to her cupid lips. She sucked it and held another out to Jack, blinking at him with her long fringe of lashes. "Would you like one?"

He kept his eyes focused on Rita when he took it. "I'd actually prefer something a little sweeter," he said, and cracked it between his teeth with a grin. Beside him, Lola's hair was dark and glossy, smooth as melted candy.

Cora took a fresh glass from the tray and pushed it forcefully into the sugar crystals to coat the rim.

"Mr. Conner?" she asked. She met his eyes.

Her hand brushed his, faintly, when she handed him the lemonade. The warmth of his skin hadn't faded before he abruptly tipped the glass and spilled half of it down the front of Cora's apron.

She gasped, the cold liquid like a bolt of ice shooting through her.

"Horsefeathers! Oh, I'm so sorry," he cried, and dropped his racquet in a rush. "I'm terribly sorry, how clumsy of me—" he said, and whipped out his handkerchief.

He offered it to Cora, and it took everything in her not to rip it from his hands. She gave him a perfectly controlled smile and said "Not to worry, Mr. Conner. Accidents happen."

"Here, I insist," he said. He apologized to the other guests and took Cora by the elbow, leading her to the back of the bath house, just beyond sight.

Cora wrenched her elbow out of his grip. There was a trail of sugar crystals drying on her arm.

"What are you *doing*?" she hissed, turning to him. "Was that on purpose, you cow?"

She mopped furiously at the spill that had darkened through her uniform. She could feel it soak through her undergarments, and her skin tingled.

"Again, I apologize," he said. His mouth took on a wry glimmer of amusement. "And—did you just call me a cow?"

He disappeared into the bathhouse, emerging with a white towel that smelled faintly of lavender. "We weren't finished last night," he said. He handed it to her. "There are still things you need to know."

She glowered at him, mopping the stain.

Three years ago, she had wound through a blue-collar neighborhood with crammed streets of wooden triple-decker houses. She had taken the train up from New York to Boston and found herself standing outside a chipped front door, green as the color of moss. An Althea Yates in Dorchester did exist. Cora had looked her up, summoned her courage, and rang the doorbell. Cora had made up a story, said she had the wrong address. And just before Althea Yates closed the door, the light hit her face. Her expression changed, and it was like seeing an echoing reflection of Jack.

Cora didn't know what had compelled her to go there that day.

She supposed she just needed to know whether it had all been a lie, or whether anything Jack had ever told her was actually the truth.

Now she took the towel from Jack and, as she stepped back, the branches of a bush caught in her hair. It made her feel like an awkward young girl again. And that made her want to be cruel.

"You told a nice story last night. But Rusty is still dead." The twinkle in Jack's eye dimmed as Cora found the place to hurt him and pressed in. "You can't explain away what happened on that island. You use people for your own purposes and leave carnage in your wake. Why would I ever help you again?"

He stiffened, and she knew her words had hit home. "Right," he said. "I thought we might be able to help each other out. I'm in a little better position to repay my debt this time. But if that's the way you want to play it—" He opened his palms in a frustrated surrender. "I'll stay out of your way, and you stay out of mine."

He tipped his hat to her firmly, like a gentleman, and turned away from her.

She whispered: "Jack."

He stopped.

"What would you want?" she asked warily. She swallowed. "From me?"

He looked both ways, then took a step toward her. He leaned forward, so that she could feel his breath on her ear. "I need to find those files. You can be places I can't. But I can do the same for you. So . . . maybe we could help each other."

She handed the towel back to him, and he clutched it.

The sense around him was eager, and almost disarmingly boyish. And Cora was struck by a recognition of that same part of him that she had known at Pelican.

But perhaps that disarming sense was what made him most dangerous of all.

"What are the files?" she asked reluctantly.

His eyes darkened. He leaned forward. "They're documenting a horrific scheme called frame-ups. Men who want a divorce pay off the police to frame their wives for prostitution. They'll be lured to a hotel room to be 'caught' with a man, arrested, then shipped off to a reformatory. They lose their children, their freedom. Sometimes they can get out if they pay an exorbitant amount of money for bail that's split among those running the scheme. Innocent women have been framed for years, and everybody's in on it. The cops, the lawyers, the judges, the politicians. If that story broke, it could take down the city."

Cora thought back to the pages she had seen hidden in his book, full of names and dates, and her stomach curled in disgust.

"How is this possible?" she whispered angrily.

"Truman has a list of every woman who has been framed by the entire system. It's a huge farce, but the mob depends on keeping these crooked politicians and judges in power so that all their other illegal dealings can carry on without interference. They will stop at nothing to prevent that information from getting out."

"And if you deliver those files back to the mob, they'll tell you who really stole the Bastion paintings all those years ago?"

"Yes," Jack whispered. "Or I'll blackmail Truman with his own blackmail."

"And what of all those wronged women?" Cora asked, her jaw flaring. "And the ones still to come?"

"Perhaps I'll make my own copy of the intel," Jack said, meeting her eyes. "Perhaps it will still make its way to the newspapers after all, once I have what I need."

He glanced over his shoulder. "But for now, I'm going to need to search Byrd's office."

"I've already done that," Cora said automatically. "I combed through it head to toe when I was first here. Those files aren't there."

He narrowed his eyes. "Why were you searching Truman's office?"

She hesitated. "Because Mabel's the one who hired me," she said. A crumb of truth, if not the whole story. She hedged her bets and, thinking quickly, steered him away from the real story. "She wants Clem gone. And I'm going to help her with that."

"Everett, what are you doing over there?" Rita called coyly.

"You should go," Cora said. "Before you raise suspicions for both of us."

"Can we agree to strike a deal? Help each other, just for a few days?" he asked urgently. He looked at her with something like a very cautious hope.

Cora gritted her teeth. As much as she hated it, she needed help. Her future was slipping out of her grasp.

"Fine," she said curtly. "I'll keep an eye out for your files if you'll help engineer some sparks between Clem and Beau."

"Deal," Jack said. His face broke into a rare true smile.

"Now go," she said.

"Wait. You have a little something—" He reached out and pulled a twig from her hair.

She felt a dip in her stomach at his gentle touch. A warning, stirring within her. But what other choice did she have? He walked away and she watched him uneasily. Wondering if she had just made a deal with the devil himself.

Twice.

CHAPTER FIFTEEN

Cora changed her uniform, then the sheets in the Astral Bedroom. On her way out, she stepped into the bathroom and spritzed two heavy sprays of Clementine's signature perfume on one of her own scarves. She would waft it outside Byrd's office later like an invitation.

It was a tricky maneuver, designing romantic, secluded moments for them, because of the way their relationship worked—a big open secret and a game, and that seemed to be the way they liked it. But she was running out of days, so it was time to force things into play. She entered the kitchen and said casually to Dorothy, the cook, "Miss Garver is requesting a private table near the party's end tonight, in the loggia of her suite. Shrimp cocktail, two bottles of the reserve white wine. And a cheese souffle."

Dorothy paused over the brining of two dozen pheasants, looking momentarily incensed. "A private dinner? But tonight is meant to be the men's night now." Dorothy maneuvered around copper stock pots of potatoes to check her pages of instructions. "Cigars and brandy and oysters on the half-shell?" she said, perturbed.

While Dorothy's back was turned, Cora nicked the heavy iron ring of keys hanging off the notch in Macready's office.

"Don't tell me it's changed again," Dorothy said, the color in her face rising.

"Sorry—" Cora said. "I must have gotten the dates wrong, then. But best make sure to have the ingredients on hand, anyway, for the next few days."

The keys dropped heavily into her apron pocket.

Dorothy grunted and turned back to her pheasants, and Cora sauntered out the door.

She almost ran right into Mrs. Macready.

"Change of plans for you this evening, Ella," Macready said. "You and Daisy are to staff the men's night out there." Macready jerked a nod toward the cascading outdoor porticos. "I'm sending some of the younger maids to serve the girls in the house tonight."

"I thought I would be serving Miss Garver," Cora said, eyes narrowing. She had been planning to eavesdrop on the conversations between the starlets. Hoping that some alcohol would loosen their tongues, and that Cora might find out something—anything—useful.

"Tonight you're being reassigned. Because I know you can hold your own," Macready said. "And the boys out there've been drinking since noon."

Cora gritted her teeth. "Fine," she said. The keys tugged at her pocket as Macready led her back into the kitchen. Cora tried to forget all about them, practicing the way her father had taught her to avoid a thought so that a mark couldn't sense it. "If it doesn't exist to you," he would say, "then it doesn't exist to them." She had used the advice many times in the kitchen when she would stare into his lined face and try not to think about Jack.

Macready began to brew a strong batch of coffee, and Cora threw spiced jerky and freshly baked cheese rolls into a basket. "We'll serve them this to soak up the booze," Cora said, placing deviled eggs with horseradish on the tray.

"Don't outright refuse if they ask for another drink," Macready said, dispatching the coffee into cups like they were miniature soldiers with marching orders. "Just . . . water it down to almost nothing."

Cora gave her a nod of acknowledgment. Byrd liked enough liquor to keep a party going, but he disapproved of sloppy drunkenness. "He likes order, and beauty; a world of cultivated excess under control," Macready had instructed Cora in her training.

"Not people stumbling around like they'd been mickied," Daisy had whispered in Cora's ear.

But Cora could tell something was brewing outside as evening approached—whether trouble or opportunity, it was hard to tell. She felt the change in the air as soon as she stepped outdoors. The late afternoon was oppressive, the kind that made clothes feel damp and a half-size too small. The keys sank a degree lower in Cora's pocket to press against her leg.

She was disappointed that the plans had changed, that the women and men would be separating. That meant that Byrd would likely stay up too late playing cards, and another night would be lost.

She steeled herself. She wouldn't think that way.

Daisy squeezed Cora's arm as she passed, weighed down with a tray of seltzers.

"Watch yourself tonight," Daisy said, giving Cora a careful look as she passed. They all knew what happened when powerful men in packs had too much to drink and started to feel entitled. Cora promised herself that before she left the Hill, she would pass on a few of her father's defense lessons to Daisy.

The men were heavy on the cologne, perspiring in their silk suits and hats. Beau Remington sipped a mint julep, bantering with Governor Gilham, Albert Boyle, and Ronald Rutherford. Truman anchored the other end with railway tycoon William Morton, banker John Hanson, and the British tennis phenom Simon Leit. Jack was somewhere in the middle. Cora balanced the tray and watched Truman. Could he possibly have known that the story he painted in his papers wasn't true? Could he have known that Jack and Leo were innocent, and framed them anyway?

She didn't know which she found worse—that the world could be that cruel and unjust to two boys who were truly innocent—or that Jack was a liar, thief, and murderer who had taken her for a fool.

Clementine came to hold court in the center. She wore a long, liquid blue satin dress that hugged her curves and flattened around her body in the wind. It was half dress, half nightgown. Her voice was sultry, a laugh deep in her throat, and the men all laughed along with her. She was sharp at impersonations, and people were always surprised to find out that she was actually funny.

"There'll be dancing tomorrow night," she was saying as Cora approached. "Which of you fine lads is going to take a spin on the floor with me?" She gave a throaty chuckle when they all jostled and raised their hands. Byrd sipped his drink quietly. "Off to the nest, now," she cooed over her shoulder, batting her lashes and sauntering away. "Be good tonight, boys."

The men broke out a round of cigars as two of the butlers brought card tables and a large bronze telescope out through the heavy front door and situated them beneath the bell towers.

"Does this thing help us to see the stars?" Hanson called to Byrd, directing the telescope toward the girls' wing. The men's laughter was boisterous but seemed good-natured, without a sour undercurrent—but Cora listened for it, lurking there, waiting for the moment when it might turn. They were dressed more casually than their tails from the past two nights. Their dinner jackets were unbuttoned, their patterned ties either knotted loosely at their necks or removed entirely. The palm fronds rustled in the breeze overhead. The sun was burning red-hot over the ocean, turning the terra-cotta tiles crimson.

"Carry on without me, men," Byrd announced, using his cigar to gesture toward his office. "I'll be back after my last editing rounds."

Byrd's early rags had tied the Bastion murders to Jack and Leo with an almost unwavering insistence that would never pass muster in his current, more respectable brand of newspapers. Perhaps that had been more than tabloid hysteria and an urge to sell papers, Cora thought. Perhaps it was to cover for someone. Someone who had a lot of money, and was very powerful.

Someone who would fit right in with the men who were on the Hill that night.

Jack remained at the edges of the group, flipping through a deck of cards, nursing a drink. He flayed out the cards and set a roulette wheel turning. A metal ball ticked around the rotating wheel. The edges of the tablecloths lifted in the breeze. Knowing Jack, he would remain sober as anything. He needed to stay as sharp as Cora did.

Parts of her hated him, and yet it was also strangely comforting to see him.

He met her eyes and then looked away without a spark of recognition. How could he be there, laughing and conversing and playing games with the man who supposedly had ruined his life? He was the picture of calm indifference. Leaning against the table, all ease and smoothness, while the sun set behind him in a burning, orange haze.

*   *   *

Jack noticed the gilded edges of the playing cards first, then the birds mapped onto their faces. The backs of the cards had an outline of the Castle, its distinctive bell towers and needle-thin palm trees. He flipped the cards through his hands, loosening their stiffness, the paper turning supple beneath his fingers. He watched the maid who had interrupted him and Cora now make her way through the middle of the pack, parting the men. Cora had called her Daisy. She looked graceful, the silver tray perfectly balanced, her apron crisp and starched, her chin up. There was a pleasant smile on her face, but she seemed careful not to make eye contact. She glided into their spaces without really being seen.

It wasn't hard for Jack to tell who among them might be trouble.

Albert Boyle was tottering off-balance, his face flushed. His short fingers shuffled through the poker chips as though he were searching for sea glass.

Daisy carefully set down the tray of lime rickeys and offered one to Albert. The glass was sweating when he took it from her, his fingers heavy with rings. He wore a suit checkered in wide windowpanes and a bowler hat, and tonight he had a cane that Jack had not noticed him carrying before. Jack eyed it, watching Albert shuffle the cards, and noticed with a quick side glance that Cora was, too. He could tell by the way she was pretending not to pay attention, her head cocked the same way it used to be when she was listening for the guards.

"Thanks, little lass," Albert said. His voice was slightly too loud, and he fumbled with the top of his cane, unscrewing the carved silver handle to take out his own hidden flask. He tipped it generously into his lime rickey. "Byrd's always got maids cute as a bug's ear. What's he serving us tonight?"

"You're in luck," Daisy said, her voice clear and strong, but Jack could see the slightest shake in her fingers. "A treat. Roast ringneck pheasant."

Albert leaned in closer to her with a grin. "But is the treat what's on the tray, or what's holding it?"

Gilham gave a half laugh and the banker, Hanson, snorted. They both turned away, as if to pretend they hadn't heard. Perhaps they thought if they didn't encourage Albert, he would stop.

Beau Remington rose, running a hand through his hair, but stopped short of saying anything. These men, Jack thought. Powerful enough to lead a country's industries like admirals, yet unwilling to stand up to a friend to cause a ripple at a dinner party. The powerful, always silently acquiescing while the innocent were targeted. For some reason, the thought that it could have been Cora angered him even more. He felt an old rage stirring in his throat.

William Morton half-heartedly tried to step in. "Care to play whist tonight, Albert?" he asked. "Or billiards?"

Daisy saw an opening and attempted to flee, but Mr. Boyle took her arm. "Wait, now, don't rush off just yet," he insisted. He placed his hand on her back, but too low. She stopped suddenly and swallowed, her face paling. Then she appeared to steel her small frame to take it.

"Byrd's been a good friend of mine for a long time," Mr. Boyle said. "And he's always so generous to share what's his." And then, in case she didn't catch his meaning, Mr. Boyle moved his hand a degree lower.

Jack stepped forward, clearing his throat. "Albert, old boy," he said, reaching up to loosen his tie. "I don't think that's the game here." His voice sank into a twang of a midwestern accent now, and he was careful that even when he was angry, the long-buried Boston didn't resurface. "So step off, now. You follow?"

Mr. Boyle sneered, but it seemed more in confusion than anything, as though he were unused to being confronted. He began to turn away, but instantly Jack was beside him. He managed to remove Albert's cane, whip a porcelain coffee cup from Daisy's tray, and push it into Mr. Boyle's hands in one smooth motion. "Drink up and let's take a little walk and at least pretend one of us is a gentleman."

Mr. Boyle guffawed. "Like I haven't seen you sneaking out at night yourself—" he began warningly, but Jack gave him a distinctly ungentle shove past Daisy. He had at least a half-foot's height on Albert, and he rose to the fullness of it to ensure that there was no room for argument. "Here you go, old chap," he said firmly, with two sharp raps on Albert's back, and began to steer him toward the main house.

Out of the corner of his eye, he could see Cora move into place, offering coffees and jerky to smooth over the disturbance. "Night's just getting started," she said, smiling winsomely at the men while she poured coffee into their cups. It was a smile that was curated: warm and maternal rather than flirtatious. The humidity from the night was making the small hairs curl at the nape of her neck and at her temples. "Need a little caffeine and a bit of luck," she said, handing Beau Remington a piece of jerky.

Jack was surprised by the jolt he felt when Beau smiled at Cora, and she flushed.

He was in a foul mood when he turned back to Albert.

"What the hell is this?" Albert asked. "Get your hands off me."

Jack ignored him and kept him moving. He barely saw Albert in front of him now. Instead, he pictured his father. His heart had given out not long before Jack's escape, likely not helped by the trial and the sentencing of his two sons. Jack hadn't even been present at the funeral of the man who had taught him how to ride a bicycle and make a chair. How to shave the beginnings of the mustache Jack had only barely been able to grow when he was thrown in Pelican. His father had raised him to give a woman flowers, to take his hat off in her presence and carry her luggage up the stairs. That your wife could be the best friend you ever had. Men like Albert, like Truman, didn't even know what they had. They could be truly known by someone else and they refused it. He yearned for what they threw away like scraps. For thirteen years, he hadn't let anyone get too close. Not because he didn't want to. But because it wouldn't have been fair.

He hadn't been perfect. He had been lonely over the years, and had sought his own comfort. But he never let anyone in deep enough to approach love. Breaking a heart was a worse thing than stealing a piece of art, in his opinion. Art didn't breathe and cry.

He took Albert's arm with enough strength to ensure that the man would comply and led him through the front door of the main house. "Where's your room, old chap?"

Albert said, "Listen, Cotter, is that your name?" His speech was slurring, but Jack could hear the warning just beneath it. "You clearly don't understand how things work—"

"I may be a newer friend of Truman's, but I happen to know that the two things he hates are messy drunks and people abusing his employees. So I'm escorting you to your room to sleep it off."

It was hard for Jack to believe that he was defending Truman Byrd's character, the man who had played such a part in his own demise. He asked the butler for help finding Albert's room and then gave Albert a firm push inside.

The old fury curled up in him like smoke.

Albert sniggered and said "Truman is going to hear about this. And we'll see who is left standing in the morning."

"Yeah, you and Truman go way back, do you?" Jack said. He deposited Albert on the bed.

"I've been friends with him since before he had anything. That's called *loyalty*. So if you think you can just waltz in here on your first damn day and start playing gatekeeper—" Albert spat. "Truman is going to kick you out on your ass."

"Albert, I didn't take you for the charitable type." Jack folded his arms, blocking the door in a subtly menacing way. "What did you see in Truman before anyone else did?"

Albert laughed.

Jack fished out a cigarette and offered it to him.

"Oh, you want to make nice now?" Albert said. But he took it. "You met him playing cards in Reno, didn't you? Had to be in on a dark circuit in order to get an invite there." Albert cocked his eyebrow and leered.

Jack gave a nod. That was true. You had to have some sort of reputation with the men running those underground card games before they would let you in. He knew that Albert was in deep himself.

"Then you know," Albert continued. "At those tables, it's not how much money you have. It's what you're willing to do." He looked at Jack. "What were you willing to do, Mr. High-and-Mighty?" He laughed again, and sucked on his cigarette.

Jack leaned in close to his face, close enough for Albert to draw back, and said in a deathly quiet voice: "Touch one of those maids again and you can find out."

Albert dropped his cigarette on the bedspread and gave a slurred grunt. Jack swore and picked it up before it could set the room on fire, and by the time he had stubbed it out in the ashtray Albert had rolled over and passed out. After reluctantly checking to make sure Albert was still breathing, Jack took the well-timed opportunity to snoop. He rifled through Albert's bureau and briefcase, then bent to look under the bed and behind the hanging tapestries. Above the four-poster bed was a magnificent gold-plated ceiling boasting interlaced patterns of shields and pendants. The center panel was an eagle with wings spread and talons out. In the closet, he could still smell Albert's heady cologne, and there were empty liquor bottles and wrappers of candy strewn on the floor amongst Albert's discarded clothes.

Albert's question crawled on his skin. *What were you willing to do?*

Jack thought of the night in the old stone tavern in Chicago. The Moss Duck, so called because the roof leaked so that the rainwater came in through the roof and clung to the stone walls, turning them a mucky green like a stagnant pond. But it was nestled in a back alley where the cops never seemed eager to venture; the drinks were strong and good; and the owner left them alone. And he served killer au jus sandwiches.

Getting involved in the underground, and, by association, with the mafia, had been like wooing a serrated knife. He had bided his time, listening carefully. He had learned who talked among the small-time crooks, and made sure to pay them extra attention. It was the trickiest work he'd ever done, weaving the next layer of a web and moving ever closer to its center. The only thing trickier had been planning his escape from Pelican.

Albert gave a snore from the bed, and Jack felt fresh annoyance that he had wasted so much of his life while creatures like this walked free and were even celebrated. He didn't bother spending any more time in Albert's room. Jack needed to find a safe. A vault. Or perhaps one of Byrd's infamous hidden passageways.

He stepped out into the hallway and closed the door behind him. He had worked his contact deep in the underground circuit for years. Virgil's mouth was normally wired tighter than a steel coil. But Jack waited for his opportunity. And that night at the Moss Duck, he got Virgil drunk. The dripping walls had reminded him of Pelican. He had listened to the rhythm of it and bought them a sixteen-year-old bottle of Lagavulin to split. Jack had waited patiently, after so many years, to tug the thread. Until they were three quarters of the way through the bottle.

"The Bastion job, years back," Jack had said. "You know anything about that?"

Virgil laughed. "That was a pretty little job, wasn't it? Practically had a bow on top."

"You know who did it, then?"

Virgil eyed the empty bar counter and cracked his neck. "Thief's honor. Even if I knew, I ain't telling."

"You ever see one of those paintings?"

Virgil quirked an eyebrow. "I might have."

"Well, if you might have seen it, I might have an interested party."

"Arright. Yeah, I saw one once. But it was years back."

Jack's heart had skipped a beat. So the paintings had been sold on the market. He'd poured Virgil another shot of Lagavulin. Waited until the barkeep went into the back.

"Can you put me in touch with the person who sold them?"

Virgil had thought for a long moment. "Not likely." He flicked his eyes toward the discarded newspaper that was stuck to the scummy floor. "But there's someone else who knows for sure."

Jack had picked up the *Post-Courant* and examined the front page. "Herbert Hoover?"

"Truman Byrd." He smiled a sour smile. "He's always known more than he's saying."

Jack had waited half a beat. Then all but whispered "What do you mean?"

But Virgil's smile had dropped. "You're talking about powerful people here," he said, eyeing the barkeep. And then he'd shut up entirely.

Jack began to walk the hallways now. He checked each of the doors, glancing inside the ones that he found unlocked, and scanned the darkened rooms for their contents. There were two closets, two bathrooms, a sitting room. Three locked doors he assumed to be guest bedrooms. His hand was on the knob of the ninth door when he heard a voice say "Mr. Conner."

He tried not to jump when he felt Dallas Winston, Byrd's security, appear suddenly beside him. He turned. The handle of Dallas's gun in his belt glinted in the shadows.

"What brings you up here, Conner?" Dallas asked. His voice was pleasant. But Jack didn't miss the fact that Dallas's hand moved toward his gun.

"Oh, thank goodness!" Jack said. "I'm looking to have a private word with Truman, but I realized I don't have a clue where his office is."

Dallas studied Jack. At first, Jack suspected he was trying to determine whether or not he was inebriated. But his eyes lingered on the places where one might conceal a weapon, and a part of Jack went cold.

"It's not on this floor," Dallas finally said. He cocked an eyebrow. "It's on the fourth. I'll escort you there." He pointedly waited until Jack turned to follow him, then led him up two more flights of stairs. The sconces flickered on the walls, and Jack heard a distant giggle waft through the open stairway. Gardenias spilled out from the chinoiserie in the stairway landings. Otherwise, the house felt eerily still.

They finally came to a stop in front of a large oak door on the fourth floor. Dallas knocked briefly and then opened it. He and Jack stepped inside.

Byrd was standing amidst a flood of white papers spread across the rug in columns, like they were building a monument.

"Conner," Truman said, looking up. He frowned.

Dallas Winston closed the door behind them.

$$* \quad * \quad *$$

Truman capped his pen with a sharp click.

"I'm sorry to disturb you, Truman," Everett Conner said.

"Not at all," Truman said. "Though I'm sure you didn't come for the interior decorating of my office?"

He exchanged a quick look with Dallas and pictured the revolver that was fitted beneath his desk, easily reachable. The button he had installed next to it would alert the local police.

Everett laughed a little. "Actually, a tour is something that would interest me. But that's not why I've come."

Byrd raised an eyebrow at Everett to continue. He felt irritation like an itch beneath his collar. He had just received notice from another advertiser who was pulling out. The Depression was hammering the economy, and it was playing out on the ink of his papers in more ways than one. He wanted to melt away into an aged whiskey, a game of craps, and a piece of butterscotch pie.

"This is a little awkward, I'm afraid," Everett said. He scratched the side of his head and then regaled them with what had transpired shortly after Truman had left to attend to the papers. Truman felt the itch of his irritation flare into a full-blown rash.

Maybe Ronald was right about Berty.

His loyalty had limits. And the hairline cracks were showing.

Truman studied Everett Conner as he stood before him. He let the silence stretch out uncomfortably between them. He had to give it to the man—if Everett wasn't there to shoot him, it was a brave thing he was doing. Something that took risk and character. After all, Truman had known Berty for decades, and Everett only a few months. He let the silence strain to the point of unbearableness, examined the scar on the top of Everett's lip. He'd never noticed it before, but the light hit it just right. Tonight, he didn't look like Truman's brother Elias.

He reminded Truman of someone else.

"The situation will be handled," Truman said.

"Thank you," Everett replied. He gave a smile but took a step backward, as if suddenly anxious to get away.

Truman stared after him.

"You know what to do," he said to Dallas, and returned to his papers.

CHAPTER SIXTEEN

Clementine slipped off her gown and hung it in the wardrobe, exchanging it for a silk nightgown dyed the color of sapphires. Kitty was in the bathroom tying her hair up in rag curls, Rita was inspecting her eyebrows, and Lola was smelling each of Clementine's perfumes.

"Mmm," Lola said. "This one reminds me of Howelsen Hill."

"I didn't know you went to Colorado," Kitty said, tightening a knot near her scalp.

"Just a few months back, on New Year's." She giggled. "Johnny took me as his ski bunny."

"I love Colorado," Rita agreed, arching a brow and plucking a stray one with tweezers. "Clem, you love Colorado, don't you?"

Clementine came into the bathroom and joined them, slipping a sheer lace robe over her nightgown.

"I've never been," she admitted.

She had always wanted to go. She had grown up barefoot in mud, making crowns and jewelry out of violets. When she was a child, she'd had buck teeth and they were poor and boys called her Mudspackle because of her freckles. She'd watched the silent movies once a year with stars in her eyes. When she was a girl growing up in Florida, she had never seen snow before, and all she wanted to do was learn how to ski. She had imagined that it might be the closest one might feel to flying.

Now skiing was becoming all the rage and she had researched lodges, selecting the one with the views of the Rockies, hot springs, and five-star cuisine. She had even purchased snow boots with fur trim back when she and Truman were planning to travel, but they had to keep a lower profile now that he was considering the run for office.

She had tried not to pout when he told her.

"So, Clem, what happens when the wife comes?" Lola lowered her voice deliciously. "Do you have to leave?"

Clementine smiled thinly, pinning her golden hair back from her face. She did. It was infuriating to be escorted out according to Mabel's whims and schedule. Mabel didn't come often—maybe once every six months to a year—but she made sure to plan it for the most inconvenient times. She had decided she was coming for Christmas last year, and gave only a week's notice, so that Clementine ended up spending Christmas at a hotel alone, drinking too much champagne and eating chocolates wrapped in gold foil. She had listened to festive music on the wireless, wandered through the lobby's elaborate display of gingerbread houses near midnight, and thought of her mother at home in Florida.

Rita had dropped by her suite for a few hours to dress and gossip, but then she had left for her own date. So Clementine had ordered herself the most expensive filet mignon, put it on Truman's tab, and then fed half of it to her schnauzer, Snick.

It was the first time since she was a girl that she had ever felt trapped.

She petted Snick now and joined the line of starlets at the mirror, slathering on face masks made from sea kelp. They peered out the slats of the Astral Bedroom, spying on the men. "Good to be away from those old fuddy-duddies for a bit," Clem declared. She brought out her nail lacquers and, beneath it, a bindle of cocaine. "Let's have a little fun."

She let her sheer bathrobe fall open so that the massive diamond and ruby necklace Truman had given her sparkled, without being crass enough to draw attention to it.

*　　*　　*

Cora reached for the worry stone in her pocket as she approached Daisy in the warm, dusky night.

"You all right?" she whispered. The men had been served and satiated and were playing cards, their low laughter hanging in the heat of the night.

Daisy hastily wiped her nose. "Aces," she said briskly. "Nothing I haven't met before, anyway," she said. She shrugged, but it looked more like a shudder. "Or you either."

Cora took her arm, and they crouched down behind the eucalyptus. "Macready will come looking for us soon," Daisy said, searching her pockets for a cigarette.

"So, let her," Cora muttered, watching the way that Daisy's hands still trembled. She took the matchbook from Daisy and lit the final match, touching it to the end of Daisy's cigarette and her own. She breathed the tobacco deep into her lungs, almost feeling it crackle, and they crouched there at the edges of the party, breathing in the nicotine and the scent of eucalyptus.

They were silent for a long moment.

"I need the money from this job," Daisy finally said. She swallowed hard. "No matter what."

Cora met her eyes and understood all that she was not saying. She nodded, feeling her throat tighten.

"Do you ever wonder if we could do something to change all this?" Daisy asked. "Or not all of it—not even close, really. But do *something* to make things better? More just?"

Cora looked at her carefully. "What do you mean, Daisy?"

Daisy shook her head. "Never mind." She blew out a breath and forced a laugh. "Wasn't expecting your Mr. Conner to be a knight in shining armor."

"Me neither," Cora said.

But was that true?

For a moment, she thought of the day the Gasper had spoken to her through the fence. She shivered.

"Maybe he's changed," Daisy said. "From when you knew him before."

Cora was quiet. "Maybe," she said.

Daisy blew the smoke out thoughtfully. "Hoo, but he is handsome, ain't he?" She sneaked a smile at Cora, exhaling wisps of smoke from her nose. "He looks good, togged to the bricks like that. Cleans up real nice."

Cora shrugged and looked away. "Can't say I noticed, really," she said.

Daisy shot her a sidelong glance and snorted. "Hope you never have to lie for a living, Ella," she said with a small push, "'cause you sure ain't much for it."

Cora laughed and flipped her the bird.

Daisy flipped her one back.

They were just finishing their cigarettes when Jack ducked between the branches of the oak tree.

Daisy rushed to her feet and stamped out her cigarette.

"Oh, don't get up for me," he said. He crouched down next to where Cora was sitting. "Just wanted to let you know that I spoke to Mr. Byrd, and our resident lecher is being demoted to a bungalow further down the hill," he said. He shifted, reaching into his pocket for his own cigarette case, and his knee brushed against Cora's. She felt a troubling zing, and quickly moved away. "If he doesn't take the hint," Jack continued, apparently without noticing, "he'll be moved again until he's sharing some sod with the lovely zebras." He offered Daisy a fresh cigarette.

"Thank you," Daisy said, and even though she was kneeling, still managed a dip of a curtsy. She took the cigarette he held out between her long, delicate fingers. "That was kind of you."

"Well, I suggested castration. But I was overruled."

Daisy smiled a little. "Got a light?" she asked shyly.

"I do," Jack said.

He reached into his pocket and took out the Dunes matchbook that Cora had stolen from him and then given back.

He carefully turned the cover over. Met her eyes.

When the match flared, she saw words scrawled across the back of it.

1:00 a.m., he'd written.

The Grotto.

"Take care," he said to Daisy.

Then he stood and sauntered into the night.

*   *   *

Byrd's bedroom light flickered off at a quarter past twelve, and then Clementine's a short time later. When Cora delivered a late-night pot of chamomile tea smelling of amber honey, two other starlets were asleep in the bed with Clem. Cora softly closed the door behind her. There was not going to be anything meaningful to catch for Mabel tonight.

With a sinking disappointment, she returned to her own room.

At seven minutes to one o'clock, she pulled on her coat and slipped her camera into one pocket and her gun into the other. She wondered how Jack even knew about the grotto, which was a fountain cleverly tucked beneath the farthest garden terrace in a wall of ivy. Part of her hoped he wouldn't show. Her feelings about him—about what she could believe to be true—were thorny and knotted. She had to pick through them carefully. Perhaps she was walking into a trap all over again, one she was setting for herself. She made her way down the path through the descending gardens, alert for guards. The air was thick with wet soil, blooming dahlias, and lavender hydrangea. Kitty was playing cards with Governor Gilham at a small table on the esplanade, and Cora could hear the distant, tinkling sound of her laugh.

Someone was already there, standing in the shadows, when she reached the overarching willow boughs. She pulled the hanging strands apart and felt a hitch in her stomach at the sight of Jack.

As the willow strands fell back into place, they almost formed a private room. She was careful to let the handle of her gun show.

"Have you come to shoot me, then?" Jack asked. He raised his hands in half-surrender, his fingers long and thin. There was a dark twinkle in his eye.

"I haven't decided yet," she said.

For a moment, she saw the flash of her father's face in her mind. The troubled look as he spoke to her mother in hushed voices in their bedroom. The door had been left open a crack, luring Cora toward it like a moth drawn to flame.

"Influenza's sweeping through," he had said. "A third of the guards are down tonight. We're trying to get backup, but I don't think they'll come in time."

"What are you going to do?" Cora's mother had asked quietly.

"Go in shifts. But there simply aren't enough of us. I'm going to have to leave the south side almost blind until—"

He'd looked up and caught Cora standing just outside the door, eavesdropping.

He'd stopped speaking.

Stood up. Walked slowly to the door.

And closed it in her face.

Cora ignored the fresh stab of guilt she felt at the memory.

"I was just standing here, wondering how long it took you to recognize me," Jack said.

Cora paused. "I thought it was you as soon as you stepped out of the car," she said. "But I knew for sure when I heard you laugh." She met his eyes reluctantly. "You?"

"I wasn't certain until the moment Lola dropped that glass. Initially, I thought I saw you in the Assembly Room. But I didn't believe it." He stole a look at her. "I thought I'd seen you a hundred times before."

That made her stomach do a funny, unexpected little jump. She felt for the curve of her gun again.

"How has Byrd not made you yet?" she asked. "Are you certain he hasn't?"

Jack shrugged and ran his hand over his chin. "The longer I stay, the more I expect that he'll put it together. But you saw my mug shot—it was terrible. Luckiest break I ever had."

"But he saw you in person all those days during the trial."

Jack shook his head. "No. He never set foot in the courtroom. Sent someone else to cover it. Truman never saw me in the flesh before Reno."

"How strange," Cora said. "It was the story of the decade. He never came to see it himself?"

"I've always wondered why not. Maybe he didn't have the guts to face us, knowing that we were innocent." He rubbed his jaw ruefully. "If I get what I came for, maybe I'll ask him."

Cora hesitated. "I might know where to start with that," she said roughly. She clutched the stolen keys tight in her hand, letting the edges cut into her palm. She didn't want to admit to herself how badly she needed Jack to have been innocent during that time on Pelican.

The night guards were patrolling the grounds' perimeters, carving through the maze of trees and marbled fountains on a scheduled gradient. There seemed to Cora to be even more of them than usual.

"The guards will pass by here at one fifteen, at two-thirty—" she whispered.

"—And switch out at ten after three," he continued. She gave him a curt nod of acknowledgment, then stuck out her hand to stop him at the crunching sound of boots. Together they ducked behind a row of arborvitae. He was so close, she smelled his skin. Citrus and pine. The last time she had been that close to a man was Bobby.

She tried to breathe through her mouth.

When the sound of boots had moved farther south, she led Jack down the slope of the hill to the rear of the main house. They crept along the shadows until they reached a slight clearing. Above it, a fresco of Dionysus glowed white in the moonlight. Cora pulled back the brambles. Beyond it was a door, mostly concealed.

It was the back entrance to the underground wine cellar—full of liquor, in case the cops ever came looking. Cora suspected that Byrd probably had them all on his payroll anyway. She stepped forward to get a clear shot at the lock and pulled out the key.

"On Pelican, we used to pick the padlock with hairpins," she whispered. "That older girl who lived there, the cook's daughter, Dina, you remember her?"

Jack cocked his head as he sorted through his memory. Squinting, he nodded.

"She taught me." Cora soundlessly fit the key to the lock and turned it.

"What were you doing picking padlocks on Pelican?" Jack whispered, sounding amused.

"Stupid kid things," she said. She hesitated. Cora had to use both hands to wrench open the door, leaving her gun unsecured and vulnerable. It was a calculated risk. "Dina wanted to meet up with the lighthouse keeper's son."

"And what about you?" he asked.

"Me?" She threw her hip into the door and felt it give. "I just wanted to see if I could."

The door swung open into a gaping darkness. Her gun stayed undisturbed in her pocket. He hadn't made a move for it.

The night would bring a hundred little tests. Temptations to show who he really was, and who he had become. Ways for Cora to regain the sight line, when Jack's version of things always threatened to disorient her again. Cora stepped inside the doorway, and the light vanished totally. Jack followed behind her, his breath close enough to faintly tickle Cora's ear. They stood together on a level entryway before the steps descended into an even deeper darkness.

You're being needlessly reckless, her father would say, fury building in his jaw.

I'm the one playing him, she would insist, her heart landing each beat with a heavy thud.

In this job, he would say, voice cutting sharp, *you only play games when you know you can win.*

"Careful," she whispered to Jack behind her, feeling along for the banister. She didn't dare light a match until they were below ground. Their footsteps echoed in the stairway, a gentle slap of sole on stone. After the expansive night, it felt small and enclosed. The air grew chillier by degrees as they descended, and Cora's nerves prickled with awareness of every sound. Jack stayed close behind her, and for half a second she couldn't help but think about how easy it would be for him to give her a hard push, and that would be the end of it for her. The only one who knew his secret.

She tightened her grip on the banister.

Perhaps she would never have closure, never be able to move on, without knowing what had really happened that night at the Bastion, and the night he escaped. But first she had to gain his trust. Trust was a thousand tiny strands threading together over time, eventually twisting into a cord thick enough to hold a piano.

"Did I ever tell you I once rode the ferry across the Bay with Joey the mobster's wife?" Cora said quietly. The first strand of trust was often a shared experience, some sense of familiarity. She laid it down between them like a single wire cable.

"Yeah?" Jack whispered back. "Joey Vino? I didn't know he had a gal."

Cora smiled into the darkness in spite of herself. It came so easy, with Jack. She stepped onto their shared memories of Pelican like a bridge.

"What was she like, then?" Jack asked.

"She wore a fur with gold-plated buttons, and she brought a cake that she held in her lap."

Jack's voice turned incredulous. "The guards let her bring in a cake?"

"Of course not," Cora said. "They threw it into the Pacific."

"A perfectly good cake!" he whispered, incensed.

"It could have had razors in it."

"Or raisins," he said, shuddering.

Cora snorted.

"I remember your mother once made a cake," he said softly. "With candy buttons." Cora almost stopped breathing. She couldn't believe that he recalled that story.

He was laying down a cord of his own. Perhaps he was playing her back. Perhaps he was coming to meet her.

Either way, she let him.

"She died," Cora said quietly. He was so near that when she turned, her shoulder brushed against the firm curve of his chest and she could feel his breathing.

"I'm sorry," Jack said. She was surprised how gentle his voice sounded in the dark. "I didn't realize."

"It was a long time ago."

The air was cool and stony when they came to the bottom of the stairs. The door to the wine cellar was made of iron. Cora inserted the second key into the lock and then gave the door a hard shove.

Inside, moonlight cut through the bars of a small window at the top of the wall, illuminating a wine cellar filled with dry wooden barrels and rows of bottles that shone along the wall like ambered jewels. Cora turned suddenly to make a crack about an aged whiskey that was older than both of them, and Jack jumped. She had spooked him, she realized. He had followed her there, alone, into a buried room. And though he was physically stronger than Cora, she was the one with the weapon, and a grudge.

"We copacetic?" she asked lightly, cocking an eyebrow.

"Yeah," he said. He held her gaze. "Sorry. Just a little on edge."

She moved carefully around the room. She had seen the blueprints that Mabel gave her to study, and she knew there was an enormous space below their feet. But there was no door or staircase that she could make out. The moonlight glinted on the bottles. The walls were all fireproof stone, and the far one was covered with a thick hanging tapestry.

"You think the files are in here?" Jack asked uncertainly. He glanced around, shifting his weight, and she knew in that moment that he trusted her about as much as she trusted him. Yet, for a handful of days, they had come to unexpectedly hold each other's fates. And perhaps that was the strongest strand of trust there was.

"No," she said.

Cora moved toward the tapestry. She examined it closely.

And then she saw it. Her eyes fell upon a small gray dove, holding a persimmon branch. Just behind it was a tie, fitted onto a latch. She stepped forward, unhooking the tie, and pulled the tapestry aside.

There was a door to a freight elevator.

"Bingo," she said.

Without looking back, Cora pulled open the grate and stepped inside. She examined the button panel. It appeared that the freight-elevator shaft went up into the main house, where it likely hid behind a locked door that she had mistaken for a closet.

"This goes up to the main house, and down to a sub-level basement," she said.

Jack's eyes lit, and he gave a low whistle. The hair on her arms prickled.

"Shall we see what Truman's been hiding down there?" she asked.

Cora didn't let him see the pulse of fear she felt. She pushed the down button and kept her hand on her gun as the elevator began to descend into darkness.

CHAPTER SEVENTEEN

"Truman seems to have a thing about birds," Jack said from somewhere next to her.

The darkness felt thick and substantial, like Cora was being submerged in it. "You've noticed, too?" she asked.

She lit a match, and it flared to illuminate Jack's face.

Cora's heart rate kicked up a notch. She knew her father would kill her himself—with Chief Bellanger's gold belt buckle and his own two hands—if he could see her then.

She watched the pulse on Jack's neck beating more quickly as the elevator came to a stop.

She pulled the grate open and stepped out, feeling along the wall for a switch; and when she found one, the room flooded with light. Cora blinked, momentarily blinded. Jack shaded his eyes with his hand and took a step forward.

His jaw went slack.

"What is this place, Cora?" Jack asked.

Cora looked around in amazement. It was like being lowered inside a secret museum: solemn and cool, fireproofed and void of any natural light. White sheets were draped over the carved arms of antique chairs, globes, and paintings. Locked curio cabinets held bejeweled eggs and ancient books that looked as though they could crumble into dust beneath a single breath.

"This is where Byrd keeps his alternate furnishings," Cora said. "They're switched out every year or so, to keep the Castle feeling fresh. If those files are valuable, maybe they're hidden down here somewhere."

Cora eyed a massive trunk with bronze latches and a label noting ancient weavings. Carved golden frames leaned against the walls, and bronze statues peeked out from beneath swathed sheets. The shelves were lined with goblets and candlesticks. She had heard whisperings once, about illegal jade and ivory. Just hints. Byrd loved beautiful things. He loved the game of acquiring them.

Jack was looking at her with an unreadable expression.

"What?" she asked.

"This is brilliant," he said. His eyes lit. "*You* are brilliant."

She flushed with unexpected pleasure. She still felt the shimmer of a spark when he was near, and it made her angry. Because he had been the first to ever make her feel those things.

She stepped forward, running her gloved hands over the sheets, pulling them free like she was uncovering ghosts. Beneath them she found a set of carved marble busts, and then a naophoros statue carved out of black basalt. She thought of the *Life* magazine she had seen once. The cover showed a flag drowning beneath a pile of money, accompanied by the line *As wealth accumulates, men decay.*

"I've been thinking," Jack said, "of asking Clem and Beau to go on a private horseback ride with me. I'll invite them, and then somewhere along the way I'll lose them on the trails."

"Good idea," Cora said. "Just let me know when, so I can ensure that Truman is made aware of it at the right time."

Her hope rose. And, with it, her courage.

She followed Jack toward the back of the room, moving through corridors of trunks and tables.

"I don't have to tell you what a big risk I've taken, bringing you down here," she said. "Now I want something in return."

"And what would that be?" Jack asked, instantly guarded.

She caught her reflection in a carved bronze mirror. "Tell me about the night of the escape," she said softly. "You didn't have anyone helping you on the inside?" The color rose in her face, but she forced herself to go on. "Anyone *else*, I mean? No crooked guard?"

The muscles in his back stiffened. He met her eyes and shook his head.

She nodded. One night, one single night that entire year, the south side of the island went unattended. Everyone at Pelican—all but Cora—could hardly believe the luck of it: how had they possibly picked the one night that would give them that advantage?

"How did you manage to get out of your cells, then?" she asked. She'd always wondered.

"Cut through the bars." He rubbed at the hint of stubble beneath his chin. At his elbow were a trove of ancient Greek vases, patterned with intricate geometrics in red and black liquid clay.

"Sure," Cora said sarcastically. She sank her hands into a chest of antique coins. Let them trickle between her fingers. "With that machinery the guards conveniently lent you?"

It wasn't the first time such a thing had been attempted. Three inmates before them had tried sawing through the bars and fences with wire cutters, which resulted in the iron being steeled against those sorts of tools. A year after that, two convicts had overpowered their guards and been shot when they climbed down the rocks. They had been bleeding too much to attempt the one-and-a-half mile swim across the Bay.

"With string," Jack said. "Coated with powdered kitchen cleanser. A makeshift saw."

She glanced at him. "Clever."

"It was Leo's idea."

Leo, she thought. She was making her way to Leo. Putting down strands, walking gingerly across them.

She didn't test the full weight of them yet. "The sawing didn't draw any attention?" she asked instead.

"We did it little by little, when Joey Vino was playing during music hour."

Cora knelt to open a display cabinet that held a collection of candelabras and wax jacks. "Good old boy Joey Vino," she said, "always playing that wretched accordion."

"Sounded like a cat in a blender," Jack said. "Cruel and unusual."

"But still," Cora said. "That must have taken more than an hour or two."

"It took us a month, give or take. We waited to finish it off until . . ." He paused. ". . . the right opportunity came."

Cora quietly studied the inside of the cabinet. Then she moved on to the next. A file cabinet. Locked. Her heart quickened. She stooped to examine the mechanism.

"The water was less than sixty degrees that night," she said. "How did you get across the Bay?"

"Leo and I collected essentials," Jack said. "Inconspicuous things that wouldn't raise suspicion during a raid check."

"Like string and kitchen cleaner."

"And rubber raincoats. We had close to two dozen by the end, trading them with other inmates in exchange for packs of Luckies. We stitched them together. They were supposed to act as flotation devices."

"Supposed to?"

Jack ran his fingertips over a ceremonial casket, with inlaid, interlocking pieces of agate, ebony, and crystal. "The waves were rough. Not sure they did much good."

She knew the Bay was rife with riptide currents that could pull someone under with a frigid vise; and occasionally sharks made an appearance, their sharp fins cresting the waves like knives gliding through butter. For weeks after their escape, the coast guards, the FBI, had searched the Bay and surrounding waters. The official story that emerged was that the brothers had drowned and washed out to sea.

The problem was, no one had ever found their bodies.

And no one had ever guessed who had been helping them on the inside.

Cora pulled a bobby pin from her hair and set to work on the cabinet lock.

*   *   *

Jack yanked the edge of a white sheet to reveal a glass cabinet. Inside were triptychs and tiny icons, glass shelves of gold-and-jewel-studded Faberge eggs, painted with a brush as fine as a single strand.

He bent to examine the cabinet's contents.

"Even if you were sent to Pelican with clean hands," Cora said, her voice muffled around the pin in her mouth, "you didn't leave with them."

Jack stiffened. "That guard's death was an accident."

"He had a name."

"Yes," Jack said tiredly.

"Rusty—"

"Weathers. I know."

"He should still be alive," Cora said. She flicked her wrist, inserting the pin into the lock. Her movements turned sharp, angrier. "All this time, he should have been living his life with his wife, his daughter. How it happened doesn't matter."

"It matters to me," Jack snapped. He paused and gathered himself. "I'm not saying my story is tidy, or even that I don't deserve some sort of punishment for what happened. But the truth matters." He met her eyes as the lock caught. "Redemption isn't possible without the truth."

She held his gaze. "Then what is the truth?"

The cabinet door swung open beneath her hands, but she ignored it. Waiting. Watching him. Jack braced himself. His memories were a path littered with broken shells. He dreaded reliving it, every step painful and tender. She stared back at him, her eyes pools of green and gold. He could tell she wasn't going to let him see inside that file cabinet without an answer.

He sighed.

"Leo always blamed himself that we ended up on Pelican Island," he began.

"Why?" Cora asked softly.

"He was the reason why we were outside of the Bastion that night of the murders. He'd wanted to ask a girl to go steady, and he chickened out instead."

Jack had always been rash and bold, and Leo had been the tentative one. The one who stopped and thought things through, to the point of agonizing over them. He would spend a quarter of an hour picking through the potatoes at the market for their ma, making sure they weren't eye-speckled or rotting. He practiced the same song on the violin for hours, until the daylight was snuffed out and there was no time left to play kick-the-can. It was the kind of thing that used to drive Jack crazy.

"If only I had got up the nerve to ask that girl out," Leo used to say on Pelican. "If only I wasn't such a bleeding coward, we'd both be free."

And in his darkest moments, Jack had thought the same thing. Loving Leo and hating him more than anyone else on the planet. There was no one else alive who could understand what had been done to them, and what it was doing to them on the inside.

"I'm so fucking sorry, Jackie," Leo had said.

"Stop it, Leo," Jack had said.

"I swear I won't let you down again. I hope I get the chance to make it up to you."

Jack had shoved him. "Just stop."

And then Cora had appeared like an answer to their prayers, a flower sprouting up out of the rock. Bearing little tidbits of information that, when fit together, added up to make something whole.

Leo hadn't been sure about the plan at first. But he felt like he owed it to Jack to try.

"You're using her," Leo had said, blowing smoke from the bootlegged cigarette they were sharing between them. "That girl."

"I'm using the information she's giving me," Jack said. "It's her choice."

"You're going to hurt her. Why on earth is she helping you?"

Jack hesitated. He had always wondered that himself.

"Maybe it's a trap," said Leo. He had wanted to hold up their escape plan like a diamond, examining every facet. Looking for all the possible imperfections.

Jack just wanted to do it and get it over with before he lost his nerve.

"So we're doing it, then?" Leo asked nervously.

Jack had nodded. "Tonight," he said.

He had forced himself to eat his dinner with shaking hands, even though his stomach threatened to reject each bite. He lay on his cot that night after lights-out, and hope and terror had run through him like two electric strands. He had forced himself to slip out from the sheets. Put on his shoes. Take silent, deep breaths when he stuffed still lumps of clothes beneath his blankets. He had clenched down his teeth and ripped out patches of his own hair to leave behind on the pillowcase.

It had almost been enough to make him laugh bitterly a few hours later in the frigid water: to picture Brutus, the guard he hated, with his horrible breath and his provoking stick, trying to rouse two lumps of clothing for morning rounds as the day broke. It had given him a final push when the water was so cold that Jack felt his muscles cramping up. For a moment, he hadn't thought he would reach the other side, and yet he kept on, waiting to hear the alarms blare, the white-hot lance of the spotlight cutting through the waters and declaring that they had failed.

But it hadn't come. Not until he had reached the other side, and freedom.

Freedom.

At a terrible cost.

It haunted him.

"It was raining that night," he said. "Leo and I got out of our cells around half past two, when the guards were changing shifts. Our cells were at the end of the row, so we didn't have to walk past many possible snitches." He rubbed his eyes with the backs of his palms. "But everyone was asleep. It seemed like God was smiling at us."

Cora was still. Watching his face.

He had to relive it one more time. And then maybe—the thought came at him with a wild desperation—maybe once he had confessed to someone, that night would finally stop haunting his dreams.

"We shimmied under the fence by the commissary and got to the civilian side of the island without being seen by anyone." Because of Cora, he knew about the part of the fence they could shimmy under where the ground washed out in the rain. Just like she had said.

"And then you went to the south side," she said. Her pulse was beating at her neck. "Because of what I told you."

He nodded. She had whispered it through the fence, her face white with a mixture of excitement and nerves. "My da says there's a sickness going through," she said. "There won't be enough guards on shift to cover tonight."

He never forgot the look on her face. The smallest smile, with a hint of sadness. "I've heard the south is nice," she said. And she had turned and walked away, her hair coming loose from her braid.

"Nobody was supposed to be patrolling the south side that night," she said slowly now. "The currents make it the toughest way to cross the Bay."

"But someone was," he said. "We were heading down the south side of the island when we ran into him, walking the grounds."

When he had first seen Rusty, he had wondered for a split second if Leo was right. If Cora had set them up and tricked them.

Cora's face was white and pinched. Listening. She was so still, she barely seemed to be breathing.

"Go on," she whispered.

"I had gone down the slope first to check things out," Jack said. "And I heard him come up behind me. I was so scared that night. Nerves like I've never felt. I kept thinking I was going to get sick or get shot at any minute. Or that Leo would."

"*Hands up,*" Rusty had shouted. *"Or I'll shoot."*

"I put my hands up," Jack said. He had dropped his sack of raincoats. He had turned around slowly. His heart had sunk.

But that's when he realized that Rusty hadn't seen Leo yet.

The rain had been cold, the visibility terrible. The light from the guard tower hadn't found them. It was just them and Rusty—and though he didn't know it yet, Rusty was outnumbered.

"I told him that I wasn't coming back with him," Jack said. "That I'd rather die instead. I just felt . . . crazed, in that moment. That my freedom was so close. I couldn't go back to that cage. I couldn't spend the rest of my life paying for a sin I hadn't committed."

"Come on, son. You're coming back with me. It's your choice whether it's still breathing or not," Rusty had said.

And that's when Leo jumped him.

"Leo came up on him from behind and tackled him to the ground. But he didn't get the gun out of Rusty's reach in time."

He was having to force the words out.

"They were both on the ground wrestling, and I came running toward them. And I remember Rusty reaching for his gun and aiming it at me."

Jack stopped. He tasted salt on his face. "And then Leo picked up a big rock."

Leo, who closed his eyes when he played the violin. Who took the better part of a week to pick out a new pair of shoes. Who was too afraid to ask the girl he liked to go steady with him.

Jack heard the sick sound of the rock when it came down on Rusty's head. It had made him stop in his tracks and sway. A sick, woozy feeling seeped into his stomach.

"Jack," Leo had said, looking down at his hands. He had dropped the rock with a thud. "I think I killed him." He had staggered to his feet and started to breathe fast and heavy, as though he were hyperventilating. "I think I killed him."

"You just gave him a good knock. He'll come to," Jack had said. He took one look at Rusty and knew it was a lie. "Come on." He had taken Leo's arm and shoved him away from the guard's still body. His mind was dizzy. All he could think about was that they had to go.

If they were caught now, his brother was never getting off that island.

"Leo killed Rusty," Cora whispered.

"He panicked," Jack said. "He did it to protect me."

Cora shook her head. She closed her eyes, as if she couldn't look at him. "What happened then?" she asked.

Jack bit down hard on his lip until he tasted blood.

"He'd been grazed by Rusty's bullet," Jack said.

He could still see the image of Leo pulling up his shirt. The crimson streak on his side.

"You're hit," Jack had said, the rain streaming into his eyes. "Shit. We should turn back."

The rain was pelting them. The alarm would go off any minute. Everything was spiraling out of control. Jack's thoughts had swum. For so long, he had wanted to escape. To get back to the house where he'd grown up in Dorchester. To climb the creaking stairs again and ring the bell, and hear his mother's footsteps come to the door.

"It's just a graze," Leo insisted. "I'll be all right."

Jack had felt it then. A warning somewhere deep within him, nudging him to turn back. To get help for Rusty. To face the consequences. Maybe Leo hadn't killed him. Maybe there was a chance he could still be alive.

But if he wasn't. . . .

Jack had let out a silent sob, into the rain. They were so damn unlucky. It was a nightmarish loop, of being put on the island for killing a guard they hadn't killed, only to kill a guard anyway.

"What have I done?" Leo said. He was starting to shake.

"He was going to shoot me. You saved my life, Leo," Jack had said.

"We should go back." Leo had grimaced, his face almost grotesque. "We should see if we can help him."

"No," Jack said, and his voice hardened. "We have to go. If we don't, we're never getting off this island. Not after tonight."

Leo had squinted toward the guard tower in that deliberating way, the one that meant he would spend half an hour going over his options.

"We can't wait any longer," Jack had said. "Are you too hurt to swim?"

Leo had stopped squinting. "No," he said, steeling himself. He had bent down and grabbed his pack of raincoats.

Jack had known then that he had to hide Rusty's body. He had bent down to confirm that there was no pulse at Rusty's throat. Wiped some of the mud and blood from his badge and his face. Replaced his hat. A stupid thing to do. It was long past mattering. Rusty stared up at him through half-closed lids. Jack unwrapped some of his raincoats and covered Rusty with them, as if he were tucking him in. He thought of his own father when he did it. He did it like he would want someone to do for someone he loved. But he couldn't think that way.

He gritted his teeth and said a prayer for Rusty's soul. He didn't bother making one for his own.

Then he shoved Rusty off the rocks into the frothing, white sea.

"Swim hard. Think of ma. We're going to make it, Leo," Jack said. "We're almost there."

He'd hugged Leo to him. Taken Leo's face in his hands and planted a rough kiss on his cheek. "I'll see you on the other side."

Then he had dived off the pier, and heard the splash as Leo followed.

He still remembered the water, like icy knives. In his nightmares, he dreamed of it pouring down his throat like ink. He'd lost Leo right away. He couldn't see anything but the rain, falling in pinpricks against the water and forcing it back up into his mouth and nose and eyes. He kept kicking and swimming toward the shore, for what felt like hours, his side cramping and his thighs burning, until he finally came to a strip of beach and pulled himself up. Retching into the sand, in exhaustion. Wringing out his clothes. Alone.

And then waiting.

And waiting.

The dread creeping over him like the coming sunrise.

"Jack," Cora said softly. She suddenly seemed so far away.

"He drowned," Jack said. "I was always the better swimmer. I should have known he couldn't have made it. Especially not wounded."

He felt the hold on himself slipping. Did he even deserve to be free? He hadn't ever pulled a trigger, hadn't picked up that rock; yet, all the same, his decisions had cost more than one life. He had felt the warning inside himself that night—but the pure temptation to be free was stronger. So he had reached out and plucked the apple, determined to take back his own life, no matter the consequences.

The knowledge of it haunted him still.

Cora came near to him. She gently put her hand on his arm.

"I'm sorry," she whispered.

The tenderness was too much. He was going to lose it entirely.

He turned away sharply.

She was close enough to him that he could smell her shampoo, rainwater and honey; see the downy hair on her ears.

"Guilt is worse than Pelican was," he said. "Because you can't ever escape it."

She nodded wearily, as if she understood. "It's exhausting," she said. "Spending the rest of your life trying to account for the worst mistake you ever made."

She took her hand away from his arm.

And in that moment, he realized what he wanted most of all was for someone to forgive him.

*   *   *

Cora didn't say another word. She bent to the file cabinet and pulled the first drawer open. The silence stretched out between them.

Inside, she found a roll of papers.

She felt Jack's eyes on her as she pulled out sheaves wound with twine; gingerly unfolded them, trying to clear her head of the picture Jack had painted. Of Leo reaching for the rock. Of its meeting Rusty's head. Of his body going limp.

Or the thing that had shocked her most of all—that when she had glimpsed the depths of his grief, raw and aching, something in her had wanted to reach for him. She was as surprised as anyone that compassion could reappear in a place long hardened with bitterness and regret. Jack had never breathed a word of the truth about himself for more than a decade. What did that do to a person? Cora's unconfessed secret had rotted inside her, twisting her from that night on, like a gnarled tree.

If she was bent around her secret, what had the loss of Jack's brother done to him?

She ran her thumb over her worry stone, feeling the grooves her fingers had worn across it over the years, and forced herself to focus on the papers in her hand. Anything to get away from that image on repeat.

Meet me at the fountain on 24th and Locust, she read.

I can't stop thinking about the way you tasted the other night.

Like malt and chocolate ice cream.

Jack cleared his throat. "Find something?" he asked hopefully.

She shook her head. "Nothing that seems related to the mob's frame-up files. The opposite, actually," she said. "They're love letters."

"To who?"

"I'm not sure. They're unaddressed and unsigned."

Her heart skipped a beat. While she was looking for something else, could she have stumbled upon something to do with Clem?

She wondered how long ago the letters had been written. There was a set of directions at the top of the first one.

Main Street. Albany Drive. Broadview Lane.

Cora drew out her camera and snapped a few pictures.

"They're not unsigned," Jack corrected her, coming to look over her shoulder. She forced herself to stay and not retreat as she felt his presence, a breath's distance behind her. He pointed. "See. There. An M."

"An M?" she said, examining it.

He was right. There, in the bottom corner, was a small, inconspicuous M. An M for Mabel?

Were these old love letters from Mabel that Truman had saved? Or had Mabel strayed first, and this was Truman's evidence of it? Cora took another photograph so she could examine them later. Then she carefully returned the letters to the cabinet and started picking the lock of the next drawer.

She could feel Jack's excitement. Smell the heightened, earthy scent of his skin.

"Does your mother know that you're alive?" Cora asked, twisting the pin. She bit her lip. "Althea, wasn't it?"

A muscle in Jack's jaw flickered. "She doesn't know anything for sure," he said. "I send flowers every Mother's Day, anonymously. I don't want to put her in a bad position, where she felt like she was hiding something from the feds. But I give her just enough to hope."

Again, Cora felt that throb of compassion. She fought it. Helping him wasn't about him, this time. It was about her. About rewriting her story. Perhaps she did deserve some semblance of happiness if he had once been innocent. If she hadn't been duped, if he hadn't manipulated her—if, when she had done her part, she had truly been helping someone who had been wronged.

It was almost too much to hope for.

Cora felt the lock give beneath her fingers.

She pulled open the second drawer.

Jack leaned forward eagerly so that their arms grazed. Cora struck a match and brought it closer so that they could see the folders hidden inside. Jack's excitement was contagious, and, despite herself, Cora felt her heartbeat pick up.

They began to search through the files. There were hundreds of papers inside. The first folder was filled with short, curt notes that appeared to be from Byrd's father, Franklin—

Needs work.

Could be better.

Just give it to Elias.

It was an odd collection of things to keep. As they went on, they found bad press clippings by rival newspapers, carefully cut out and gathered together. Things about Truman—about his stake holdings, satirical pieces about his wealth and his looks. What sort of man kept these reminders of slights, holding on to them like keepsakes?

Jack picked through the files with a fine-toothed comb, but the lists of names and dates from the frame-ups weren't there.

He sat back on his heels, exhaling.

"I really thought we had something there," he said.

He sat for a moment, then rose to his feet.

"Need a hand?" he asked, extending his arm to her.

She turned away. "I'll just get this back in order," she said. "There are a few more closets over there we haven't checked yet."

Cora waited until he'd left her side. She had spotted something that she wanted to get a second look at, without him there. She pulled out one of the final papers and examined it. A notice, for Truman Byrd.

You are overdue six weeks of payment, the notice said. The letterhead was from Turning & Blackburn Printing Press. *We will be shutting down your paper and pursuing legal action if you do not settle your debt.*

It was dated March 11, 1915. Roughly two weeks before the Bastion murders.

Cora brought out her camera and took a picture of the notice. She felt a thrill crackle through the fatigue that was beginning to gather at the base of her eye sockets.

"Find something interesting?" Jack called, and she jumped.

"No," she said. She quickly tucked the notice back into the cabinet.

Truman's paper hadn't always been successful. At some point, he had owed a significant amount of money. Where did that money come from?

An idea was beginning to form. If she was going to find out what really had happened at the Bastion, she knew she couldn't take Jack simply at his word. But maybe there was another way to find out for sure.

Cora shut the cabinet door and refixed the lock.

"We should go," she said.

Jack looked tired, shadows beginning to gather beneath his eyes. It was three o'clock in the morning.

They were silent as the elevator rose. Perhaps it was the fatigue setting in, but Cora found herself so unbalanced that she almost felt drunk. Something had changed for her, she realized. A weight had shifted, one that she had carried for so long that it left her feeling vaguely lost.

"Are there any other places like this in the house?" Jack asked, and she could hear the desperate note of hope in his voice.

"I'm not sure," she said.

There was someone who would know for certain. But she wasn't willing to give up that bargaining chip quite yet.

"I'll hold up my end of the deal," he said. "Clem and Beau on horseback, together. Tomorrow."

"Great," she said.

She stared at him.

"What?" he asked.

"I need to see your pockets," she said.

He looked at her like she was kidding, his amusement fading when he realized she wasn't. He sighed. Slowly, exaggeratedly, he turned them out for her to see.

"Satisfied?" he asked, showing that they were empty, save for his room key. When Cora didn't answer, he carefully reached up to unbutton his shirt. He pulled open his collar just enough to show that there was nothing hiding beneath.

She caught the slightest curve of his chest in the moonlight, the skin there tanned by the sun. She took a step closer, and he held up his palms and let her search him. She felt the solidness of his body beneath her hands.

A strange heat flooded through her, unbidden.

As he rebuttoned his shirt to the collar, a warmth kindled within her, like long-simmering coals. She didn't want it. It was much less confusing to hold on to the anchor that had moored her for so long that it had become a part of her. Anger. Bitterness. Regret.

Now there were too many things to think about. Dead Rusty and drowned Leo. Anonymous flowers to Jack's grieving mother. Truman needing money right before his paper mounted its case against the Yates brothers.

She opened the latch on the door, glancing quickly at her watch. The next guards were coming by at 3:10.

"Cora—" Jack whispered urgently. "Wait." He reached for her.

But she was already out into the cool night. Away from the bewildering parts of her that threatened any empathy and that dangerous, stirring warmth.

And that's when she realized that the guards were running four minutes ahead of schedule.

∗   ∗   ∗

Jack saw her stiffen the moment she noticed the patrol guard. Barely ten yards away from her, and already turning back at the sound of her feet on the gravel.

Instinctively, her hand went to where she had hidden her camera.

And her gun.

He didn't want to guess what might happen if they found her roaming the grounds, armed.

"*Dammit,*" he growled. "Get down."

He started to sing loudly, drunkenly. She crouched and hid behind a dark clump of sagebrush.

> *"Now what of the wedding and the christening,*
> *And the wake when your dear friends die.*
> *Oh, How are you goin' to wet your whistle,*
> *When the whole darn world goes dry?"*

Jack whistled and stumbled a bit, and the guard turned on his heel and marched toward him.

"Sir?"

He shone a torch in Jack's face. Jack blinked, holding a hand up to shield his eyes.

"What are you doing down here, sir?"

Jack clapped him on the back a few times. "Fine and dandy, yessirree."

"Are you a guest at the estate?"

Jack laughed.

"What's your name?"

"Name's Conner. Everett Conner."

"What are you doing down here, Mr. Conner?"

"Would you believe I was trying to find the john?" He winked, and made an exaggerated gesture with his hands to indicate that by "john," he meant liquor.

"Right. Why don't you come this way with me, Mr. Conner?"

Out of the corner of his eye, he watched as Cora hurried away. Her shadow slid along the path, growing smaller.

Jack swallowed.

"Right this way, yes. That's it," the guard said. The man nodded to his partner, and together they stopped Jack and patted him down for weapons. When they found him unarmed, they made a motion to let him go.

Jack gave them a salute and turned on his heel, breathing a sigh of relief.

Until Dallas Winston stepped forward from the shadows, the moonlight cutting down his broad face. "Hello, Mr. Conner," he said. "Looks like we meet again."

CHAPTER EIGHTEEN

WEDNESDAY, APRIL 30, 1930
~ Day Four ~

Truman awoke not to his alarm, but to his personal telephone line jangling next to his head. It was four minutes past six o'clock.

"Hello?" he answered, with a slight growl in his throat.

"Truman."

He knew the voice instantly and rubbed his eyes, which had started to feel gritty. Mabel knew exactly what she was doing. She knew he set an alarm every morning to awake at 6:16 a.m. It was a quirk he had picked up in his early twenties, an almost superstitious tick. But Mabel was three hours ahead of him in New York, and she would love nothing more than to upset the balance of his day by starting it off on her own terms.

"Mabel," he said. Even despite the distance, the telephone connection was clear. He could hear her breathing. Almost smell her perfume, nestled into the skin that was beginning to sag at her neck.

"Were you sleeping?" she asked. Her voice brimmed with polite animosity.

He stood and poured a glass of water from the pitcher on the washstand. "No," he lied. The water felt cold going down his parched throat. He examined his reflection in the mirror. His skin was a little tinged with gray. He looked old and tired.

It made him angry.

"What is it, Mabel?" he asked, with irritation.

He heard the shift of the telephone against her cheek, the curve of her smile. Truman had given her the satisfaction of knowing that she was the one person who could still get under his skin like no one else—no one, perhaps, other than his father. Thirty years ago he had loved her for it. They would dare each other on dusky fall nights riding on a sooty streetcar—how quickly she could get someone to give her a cigarette; buy her a drink, or even dinner, when their money was tight. She would order enough for two and bring the rest home in a doggie bag, leaving the poor hopeful sot with little more than a chaste kiss on the cheek.

How he loved the scams and the games, when they were in on them together. Before they'd turned into something darker.

He had fallen so hard for her, he used to steal into orchards to pick her peaches and daydream of tracing the line down the back of her stockings with the tip of his finger. He used to love her laugh, throaty and wicked.

"I've got plans for you," she said now. Her voice sounded hoarse and thick with smoke. "You might want to pull out your date book."

He paused in front of the mirror, unbuttoning his nightshirt.

"I'm fairly sure you stopped making my schedule back in 1927," he said coolly, stripping off his pajamas. He let the double meaning sink in like claws: neither planning his schedule, nor being found anywhere on it.

"Well, good news, darling, I finally found *something* we can do together that will give me a bit of pleasure and last longer than a minute and a half."

"Mm," Truman said. "I think I'll pass, love. You know I never indulge in things past their expiration date."

"It's funny, Truman," Mabel said, without missing a beat. "Do you remember those poor saps I used to hoodwink into buying things for us?

How we would laugh at how pathetic they were behind their backs?" she said. She tsked. "How *is* Judy, by the way?"

"What do you want, Mabel?" Truman said sharply.

Truman had long been attracted to Mabel because she went toe-to-toe with him. She never shrank back. He felt nothing like his father when he was with her. His father had dominated his mother her entire life. It struck him like a gong that perhaps he liked Clementine less for her gorgeous young languid body and more because he held almost every ounce of power over her. Maybe, despite his best intentions, he had become his father after all.

Mabel let a long silence fall, as if to remind him who was in command of the conversation.

"Trudy is co-hosting a gala benefiting the General Education Board," she said. "It's the biggest social and philanthropic event of the season."

"And let me guess. You don't want to have to face Trudy's sneer if you show up alone," Truman said.

Mabel paused. "She is quite ugly when she sneers."

"With girlfriends like these. . . ." Truman said, cocking an eyebrow.

"If you're serious about holding an elected office some day, you'll want to be there."

He knew Mabel well enough to understand that this had nothing to do with him or his dreams. It was about control. He was a cat toy, being batted between swipes.

"When is it?" he asked begrudgingly.

"It's at Trudy's Newport estate. On the fifteenth of June."

The fifteenth of June. That was the weekend he was supposed to be meeting Clementine in Los Angeles after weeks away. He had promised to take her to dinner to cement her role in a film with an old director friend.

"A good portion of the Senate and the president's foremost political adviser are expected to be there," Mabel said. "Or you can try to explain why you've found something better to do, as I've already RSVPed 'yes' for us both."

He sighed. "Fine."

"And for God's sake, don't wear anything green: it makes you look like a corpse," Mabel said, and then he heard the phone click in his ear. He couldn't remember the last time someone had hung up on him. To think that, once, that would have turned him on. Now it felt like she had climbed into his lap and rubbed a piece of sandpaper into his eye.

Truman dressed, forcing himself not to hurry. He went to his wardrobe. Selected a green tie and examined it in the mirror. Then he snarled and tossed it aside.

At a knock on the door, he called "What?"

Dallas Winston poked his head in, looking apologetic.

Truman gestured him inside with a jerk of his hand. Dallas smoothed the cuffs of his shirt and set down a cup of black coffee on Truman's bureau.

"I wanted to keep you apprised of a developing situation," he said.

"What is it?" Truman asked. He selected a blue bow tie with hints of green in it.

"One of our patrols found Everett Conner wandering around the south side of the house in the early morning hours," he said. "It was the second time last night that he was found somewhere he wasn't supposed to be."

The back of Truman's neck prickled in warning.

He watched his own reflection as he tied his tie. It was a rote motion, done a thousand times before, but he wasn't really seeing it.

"Is that so?" He tightened the bow tie at his throat. "How interesting."

*　　*　　*

Just before dawn, Cora stood outside her room, smoking a cigarette in the dark.

She could still feel the panic of almost having been caught by the guard, dizzying and electric behind her eyes. But, thanks to Jack, she had made it back to her room without being seen.

Jack had drawn the attention to himself. Sacrificed himself for her.

And not, she admitted to herself, for the first time.

She inhaled sharply and the cigarette bloomed with light.

She hadn't thought of the Gasper in years, but she still remembered what it felt like to be in his presence. He would laugh at off times, an unnatural sound that would send a surge of ice water through Cora's veins. It felt like seeing a broken limb that had been twisted the wrong way.

She remembered little flashes from that fateful day in late spring, sharpened to a crisp point. The way the Queen Anne's lace shivered against the rock. Wearing her new dress with its dark plaid tailoring. She had tied a grosgrain ribbon in her hair.

When she had approached the fence, someone had been there. His head was bent, his back turned, in the Pelican blue chambray shirt. Cora had noticed his scrawny shoulders first, and the words "I've just read a good one, you're really going to like—" died on her lips when the man turned around.

It was him.

Her breath had caught in her chest.

He looked at her with interest. One of his fingernails was long and sharp—the index finger on his right hand. A stringy dark hair was growing out of the mole on his cheek.

"Hi, little lady," he had said. His voice was high and thin. "You're a pretty thing. You remind me of a rabbit. What's your name?"

Lightning-fast, he'd seized her wrist through the fence, bending it at an angle that hurt. She had made a noise and thrown a panicked look toward the silent guard tower, with its dark, blank windows. When she looked back, drawn by some impossible force, Gasper had cocked his head. "Are you afraid?" he had asked, and smiled. His voice had turned low and hollow. He looked pleased, relishing it, as if Cora's fear had a taste, and he liked it.

Cora had tried to pull away, but his grip was too strong. Her eyes began to burn and water with terror that she tried to hide. She didn't even blink.

"Your daddy a guard here?" Gasper sang. "5576. Head Guard McCavanagh, innit?"

He reached through the fence with his other hand and traced his index finger with the long nail across her cheek. He whispered "I could kill him if I wanted."

And then he had smiled.

Cora had made a noise. Terror pressed a heavy foot at the base of her throat, cutting off her air.

And then she had heard a voice.

"Cora?"

Her head whipped around. When she saw Jack, a grateful sob erupted from deep in Cora's chest. Jack took one look at her face and his body had gone rigid. He dropped the cluster of weeds that were in his hand.

"What are you doing?" he said, advancing on the Gasper, his fists already curling.

Jack's presence sliced through the fear that held Cora like puppet strings, and Gasper finally let go. She turned and ran, shuddering and sobbing until the blood in her lungs burned. Her hand had trembled on the front doorknob, and she crept past her mother's bedroom door because she couldn't face any questions and couldn't explain what had happened without being barred from going back. Instead, she had climbed under her covers, beneath the hanging pictures of horses and *Life* magazine covers, and cried silently, cried until the fear was finally emptied all out of her. When Cora's father returned home that night, Cora had given him a rare hug, resting her ear to his chest, breathing in his faded scent of pine smoke and the wool of his uniform.

"What's all this, Cora-thorn?" he had asked. He had drawn back to examine her at arm's length.

"Nothing," she had insisted. She knew that her eyes were swollen and red. He had given her a long look. But he didn't press.

"Smitty and I broke up a fight today," he had told her mother later that night. Cora had crept to press her ear against the wall, her heart rising to beat in her throat. "Something got the inmates rowdy. We sent two to cool off in solitary."

She hadn't seen Jack again until almost a week later.

Cora had approached him, saying his name tentatively; when he had turned, his cheeks were dappled with sallow bruises, just beginning to fade into yellow and green. There had been a deep cut at the edge of his upper lip.

She had examined his face through the fence.

"Thank you," she said.

"For what?" he asked roughly, dismissing it. He had bent to pull fresh weeds from the soil.

Some nights when Cora was tired of hating what she and Jack had done, she took out that precious memory, hidden in the deepest crevices of herself, and let it glow. Never too much or too often, so it wouldn't fade away. She thought of it as she waited in the darkness.

Realizing that a part of her was afraid to take it out now and find it still glowing.

She pulled on her cigarette, trying to stay awake. The film from her camera needed five more minutes to develop. She'd rolled it inside celluloid, dropped it into its galvanized can, then hidden it in her daylight loader. She checked her watch.

And she turned her head instinctively toward the sound of a low giggle.

Cora extinguished her cigarette and crept to peer over the ledge of the open balcony. In the moonlight, she could see Liam's silhouette beneath a tree. Another smothered laugh drifted on the night air. A woman's fingers snaked through Liam's hair, and then their voices turned hushed and urgent.

Cora turned away, trying to give them privacy. She had just made her way back to her room and unlocked the door when Daisy and Liam appeared in the hallway.

Daisy instantly dropped Liam's hand. "Ella!" she exclaimed. "Just where have you been all night?"

"I could ask you the same question," Cora said, cocking an eyebrow.

Liam tipped his hat at her. "Morning, Miss Ella," he said in his thick Irish brogue. He bit his lip and flushed as he waved goodbye to Daisy.

Cora whistled under her breath, grinning.

"Criminy. You almost gave me a heart attack. I thought you were Macready," Daisy said, pushing Cora into their room. She crossed herself and shut the door firmly.

$*$ $*$ $*$

Cora ate from her tin of emergency biscuits on the bathroom tile and examined the photographs she'd taken. Once, justice and mercy had been two separate ideas to her. Cora had relished their distinct edges as a girl. Her mother had exuded mercy, her father justice, and Cora had believed that people who did bad things simply got what they deserved.

Until she met Jack. He had been like a magnet, skewing everything that up until that point had directed her toward true north. She shifted uncomfortably on the cold tile, unwilling to admit to herself that it might be happening again. She saw him pretending to stumble into the path of Truman's guards earlier that night; raising his fists to call the Gasper's attention away from her when she was a girl. Distorting the neat lines around justice and mercy again. Just like he had on Pelican.

She shook her head to clear her thoughts and carefully examined the prints she'd made. She'd developed them large enough to better make out the words on them. A name, a telephone number. A plan was beginning to develop alongside the photographs.

Turning & Blackburn Printing Press.

As she dusted the crumbs from her lap, she examined the love letters she'd also photographed. In the cellar, she'd been moving too quickly to notice that there were random headings on top of each one. But now she noticed that they must make some sort of pattern; it couldn't be a coincidence that five items were included each time.

Main Street. Albany Drive. Broadview Lane. East Court. Lover's Lane.

Magnolia, astor, begonia, evergreen, lily.

Midway above, behind the edge, left.

She flipped back and forth between them. It took her a half a moment to realize that they were all a code, spelling out the same word.

Mabel.

CHAPTER NINETEEN

Clementine slipped into a bathing suit while Lola and Kitty stood next to her in the bathroom, smoothing cream onto their faces and examining her line of toiletries. "You have Mademoiselle Crimson?" Lola asked, grabbing for an ivory tube of lipstick ringed with copper. "How did you pull that one? This isn't available yet!"

"Coco sent it over," Clementine said. "She and Eliza Schiaparelli are always trying to one-up each other, it seems." She spritzed herself with the lightest mist of perfume as Lola played enviously with the copper sliding mechanism on the lipstick tube.

"You can try it on," Clem said generously, pulling a brush through her lush, honeyed hair. She would wear a straw hat to keep the sun off of her skin. Her body quickened at the thought of seeing Beau, and she tried to ignore it. She didn't really want to betray Truman. She had come to feel fondly toward certain parts of him. Fond, but that was it. It would be easier for her—easier, and much more dangerous—if she were madly in love with him. She raised her pretty eyebrows and applied the Mademoiselle Crimson to her lips. She mostly just felt indifferent.

When she had grown into her teeth and her eyes and her body had filled out between fourteen and fifteen, it was as though she had inherited an unexpected fortune. She had come into her beauty and Truman had come into his money, and they both relished the power it offered them.

She did whatever she could to enhance that fortune now. Because, unfortunately, Truman's fortune would continue to grow, compounding on itself, while she was all too aware that hers would diminish year after year. Now she had to make it last as long as possible.

"I'm off to dress," Lola said, examining the red in the mirror. Her skin was dewy, her eyes luminous. This was a woman who glowed even when she was sleeping. "I forgot the shirt I wanted to wear today." She held up the lipstick. "Can I pop back in and reapply this later for the party tonight?"

"Of course," Clementine said.

Lola gathered her own toiletries and planted a red air kiss just to the left of Clementine's ear. "See you at the pool."

Kitty moved sinuously. She was so lovely, with her dark hair and crystal blue eyes. It was intimidating, threatening, and unusual to have someone else in the room who was as beautiful as Clem was, but she was also enchanted by it. Sometimes she stole glances at her friends when they weren't looking.

"Do you ever feel guilty about the wife?" Kitty asked as soon as they were alone.

It was an impertinent question that sent color flooding into Clementine's cheeks. She knew well enough what her own mother thought about it. Disapproving. Judgmental. But Clementine actually loved Kitty a little for asking it. It was the deepest question anyone had asked her in months.

"No," Clementine said. "Truman says she's a horrid shrew. Now she just wants his money." She led Kitty into the bedroom, where she poured them each a coffee from the carafe on her tray. The rest of the food remained largely untouched. "But society being as it is, he has to play along." She fed a piece of croissant to Snick and to Kitty's terrier, Poppet. Poppet licked Clementine's hand in gratitude.

"If I play my cards right, maybe I'll leave this week with a sugar daddy of my own," Kitty said. Her lipstick left a red mark on the coffee cup.

Clementine smiled wickedly. "I'm in." She rose and led Kitty out the doors. She loved the way the air came in through the opened windows. She loved the appreciative way Kitty looked out at the Castle grounds, the view of the sea, and with a touch of envy said *I can't believe you live here.*

"I'll talk to Truman about seating you with someone at dinners, if you'd like," Clementine said. "Anyone you have in mind?"

"Beau, of course," Kitty said, and it made Clementine's stomach hitch the slightest bit. She hid it with a broad smile. "Of course. And second choice?"

"I wouldn't kick Simon Leit out of bed for eating crackers. I like the way the tennis has shaped his calves. Meow."

Clementine laughed.

"Actually," Kitty continued, "I'll move him to first choice. He has a more assured income. For now."

First choice. Was she Truman's first choice? She couldn't be—not as long as she still played second fiddle to Mabel. She hated that she was wasting her golden years in a precarious position with little to no permanence. She could be so easily replaced by any young up-and-coming thing. At Truman's slightest whim, she could be moved down the hill as surreptitiously as his old friend Albert had been.

She loved this house, but she never let herself love it too much. It didn't belong to her. And it this rate, it never would.

She gave a brittle smile. Perhaps, in the end, she was only a slightly longer-term guest there than Kitty was.

*   *   *

Cora slipped into the telephone booth and locked the door.

She pulled out the prints she had made. Her plan involved the notice threatening Byrd's paper, but she glanced down at the love letters again.

Who had written Mabel Byrd these messages? Someone who had wanted to remain anonymous, who signed them simply *M*. Who had loved Mabel this way once, and how had Mabel ended up where she was now—bitter, alone, and nursing a grudge against her husband with the attentiveness one might give to raising a child?

That bitter resentment was the exact opposite of the way Cora's own mother had been, and it made Cora miss her. There had been a lightness about Alice McCavanagh as she walked through life casting blessings the way most people threw stones, even at those who talked down to her, who cut her in line for the tram or tried to cheat her at the market. She would walk the craggy island on Pelican, the wind sweeping her hair, and Cora knew she was praying for the prisoners because of the way her cracked lips moved with silent words. Cora wondered what her mother had thought after everything went so ghastly wrong despite all those years of her prayers. If she had ever come to believe that they had been little more than wasted breath.

Perhaps she had.

But they still sang "What a Friend We Have in Jesus" from the hymnal at her funeral, at her own request.

Cora picked up the telephone.

"Hello," she said. "Is this the number for Turning & Blackburn printing press?" She examined the photograph she had taken, the one that showed the threatening note Truman had received in the spring of 1915.

"It is. How may I help you, ma'am?"

"I was hoping to speak to Mr. Edwin Turning."

"I'm sorry, Mr. Turning doesn't work here anymore. He retired a little over a year ago."

"Oh," Cora said, the disappointment shadowing her voice.

"But I'm his son. Can I help you?"

"I'm not sure," she said. "Were you working at the company in 1915? I was hoping to speak with him about something that happened in the company's history."

"Afraid I wasn't. Listen, doll, do you have a pen? I can give you a number to reach him at home."

After thanking him, Cora hung up the phone and dialed the new number. Mr. Edwin Turning picked up after three rings. Cora affected a vaguely Southern accent and launched into her cover story.

"Mr. Turning, hello. This is Betty Campbell, with *Reader's Digest* magazine? I was hoping to ask you some questions about a story I'm doing."

"What kind of story?" His voice was instantly suspicious, and Cora took a deep breath.

"It's a human-interest piece. About Truman Byrd."

"Yeah?" He made a noise like he was spitting tobacco. "What about him?"

Cora forced a smile into her voice. "Mr. Byrd started his career printing papers with your press. He's a millionaire now, but rumor had it at one point he didn't have two nickels to rub together. Is that right?"

He turned even more cagey. "I don't know if I want to talk about that. Truman and I had our differences from time to time, but I don't want to get on the wrong side of him now. It all turned out all right."

"Oh, please don't get the wrong idea!" Cora said, changing tactics. "This is meant to be a feel-good piece. Rags-to-riches kind of thing. Everybody wants to hear that story these days—how someone's luck can turn on a dime. This is a story our readers will positively eat up."

She heard the sound of Edwin Turning shifting. When he spoke, he still sounded wary. "All right. But I don't want you to quote me."

"Perfectly all right. This will be off the record." *More off the record than you can imagine,* she thought.

"Mr. Byrd himself has admitted that his finances were in a rocky state at the beginning of his career. It sounds like for a while he was looking at having to shut down his paper. Stroke of luck when he broke that story about the Bastion murders. Readership must have started to soar after that," Cora said.

Mr. Turning grunted.

"Was that the story that turned his fortunes, would you say?"

"His readership was growing, all right," Mr. Turning said, "but that's a slow business."

"But it was enough to put him in the black, it seems?" she said. "So he could continue to publish *The Post-Courant?*"

Mr. Turning paused. "No, I don't think so."

"So if not for the increase in readership, where did the money come from?" Cora asked casually. "A business loan, perhaps?"

"No." The voice on the other line suddenly sounded distant. "His father was the only one who would loan him money at the time, and that was running out too. He must have had another source of income. Some windfall, like an inheritance or something. As long as it's coming in, it's not my business. But he paid it upfront and never had an issue since. Even gave me some extra, for the trouble." Mr. Turning paused. "But I doubt that's the kind of story your readers want to hear."

"I see. Perhaps you're right. We might need to take a slightly different angle, then," Cora said. "Thank you for your time." She hung up the telephone with a twinge in her gut. She might not be able to trust Jack, or possibly even her own judgment. But the facts, for now, were lining up with Jack's version of the story.

Could someone have truly bribed Truman to frame the wrong people? To shift the spotlight and tell the story they wanted him to tell? Whoever paid him off had found him at just the right moment—when he was at his most desperate.

Cora tucked the photographs into her waistband, wondering if some things were beyond mercy. She'd always thought she was much more like her father anyway. Upturned lip, quick to mete out justice or hold a grudge. Sometimes Cora had wanted nothing more than to see her mother be human. She would feel that itch and would egg her mother on relentlessly, not letting up until she finally snapped. Breaking through that almost impenetrable fortress left Cora feeling a sense of disappointment combined with a sweet, sticky satisfaction. A reassurance that she wasn't quite out of Cora's reach, yet.

So mercy was a land her mother lived on alone, more of an island than Pelican itself.

And Cora could only wonder what her mother would think if she saw her now.

*   *   *

Jack had spent the day trying to keep a low profile. He followed the buzz of the party that was forming down the hill. Waiters were serving hors d'oeuvres of speared caprese and chilled watermelon soup on silver trays. Lanterns bobbed from lines strewn overhead, creating a canopy. Jack wove through topiary bushes carved into the shapes of wild animals and took a glass of champagne. Cora was nowhere to be seen. He looked beyond the starlets, who were playing a competitive game of horseshoes in sheer silver gowns that looked spun from gossamer. He drank a sip of sparkling lemonade, letting the bubbles hit the back of his throat and burn a little on the way down. He hadn't seen Cora all day. Surely she had made it back to her room last night, after he had distracted the guard?

He watched the birds in the aviary and glanced over his shoulder. Albert was there, dressed in a white linen suit, looking slightly disheveled. He caught Jack's eye and stared daggers at him. Jack ignored him and turned away. He knew he was under surveillance. Though Dallas Winston was subtle, Jack was intimately familiar with the feeling of being watched.

Jack exhaled. He was paying the cost of his decisions last night. He eyed the birds, the yellow finches, bluebirds, and doves. Watching for Cora. Knowing he had to be exceedingly careful tonight.

He took another sip of lemonade and approached Beau.

"Beaumont," he said warmly. He stuck out his hand. "Everett Conner. We haven't been formally introduced."

"Everett. The card player," Beau said, shaking his hand heartily. He grinned.

"And aspiring cowboy," Jack said, grinning back. "I saw you in the Western on that Arabian stallion. Where did you learn to ride like that?"

"Growing up in Missouri," Beau said. "My grandfather owned a farm in a little town called Buffalo. What about you?"

"I spent my childhood in a modest little family home exactly like this one," Jack said airily, gesturing toward the Castle.

Beau laughed.

"Would you be game for a ride tomorrow?" Jack asked. "I'd like to see more of the land. I know Truman's up to his ears in work right now, but Clem had mentioned earlier in the week that she could possibly give us a tour."

Beau glanced at Clem, who was dripping in silver from head to toe. She felt his eyes on her and turned.

"Certainly," Beau said. He smiled at her.

And though she couldn't possibly hear what they were saying, she smiled back.

$$* \quad * \quad *$$

Daisy was the one who came to Jack, appearing at his elbow. "Go into the maze," she said pleasantly, "and find the back wall." She took his empty glass and handed him a full one. "Ella will be waiting on the other side of the hedge."

"Cheers," he said under his breath.

She adjusted the grip on her tray and moved on to serve Governor Gilham.

Behind Jack was a yew labyrinth twenty paces away with tall, manicured hedges—significantly larger and more impressive than the boxwood maze near the main house—and it provided the perfect place to get away from Dallas Winston's prying eyes. Jack waited a few more moments, watching a rainbow lorikeet in the aviary clean its wings. Then he turned toward the maze and wandered in.

He made his way through the walls of green. The setting sun striated the sky with stripes of pink and blue clouds as he made a wrong turn into a dead end, then corrected himself. Eventually he found the back wall of hedge.

"I seem to have gotten lost," he said aloud. He glanced behind himself, but no one seemed to have followed him.

"Perhaps I'll send a waiter in after you," he heard Cora say, "so you don't starve in there." He moved toward the sound of her voice. She stood on the outside of the hedge, so that no one could glimpse them together as they talked. The hedges were thick and well pruned, but he could catch a glimpse of an eye, her full lips, through a small gap.

"I've invited two guests to join me on a horseback ride tomorrow," he reported.

Her lips parted.

"Were you all right last night?" she asked quietly. "Did you get into trouble?"

He sighed. "I'm not rooming with Albert down the hill yet," he said. "So there's that mercy." He kept a trained eye on the corner of the maze, waiting for someone to come around at any moment. "And yet—I think Dallas Winston is watching me closely."

"Listen. There's a hidden entrance to the bell tower. There are mosaic tiles in the garden paths," she whispered. "Look for the ones near the outdoor pools, in the shape of hexagons."

"Hexagons."

"Normally the pattern is blue, yellow, red, green, but you'll find one that is blue, yellow, red, white instead. Look for the white tile. That's where the entrance is."

Of course. When trying to find something, the first place to look was for anything off. A loose thread to pull.

"There's a tunnel there," she whispered. "And a secret staircase that brings you to the top of the bell tower.

"I'll be there at 11:30," she said, and then she was gone.

CHAPTER TWENTY

A
t 11:20 p.m., Cora changed out of her uniform and pulled a shawl over her hair. She followed the tiles to the hidden entrance and climbed the staircase of the eastern bell tower, stealing a glance at the Astral Bedroom when she reached the top. She couldn't see inside, but she could tell when the light went out—and she could keep an eye on exactly when the guards passed by below, in case she grew desperate enough to scale the wall.

Her heart flickered as she eyed the height.

The fall could break her neck. Likely even kill her.

How badly did she want this? What was she willing to do in order to avoid leaving a failure?

Failure. It was like the dog tag she could never take off.

She tightened the soft threads of the shawl around her shoulders. The bell tower was a hexagonal room formed by twelve arches of colorful polychrome tiles, with twelve carillon bells hanging suspended between them. The moon was high and white-bright, throwing off enough light to illuminate the thin cushions, the decks of cards and row of bottles that Liam kept stashed there for their occasional game nights with Daisy and Matias.

She listened for the sounds of Jack approaching. When they were on Pelican she had sometimes heard Jack laughing with his brother, their Dorchester accents emerging against each other. Leo had a rich singing voice. Jack's was rougher and sometimes a little off-key, but he was much better at handling people, and the flowers. He had a gentle way about him that made things warm and soften. Telling her how arches made of stone didn't even need mortar to hold them together. About the way his grandmother, Dearie, used to cut a cross in the soda bread she baked to let the fairies out. Cora had donated her favorite mysteries to the penitentiary library so that he could read them.

"It doesn't seem fair, though, that you have to lose the very ones that are your favorites," Jack had protested.

"I don't mind," she had said. And she didn't. She liked the way they picked apart the mysteries together, the way Jack's mind tried to crack the lock of them.

She had felt a white-hot slice of satisfaction every time she made him laugh with clever jokes, a feeling that made her body feel strange and flushed. Cora even stopped protesting and sat down with her mother to look through the Sears catalogue, and her mother ordered her two new dresses that she only got to show Jack once.

She glanced up with sudden nerves at the sound of the door creaking open.

$$* \quad * \quad *$$

Jack found her smoking a cigarette, her long legs folded beneath her.

"Were you followed?" she asked, rising.

"No," Jack said. "I made a show of saying good night and retiring to my room. Then I climbed down from the loggia." He didn't mention that he was fairly certain Mr. Winston had posted a guard standing just outside his room, watching the front door.

"These won't be missed," Cora said, bending to rummage in a crate near her feet. "Take your pick." She held out an ambered whiskey and a bottle of red wine.

He pointed to the whiskey, and she handed it over.

As he opened it, she placed a set of photographs on the table. "I found something last night," she said. "Proof that Truman was in a lot of debt two weeks before the Bastion murders."

Jack took a swig of whiskey and pulled the photographs closer to him. He noticed that her hair was down and loose tonight, cascading in waves.

"How did Truman get out of this debt?" he asked.

"I called the printers to inquire about that today," Cora said. "Apparently Truman paid it off with a lump cash sum shortly after this notice."

Jack looked up at her sharply. "It was the same story with the witnesses," he said. "They were all paid off."

"How do you know?"

"The eyewitness testimony from an unrelated man and woman was what really sealed the case against Leo and me. We had a fighting chance until that point. Well, I looked into the male witness a few years back. I paid handsomely, and one of my guys was able to dig up some info on him. Turns out he was already well known to them—in a ton of debt, gambling type of stuff, until he came into a big chunk of change and settled up shortly after my conviction."

"Interesting," Cora said. She watched him through her eyelashes as she opened the wine and took a drink straight from the bottle.

"The female witness who testified against us had an ill kid at the time. But both witnesses were sitting pretty by the time I escaped Pelican. The woman's sick daughter was set up in a nice new brownstone and was being seen with the best doctors and care. You don't find that just a bit suspect?"

Cora paused, her eyes narrowing. "What were the witnesses' names?"

"Dean Fischer and Lily Davis," he said.

Cora could double-check his story, and he knew she would, too.

He had fought hatred for those people for years. But how easy would it be to tell one lie if it would take care of you for the rest of your life? If it could get you out of debt with a mobster? Or save your kid's life? He'd done the same. Exchanged lives for his own purposes.

He picked up a deck of cards and began to shuffle them, his mind quickening. "So Truman needed money. Perhaps someone approached him. Someone rich and powerful enough to bribe Truman and the witnesses. To swing the public opinion and the trial toward Leo and me."

To cover someone else's tracks. The cards fell in a waterfall between his hands. Who had Truman been protecting all these years?

Jack needed to find those powerful files, or something else that would get Truman to talk.

He wrenched the whiskey bottle open again, feeling the pungent alcohol hit his nose. Cora was staring at him again with those hazel eyes, the ring of gold in them blazing like a corona. Last night, he had tried not to notice the way the hem of her skirt skimmed her calf as she bent to go through the locked cabinet files. He turned now to look at the rows of vintage clarets and bottles of bourbon, the decks of cards scattered amongst the cushions.

"So, Truman caused all of this destruction to gain a valuable ally while he was on the rise," Cora said. She brought the bottle to her lips again. "He really is a bastard."

Her eyes brightened with something like anger, and it ignited something in him that he had fought so hard to keep dormant. Jack took a long drink of whiskey and tried to keep both at bay—the alcohol, and his desire to make someone pay. For so long, he had wanted someone beyond himself to suffer, and he could feel the way it was turning his insides to rot.

"How did you get here, Jack?" Cora asked. She licked a crimson drop of wine from the edge of her mouth. "Rich enough to garner an invitation to the Hill, when you were starting with little more than your own shadow." She studied him. "You must have had help?"

Jack took another gulp of whiskey. "I did. A man by the name of Luis Lozada."

"Never heard of him," Cora said.

"That's not surprising, seeing as he was a cattle farmer," Jack said. He closed his eyes. How much a single person could do to another: one man had ruined his life, another had saved it. "And he went by the name Hank Ritter."

"He took you on?" Cora asked. "With no identification papers?"

"He must have suspected I wasn't working under my real name, but he was an immigrant working under a new name too. He thought I was a hard worker. Liked my gardening know-how."

"He . . . must have paid you handsomely, then?" Cora asked, and he heard the skepticism that crept into her voice. She was so much more guarded than she used to be.

"I worked for Lozada in the field for a few years, and then eventually I used the knowledge of his fields to help design an irrigation system."

"You became an engineer after all, then," she said.

He smiled, almost wistful. "Can you believe it? That time in hell on Pelican helped me after all. The system I came up with helped turn the arid desert land to grass. Revolutionized his acreage and managed to double Lozada's fortune practically overnight."

Jack still remembered the taste of the fried potatoes dripping with grease in the mornings. Lozada was unmarried and had treated him like a son. He had taught him to ride a horse bareback and fly-fish in the Nevada creeks. For a few months, Jack had almost forgotten everything. His dreams of returning to Massachusetts and seeing his mother again. Of clearing his name. It was only the fresh fry of fish on a skillet over an open flame, of dirt under his nails, of the howl of coyotes at night under a sky littered with stars. How Lozada had taken them out for a steak dinner with corn mash after the first pipe had gone in, already convinced that Jack would be a success. "He died a couple of years later and left me most of his fortune. I gambled some of what he had left me and made it into more. And my expensive card playing found me a way to get in front of Byrd."

Cora nodded, the delicate curve of her throat bobbing. Her skin was so smooth in the moonlight. It was so strange to see the echoes of her as a girl, now a woman, and the noticing of it was prompting things in him that he did not want to acknowledge.

He shut that down as hard as he could manage.

"And you grew up to become a private investigator," he said. "Just like you wanted."

"Yes. What a private investigator I am," she muttered darkly, "drinking stolen booze with the most wanted con in the country."

He laughed at that. "So, Mabel Byrd's aware that Mr. Byrd's been taking a left-handed honeymoon with Clementine Garver? And she wants her gone?"

Cora took a long sip of wine. "Clementine's the worst-kept secret in Hollywood," she said. "It's a horrible sort of game he plays. Everyone knows, but Byrd still won't grant Mabel a divorce."

"And divorce law would always favor the man. Especially rich and powerful ones."

"Right." She paused. "And the only way that Mabel would have any leverage in the court is if she can prove beyond a doubt that Truman was responsible for the divorce due to his infidelity."

"Ah," Jack said. "So you're not just looking to merely get rid of Clem, then."

Cora hesitated. "No," she admitted. "I need photographs. The only story Byrd can't spin is one that people have seen with their own eyes. Especially if there's something incriminating the rival newspapers could run and turn public opinion."

"But Byrd has to know that too."

"Yes. That's why he and Miss Garver are so careful. It's been difficult to catch them in a compromising, ah. . . ." She trailed off and took a quick drink of wine.

". . . . position," he supplied helpfully. He was trying to tease; but when he caught the lovely flush gathering at the base of her neck, something stirred deep inside him. He set the whiskey bottle down roughly.

No more drinking.

"What can I do?" he asked quietly.

"Take Clem and Beau on that ride and get them alone. There's going to be a ball tomorrow night. And I need Truman to be made very jealous, and then for him and Clementine to be together as much as possible. I'll scout out the location. And then I need for you to get Truman into it for me."

"I thought you were done making deals with the devil," Jack said.

"Perhaps I'm not sure who he is anymore," she retorted.

There was a small tentative quirk at the corner of her mouth. She took another sip of wine.

He warned himself to be careful. Being around her was feeling dangerously good. The sleepless nights were leaving everything feeling a little blurred around the edges and sepia-toned. He never let his guard down like this with anyone, and something about doing it with her gave him a thrill.

She refolded her legs. "I've staked them out from afar, got myself situated as her private maid," Cora said. "Gathered information to be in the right place at the right time, and give them little pushes as I could."

"And?"

"I almost got something a month ago," she said wistfully. "You can tell it's Clementine in the photograph, but the lighting wasn't good enough, and Byrd's too blurry to bank on." She ran the tip of her finger along the lip of the bottle. "But my time's running out. I only have a few days left. I can't afford to be as patient, or as cautious."

He watched her hands trail from the bottle's lip to clutch its slim neck. The same fingers that used to curl through the wire fence, often caked with dirt, almost always holding a book. His mouth suddenly felt dry. He realized then why he might feel so drawn to her. She was a slow-burning sort of lovely. But she had also known him when he was still partly himself—hopeful that justice would someday be served. That he and Leo would make it back home someday. The true him had been present in those moments with her, even though she had just been a kid. She had reminded him of goodness.

"And you found some sort of proof last night?" he asked. "That's why you were taking the photographs?"

"I thought so. But I realized earlier today that these don't have anything to do with Clementine. It's a code. See this pattern? *M* is for *Main St.* and *magnolia.* They're written to Mabel." She tapped the photograph. "But from someone named M."

Jack bent to examine the letters closer. He noticed that her skin smelled like gardenias.

"What if that's not meant to be an *M*?" he said slowly. "What if it means something else?"

She looked again, and he noticed that she had drawn infinitesimally closer to him. "You're right," she said, the ends of her hair lightly tickling his arm. "I think that's a symbol of a bird."

CHAPTER TWENTY-ONE

THURSDAY, MAY 1, 1930
~ Day Five ~

Clementine woke and dressed in tennis clothes: navy wide-legged trousers, a crisp cotton shirt. She tied a silk scarf with a navy-and-persimmon pattern at her neck, poured a cup of coffee that Ella had left on the tray, and headed down to the clay tennis courts. Clementine spotted Beau before anyone else. She felt warmth grow in her body, as golden as the sunlight.

"Ladies," said Simon Leit. He gave a slight bow to them, and Kitty sauntered toward him, laughing.

"Will you be on my team?" Beau asked Clementine, twirling the racquet that rested on his shoulder. His eyes were the color of cloudless sky. He had a million-dollar smile—the kind of smile that might make Clementine willing to give up a life worth more than that. She grabbed a wooden racquet from the stand and gave him a smile in return that was unmistakably flirtatious.

"What makes you think we'd be a good one?" she purred.

He laughed. "For starters, the scenery is already infinitely more beautiful than it was last night."

She laughed back. "Charmer." She took off the scarf from her neck and tied it around his wrist. "A charmer deserves a good-luck charm."

"And you're going to need it!" Simon called across the net.

"We're doomed," Beau said conspiratorially to Clementine as he settled in behind her for a doubles match. "Rest in peace to my vanity."

"Speak for yourself," she said, expertly returning the first volley. "Mine's still alive and well."

Beau whistled behind her and it was all she could do not to smirk. She bent down to pick up the ball in a way that made sure her pants hugged the curve of her backside. The smallest, sun-kissed sliver of skin showed at her waist. Clementine knew how to tease. Was she throwing away her chance at true love to be someone else's side piece for a few short years? A playful distraction during her golden years? She needed to secure her own future, one way or the other.

She felt sorry for Truman, sometimes. No one could know the shrew that Mabel Byrd had become, the torture of being with her. He was a victim, see.

But Mabel still had the name Byrd. The permanence. And she didn't.

Jack sauntered over after the game, twirling a racquet on his shoulder. Clem wiped a glisten of perspiration from her forehead.

"Maybe next time you'll let me join them on the court," Jack teased to Simon. "It might be a fair fight at three against one."

Simon laughed good-naturedly and begged off to practice his serve.

Jack turned toward Beau and Clem. "What do you say about that ride? Meet you at the stables in an hour, then?"

They finalized the plans and Clem made her way toward her room to freshen her makeup and change into her riding gear. But first, she climbed the stairs to Truman's office with Poppet yipping behind her. Truman loved to ride his Appaloosa mare along the sloping vistas, informing his guests about the features of the land, and he might want to join them for the afternoon. Besides, she thought—it might be just the thing to get Truman on board with Beau as her upcoming costar. She was about to knock on the closed door when she overheard his voice. Something in his tone made her pause. She gave Poppet a treat to stay quiet and leaned in closer to listen.

Truman's voice was elevated. She caught a snippet of *Newport*.

And *what Mabel wants*.

Mrs. Macready, the head of house, responded with something just out of hearing.

Clementine pressed her ear to the door.

"I haven't told Miss Garver yet," Truman said. "But cancel my June trip to Los Angeles."

Clementine stepped back from the door. Inwardly, she seethed.

She stalked down the hall with Poppet at her heels. On second thought, she wouldn't tell Truman about the ride after all.

*   *   *

Cora caught herself in the reflection of the mirror as she gulped down a cup of black coffee in the kitchen with Daisy, waiting for the caffeine to hit her blood. Her eyes looked tired.

Three days left.

"Mr. Conner hasn't been feeling well and requested brunch in his room this morning," she said to the cook. She was careful to avoid Daisy's eyes, and Daisy loyally buried her face in her coffee mug to hide any expression. "Shall I take it to him?"

The cook sighed. "Macready's still meeting with Mr. Byrd . . . ," Dorothy said, clearly not wanting to make a decision without the head of household. "Fine, go ahead," she said gruffly, adding a cup of heavy cream to the pan where she was making a soufflé. Cora quickly loaded up a tray before Macready could return. She swept past Daisy without sparing her a look.

She quickened her step over the mosaic tiles of the esplanade, then paused outside Jack's door. She balanced the tray and knocked. She supposed she should feel exhausted, but instead she felt strangely alive.

Perhaps Jack could actually help her get what she had come for. Perhaps she wouldn't have to do this entirely alone.

Jack's face registered the slightest surprise when he opened the door, his bathrobe barely concealing the skin of his chest.

"Breakfast?" Cora asked.

He stepped back to let her in.

Cora looked over her shoulder and then slipped inside.

Jack must have been fresh from a shower. The bathroom was heady with steam, the mirror dewy. The balcony doors were open toward the swath of ocean. She could smell the fragrant wave of flowers beneath them. The bed was unmade, the sheets rumpled. She slid the tray onto the table, and, on looking at the distant base of the hill, spied two zebras grazing.

"Did you sleep at all?" he asked.

"That's what coffee is for," she informed him.

"Are you hungry?" he asked. He gestured to the tray.

"I really shouldn't stay," she said, glancing toward the door.

"Are you sure . . . ?" he asked, and, with a wicked look, uncovered the first silver dome with a flourish. Her resolve wilted the moment the greasy scent of bacon hit her nose. She saw the plump, flaky pastries nestled next to one another.

He moved to the edge of the bed and sat down.

"Sit and eat," he said.

"Fine," she relented. "But I can't promise to save you any." She uncovered the rest of the food, revealing blueberry hotcakes, fresh-cut mango, a ramekin of cheese soufflé.

She dipped her spoon into the soufflé, trying not to notice the way his bathrobe hugged his waist when he slipped into the bathroom to change. She moved on to the mango; and when he emerged dressed in a crisp day suit, he suddenly looked young, a tuft of hair sticking up from his head. For a moment, Cora could almost imagine what he must have looked like when he was a little boy.

He watched her with amusement as she spread jam onto a croissant and almost sighed with delight.

"You're enjoying that," he said, taking a croissant for himself.

"This is the most fun I've had in someone else's bedroom for a long time," she said.

He cocked an eyebrow and laughed the way he did when she surprised him.

"Does that mean you have a fella waiting for you somewhere, Cora?" he asked.

She eyed him. "There was someone, once," she said.

"Not anymore?" he asked.

"I have trust issues," she said lightly. "Imagine that."

Jack nodded and let that sit for a beat. He handed her a cup of coffee and she felt the brush of his fingers.

"What about you?" she asked. "You have a doll somewhere, just waiting for you to finish your business here?"

"No," he said. "Nothing serious, anyway. Intimacy is a bit tricky when you have to lie about every aspect of who you really are."

She took a hasty sip of coffee that burned her mouth.

"So," she said. "For tonight. I scouted the location."

He nodded. "Draw me a map." He fetched her a pen and paper.

"When I give the signal, you're going to lead Truman up here." She traced the route with the tip of her pen. "Jack—this might be my last good shot to get what I came for. Tell him whatever it takes to get him there."

"Are you condoning deceit?" he asked, teasing.

She took another sip of coffee. "My mother always said 'Wisdom heeds all rules and occasionally breaks them.'"

"Ah," he said. "I like that."

"You would have liked her," Cora said.

"Oh, I did. I met her once," he said. "She came out to the fence and spoke to me."

"What?"

Cora set down her mug.

She could almost see her mother standing there, in her long cotton dress, the wind pulling at the pins in her hair. It hurt to think of her mother's touch now, and the certain things made only by her hands. Sweet maple bread with hunks of cheese. The careful way she had tucked basil seeds into dirt. "Cora?" she used to say, in a gentle voice a half-step above a whisper. She'd sweep the fine hairs along Cora's temple away with her fingers like they were spun floss. Lower her lips to Cora's ear. "The day is calling for you, dearest, and it's time to answer her."

"She wanted to know what seeds I was planting," Jack recalled. "I told her they were for a rose named Madame Butterfly. And then she came closer and asked for my name. She told me that 'The Lord could restore the years the locusts had eaten.'"

"Joel 2:25," Cora said, her voice almost a whisper. Her mother had had her memorize it out of the big King James Bible, though Cora was never quite sure she knew why.

> *So I will restore to you the years that the swarming*
> *   locust has eaten,*
> *The crawling locust,*
> *The consuming locust,*
> *And the chewing locust,*
> *My great army which I sent among you.*
> *You shall eat in plenty and be satisfied,*
> *And praise the name of the Lord your God,*
> *Who has dealt wondrously with you.*

"I never forgot it," Jack said. "The kindness to give a promise like that to a prisoner whose life was all but already over. She thought I murdered guards, people like her own husband. She gave me hope like an object I could hold onto in my hand. 'I will restore the years the locusts have eaten.'" He looked back at her. "You grew up to look like her, a little," he said. "You always had her kindness."

Cora turned away, touched to the core. He couldn't know that that was the thing she had most wanted anyone to say to her. That she was like her mother.

"I haven't spoken of her in so long," she said. Her father never wanted to, always changing the subject right when Cora needed him not to. When Alice had died, it was as though the tension of what held Cora together fell away. There were no guardrails or ramparts left to hold her in place anymore, to bump up against and reorient.

And there was something about the knowledge that Jack had seen Alice alive—moving, breathing, speaking. Cora didn't have to try to conjure her mother for him. Her memory could meet with something of his own.

Cora hesitated. "She used to pretend to crack an egg on my head." The memory was so intimate that it felt like stripping pieces of clothing off of herself. "Too many gray days in a row would make her ornery and melancholy."

"Pelican must have been hard, then."

"Yes. Her moods were like a weather vane." She used to read Cora books about little mice that drank blackberry juice and went on picnics. She talked about prayer like it was a real thing that accomplished something. Whispered words that could turn back pandemics like breakers and sea walls. Each one was like a piece of glass, putting together a beautiful, intricate mosaic, built somewhere they couldn't yet see.

Cora set down her cup. Something had broken inside her, a floodgate opened by the crack of remembering her mother and the almost unbearable intimacy of sharing it with him. And now she was stumbling backward, trying not to fall, but it was too late.

She felt the hairs on her skin prickle and rise. Something awakened in her. A fierce wanting, reigniting something long dormant. Her first love. She could feel it sweeping through her veins again, the dizzying yearning and pure shot of adrenaline of just wanting to be near him, like a drug that she knew would destroy her, but she didn't care because she just wanted more of it. She had told herself that she had felt the same things for Bobby, but here it was now, potent and electrifying, and she knew it had never quite reached what she had felt for Jack. She wanted to feel more of that, and it scared her to death.

"In exchange for your help tonight," she said, "I have something for you."

"Oh?" he asked. "And what might that be?"

He looked unguarded. She smelled sandalwood and mint; was close enough to see the stubble shadowing his jaw like dusk. Cora scrawled down a name, moving away from the unmade bed before she made a big mistake. "The architect of this place," she said. "She'll know of any secret places in the Castle." She held out the paper to him. "Her name is Florence Abrams."

∗   ∗   ∗

Albert Boyle was nursing a dull headache and a foul temper when he opened his door. He leaned against the railing in the shadows, preparing for the sun to hit his eyes, still feeling the grime from last night on his teeth. It was a longer walk up the hill to the main house now, and he felt the resentment stirring in his belly. "A little change of scenery," the butler had said when they'd escorted him to the guesthouse down the hill.

Albert lit a cigarette, preparing to make the trek to the main house for some coffee and greasy sausage. He had watched Everett Conner at the party last night, wondering who he thought he was, anyway. Some self-righteous, new-money, Midwestern blowhard who happened to be good with cards and . . . cattle?

And that Truman would listen to him anyway. It was insulting.

But then Albert straightened. He stepped back into the shadows, his lips cracking drily as he noticed something very interesting.

A young auburn-haired maid, trying very hard not to be seen as she left Everett Conner's bedroom.

CHAPTER TWENTY-TWO

At a quarter past eleven, Jack met Clem and Beaumont at the stables. Clem was already astride an Appaloosa, and one of the stablehands was saddling a roan Arabian for Beau.

"You've chosen intriguing footwear for a trail ride," Clem said.

"I'm afraid something's come up for business," Jack said. "You go on without me."

He walked away just as Beau was climbing into the saddle. He saw them off, giving them a wave.

Then he arranged for a car to take him down the hill into town.

Cora had written out the name of the diner in Harmony where Florence ate every Wednesday without fail. "If there's something else hidden here, she'll know where," Cora said. "She orders the same dish and sits at the same booth, like clockwork. She'll be there at noon."

"Then so will I," Jack said.

The day was clear, but the air was pregnant with a coming storm when Jack climbed into the chauffeured car and watched the house recede behind him: the cypress trees, the bell towers. And somewhere hidden deep within the grounds, Cora.

There was a strange new crook in his gut, a filling where he had felt the daily ache of loneliness for more than a decade. So unfamiliar it bordered on uncomfortable. He watched from the window as the automobile snaked along the road, hugging the cliffs where the Pacific dropped dangerously below.

He envisioned the curve of her collarbone peeking out from beneath her uniform. She had a slow-blooming beauty that unfurled itself more each time he saw her.

But he knew he couldn't afford to notice such things. He needed to stay the course he had made, of becoming strategic and cynical. It was what he knew. What he could trust. It filled the places where the hope used to live.

He had come to know despair in the coolness of the desert nights while on the run from Pelican, watching horned lizards skitter patterns across the sloping dunes after the sunset had scorched the sky. He used to lie under a fringe of stars and think about how easy it had once been to turn the thoughts in his head into words to trade like smooth stones or coins. Bantering with Leo over sausages frying on the stove; singing a clever, cheeky little ditty to May Rollins down the street while she swung her legs from a perch on the fence post. As a fugitive, he formed words that lay empty and dormant in his mouth and wondered if it was possible to go mad from loneliness, anger, regret. What he learned was that those were places you could live in, realer even than the numbers of his address. A deeper world. And sometimes he wondered if, for some people, hell started well before you died.

Jack straightened his cuff links and directed the chauffeur to stop at a small turnoff in front of the Harmony Diner. The restaurant was situated on a cliff, where waves dashed into foam at the base of the hills and then slunk back into the sea. Elephant seals gathered on the beach below like wet tires, and the air smelled of fresh grass, brim, and rotting kelp.

"Give me an hour?" Jack asked, tipping the chauffeur heartily. The automobile drove off, dust swirling into eddies behind it. Jack turned toward the diner, a bell tinkling over his head when he opened the door and stepped inside.

It was a tight, cramped space, made bearable by the vast views of the Pacific through the back wall of windows. Jack stood in the doorway, hit with the scent of brewed coffee, grease, and fresh buttermilk. There were ten booths, seven of which were occupied. He recognized Florence immediately, sitting at the window in the back corner, just like Cora had said she would be. She was examining what looked like rudimentary blueprints, her head bent over a half-filled cup of coffee.

But he didn't go to her right away.

Instead, he asked to use the telephone.

"Muddy Dahlia," someone answered on the fourth ring.

"Virgil. It's Conner," Jack said. He played with the matchbook that Cora had stolen and then given back to him.

Virgil's voice immediately turned cagey. "Conner. You got the goods?"

"No. Listen, I didn't want to call from the house. I don't have it yet, but I'm . . . following a new lead." His eyes landed on Florence.

Virgil sounded agitated. "Byrd put out another hit piece on our candidate today. The boss is fuming. I'll try to hold him off a bit longer, but I can't promise anything."

"Hold him off from what?" Jack asked.

Instead of answering, Virgil hung up the phone.

Jack gently replaced the receiver.

"What'll it be?" the cook barked.

"Hash with heat, please," Jack said, and moseyed over to the back-corner booth. He tried to shake off the way the call had unsettled him.

"Miss Abrams?" he asked with a polite amount of hesitation. "Is that you?"

She looked up through her blunt fringe of hair, examining him with shrewd, intelligent eyes.

"Do I know you?" she asked.

"I'm sorry, no. Everett Conner," he said, extending his hand. "I'm staying with Truman up at Byrd Castle this week. Which I know you designed." He sidestepped the waiter, who slid a plate of steaming hash across the table to Florence.

Since he was a kid, Jack had had an innate sense for the locks that people carried within them. Locks that needed the right key to open. He had never had trouble making friends, or getting other people to trust him. That was how relationships were forged, and he had honed this skill with the same intensity as someone learning to sculpt bronze or brandish a carving knife. But sometimes Jack knew his skill was wielded as a weapon. There was a line between friendliness and manipulation. There had been times in his life when he wanted something. When he knew exactly what he was doing, and finding the right key was a surgical, almost violating thing.

He always sensed when he was nearing that line. As he was about to do now.

He flashed her a broad smile.

"I don't want to interrupt your lunch. I'll leave you to it—I just have to say, the engineering marvel of the water reservoir you designed, with the gravity-based system making use of the artesian wells. Well, it was genius."

He took a step back to leave, gesturing toward her steaming plate, and she eyed him, her fork raised.

She used it to point to the booth opposite her.

"Sit, Mr. Conner," she said.

"Coffee, please," he said to the waiter, and slid into the booth.

"How did you come to know so much about the water system? Are you an engineer by trade?" she asked. Her fork bit into the egg next to the hash, sending marigold yolk spilling across her plate.

"Somewhat." He spoke in detail, telling Florence about designing his own agricultural system for Lozada. She examined him with reserved interest as though she were sizing him up.

"I'm curious, though," Jack said, tucking into his own plate of hash. It was piled high with jalapenos, and he added Tabasco sauce to it, so that the first bite made his eyes water. "Tell me about the choice to use Caen limestone for the exterior of the castle." It was one of the first things he had noticed, and he had reached out to touch one of the outer walls. It was so smooth that it looked like poured cream, ready to ripple beneath his fingers.

"Mr. Byrd had a penchant for Caen, and it withstands the elements quite well," she said. "The high winds and the salt air."

"The very same stone used to construct the Tower of London and Westminster Abbey, isn't that right?" He took another eyewatering bite of hash. "Formed in the lagoons of northwestern France."

"Yes," Florence said, cutting him an approving look. "And dating back to the middle Jurassic period."

Jack relaxed into the booth and grinned at her. She gave him a genuine smile back. There was something healing in that moment, sitting across from Florence Abrams, watching some of the time he'd spent on Pelican being redeemed. He had used it to soak up all sorts of the information he would eventually need: To escape from Pelican. To make the tributaries for the desert where he had made his fortune with Mr. Lozada. And now to open the lock that was Florence Abrams. He had a niggling sense that she was going to be the key to the whole thing.

"There are rumors of a bridge project to connect the coastal highways north of Byrd Castle and make the travel easier to San Francisco," he continued, pushing away his emptied plate.

"Yes. That bridge is necessary. But the falsework will be complex over Bixby Creek, to construct the span of that gulf amidst high winds and waves," Florence mused.

Jack stroked the cut of his chin. "Would it make sense to use steel, then?"

"No," Florence said decisively. "Steel requires more upkeep with its exposure to the elements." She watched the waiter approach with her dish of strawberry shortcake.

"I'll have one of those too, if you please," Jack said, eyeing Florence's plate.

"I'd employ concrete," Florence said, her fork sending a strawberry to slide down the mountain of cream, "which could help stabilize the cost and perhaps allow for more profit to the laborers."

"Interesting," Jack said. "I can see why Truman likes you."

"The jury's still out on you," she said demurely, licking her fork. Jack laughed, and they plunged into an animated discussion on corbels and crestings, pilasters and crenelations. Jack illustrated and smoothed lines through the air as though feeling the wood and limestone and steel beneath his hands.

And then he checked his watch. "Damn. I'm afraid I have to go." He put his napkin on the table and paid both their bills. "Thank you for this enchanting hour, Miss Abrams. Will you be at the party tonight?"

She waved that off. "I'm not much for Truman's parties."

"Nor am I," he admitted.

"Gaudy and awful, if you ask me. I'd rather pour wet concrete into my boots."

"Agreed. Especially seeing as tonight's fête requires a costume."

She shuddered.

"Yet I'm only here for a short time longer." He checked his watch again, leaning toward her. "It's terribly forward of me to ask you to be my deliverer, as we've only just met. But—won't you come? It would be the highlight of my day if, instead of dancing and making painful small talk tonight, I could have an architectural tour of the castle. Behind the scenes. I promise to appreciate every last bit of minute detail you want to include."

She pursed her lips, glaring at him a little.

He felt nervous, waiting for her answer. That was the trouble with him: he had an end goal with Florence Abrams in mind, but he also genuinely liked her. She was sharp as a tack and perhaps, if he was willing to admit it, he found her even the slightest bit intimidating.

"No costume," she said curtly.

"Unless it involves concrete boots."

"Not even then."

"Fine. I'm willing to wear something grotesquely frilly in your stead."

"And I'm leaving if anyone tries to make me dance, discuss politics, or eat any food shaped like a swan."

She gestured to the waiter to refill her coffee cup and snapped open her binder, as if dismissing Jack.

He grinned. "I'll see you tonight."

She waved him off without looking at him.

He paused at the counter on the way out. There were candies and truffles for sale behind the glass display. He remembered Cora once telling him through the fence that yellow candies were her favorite—banana, lemon. Somehow that detail had stuck in his mind across the miles and years.

He caught the waiter's eye. "I'll take some of those, please. The yellow ones."

He felt a sense of elation as he climbed into the back of the chauffeured car, a white package of saltwater taffy tucked beneath his arm. As the car wound along the coastal highway back toward Byrd Castle, for the first time he wondered if he might finally find out what had happened to him all those years ago. And then what? He could never be Jack Yates again. He would have to shed that name like he'd shed the boy he had once been, in order to survive. But perhaps, once he'd found the person who had done this to Leo and him, he could finally become someone new.

"I've made some mistakes in my life," he had once admitted to Lozada beneath a star-spattered sky. "Done bad things. Some real shit."

Lozada had crouched and thrown a log on the fire, sending up a spray of sparks. "You know what they say about shit," he had said as the dry wood caught.

"Afraid I don't," Jack said.

"You give it to a gardener, and you know what it becomes?" Lozada had grinned up at the heavens. "Fertilizer."

Jack hadn't believed it. That, somehow, anything good could grow up out of the soil of even the worst things he'd ever done, or that had been done to him.

He had downed too much whiskey that night and ended up lying out across the ground with his arms and legs splayed wide, a half-drunk snow angel in the desert. And he had let himself believe enough to pray, just that one night, that it might someday be true for him.

Nothing had happened, of course. Just as he'd expected.

He had almost forgotten it.

Until two years later, almost to the day, when he was playing the winning ace at a table in Reno and Truman Byrd walked in.

∗   ∗   ∗

Mabel Byrd was sitting in the dining room, having a late lunch of tea sandwiches and chicken salad with her oldest friend, when the butler came with the telephone.

"A Miss Ella Duluth, for you, madam," he said, standing in a golden strip of sun. The rest of the room was dim, with the heavy silk drapes pulled almost shut.

"Excuse me, Trudy," she said, laying her napkin down. Trudy waved her off with a manicured hand that glittered with rings of jade and opal the size of robins' eggs. Mabel had slipped off her leather mules under the table. Now she put them back on and rose to take the call in her private sitting room.

She took her time, lighting a cigarillo and sitting down in a plush armchair she had furnished with peacocks. As a girl, she had loved the show they put on. She had seen them once at the circus—a simple brown bird with a dull tail trailing like a feather duster. And then it had exploded into a fan of color. It had delighted her, surpassing her expectations. Those moments in her life had been few and far between.

"Hello?" Mabel finally said into the receiver. There was something powerful in making people wait. The smoke curled in plumes to catch in the velvet curtains.

"I received your message," a woman's voice said on the other end. "And I'm well aware that the deadline you've set is approaching."

"Yes. Well. You've been a disappointing investment." Mabel's voice was clipped and exacting, and wielded to inflict pain. "And I'm smart enough to spot when a stock is going down."

"I still have three days left to deliver what you've asked," Cora said, and Mabel could hear the way her voice took on a blade of its own. "And an idea to ensure that you get what you want."

Mabel sucked on her cigarillo. "And what is that?"

"I'm going to ask Mr. Byrd to let me stay on as Miss Garver's maid during her travels," she said. "So I will be there when they . . . reconnect after a long absence. I know that they have plans to meet in Los Angeles in June."

"I'm afraid that won't be happening anymore," Mabel said. "And to be frank, I've run out of patience with you."

She had really let herself believe that this girl could deliver what she had promised. She was annoyed—mostly at herself. That was a vulnerability she hadn't allowed in years. People were nothing if not disappointing. Full of empty promises. Especially the ones who had once held her highest hopes. Weren't dashed dreams a form of debt that should be repaid?

Mabel would be coming to collect on hers, one way or the other.

"I'm flying to San Francisco for a society function tomorrow," she continued. "I will be staying at the Fairmont with some of the most influential women in the country. We both know a man isn't ever going to hire you. But these women would. Give me what I want, and you'll be the first name on a list of the most powerful and wealthy females with the sorts of discretionary private jobs you would die to get."

She hoped the girl wouldn't try to apply to her sympathies by growing weepy or, worse, pleading. She hated that. Sadness, she had decided long ago, was a useless emotion. The one that got things done was anger.

"Or you can fail, Miss McCavanagh, and it would be easy enough to ruin you beyond repair." The smoke turned her voice to gravel. "So don't call unless it's good news."

"Thank you, ma'am," the girl said pleasantly, and Mabel's estimation of her raised a hair by the way she remained smooth as silk, without the hint of a waver. "We'll speak soon."

Mabel hung up the phone and put out her cigarillo. Everyone else thought they were running the show. But she was, even from across the continent, and it gave her an old thrill of satisfaction.

Truman had pushed her back into the shadows like an old forgotten doll.

But when the time was right, she'd come out.

CHAPTER TWENTY-THREE

Cora should have known better than to expect anything resembling mercy from Mabel. Her voice echoed in Cora's head, ricocheting like a bullet, and Cora felt a sudden desperation. Tonight had to work. Her dream was slipping through her fingers, its heartbeat fading. And she knew all too well that nothing hurt worse than hope did when it began to die.

Cora ran her fingers over the new serving uniform laid out on her bed. It was satin instead of cotton, with woven black feathers at the hem. For some reason, an image of Jack seeing her in it flashed unbidden through her mind. She wondered if he'd had success with Florence that afternoon—and if he had, if anyone that good at disarming people could really be trusted.

On the other side of the room, Daisy was silent. She was scanning the contents of a letter, her uniform hanging open and loose at her back.

"Did they get your measurements wrong?" Cora asked, coming to help Daisy with the black shell buttons. Normally their uniforms were tailored to fit them like a glove. But this time, even when Cora had buttoned the uniform to the top, Daisy's swam around the chest and waist.

"Does it ever make you sick?" Daisy asked, folding up the letter briskly. She had the pinched look on her face that she always got when she heard sad news from home. She turned toward the windowsill, looking out over a carpet of freshly planted lilies. The gardeners had worked all day to make the landscape awash with blooms, just in time for the thunderstorm.

"How much do you think it cost to plant all those flowers?"

"I can't think about it," Cora said. "But starving yourself here isn't doing Anette and the baby any good," she added gently. She turned and let Daisy sweep her auburn hair back to pin it.

"Liam says that at some of the other manor homes, at least they offer services to help the poor. Teaching reading—using space for field hospitals during times of emergency. This is just parties and frivolous waste."

Part of Cora agreed with her. And yet she found herself saying "Is beauty ever really a waste?"

"It is, when people are starving."

Cora picked up a brush and began to pull it through Daisy's hair. "I grew up in a place that felt starved for beauty. And goodness." She hesitated. "At least one of those is in supply here."

She drew out the worry stone from her pocket.

"When I was six years old," she said, "I learned that my father worked a dangerous job. One day, I gathered handfuls of rocks and put them in his work boots, where he would keep them by the door. I thought maybe it would stop him from leaving." She gave a painful little laugh. "When he found them, he came and knelt down beside me. I remember it so clearly because he wasn't usually affectionate. But he gave me one of the stones from his shoe."

She held it up. It was striated with white, and shaped almost like a heart. Daisy was watching her with unmasked attention, because Cora so rarely offered stories about herself and where she came from.

"A worry stone," her father had said gruffly that day. "You rub it until you don't worry anymore."

Cora's mother had overheard them. "Or a prayer stone," she had said, a note of teasing in her voice. "That would be more effective."

Cora had used it as both over the years, and now it was as smooth as silk.

"Can I see that?" Daisy asked. When she reached out to touch it, Cora was surprised to see that she was practically trembling.

"Are you sure you're all right?" Cora asked. "You look quite pale."

"You've been a good friend to me, Ella," Daisy said. "No matter what, I'll never forget that."

"Come, now," Cora said lightly. "It almost sounds as though you're telling me goodbye."

Daisy stroked the stone. "We should go," she said.

She held out the stone and Cora hesitated before she took it back, wondering if the sense of finality in Daisy's voice was something she was merely imagining.

✳   ✳   ✳

Cora and Daisy latched all of the windows in the main house, lighting candles on the mantels. Fires flickered in all the grates. The sunny, breezy parties of the other nights were replaced by candelabras and lengthening shadows that seemed ready to detach and sail through the corridors. Wind rustled through the espaliered trees, and the air took on undertones of chill. A storm was coming.

Cora made her way to the outdoor ballroom, stealing up to the second floor to hide her camera.

She returned to the ballroom floor just in time for the ghosts to appear.

Rita Blanchard was almost unrecognizable, in costume as Marie Antoinette. White curls piled high atop her head and roses spilled across a dove-gray dress. Rita held a fan above her bee-stung lips, and, when she spied the railroad tycoon William Morton dressed as a Viking, she let out a throaty cackle. Cora could smell the hint of pears as she passed.

The ballroom felt intimate that night, dreamlike and cloistered, while the storm swelled outside. Cora scanned for Jack as a string orchestra began to play softly from the second-floor balcony.

Byrd entered the ballroom draped in white robes and a crimson sash, a gold-leaf headpiece encircling his head. Cora knew that some of the costumes had been made just for tonight, commissioned from tailors by Byrd himself and left in ribbon-tied boxes on the beds of each guest. Others were officially on loan from film sets or museums.

There was no sign of Jack, but the British tennis player Simon Leit was dressed, ironically, as George Washington, with a tricorn hat and leather boots. When Cora approached him and offered him a canapé, he took three in a napkin emblazoned with a golden harpy eagle and Byrd's stitched monogram.

Clementine appeared in a white toga with a slit up to her thigh, her blue eyes lined with thick kohl and a gold headdress wrapped around her forehead like a serpent. She wore a blunt black wig with a jewel hung suspended between her eyebrows, and her lips were painted a shocking red. Cleopatra, to Byrd's Caesar.

He lifted his glass to her in approval from across the room.

Cora's gaze drifted to the entrance through fragrant smoke curling from cigars.

Had she imagined the way she had felt in Jack's room that morning? The familiar scent of him, on his sheets. The cut of his jaw, and the way he looked at her with those eyes she had thought she would never see again. A delicate shiver tingled down her spine. Had he felt anything in return? Perhaps it was all in her imagination. Wanting to see something that wasn't actually there. Just like on Pelican.

She turned now and saw him across the room. Something in her body curled.

He was dressed in a velvet suit the color of plums with a white neck-cloth. It was tailored to him even better than Cora's uniform had been made for her, and he wore a wig the color of fresh snow that was tied with a matching plum ribbon. Kitty stood next to him, her long, delicate fingers wrapped around a goblet. "And who are you tonight?" she asked, tilting her head as she examined him from head to toe.

"'I can calculate the motion of heavenly bodies,'" he quipped, spinning an apple on his finger, "'but not the madness of people.'"

"Sir Newton," William Morton said, mock-bowing. "Shall we take turns shooting arrows at your head?"

"That part comes later," Jack said. He tossed the apple and caught it. "And only once I'm good and zozzled."

"Where's Berty?" Rita asked, craning her neck to look around the room. "I've been simply dying to see him as Napoleon."

"I heard he was experiencing some unpleasantness of the stomach," Jack deadpanned. "Messy stuff, I'm afraid." Jack's eyes flitted ever so briefly to meet Cora's, as if he knew exactly where she was, and her own stomach dipped.

"Oh!" Kitty spluttered. "Dear."

"Wait, no—there he is! Hello, Berty," Jack called, waving from afar.

Albert Boyle arrived just as a heavy rainfall spattered against the ballroom's skylights. He was dressed in a black hat and gold epaulets, his sash studded with twinkling medals. A long sword was slung at his side, and Cora half-wondered if it was real, though surely Truman wouldn't be so stupid. The liquor was already drained from the glass in his hand. Albert watched Jack with an unnerving coldness.

Jack didn't seem to notice.

"Now, let me see, doll," Jack said, twirling Kitty around to examine her. "Who are you channeling tonight?"

Kitty's blue eyes were lined to a razor point, the fit of her toga pressed against her stomach and trailing down her legs. Her dark hair was coiled, snakelike. She was a fitting Medusa, all crisp sheet and curves. Her eyes lit up when Jack looked her over.

Cora's stomach plunged. No matter how fitted or fancy the night's livery was, she was still just a maid in a uniform. And she had let herself get distracted. Her focus returned to Clem, where it should have been all along.

She abandoned her tray and ascended a stone staircase to the second floor.

The first door on the left led to a simple bedroom with warm pinewood boards and mullioned windows. Cora stepped inside. There was a four-poster bed with an embroidered quilt, and a fireplace with a hearth that smelled of spices and kindling.

There was also a connecting closet between the first bedroom and the second that functioned as a go-between for the servants. Cora crossed the room. The door was a hidden panel seamlessly fit into the wallpaper. It was covered, she noticed, in a pattern of nightingales. She opened it and stepped inside. The long, narrow closet smelled of pine. She felt beneath the pile of towels, and her hand clasped around her camera.

She recognized the warm spice of his cologne before she saw him.

"Cora?" Jack whispered.

He slipped into the space beside her and pulled the door closed until there was nothing but a sliver of light between them. The orchestra music dimmed and grew distant. She could hear the sound of her own breathing.

"Hello," he said.

"Hi," she whispered back.

He slipped off his wig and ran his hand through his hair.

She had found him attractive before, a girl of fourteen with a crush. Now, at twenty-eight, she found him almost devastatingly handsome.

231

But he was a means to an end. Someone she had long held responsible for ruining her entire life. It was ludicrous to think of him even as an ally tonight, much less a friend.

And yet she realized that part of her did.

"So the plan," he said. "I'll get Truman here tonight."

"On my signal," she reminded him.

"And you'll be set up here. Will this work for a photograph, then?" he asked, turning toward the small shaft of light.

She nodded. "It should. But only if they're distracted. They have to be good and hot. Or I'll get caught when I slip open the door."

"I won't let that happen," he said. He met her eyes and held them. There were faint echoes of tipsy laughter from the party far away, the tinkling of heels on marble.

Cora's heart skipped a beat when he didn't look away.

"Did you find Florence?" she asked.

Jack nodded.

"Is she coming?"

Jack's eyes traced down her face, and he hesitated. He nodded again. Then he reached up to brush something from her cheek. At the gentle stroke of his fingers against her skin, hope for something that should not be sparked inside her. Her whole body quickened. It felt like a betrayal.

Her eyes fell to his frilled neckpiece. "This costume is absurd," she murmured.

He laughed low in her ear, and every part of her smoked and caught fire.

She closed her eyes. "I had a thought," she said. Her heart was racing. "Mm?"

Jack took a step closer to her. Their hands brushed in the darkness.

This time she didn't pull away.

She reached out and gently stroked her thumb once along the ridge of his knuckle.

He went very still.

"A thought?" he asked. His voice was low and strained.

"About the letter, signed with a bird," she said.

He played with the end of a feather on her uniform, skimming her wrist, and a white-hot heat shot across her skin, down past her belly. Then he brought his hand up, grazing along the curve of her waist. His touch practically melted into the satin.

Cora closed her eyes. "It made me think of all the other birds in the house," she whispered. She could feel his breath on her neck.

And then she heard the soft whine of hinges. The door to the bedroom opened, and Liam stepped inside.

Jack swore under his breath, his hand tightening on her waist. He pulled her away from the door, and they moved to the opposite side of the closet, pressing into the wall as they tried to stay out of the light.

She felt his breath catch the moment her body fit into his, and he instinctively drew her even closer. He tilted his face down, as if breathing her in, and made a low sound in the back of his throat.

She pressed into him, feeling the delicious way his body met every part of hers as she searched for the door handle behind him. Her hand clasped around the knob, and she turned it.

They spilled out into the second bedroom, and Cora shut the closet door behind them just in time.

*　　*　　*

What was that? Jack asked himself.

Cora smoothed her dress, turning away from him. He suddenly wanted to draw her close again, to fit his hands around the arc of her waist like it was the most natural thing in the world; for the scent of her hair to flood his nostrils again and to feel the gorgeous curve of her body beneath satin.

You do not have the luxury of distractions, he admonished himself.

When she turned toward him again, her face was flushed.

"Cora—" he started to say, but she interrupted him.

"What I noticed," she said quietly, as if nothing had happened between them. She pointed toward the door they had just come through. It fit perfectly into the wall, almost disappearing. He tried to ignore the unexpected disappointment that was settling into his belly.

"The nightingales," she whispered to him, moving to skim her fingertips over the patterned wallpaper. "There are birds on the other end, as well. I think it must be some sort of code."

"A code?" he asked.

"Like the letter. A code, or some sort of clue, maybe. There was a dove to show the way to the freight elevator in the basement."

"And the missing heron beside the grand fireplace," Jack said. He was still clutching the wig in his hand. He forced his racing heart, his breathing, to return to normal.

"Mm," Cora said. She still didn't meet his eyes. "There are always birds leading somewhere." She examined the door, and he saw how full her lips were, the delicate slice of her collarbone. "I wonder, if we pay attention, if they will lead us somewhere we need to go."

He dragged his gaze away from her, running his hands through his hair. He gave it an extra tug, hard enough to hurt. "Good thinking. I need to go meet Florence." He placed the wig back on his head. "But I'll be back in time to help with Truman."

Finally she looked at him. Her eyes were bright and luminous. "On my signal," she said.

He nodded. "On your signal," he confirmed.

She smiled. "I hope you get what you want tonight," she said, brushing past him. He caught another whiff of her hair.

"Me too," he said under his breath.

The problem was, he was no longer entirely sure what that was.

CHAPTER TWENTY-FOUR

Jack took the stairs. The orchestra was beginning to play Schubert. He
paused at the fountain, feeling the slightest bit of mist hit the skin at
his wrists. It helped to take the heat off, and he took a glass of water from
a passing tray, but it was more of a prop. He sipped it to have something
to do.

What had he even been hoping would happen up there in the closet? As
if his and Cora's history wasn't tangled and thorny enough. The last thing
he needed to do was add another layer of complication. But he could still
smell the scent of honeysuckle. The feel of her waist beneath his hands. How
fiercely he had wanted to pull her to him and kiss her lips, her neck. . . .

He took another sip of water, forcing his mind to the task at hand. He
had several jobs to do tonight, and he couldn't be caught in this strange,
disorienting fog. He ordered a cupcake for himself, and, in a moment
of optimism, for Florence. The icing was whipped and airy, and the taste of
strawberry bloomed in his mouth.

Exactly at the strike of nine, she appeared. Florence was dressed in
a tartan kilt and tie, with a calfskin sporran slung around her hips. She
nodded at him across the room and tellingly drained her martini glass in
one slug.

"You look lovely," he said, approaching her. "Mary, Queen of Scots?"
he guessed.

"I'm J. M. Barrie," she said. "And your flattery will get you nowhere."

"Will this, then?" He offered her a flute of champagne and the cupcake. He was immensely grateful to her—for giving him a tour or for providing an effective distraction from Cora, he wasn't sure which.

Florence raised the cupcake to her nose, sniffed, and then took a bite. "It's like the seventh circle of hell in here."

"The cupcake, though. . . ." Jack said.

She acquiesced. "The cupcake is divine. A cloud constructed of strawberry. I wish I could live in it."

"If anyone could figure out how to do such a thing. . . ."

They leaned back against the wall of nasturtiums, observing the party in comfortable silence.

"Why did Truman want a separate ballroom set apart from the main house?" Jack asked. "It seems like a lot of trouble."

She harrumphed. "Why does Truman do anything?" she asked. "It was beautiful, and it creates drama. There's an indoor pool beneath us; did you know that? With the added bonus that it made my life more difficult."

He smiled, crumpling his napkin in his fist. It was then that he noticed the eagle on it, emblazoned in gold.

"Shall we start in the main house, then?" he asked.

She took another flute of champagne from a passing tray and adjusted her sporran. "I'll lead the way."

*　　*　　*

Clementine loved the way the toga slipped around her golden legs like poured cream. She ordered a Clementine, her signature drink—gin, lemon juice, orange blossom, and local honey—and by the time she'd finished it, she felt a pleasant buzz. The lights had dimmed, the alcohol had set in. She moved through the leafy aisles, smelling the verdant ferns, feeling their waxy fronds beneath her fingers.

Beau sauntered toward her as the orchestra music swelled. He was dressed as King Arthur, his chest swathed in a mesh of chain, his skin golden from their day riding in the sun. He had told her all about his childhood during their ride. How he'd wanted to be a concert pianist, or a sea captain.

"I heard that Albert Boyle is looking to cast his new musical soon," Beau murmured suggestively, sipping his drink, in a voice just loud enough for only her to hear.

She turned toward him, interested. "Can you sing and dance, Beaumont?"

Beau arched his eyebrows with a look of mock offense, and she laughed. She'd enjoyed the ride with him that afternoon, unexpectedly alone on the vistas. She'd told him about growing up in Florida; her mother's endless disapproval; and how her older brother had taught her how to play the fiddle. She couldn't help but notice the way his hair caught the sunlight, his laugh quick and full.

"Shall we show Mr. Boyle what he could have?" she asked now.

He led her to the very center of the ballroom and made a show of clearing his throat and offering her his hand. The orchestra conductor peered over the balcony at them, baton raised. The room seemed to dim further in the storm, and she noticed how Beau smelled so different than Truman. Cloves, and cinnamon.

She took Beau's offered hand and felt the chemistry crackling through her body like lightning. He whispered "Not to make you nervous, but Albert's watching."

"I hope you're as good as you think, then," she said. As if her body wasn't practically trembling to be near him.

"You'll have to let me know," he murmured, and the orchestra shifted into a ballroom waltz for them. He took her around the waist, his large hand making her feel impossibly light, and looked deep into her eyes. She couldn't tell whether he was merely selling the part for Albert, or whether it was real.

"You're not half bad," he said, sending her out for a twirl. She felt her toga sway when he dipped her, and she leaned into it, showing the white expanse of her throat. She loved dancing; but the more fascinated Truman became with his political career, the more photographers he began to invite to the parties. Which meant they were forced to stay apart, never quite touching. Not a hint of impropriety. She was vaguely aware that a small crowd was forming along the edge of the ferns, crowning them in a circle. She did not let herself look up at Truman, but she could imagine him standing with arms crossed. Watching; a carefully masked expression on his face.

The way Beau was dancing with her, he either truly didn't know she was with Truman or he didn't care. It emboldened her. His hand grazed her stomach when he twirled her, and at his touch her insides felt as though she were falling from a great height. She had never been able to be with Truman the way she wanted. Never in public like this. Or with anyone else, either.

For a moment, she let herself go.

The orchestra played along, leading them into a song that was buoyant and peppy. They seamlessly transitioned to a tap dance. Clementine did it in her heels, flashing some leg as she mirrored Beau's lead and did the Charleston. She kept in perfect step with him, laughing at the cheers that sounded, the eruption of thunderous clapping. They turned and faced the crowd, bowing together, her chest heaving from breathless exertion. The bulbs flashed again as she reached out and coyly straightened the crown on his head, and he looked like he could eat her.

When she finally turned to face him, Truman was staring at her across the room. Albert was laughing, clapping him obnoxiously on the arm. She could sense the flare of his emotions in the heated expression on his face, the telltale clench in his jaw. She had only ever seen him that way after being with Mabel. The thought gave her immense satisfaction.

She forced herself to walk away from Beau so as not to prolong the moment, her heart thundering in her chest. Wondering if, in Truman's eyes, she had just gone too far.

Wondering if, in her own, she even cared.

$$* \quad * \quad *$$

Cora set up a tray of chocolate-dipped strawberries in the upstairs bedroom. Being with Jack had set her feeling off-balance. She felt like she was fifteen again, awkward and unsure. Wanting something she could never, ever have.

Her body still felt flushed and aching with longing.

She hadn't fully realized how much she actually wanted to trust someone. Enough to be vulnerable and to show them the very depths of herself. She had no partner in work, no partner in life. Instead, she was always alone, outsmarting people, deceiving them. Keeping them at arm's length. Perhaps she hadn't wanted to become a private investigator merely to try to reset the balance of her life, but because it allowed her to pretend to be anyone but herself.

She hadn't anticipated how little relief it would be, playing a role when no one in the world knew who she truly was.

She pulled a ring of keys from her pocket. Then she closed the door behind her and turned into the hallway.

A sudden burst of cheering and clapping set her leaning over the stone railing to observe. Clementine and Beau were dancing together, and Clem's toga was slit so that when Beau twirled her, it unfolded in a sensuous fan, then back to embrace her thighs. Cora stole a glimpse at Truman's face. He looked irritated, a flush creeping up from his toga. Albert was slapping him on the back, laughing, which only seemed to incense Truman more. For a man who usually hid his emotions, this was a stunning admission.

Her hopes were beginning to revive again. Tonight would work. She would call Mabel triumphant.

She turned at the soft sound of footsteps just behind her.

"You've got to stop sneaking up on—" she started to say, but the words died on her lips when the man stepped forward. It wasn't Jack, in his white wig and velvet suitcoat.

It was Albert Boyle.

A slight chill hit her veins. She glanced across the open expanse of the dance floor to the other side of the balcony, where the orchestra was playing too far away to be of help. The rest of the party was downstairs, taking to the dance floor. No one seemed to notice her and Albert in the shadows. She swallowed.

"Can I help you, Mr. Boyle?" she asked. She took a step backward and slipped the blade of the key between two of her fingers.

"Where is he?" Albert asked. He was smiling—pleasant, even—but she could smell the alcohol on his breath.

He took another step toward her, advancing on the distance she had created.

"Mr. Byrd?" she asked.

He gave her a bemused look.

"I think I saw him downstairs," Cora said, confused. She was careful not to allow herself to be backed into the locked door and cornered. "Shall I help you find him?"

"Yes," he said. "Perhaps we should do that together. I think Truman might want to know a little something very interesting."

Her heart pounded a warning. "And what is that?" she asked in a low voice.

He smiled again. "That Everett Conner has been playing the role of chivalrous knight while dipping his own sword in the pot with you." He leered at her. "That's the richest thing I've seen this week. And on the Hill, that's saying something."

Cora grimaced. She had thought she caught a glimpse of Albert's shadow that morning when she had left Jack's bedroom. She had hoped she had been wrong.

"What do you want?" she asked.

He took a distinct glance at the bedroom door behind her. "What do *you* want? I'm not a monster, you know. I'm sure we could come to an agreement. Something we would each find mutually beneficial."

"Aren't you married, sir?" she asked faintly.

Albert ran his thumb over the wooden grain of his cane. "I keep the money rolling in for her to spend; she doesn't ask many questions," he said. "I mind my business, and she minds hers. It's a shame your secret fellow couldn't do the same."

"Your business," Cora echoed him. Albert nodded, still smiling. He looked at her with hungry, bloodshot eyes. A look bordering on patronizing.

That was about to change.

"It's an interesting thing, your business," she said. She scratched her eyebrow, as if in thought. "Your wife might not ask many questions, Mr. Boyle, but perhaps the emerging Federal Bureau of Narcotics should?"

The gleeful smile on his face instantly shuttered. "I'm sorry?"

"You heard me." She kept her voice hard. She needed to make sure Albert Bloody Boyle kept his mouth shut. He couldn't leave that hallway until she was certain she had covered herself.

Albert Boyle narrowed his eyes, finally realizing that he might have misjudged her. "I don't know who you are, doll, but I do know this: you're messing around in things that are way above your station."

"Yet I know *exactly* who you are," Cora said. "It *is* Albert Boyle, or do you prefer Bertie McCoy?" The unsure fifteen-year-old girl had vanished. She had found her balance. She watched with satisfaction as his lips faintly parted in surprise. "The same Bertie McCoy who was arrested for possession and intention to traffic heroin and coca leaves, isn't that right?" She remembered every detail with crystal precision from her father's old case. "Perhaps the FBI allowed jail time to slide several years back because of that insider information you provided—" at this, splotches of red began to bloom across his face—"but I'm fairly certain that the Bureau of Internal Revenue probably wouldn't look kindly on your skirting taxes on a million cash in laundered drug money."

"What the hell are you talking about? You're a—a *maid* with no evidence of any of this." His face was turning the faintest shade of purple.

"Just because I'm a maid doesn't mean I'm not well informed—or well connected. Yes, those two bureaus are separate entities; and though the scandal was effectively buried, you would still owe considerable taxes on that income, vis-à-vis the Harrison Narcotics Tax Act of 1914. How do I know this? Because Commissioner Douglas is practically my godfather."

She smiled a little. In truth, she'd never met Commissioner Douglas in her life.

Cora advanced toward him and took him firmly by the arm. "Now, I'm very sorry, Mr. Boyle, to hear that you suddenly aren't feeling well, but I'll be sure to relay the message that you had to return home post-haste."

"Are you—? Is the Bureau—?"

"Be gone by morning and I can be persuaded to keep my mouth shut," Cora said swiftly. "But if I hear one whiff of a word about Mr. Conner being seen with any sort of the household help, I'll be sure to give my Uncle Douglas a ring."

Albert Boyle's eyes glittered like tiny dark flames. Then he turned, slamming his hand with a crack against the wall near Cora's head. When Cora didn't give him the pleasure of flinching, he adjusted his costume in an attempt at dignity and stalked away.

Cora breathed out. Caught her reflection in the mirror. Her eyes were bright and emboldened. There was no trace of the awkward, unsure girl left, but only a grown woman. And this time, when a man had caught her unaware, she hadn't run away to Jack or to her father.

She had handled it herself.

She picked up her tray and strode down the stairs, weaving through the costumed guests.

"I put some of your favorite snacks and drinks in the first room upstairs," she whispered to Clementine. "In case you need a private moment to slip away."

Clementine thanked her, but Cora had already moved on. Her mouth was set with a grim determination. She hadn't done it out of kindness: she had done it to plant the final, treacherous seed.

CHAPTER TWENTY-FIVE

In the main house, the fires were lit in the grates and rain slid down the windows in rivulets of lace. Jack and Florence moved through the arched hallways, past the tapestries of wool and silk once owned by King Louis XIV. Jack listened attentively as Florence described the choral stalls that had been shipped from Burgundy. Set away from the revelry of the ballroom, the main house felt vast and quiet. Almost private.

He was growing frustrated at how often his mind kept drifting to Cora.

Florence was noticeably looser, away from the trappings of the party. Her gestures grew more animated, yet the smile she was giving him was almost shy, as if she were sharing an intimate piece of herself in the presence of a kindred spirit.

"I've touched every aspect of this house," she said. "It's like showing off a child. A large, overgrown, fastidiously decorated child."

"You seem to work well together," Jack observed. "You and Truman."

They stopped in front of a fireplace that was so large, it could have hosted a small dinner party inside it.

"We argue mostly over the scale of things," Florence said. "Width of stairs, the height of the plantings outside. The animals from his zoo trampled the seedbeds when we were first planting the gardens, proving the need for walls I had angled for from the beginning."

"Never angle with an architect."

"He has the vision. I bring the scale and proportion." She paused. "He's particular about every detail. The tiles couldn't just be white, for instance," she said. "They had to be *Dutch* white."

Their steps echoed in the foyer, among the potted ferns and the hanging tapestries. "It's like being in a cathedral," Jack said.

"'A cathedral to excess,' I believe is what the rival newspapers call it," Florence quoted.

"Yes, but . . . there's something else, too," Jack said. It was ostentatious, to be sure. A display of wealth that was at times brash and almost garish. But occasionally he also saw glimpses of something almost otherworldly. The way the light hit the tiles. The orchestral music and the lapping fountains, the ocean salt and the perfumed flowers playing on the breeze. Opposite in every way to Pelican Island.

He and Florence came to a stop in front of an enormous painting. It showed Mary, angels, and—his eye caught on it—a snow-white dove.

He thought of Cora, her lovely face flushed as she pointed to the nightingales on the door. Her satin dress. The curving hint of her smile. The candies he had bought for her at the diner, which he had decided at the last moment to leave in his room. He thought of the secrets he had shared with her in the wine cellar and the bell tower, secrets that he had never breathed of to anyone else.

He realized he wasn't even listening to Florence.

"The Annunciation," Florence was saying, examining the painting in front of them. "Painted by Spaniard Bartolomé Pérez de la Dehesa. He was appointed as a painter for King Charles II beginning in 1689. We planned entire rooms—sometimes even entire guest houses—around the art that Truman wanted to display."

"Is he a collector of religious art?" Jack asked.

"He's a collector of everything," Florence said. "He never met a trinket he didn't like."

"What about you?"

"I prefer blueprints. Crisp, clean lines. Order."

"Do you decorate your home with the plans of others, then?" he asked.

"I do," she said resolutely. "My office is covered in exquisite blueprints, and they are no less art just because they're functional."

He had been so single-minded for so long. A decade of deceit, even violence, to get there. And now he was there, walking the house with its own architect, never dreaming he would get this close. And all he could think about was the small scar between Cora's eyebrows from a fall she'd gotten on the ferry as a girl; the way her fingers brushed along the curve of her lips.

What was wrong with him? He was going to give it all away for nothing.

"Speaking of blueprints," Jack said, seamlessly shifting gears, "are there any places in this house that are . . . off-limits to the regular tour?" He turned to her with a conspiratorial grin. "Any unusual collections of art or architecture, perhaps, just waiting for the right gentleman to appreciate them?"

She appraised him for a long moment.

"Truman isn't known for his restraint when it comes to displays," she said finally. "There's a basement storage area, beneath the wine cellar, that is not fit for guests to tour. But if you had interest in a particular subset of works, I'm sure Truman would be happy to oblige. You might have guessed that he enjoys a bit of preening."

So the basement storage area—the one that Jack had already explored from top to bottom—was a dead end; and, as far as Florence knew, there were no others. His heart sank.

"As for things of architectural interest, there are catacombs left beneath the West Terrace," she said. "Truman tends to change his mind quite frequently;

and, as the castle and grounds have evolved, the old structures were merely buried and covered over, rather than torn down."

He made note of that.

And then he noticed that they were not alone.

There was someone there in the shadows. Jack stole a quick glance behind him. The figure was ten paces away, and had stopped in the hallway, hands crossed over his hulking chest. Dallas Winston. He tipped his cap at Jack, and Jack gave him a nod back. Had he been keeping tabs on them? Trying to eavesdrop on their conversation?

Jack decided to change tack as he stooped to stroke his fingertips across the floor tiles.

"Tell me about these," he said, feeling the head of security's eyes still on him. "The detail in them is exquisite."

It was then that he noticed. They were of ravens, bluebirds. Doves.

"I designed those myself," Florence said, her small chin rising a fraction. "There are bird themes woven throughout the house. Surely you've noticed." Jack decided not to feign ignorance. At his nod, she continued: "But there are additional layers there to find, if one has an exacting eye. Do you notice anything particular about those birds?" she asked.

"I don't recognize this one," he admitted. He pointed out a tile with a small brown bird on it. It looked like it was wearing a bandit's mask on its face.

"A yellowthroat," she said, and the way that she was watching him for a reaction made him look at the tiles again.

Raven, dove, bluebird, yellowthroat. In a repeating pattern. He stood, thinking back to the love letter Cora had found from Truman to Mabel. If he looked at the tiles in another way—

"They spell BYRD," he said.

"Bravo," she said. She gave him a sly look and moved on down the hall-way. "Truman likes those hidden riddles, for those who pay attention and look close enough."

The carillon bells rang out in the tower.

Jack stole a fleeting glance at Dallas Winston.

"Can I interest you in a dance?" he asked Florence.

She guffawed. "Absolutely not. But I'd like to tell Truman hello before I say goodbye."

She offered him her arm, and Jack felt Dallas's eyes follow them as he led her back to the ballroom.

*   *   *

Truman eyed Ronald Rutherford's suit and tie over his tumbler.

"Rutherford," he said, "you seem to have forgotten your costume."

Rutherford pointed to his pocket square, where he had tucked a monocle. "People can make of it whatever they may," he said. He leaned his elbows against the outer railing of the ballroom. "But I'll be damned if I'm going to strut around like a turkey."

"Ah—but isn't it fun to make you try."

Truman leaned his weight next to his old friend Rutherford's and clinked his glass. His vision was starting to swim. "You might have had the right idea," Truman said, adjusting the golden laurel wreath. "This is worse than being strangled with a necktie."

"Heavy is the head that wears the crown," Ronald drawled as Truman reached up and pulled the metal into a more forgiving shape around his head.

"If only Clementine could be plied as easily," Truman said.

Ronald snorted. Truman kept his eyes on Clementine. She had strayed too far, and she knew it. Yet she was gaily laughing with her friends. The toga looked like it had been poured onto her. There were gold circlets at her delicate wrists and around her waist. She had never been the simpering sort. It was why Truman found her interesting. Her spark was somewhere in between Mabel and his mother.

He was stalling. For once, he did not go to his office to mark up tomorrow's news. The photographer he had invited was there, flashing bulbs. Truman himself would select which pictures would run. He had yet to decide whether Clementine and Beau's dance would be buried or splashed across the fronts of the tabloids as fodder. Someone's pain always served as the kindling to sell more papers. Sometimes even his own.

Beau whispered something in Clementine's ear, and her eyes widened, and then she leaned her head back and laughed, exposing her beautiful neck. Rutherford kept keen eyes trained on them.

"Is Clem *trying* to—"

"Don't," Truman said, a warning note in his voice. He threw back another drink.

Ronald ordered him a coffee.

Truman was getting pissed, in all senses of the word. He watched as Beau led Clem back out onto the dance floor. He smiled, cold and small. If only Beau Remington knew what had happened to the last man who'd tried to flirt with the woman Truman had claimed as his own.

Mabel had been wearing a red dress that day, the same one she always wore when they went out for a highbrow activity, like the opera or a museum. They'd usually had to go on the crowded, free-entry days, because they'd been flat broke back then. But they loved to walk through corridors filled with embroidered costumes, tapestries, and sculptures, and pretend for a moment that they were home.

Now he'd made one for himself. Built it on all the hopes and dreams he'd had as a man standing amidst treasures with worn soles, beans in his stomach, and not even enough money to pay the entry fee.

And the man who had once tried to cop a feel from Mabel in front of him—well. Without that ill-fated decision, perhaps Truman wouldn't be where he was today.

Truman brightened imperceptibly at that thought and at the sight of Florence, making her way toward him on Everett Conner's arm.

"Florence! In a costume!" Truman crowed. "What, ho! Is it hailing in hell?"

"You'll have to tell us when you get there," she said.

"Oh, come. Have a sandwich shaped like a pineapple."

"You know how I hate foods shaped like other foods. I've come to bid you adieu."

Truman sloshed a bit of his drink out of the glass. "You've only just arrived!"

"I've been here for longer than I intended. I was giving him a tour." She nodded at Everett Conner. "Very interested in art and architecture, this one."

"Well, why should it end?" Truman asked. "I'm not feeling particularly in the party spirit tonight myself. Let's go to the billiards room, shall we?" His eye twitched. He knocked back another drink. "Come now, Conner. Rutherford. I'm in the mood to shoot something," he said darkly. "It might as well be pool."

*　　*　　*

Jack could tell that Truman Byrd was drunker than he'd ever seen him.

It was unusual. Byrd was often buttoned up without a hair out of place. Clementine and Beau must have really gotten to him. Exactly as Cora had hoped.

Jack gestured to a maid for a new drink. Grabbed a bite of salmon and caviar puff pastry.

But it was Cora who appeared with the tray. Jack was careful not to meet her eyes as he took one of Byrd's signature drinks from her.

"Can I get you anything, Mr. Byrd?" she asked.

"No," Truman said curtly.

"I'll take a cupcake," Florence said.

Cora nodded; and as she turned, she gave Jack the signal.

This was it. He was meant to tell Truman that Clem had a message for him. That she wanted to meet him in the bedroom at the top of the stairs. He watched Clem beginning to climb toward the second floor. Cora followed, heading for the secret corridor in the next bedroom, where she would get into position. Cora stole one last, expectant glance at him.

He met her eyes. He could still smell the scent of her hair.

He felt a sharp tug in his gut.

Why was he there, after all? he asked himself sharply. Had he lost sight of it so quickly?

He thought about the way Leo always blamed himself for the way they had gotten onto the Island—and how much Jack blamed himself for the way they had gotten off of it. He thought of his only brother drowning alone. Labeled a criminal. Left to rot without even a tombstone or a good name left to put on it.

How much he missed him.

"Come, Conner. I'll show you the best part of my collection," Byrd wheedled.

"Things you haven't shown anyone?" Jack asked coyly.

"Perhaps."

Truman's eyes were bloodshot. Watching him.

Jack steeled himself. He hadn't spent a decade on the run to throw away a chance like this one. He was letting unbidden feelings for Cora get in the way of his entire purpose. And for what? This arrangement between them only worked for as long as they both needed something. What would she do once she had what she had come for? What would he be left with once he wasn't of use to her anymore?

He threw back his drink. Turned away from the rest of the party, from Clementine and Cora waiting upstairs, and said: "Well, then, I'm game."

*   *   *

Cora still remembered the sick feeling she'd had when she ran out of the house the morning after Jack and Leo escaped, and watched as Rusty's body was covered with a white sheet and carried to the ferry. Her mother had believed that Cora was crying for Rusty; and she had been.

But it was the realization that settled in her stomach like the darkness of night falling. She had been fooled.

She had been a fool.

She felt it again as she turned from the top of the balcony and watched as Jack led Truman away from her, diverting him from their plan and from where Clementine stood waiting. The feeling dawned again. A stone dropping, finding new depths within her.

She curled her hand around the banister as though she could splinter it, and the feeling of betrayal shifted to make room for something else.

Fury.

CHAPTER TWENTY-SIX

J ack followed Truman, and they met Governor Gilham on their way to the billiards room. Gilly was dressed as Shakespeare, sporting a wig and high-collared velvet robe, holding a cigar in one hand and a bleached skull in the other.

Truman opened the door and ushered them in. The lights were dim, and the room smelled of scotch and leather. Florence immediately drew Jack's attention to the pool table, pointing out its panels of walnut burl, satinwood, and maple.

"Those diamond sights look like pieces of ivory," Jack said.

"That's because they are."

"Welcome to the bachelor wing," Truman said. "Where I keep some of the finest pieces in my collection."

He pointed to a large hanging frame. It was Rembrandt van Rijn's *Judas Returning the Thirty Pieces of Silver.*

"Is this what it's going to look like when you give back all the money you hornswoggled from me last night?" Governor Gilham asked, coming over to examine the painting with them. He pulled off his wig and set his skull on the table. "At this rate, I'm beginning to wonder if you invited me here simply to take me to the cleaners."

Truman slapped Gilham on the back. "Come, now, Gilly," he slurred. "Someday you're going to know when to walk away from the races you can't win."

"I'll stick to politics, then," he said, taking the final sip of his whiskey. He set his icy tumbler on the rim of the billiards table. A maid quickly swooped it up before it could leave a mark.

"Shall we shoot?" Gilham said to Rutherford. Rutherford grunted and began to set up the table.

Jack was careful not to look at the Rembrandt. He had been following the art world ever since Pelican, and he remembered reading about it in the papers when Byrd bought it at auction for hundreds of thousands of dollars. Jack glossed past the painting and instead stopped in front of a framed picture depicting a sprawling white house. Underneath it hung a plaque that read *The Rows.*

"What's this?" Jack asked, examining it while he polished his cue stick. "Another property of yours?"

Truman nodded. "I bought it for my mother."

Jack gave a low whistle. "She's a lucky lady," he said.

"Decidedly not," Truman said. He poured himself a tumbler of brandy. "She was married to my father."

"Does she live there now?"

Truman picked up another cue stick and inspected the end of it. "Unfortunately, no. She never even got to see it."

Jack let that sit for a moment. He felt the tug of a lock, waiting to be fitted with the right key. "'The Rows,'" he read. "What is it, then?"

"It's an art school."

"Ah. Philanthropy?"

"That. And payback."

"That sounds like a good story," Jack said.

Truman flipped his new cue stick, still surprisingly adroit. "My father was a real bastard. Spent all his money on drink, never let my mother do anything, least of all take the art classes she desperately wanted to take. I grew up in Chicago; you familiar?"

Jack shook his head. "Not much."

"Well. My father, good old Franklin Byrd, used to take us out to Lake Forest once a month to look at the mansions along Lake Michigan. This was the one house in particular he always dreamed of." Jack examined the photograph. It was white, massive, clean, with a huge wraparound porch and blue stone terraces, gabled windows, and sculpted greenery set in front of it like a maze. "My father always talked about how one day, when he'd 'made it,' this house would be his." Truman came to stand next to Jack.

"But he never did. So when I made my first million, I bought it instead. Named it after her—Rose. A little wordplay."

"And then you made it into an art school."

Truman smiled into his drink. "I did."

"Out of love for her, or spite for him?"

Truman smiled. "The heart is a mystery, isn't it."

Rutherford and Florence were watching them. Rutherford's cigar wisped smoke in the dim light. Jack could see the movement of Dallas Winston's shadow just on the other side of the door.

"We used to visit the Chicago Institute on Sundays growing up. It was our own version of church. Took on new meaning after my older brother died." Truman brought the cigar to his nose and smelled it, closing his eyes. "I bought the *Judas* in honor of her, too."

"She loved Rembrandt?"

"One painting in particular."

"Oh?" Jack asked.

"She used to go to the museum and stare at it for hours," Truman said. "On loan the summer after Elias died. It was called *The Raising of Lazarus*."

Jack froze.

He stole a furtive glance at Truman, but Truman's face was blank.

Was this another one of Truman's twisted games?

Jack breathed out slowly. He set down his glass.

The Lazarus. One of the five paintings that had been stolen from the Bastion.

He couldn't hide how badly his fingers were shaking.

Truman was clearly drunk, his own hands struggling with the matchbook. Fumbling.

Out of the corner of his eye, Jack saw the faintest movement. A panel, slipping aside. He looked up, expecting to see a maid coming through the wall. Instead, he—

"Get down!" he yelled, and threw himself against Truman as a bullet exploded into the wall behind him. Wood splintered in shrapnel as another bullet hit near Jack's head. Florence let out a short, pierced cry as Jack threw himself on top of Truman, waiting for a bullet to find him. And all he could think in those final moments—was he really willing to die for a man he'd dreamed about killing himself?

Dallas was sprinting across the room and wrenching the secret passageway open. Ronald Rutherford ran to a panel in the wall and picked up a telephone, yelling into the receiver for the guards to cut off the intruder at the other exits. Jack's ears were ringing, his vision tunneling.

"Are you all right?" he asked. Truman was white, and breathing heavily beneath Jack. "Were you hit?"

It was then that Jack noticed the blood that was seeping through the velvet of his own suit.

CHAPTER TWENTY-SEVEN

S omething was wrong.

Cora's trained eye could tell by the sudden tensing of the guards at the front of the ballroom. The way they turned in unison, hands reaching for their guns.

Her stomach curled, and a sick dread filled her.

Something was happening in the main house.

"Ella?" It was Clementine. "Have you seen Truman?"

Clementine was sharper than the rest. She knew enough to register the different tone of the guards, that this was not normal. Her face paled a little. The rest of the party was too loud, too drunk. No one else had noticed the way a guard was standing at the door's entrance, weapon subtly drawn.

Clementine's hand skipped up to her throat. Cora looked urgently for Daisy, and that's when she realized that she hadn't seen her once since the start of the party.

"Come with me," Clem said. She led Cora out the front door, ignoring the guards who tried to stop her. More and more lights were flickering on in the main house. The rain had settled into a fine mist, and the ground was drenched.

Cora thought back to the night that Jack had escaped. A night that had been so much like this one.

There were more guards gathered at the front door when Clementine tried to move past them. They stepped forward to bar her entrance.

Cora's dread grew.

"You can't go in there right now, miss," they said.

"And why not?" Clem asked. Her voice shook a little. The guards exchanged a look and wouldn't answer.

"We've been instructed to insist that all guests return to the party," one of them said.

All traces of pleasantness melted from Clementine's face. "I'm not a guest here," she said.

There was a panicked shout from inside the house, and Clem let out a cry. She forced her way through the guards, with Cora on her heels.

*   *   *

Daisy had been in the Gothic Library, eyeing a crystal vase. It had been exquisitely crafted to look like a cascading splash, and she was trying to get up her courage to touch it when she suddenly turned in horror.

Were those the sounds of bullets?

She slipped on the marble floor and righted herself. She tasted fear in her mouth, as though her blood had climbed into her throat, like when she had fallen from a tree and broken her arm. Worse even when her sister Anette had fallen through the ice in the lake behind their house. Disappearing, under the waves, almost without time to make a sound.

Just like she had done then, she ran toward danger.

By the time she reached the first floor, Daisy could already smell the iron tang of blood. Her dread deepened.

She followed the noises coming from the billiards room and came to a halt just inside the doorway.

"Truman!" Clementine rushed toward where Truman Byrd had collapsed. "Help! Call the police!" she cried.

"I already have," Rutherford said. He returned a telephone to a hidden panel in the wall.

"Truman, what happened?" Clem asked, sinking down next to him.

Dallas Winston was on the floor with his knee pressed into a man's back. The man was struggling as Dallas wrested his arms behind him.

"I was almost shot," Truman said calmly. A gun lay on the floor near Dallas's foot. Rutherford bent and picked it up. "The first bullet was aimed for me and missed. The second went off when Dallas here burst in and tackled the man."

Daisy watched as Ella appeared just behind Clementine. She examined the room, her face ashen. Her gaze came to a stop on the would-be assassin.

Dallas rolled the man onto his back, and that's when Daisy saw who it was. *Liam*, she thought.

She froze, her breath sucked out of her chest. She remembered the softness of Liam's lips on her neck. The feel of his ribs shuddering beneath his shirt when she said something that made him laugh.

"I'm fine," Truman insisted gruffly to Clementine. "As fine as I can be, after almost being assassinated by one of my own bloody staff. Thankfully that man, Conner, fine old chap," Truman said, "managed to stop him."

"You're bleeding," Rutherford informed Conner.

Conner nodded, then slumped over in a chair.

"He needs help," Cora said. Her face was pale.

"The police will be here any moment," Rutherford said. "But I want a chance to talk to the butler first. Alone."

Daisy's breath caught in her throat as she, Clem, Florence, and Cora were ushered out.

"Close the door," Dallas said in a low voice. "And don't open it again until we're done."

Daisy forced herself not to look back as Liam let out a groan.

* * *

The police arrived without sirens, climbing the Hill stealthily. Under Truman's strict orders, the party went on undisturbed. Cora gave Clem a draught to conceal her shaken nerves, and by the time she returned to the billiards room, Liam was gone. There was a bloodstain on the floor, and Truman's private physician attended to Jack in the corner.

Jack sat in a leather armchair, hunched forward, his coat and shirt stripped off and discarded. He winced as a doctor wrapped a piece of gauze around his upper arm. He was alive. Cora felt her throat close. She remembered the feel of his hot, furtive breath on her neck. How his eyes had lit like embers in the darkness when he looked at her.

And she hadn't failed to notice that when he'd deviated from the plan, Jack had happened to lead Truman straight to where an assassin was waiting for him.

Cora found Florence sitting outside the kitchens. She fetched her a glass of water.

"I told him those hidden passageways were a ridiculous idea," Florence said, taking the glass. She was shaking, and Cora brought her another cupcake.

She snorted. "Thank you, love," she said. She closed her eyes. Cora crouched next to her until the shaking had passed, then helped to call her a car.

"Have you seen Daisy?" she asked Matias.

He shook his head. "Is it true?" Matias said, rubbing his temples in disbelief. "Liam, really?"

She could hardly believe it either. The four of them had laughed together in the bell tower, smoking cigars and playing cards as Liam imitated Macready with pitch-perfect inflection. She remembered the urgent whispering between Daisy and Liam the other night, right under her nose. How nervous and jittery Daisy had been before the party started. Cora's heart sank. This was why she couldn't afford to trust anyone. Multiple betrayals in one night, and she hadn't seen any of them coming.

*   *   *

Cora opened the door to her bedroom without making a sound. She stepped inside, careful not to draw Daisy's attention. She simply watched.

Daisy was throwing things haphazardly in a satchel. Panicked.

Cora drew her own conclusions about that.

She cleared her throat.

Daisy jumped and whirled around.

She let out a forced laugh and looked toward the door. "You scared me."

Cora closed it behind her with a soft click.

"Why are you packing?" Cora asked.

She took a step forward. Toward this girl who, she realized with a pang, she had never really known at all.

"I have to leave," Daisy said.

"Why? What's going on tonight, Daisy?" Cora asked. "Is that even your real name?"

"Of course it is," Daisy snapped. She clutched a faded dress to her chest. "At least since I was five years old and my mother changed it from Elżbieta."

Cora stole a glance toward the place where she had hidden her gun.

"I have to leave because of what it looks like," Daisy said. "You know I was involved with Liam. What are you going to tell them about me, when they come asking?"

"I wasn't planning to say anything yet," Cora said carefully. She took another step forward. "But only if you tell me what's going on. You were nervous earlier, when I showed you the stone. I could tell." She remembered the unsettling finality she had sensed in Daisy's words. "Because you already knew something was going to happen tonight, didn't you?"

Daisy's eyes flashed defiantly. "And what about you, Ella? You're up to your neck in something here too. I've seen the way you sneak around with Mr. Conner. There's more to why you're here than what you've said."

They glared at each other across the expanse of the room.

Cora caught the faintest hint of Daisy's perfume. Over the months, she had come to like falling asleep with the scent of it.

"Why did you want to shoot Truman?" Cora asked. "How could that possibly help anything? How does that help Anette?"

Daisy's eyes spilled over with angry tears. "I didn't want to shoot him! I swear, I had no idea Liam was planning that."

"Right," Cora said flatly. "Then why were you so anxious tonight? You all but told me goodbye."

Daisy wiped her tear-streaked face with her arm and turned to look at Cora. "What Liam did wasn't the plan. We . . . we were going to steal something tonight."

"Steal what?"

"A vase from the library. We were going to sell it for the money and send it to his brother and my baby niece to survive. So yes, I *was* nervous—*I* was supposed to do it tonight when Truman was distracted with the party. I didn't even think Truman would notice it was gone. But then—Liam—" she said. Her eyes reddened and filled with tears again. "We'd talked a lot about the injustice of it all, but I never thought Liam would *hurt* him."

Cora was silent. Thinking about how so often, in trying to correct wrongdoing, it was possible to become complicit in something even worse.

"And what about *you*, Ella?" Daisy asked. She threw the dress angrily on the bed. "What were you up to tonight? Trying so hard to get Clementine away from Truman. Was that so that he would be alone?"

"No—"

"I know you and Mr. Conner were working together. And he was with Truman when he was shot."

"That wasn't part of the plan, I can assure you," Cora bit back. She took a deep breath, calming her nerves. The night could not have gone worse. "But I can promise you that no part of me wishes Truman dead."

"You can see why the police might be interested in hearing about the extenuating circumstances of tonight, though. If I were to be asked, I mean."

Cora narrowed her eyes. "Is that supposed to be a threat, Daisy?" she asked slowly.

Daisy swallowed nervously. "I'm just saying that depending on who is telling the story, neither of us looks very good in this situation. So . . . maybe we could help each other."

Cora closed her eyes.

One messy alliance ends, she thought, *and another one presents itself.*

"What did you have in mind?" Cora asked.

"I swear I didn't know that Liam was going to hurt Truman. I would never hurt him. I need you to believe me," Daisy said in anguish. Her tears welled up again. And somewhere deep within her, Cora did believe her. Daisy had been angry, but hurting Truman didn't help her at all. And beneath that, Cora could recognize a feeling she herself knew well.

It was betrayal.

"Was Liam part of the mob, then?" Cora asked. "Did they send him to kill Truman?"

"If he was, he never said it outright," Daisy said. "We talked about the politics of it all, of course. To be honest, I thought I felt more passionately about it than him. Sometimes I thought he was just feigning interest because I cared so much about it." She gave a short, humorless laugh. "But he had a phone call from someone this afternoon and then he started acting different. I thought we were both just nervous about the plan." Bright spots of anger appeared on her cheeks. "He never told me it had changed."

"So what do you want to do?" Cora asked.

"You're the only one who knows we were seeing each other. Liam cares for me, I know he does. He knows I was in the dark about the shooting. In order to protect me, he didn't tell me about it. But I need *you* to keep your mouth closed. And if you stay quiet about my end, I'll be quiet about you and Mr. Conner."

Cora weighed her options. "I'm willing to keep my mouth closed about you and Liam, and your original plan," she said slowly. "But I'm going to need help from you with a little something else in return."

Daisy shot her a wary look. "Is it anything illegal?" she asked.

"No," Cora said.

"Does it involve the mob at all?"

"No," Cora said.

Daisy sighed, burying her face in her hands. "Fine."

"All right. Then your secrets are safe with me," Cora said.

Daisy walked over to Cora's bed and sank down beside her. Then she wrapped her arms around Cora, and with a kiss on the temple, she whispered "Thank you."

*   *   *

Over breakfast, Byrd sat in front of his portrait. He could just glimpse it through the violet petals of the orchids, reflecting in the window glass. He poured himself a cup of coffee and stirred in a rich swirl of cream. The morning was chilly and the braziers were smoking with embers of orange peel. A fire was lit in the grate. He looked up at the portrait he had commissioned from Celeste Lourd. The painted strokes of his own face.

If he had died at the hand of his own butler last night, who would inherit what he had built? He had no children. No obvious heirs.

He took a sip of coffee. He had never wanted to be a father. Mabel had tried to pressure him into it, but he had been resolute. His deepest fear was that he would turn out to be like his own. So he had decided to plant seeds of his permanence and his name in other ways.

He stretched out his hand, which sometimes ached in the mornings. He had succeeded everywhere his father had not. He wasn't a drunk or an abuser. He had even bailed his father out when his father needed money. He had done it gleefully. It was the final turn of the knife. Franklin Byrd had come to him groveling. And Truman had paid for him to live in a home in Illinois with a nurse. Truman didn't spare any expense. It was like pouring ashes on his head. And every month, he had Macready send the house a bouquet of roses. Just like his mother. So his father would have to smell them.

At one point, he had considered shedding his father's name like skin. But it had also been his mother's name, and Elias's. So he embraced it instead. Made it something new, entirely associated with himself.

His greatest revenge. And hadn't he soared.

"I wanted to thank you for your assistance last night," Truman said. Everett Conner sat in front of him, showered and freshly shaved. Everett took a long sip of coffee, and one of the maids served him a Danish and a fresh glass of orange juice.

Just before he had invited Everett Conner for a private breakfast, Truman had studied the bullet hole in the wall meant for him. It shook him more than he would show.

"I'm grateful for your service. And embarrassed that with a house full of security, one of my guests had to be the one to stop an attempted assassination."

Everett raised his hands in an effort to deflect the compliment.

"I appreciate the police chief's discretion," Truman continued. "And yours."

Truman did not want this getting out. That he had almost been assassinated by his own staff within his own home. He controlled the news. And this one would stay so buried, he would go to his grave with it.

He had been plagued with nightmares about a pine box throughout the night—just like the one he'd seen his brother buried in, a coffin Elias had made with his own hands. And all Truman could think was that he had spent his whole life doing great and terrible things, only to end up in exactly the same place.

Dallas Winston knocked and entered the room. "Excuse me, sir," he said, drawing Truman aside, "but I thought you should know that Mr. Boyle departed the Hill early this morning. Said it was a family emergency. We spoke with him before he left, but he did not appear to be aware of the incident last night."

It was suspicious. Someone attempted a hit on his life, and Albert left unexpectedly that same night. Thanks to his drug-running, Albert had plenty of connections with the mob.

But that was ridiculous. What could his old friend Albert possibly hope to gain from his death?

Truman felt a crawling up his back. He'd always been able to trust his instincts in the past. But he'd been looking in the wrong direction this time.

He studied his head of security. Or perhaps he had been *pointed* in the wrong direction. After all, Dallas had tried to cast suspicion on Everett Conner, while the real threat was close enough to slit his throat. The creeping feeling intensified. And where had his head of security been when Truman had needed him the most?

Perhaps he couldn't trust anyone.

He felt the train in his pocket now, where he had slipped it like a talisman. A weight to keep him in reality.

Was this the cost of wealth, of making a name for oneself? Barely missing a bullet to the head, and an unsettledness that left him feeling itchy and vulnerable—was that his punishment for the things he had done to get there?

According to the police chief, the young butler hadn't talked. But it was looking like the mob had infiltrated the Hill after all.

The train fell from Truman's grasp with a new, even darker thought.

Or perhaps it was Mabel, instead. Coming to cut free of him and take her share of the wealth, no matter the cost.

$$* \quad * \quad *$$

Jack studied Truman from across the table in the morning light. He stared briefly at the portrait above Truman's head. It looked nothing like the tired, shaken man who was sitting in front of him. Jack's gut tightened.

He had been too wired to sleep last night. Every time he'd closed his eyes, he'd seen the secret passageway slide open, the barrel of the gun glinting in the light. He took a shower, careful to shield his bandaged arm, and scrubbed his skin until it felt raw. He knew he'd screwed things up with Cora, and he didn't want to admit to himself how that almost felt worse than being shot. He had ended up pacing his room in his robe and telephoning

Virgil at three in the morning. It was growing increasingly dangerous to have any contact with them, especially after the stunt they'd pulled last night. But he had to know.

The mobster who answered at the Muddy Dahlia patched him through to Virgil.

"'Ello?" a husky voice had answered. Jack could picture him sitting up in bed, wearing too much cologne. He had a mouth that puckered like a smallmouth bass around a gold filling in his front left tooth.

"Virgil," Jack said. "It's Conner."

"Conner, listen—" Virgil said, instantly sounding awake.

"What the *hell* was that?" Jack hissed.

"I know, I know—"

"You are compromising my mission here. Security is going to be so high now. Dammit, Virgil—you couldn't wait two more days?"

"Listen," Virgil said. "I'm sorry. It wasn't my call."

"You've put me in a bad way here. I'm about to walk."

"Now, now," Virgil said, his voice turned soothing. "The stakes just went up for everyone. What if we increased your take for bringing the good stuff home?"

Jack paused, considering. "You want me to stay, you've got to give me a little more up front. And what I want is information."

"I'm listening," Virgil said.

"Who sold those pieces from the Bastion theft?"

Virgil snorted. "I'm not giving that up yet."

"Then at least tell me where they ended up. You can give me that, can't you?"

Jack could hear the distinct sound of wet tobacco being gummed in the cleft of Virgil's cheek.

"They were all sold but one," Virgil finally said, and Jack held back a deep exhale. "The fifth never entered the market."

"So the thief might still have it."

"Yeah, we never saw it. The thieves kept it, or burned it, or buried it before we got it."

Jack had a tingling sensation.

"Which one was it?" he asked.

"The Rembrandt."

Jack whispered, "The one about Lazarus?"

"Yeah," Virgil had said. "I think that's the one."

Now Jack stared across the expanse at Truman, his injured arm lightly aching. He had foregone the painkillers the doctor had given him, because he needed to stay sharp and alert. After the events of last night, he knew that Truman had come to trust him more.

But he was beginning to trust Truman even less.

CHAPTER TWENTY-EIGHT

FRIDAY, MAY 2, 1930
~ Day Six ~

"There's a call for you," Daisy whispered. She jerked her head toward the telephone booth on the first floor as she picked up a breakfast tray.

"Who is it?" Cora asked. But Daisy had already moved on, her head bent to mask how red and puffy her eyes were.

Cora furtively made her way to the telephone booth. They'd all been searched that morning prior to being allowed into the house, and Cora had a feeling that their every move was being watched more closely than ever. It made her nerves feel tight and coiled.

"Hello?" Cora said, picking up the telephone.

"Cora-thorn," her father said on an exhale.

Cora battled a bolt of surprise. "Da?" she asked. They weren't supposed to talk until tomorrow.

"Are you all right?" He lowered his voice. "I heard about what happened last night from my friend Johnny at the San Luis Obispo department."

Cora's surprise crept higher. Apparently Truman's lid didn't contain leaks quite as well as he thought.

"I'm fine," she insisted, touched that he had called; at the worry she could hear in his voice. "I wasn't anywhere near when it happened." She twisted the cord around her finger, cutting off blood flow. Despite the distance that had grown up between them like weeds, part of him still did care.

If only he knew *who* had saved Truman's life last night.

She tightened the cord, suddenly feeling nauseous about all the secrets she was keeping. Would she ever stop lying to him? They could never have a real relationship if she didn't.

But would they have one at all if she did?

"Did this new development wreak havoc on your plans?" he asked, and she heard the unmasked interest in his voice. "Do you need to talk through anything?"

She hadn't realized just how much he had been living through her and this mission until that moment. How he must hate his job. How her victory, in some ways, would be his too.

"It's making things a bit more difficult," she admitted.

"Right," he said, and his disappointment cut through her like a paring knife. "Well, listen. I was talking to a friend here in Bitterlake who is looking for a secretary."

"A secretary?" Her face fell.

"I know, it's not what you were thinking. But perhaps if—well, if things don't go according to plan there—"

The feeling of failure was opening up in Cora's chest like a hole.

"—it might be for the best. Perhaps . . . well, what if you came and lived with me for a bit?"

She let go of the telephone cord. Watched the blood flow slowly back into her finger.

It was both everything she had wanted for so long, and everything she hadn't.

"I'll think about it," she said softly.

And in that moment, she almost asked him.

Did you know I was listening that day? Did you change the plan and send Rusty to the south side because you knew I couldn't be trusted?

All along, have you blamed me?

"I better go," she said.

"Call me tomorrow at eight, before the chief gets in."

"I will," she promised.

"And, Cora-thorn—" he hesitated. "Be careful."

*　　*　　*

Truman looked up as the door slid open. Clementine walked in, wearing a long satin dress the color of persimmons. It trailed across her like smoke and shadows. The jewel he had bought her hung low and heavy between her breasts.

She came toward him. Leaned down and brushed her lips against his temple, so that he could smell violets on her skin.

"You gave me a good scare last night," she said. She traced the skin along his hairline, so delicate that it sent a shiver down his back.

He took her by the arm. Whispered in her ear, low and dangerous: "Are you sure? As memory serves, you seemed to be having a good time."

He gestured to the chair next to him and said, curtly, "Sit."

She slid into it. But first she poured herself a glass of orange juice that was mostly champagne.

"How do you feel this morning?" she asked.

"Alive," he said. "And more determined than ever to not waste my own time."

She narrowed her eyes as he leaned back and steepled his fingers.

"Are we going to talk about what's going on between you and Beaumont?" he asked.

Clementine shook her head a little and laughed. "I'm not sure what you mean," she said.

"Do you think I'm a fool, Clem? Perhaps I am. Letting you toy with me in my own home."

Clem bit her lip. She looked out the window, far away, at the Pacific. "It's not fun, is it?" she asked.

"What do you mean, darling?" he asked with exaggerated patience.

"It means that I'm tired, Truman. Tired of feeling like a doll dangling on a string. Just waiting for you to grow weary of me. I have no permanence here, no status—"

Truman sat forward, waving her off. "I've given you everything you could ever want, Clem. Raised you up from nothing."

She laughed, the sound of it like a drink laced with bitters. "As if you didn't come from nothing, too. I think sometimes you've forgotten that."

"I never forget," Truman said coldly. And he didn't. It was always there, lurking like stale cigarette smoke. Especially whenever he talked to Mabel.

"You know I care for you," Clementine said. "Yet you doubt me."

"You care for me," he retorted, "yet you would humiliate me in my own house in front of my guests."

"You humiliate me all the time," she said, rising. "A side piece. A harlot." She began to pace around the room. "Why won't you divorce her, Truman? Do I mean so little to you? All you care about is money and status. When will it ever be enough? Why can't you be content with it all?"

"I could say the same for you," he said. He examined his fingertips. "Isn't that exactly what this little tantrum of yours is about?"

"Maybe I'm growing tired of waiting," Clem said. She paused. "Perhaps you should go after your true love—status, and politics, and getting back at your father. And I'll find someone who—"

"Don't," he said. A one-note warning.

She emptied her glass and set it down on the table. "Well, why don't you think about what you really want," she said, coming around to face him. She traced a line across his lips, bending down to flash the skin of her leg. She whispered in his ear, "And so will I."

Then she left, her skirts whipping behind her, not letting him see that she was shaking.

*　　*　　*

"Are you all right?"

Daisy looked up from gathering the breakfast dishes as Jack approached. Her eyes were still raw, and he did a double-take when he saw her face.

She nodded briskly and looked at his bandaged arm. "You?"

"Just a graze," he said. The moment he'd heard the phrase cross the doctor's lips, he'd instantly thought of Leo.

"Daisy," Jack lowered his voice. "Do you know where Ella is?"

Daisy looked down at the stack of heavy silverware and sighed. "I don't think she wants to talk to you."

"Please," he said. "It's important."

She picked up the tray and shot him a look of exasperation. "You're going to get me in trouble."

He waited outside the kitchens for her to deposit her tray, and then they wound through the back labyrinth of the house. Daisy led him through the corridors until they came to a stop in front of a slightly open door. Jack could see Cora, dressed in her regular maid uniform, reaching as she scrubbed the inside of the windowpanes.

"Morning, Ella," Jack said, pushing open the door. "Can we talk?"

Cora stopped scrubbing, but kept her back to him.

"I can watch the door," Daisy said. She looked at Jack. "You get five minutes."

He closed it behind her.

"Are you all right?" Cora asked in a low voice. She didn't turn to look at him.

"Fine, yeah," he said.

"So you ended up saving Truman's life," she said.

He gave her a short laugh. "Don't think I wasn't conflicted about it."

"Good thing you were there, then. Instead of following my plan."

His smile tightened. "Don't think I wasn't conflicted about it," he repeated.

Her voice turned to ice. "Glad you're at least a little conflicted every time you betray me."

"Cora," he began. "I came to say that I'm sorry—"

"Trusting you always turns into my greatest regret," she said firmly, cutting him off. She squeezed the rag until her knuckles whitened. "Because you're the same person you've always been, and shame on me to believe you could ever change."

"I didn't mean to hurt you, Cora," He clenched his jaw. "I came here for one thing. I saw a chance for that thing last night, and I took it."

"Actually, it was *my* chance you took." She looked at him, her eyes blazing. "For as long as we have known each other, I have helped you. At every turn. At great risk and at incredible cost to myself." She threw her rag in the bucket. "So you're on your own, just like I've always been."

She pointed at the door. "Now get the hell out."

*　　*　　*

Jack left his meeting with Cora feeling wretched.

This week was giving him so much more than he'd bargained for. He had forgotten what it was like to owe anyone anything. To have someone depend on him. To care about someone other than himself.

Jack tried to shake free of it. He didn't know why he cared so much what she thought of him; what she must have felt when he diverged from the plan, or if it had mattered to her when she realized he was hurt. He couldn't lose sight of the goal. He had chosen himself over Cora last night. Then, in the moment, before he could think things through, he had instinctively saved Truman Byrd's life. Who was he at his core? Maybe that mattered less than who he wanted to become.

Before Jack ever met Lozada, before he had even learned how to play cards himself, Jack had gotten a job working security at high-stakes card tables. He was there less for the money—it paid a pittance—and more for the sort of information he could siphon right out of the air. It was amazing what tips could slip out when people started winning and drinking too much because of it. He could take those tips, tuck them away, and present them like shiny coins at just the right opportunity. Which black-market trade might be coming off the coffers next. Which horse would win. Who was searching for a score of heroin.

Jack gleaned information and used it to make inroads on the black market, to get the intel he wanted. He made significant headway with his contacts over one single tip: the location of a known enemy to the Perralta family. Jack learned that the man would be staying at a certain hotel on a certain night. Knowing that if he passed the information on, he would have the man's blood on his hands. Even if he wasn't the one to pull the trigger. Even if it was just words.

He'd done it anyway.

He had fallen asleep that night with a sick twist in his gut, knowing that he had gone too far. He had given information that killed a man.

The next time, he held it back to save another.

He had come to Enchanted Hill knowing exactly what he wanted. Once Leo died, he was entirely on his own—and it had been safer that way. Cora, with her own wants and needs, made things confusing.

But Cora hadn't known what it was like to be kept inside Cell Block D, built behind dense clusters of barbed wire that snaked along like vines covered in thorns. It was dank, and Jack often heard a perpetual dripping sound, slow and steady, all night long. Living within it was like climbing down the inside of a sewer drain.

Jack knelt on the floor of his suite and opened the false-bottom drawer with the blank journal that he was too afraid to write anything personal in. He remembered the way the iron bars had once stretched from ceiling to floor in front of him, like a row of strings just waiting to be strummed. The cell across from his held a painting of poppies inside, and they were brighter than they should have possibly been. Colors and sounds were all distorted in that place.

The longer he had been on Pelican, the more he had felt himself starting to go wrong. He lit a cigarette, thinking about one Christmas Eve, when the children and wives of Pelican Island officers had filed into D Block to sing Christmas carols for them. He remembered the reverent, watchful silence as they walked down the corridor between two floors of cells. Some of the youngest children had looked into the cells, even waved joyously. Others watched their shoes, the reflection of the dull lights on the linoleum floor.

The inmates had sat on their cots, watching with a hungry look in their eyes that told Jack these were some of the only women and children they had seen in years. Cora's hair had been pinned back when she stepped inside. She wore a green dress with a ribbon. Her gangly elbows hung by her sides. He had been planning to give her a smile, or hold up his cup of iceplant flowers when she walked by, so that she wouldn't be nervous. But instead, at the last

278

minute, he had stepped back into the shadows of his cell. He hadn't wanted her to see him in his cage. Or she might never have looked at him the same way again.

Because it was Christmas, a few inmates were granted permission to accompany with borrowed instruments—the warm brass of a trumpet, a mournful French horn. Someone had even found Leo a violin, and his face was bliss as he touched the bow and let the music out. But mostly it was the sound of the voices, shining like a beam of pure light through a pit. The visitors had lined up on a second-floor bridgeway, right in front of the guards' locked arsenal of weapons.

Long lay the world in sin and error pining, they sang
Till He appeared,
and the soul felt its worth.

Jack had listened while watching a disembodied hand wrapped around the iron cell bars. And he had wondered, were souls worth less when they were on Pelican Island?

He remembered how Cora had kept her eyes closed tight the entire time she sang, as if she knew he didn't want her to see him.

Why did it matter to him so much what she saw when she looked at him now?

For so long, he'd been in it only for himself. It had become almost frighteningly natural to live in this world he'd created, where nothing—and no one—mattered beyond getting justice and revenge.

He desperately wanted to clear his name of the things he hadn't done, and be forgiven for the things that he had.

But perhaps he couldn't have both. And he was starting to wonder, if he had to choose between them, which one would truly set him free.

CHAPTER TWENTY-NINE

Clementine's hands shook when she sat down at her vanity.

She examined the hollows beneath her eyes, then patted the powder in the makeup tin and began to cover over the shadows. Sunlight streamed through the mahogany slats of the Astral walls. She dabbed perfume on her wrists, behind her ears. She inhaled the signature scent of it, and it instantly made her mood rise. She examined herself as her skin became smooth and even.

She didn't know if Truman would choose her over Mabel. Over his aspirations. All she knew for certain was that Truman liked games, and this was one that she was going to win. She had to establish her own future.

Either with him, or in spite of him.

She suddenly had no patience for a set of tennis with the girls, or even soaking up the sun by the pool in her bathing suit. She was tired of entertaining, of pretending. She wanted to know she was home, and walk down to the animals and feed them apples and hay. To come back with her arms full of flowers and her hair slightly wild, without having to look pinned together and perfect.

She would slip away for the afternoon. Look at the zebras, or perhaps take Kitty with her on horseback to ride the trails. Anything to feel less like she was just one more of Truman's kept animals.

Her hand was on the banister when she met Everett Conner on the staircase.

"Morning, Mr. Conner."

"Good morning, Miss Garver," he said. They stopped together on the landing.

"What you did last night was incredibly brave," she said.

She jumped at the distant sound of a door banging.

"Are you quite all right, miss?" Jack asked. He reached out and gently touched her arm.

"I'm not altogether sure, to be honest," she said. She surveyed him. She had never spared him too much of a thought, this man that seemed more of Truman's plaything. A card shark. A farmer. Yet she was surprised to realize that this man was handsome.

Not noticeably, movie-star handsome. Not Beau. But assured. Young. There was something about his eyes that was alluring.

She couldn't remember the last time someone had cared enough to ask if she was all right.

"Were you on your way out?" he asked, gesturing toward her sun hat. He leaned back, instead of forward. But it almost seemed like an invitation.

There was something about his presence that she liked.

"I was," she said. She hesitated. "Have you seen the aviary down past the gardens?"

"I haven't."

He smiled at her.

She smiled back.

"Would you . . . like company?" he asked slowly.

She felt the brittle texture of the hat beneath her fingers. There were other affluent men in the world. Not as rich and as powerful as Byrd, but at least they weren't married. Who wouldn't put her aside for their own insatiable dreams.

Something had to change. She knew it deep in her bones.

And so she said yes.

*   *   *

When Cora returned to her room, she found a small white paper bag on the nightstand.

Next to it was a note.

She crossed the room in three steps and tore into the envelope.

I'm sorry, Ella. I know you're furious. But I learned something from Florence. Byrd's hidden his name all over the house in code, just like those letters you found for Mabel.

She opened the bag and found the taffy.

P.S., he'd written. *I thought I remember you liking the banana ones.*

For a split second, she saw the dappled afternoon when Bobby had slid down on one knee.

He had knelt there in the grass, the wet beginning to stain his pants, and he had looked up at her with a small ring. He had called her father to ask for permission. They had never even met each other, but her father had said yes. And so had she. She had felt a sudden wholeness when he slipped the silver ring on her finger. She had watched the small stone catch the sunlight, when no one else was looking. She had felt a pure euphoria that had lasted for a week.

And then, only a few days later, Cora thought she saw Jack. It probably wasn't possible, given that he had spent his last several years in Nevada—but maybe that was all a lie too. Maybe she really had. She had turned her head and lost her breath, watching the man walk down the street near Fifth Avenue. She had stood up so abruptly that her chair had clattered to the floor behind her, and Theresa had exclaimed "Cora, what's wrong? You look as if you've seen a ghost!"

Cora had left the table and followed the man, watching as he stopped to glance in a department-store window. He had a hat pulled over his face, so she couldn't be sure whether it was him or not. And then he had disappeared into the crowd forever.

And in that moment, she had known, with a sinking feeling. The wholeness had been punctured clean through, like it had taken a bullet. Her fiancé didn't know the real her, and she was too afraid to ever really tell him. They had gotten too far down the road. He had fallen in love with a person who didn't really exist. And she couldn't take the chance for any more rejection from a man she loved. She wouldn't be left again.

How quickly feelings toward someone could ripen—but that didn't hold a candle to how quickly they could rot.

She picked up the candies and threw them in the trash.

*   *   *

Jack stood beside Clementine, and they watched the zebras grazing at the foot of the hill.

"They're called a dazzle, you know," Clem said. "When they're in a group."

"Why zebras?" Jack asked.

Clem took off her satin gloves. "Truman brought them over from Africa. The rest of the zoo plans failed, but the zebras remained and they're completely wild. No one even feeds them. I've always wondered what it would be like to pet one," she said.

"Why don't you, then?" Jack asked.

She smiled ruefully. "Because one kick can break the jaw of a lion."

"Ah," Jack said.

"Plus, they bite." Her dress caught in the breeze as she turned to him. "Does your arm hurt much?" she asked.

"Hardly at all," he said.

"The police said the mob was behind it," Clem said. "The hit man wasn't associated with them before, or it would have turned up in the background check, but they got to him somehow." She shook her head, looking toward the crash of the ocean. "Truman didn't really think they could reach him. I think his hubris got in the way of common sense."

She touched Jack on the arm in a way that seemed both gentle and loaded. For just long enough to make him wonder.

"Good thing you were there," she said.

He didn't answer. Instead, he smiled at her and moved down toward the shadows of the aviary. He examined the birds fluttering through the enormous dark metal walls. *Rainbow lorikeet*, the plaque said. He watched a budgerigar shiver and clean its scalloped wings. Inside the aviary were miniature fruit trees and, according to the plaque, bright crimson bottlebrush flanked by budgerigars, yellow-collared lovebirds, and a single dollarbird.

BYRD.

"Gives you a certain amount of clarity," he said. "Getting shot at."

She nodded. "Yes," she said.

"Or watching it happen to someone you love," he continued.

She bit the curve of her bottom lip and turned her head away.

"I'm not trying to pry," he said. "I just thought it was no use pretending. If you needed someone to talk to about it."

She looked up at him in surprise. Her eyes wide and haunting.

"You know, I actually believe you," she said. Her famous face softened, and she almost looked amused. "At first, I wondered whether you wanted my company today in order to share my bed."

"Oh, not your bed. Surely nothing as civilized as that. The barn, maybe," he deadpanned, and she laughed.

"What is it that you want, then?" Clem asked, with an unbearable hint of sadness. "There's always something people want."

And buried beneath it all, Jack felt a twinge of concern for her. So much that he almost couldn't go through with it. He met her gaze.

"What if I did want something," he said slowly, "but it would help you, too?"

She tilted her head. Listening. "And how do you know what I want?" she asked.

"I think it's possible," he said, "that you and Mabel Byrd both want the same thing."

She snorted at that, surprised. "I can't possibly imagine that's true."

"I think you both want her to divorce Truman."

Clem cocked an eyebrow. Leaned a hair forward. "All right," she said cautiously. "I'm listening."

"A divorce might require a large portion of Truman's fortune, of course."

"There would still be plenty to go around," Clem shot back.

"And it might cost him his political aspirations," Jack continued.

Clem grew quiet.

"But it would mean that Mabel was out of the way," she said softly.

She traced her delicate fingers along the aviary's bars. Her ring finger was bare.

"I know what it's like to feel trapped," he said. "And that sometimes the only way out means hurting someone you care for."

She looked deeply into his eyes. He looked back and thought of the blackmail he had come for, tantalizingly within his reach. Of finally finding out who had framed him and Leo all of those years ago.

"What did you have in mind?" she asked throatily.

Jack offered her a cigarette, smiling.

* * *

In the main dining room, Cora was meticulously measuring the space between the silver utensils and the patterned china for supper when Daisy entered the room.

"I've been looking for that heavy candelabra," Daisy said.

"Which one?"

"The ridiculous one with the clusters of grapes and the mermaids," Daisy said. She came closer, then looked over her shoulder to make sure they were alone.

"Any updates on Liam?" Cora whispered.

She could smell the star jasmine through the opened windows, spilling over the wall in a wave of verdant green and flecked with blossoms like whitecaps.

Daisy shook her head miserably. "I've been listening to see if I hear anything. All I know is that he's being held at the San Luis Obispo police station."

"Are you worried?" Cora asked. She saw the twitch of a pulse in Daisy's temple, the shadows beneath her eyes.

Daisy nodded. "I know he lied to me, but I still care for him," she whispered furtively. "I was starting to picture a future for us." She shook her head to clear the gathering tears and steeled herself. "What a fool. Now I doubt I'll ever see him again."

They looked up as one of the butlers entered. They separated and went about their tasks while he cleaned the grate of the fireplace.

That's when Cora noticed the pattern on the wallpaper.

Byrd's hidden his name all over the house in code, Jack had written.

She had never paid it much attention before, but it was a repeating pattern, almost a coat of arms—a honeycomb swirling with bees, a clipping of green yew spilling into vibrant red roses and an antlered deer.

B. Y. R. D.

She began to set out the wine glasses until the butler left the room again.

"I learned something else, though," Daisy whispered. "I was trying to find out about Liam, and I overheard Truman and Miss Garver arguing." She cocked her eyebrow and said, meaningfully, "Tonight will go one of two ways. And one of them might be exactly what you were hop—"

Mrs. Macready entered the room and cut her off, this time with the groundskeepers behind her, their arms overflowing with blossoms to make the new centerpieces.

"Daisy," Mrs. Macready said, eyes narrowing as she inspected their work. "Miss Duluth can finish up here. I need you in the kitchen."

Daisy curtsied. "Yes, ma'am," she said.

She waited until Mrs. Macready had turned her back and then hastily scribbled something on one of the doilies. She crumpled it and, without looking back, kicked it to the floor.

Cora forced herself to slowly make her way around the table, setting wine glasses at each spot. Then she subtly bent and retrieved the note.

Bell tower at 8 p.m., Daisy had written. *Camera ready.*

Cora crumpled the note in her hand.

CHAPTER THIRTY

At a quarter to eight, Cora entered the bell tower. The sun was beginning to set.

"Daisy?" she whispered cautiously, pushing open the door. She saw the cushions, the cards, the bottles of booze. The last time she had been there was with Jack.

She wouldn't think about that.

The room was empty, and she cleared out the ashtrays and readied her camera. She knew the guests were all settled in the dining room for warm beet salad with pear and walnuts, pommes de terre à la Sarladaise, mashed pumpkin, and duck confit with juniper berries.

But Clementine wasn't with them. She sashayed out onto the mosaic tiles of the third-floor balcony, looking lovely in a dress that showed her entire back. The satin was the color of pears, and a gold pendant traced down her spine to land a whisper above where the dress began. Then she disappeared inside again.

Cora's risky decision to bring Daisy into the fold was going to pay off, apparently. Cora brought the lens to her eye and adjusted it for the distance to the main house. She kept seeing the way Jack had knelt beside her just a few nights ago. The hope she had felt when they had examined the letters together and made the plan for the ball. She was careful to keep her feelings about him at bay, locked behind a door, though her heart felt like a bruised piece of fruit. She would not think of him. She had a job to do.

But jobs couldn't fall asleep next to you at night. Nuzzle your neck. Give you children, or mourn you when you were buried.

And Cora understood in a new, raw way that she was just so damn lonely.

It reminded her of the morning her mother took her to pay a visit to Dina, barely two months before Jack's escape. They had ridden the ferry across the Bay and boarded the cable car, stopping by a general store along the way. Dina had gotten pregnant and sent off the island, and was renting a dirty little room in the Tenderloin. Cora stole curious glances at a belly just beginning to swell. The baby's father—presumably the lighthouse boy—was still living on Pelican; on the way, Cora saw him flirting with another girl near the Bayside pier.

Cora's mother had stocked up Dina's pantry with cans of food and supplies. Cora knew she was being brought along to demonstrate a lesson in kindness—and also, perhaps, a caution. Perhaps her mother had sensed how Cora's heart was full and trusting and ripe with loneliness, like dry kindling ready to light at the first hint of connection.

The fog had already descended when they returned to the island later that afternoon. Cora's heart leapt beneath her breastbone at the sight of Jack outside. She had slipped out the back door and gone to meet him as he weeded, and he had listened when Cora told him, haltingly, shyly, about visiting Dina. How confusing it was. She had gathered dandelions as she talked, weaving them into an anklet that made her skin itch.

"Do you know how bridges are constructed, Cora?" he had asked. He had explained how bridges were painstakingly built, piece by piece, over bodies of water. How they each started on their own side to meet somewhere in the middle. How the tension of the other was what held the bridge aloft, or else one side—or both—would crumble into the ocean.

"Do you get what I'm saying, Cora?" Jack had asked, and she had nodded, though she wasn't entirely sure. She just knew that she loved the cut of his jaw, the way his soft mouth pursed when he was concentrating. He had thrown a dandelion over the fence to her, the last to complete her anklet, and said "Just be careful who you give your heart to someday."

He'd had no idea the person he was warning her against was himself.

The bell towers began to ring eight, a deafening sound that made Cora crouch and shield her ears. And that's when the light went on in Clementine's room.

Cora crept toward it. With the rest of the party downstairs, enjoying their six-course dinner, Clementine opened the Astral bedroom shutters. She wasn't in her peach dress anymore. Instead, she was wearing a white silk nightgown.

Cora's heartbeat stuttered. Cautiously, she lifted her camera again.

And then Truman appeared behind Clem, cast mostly in shadow.

Cora's pulse warmed in her ears. She hid behind the balcony of the bell tower, aiming her camera. She couldn't make out Truman. He was too blurry.

She was hidden by the ledge, but the way Clementine and Truman were standing wasn't going to work for a good enough shot. *Move*, she begged them in her mind. But they stayed just out of reach for her camera lens.

She swallowed hard. Daisy was the one with the fear of heights, but Cora was suddenly aware of how far the ground was below her. She gave her worry stone one firm stroke and climbed out of the window opening. Her view wasn't quite direct into the Astral Suite; but if she dropped down a few feet onto the ornamental ledge, she might get the perfect shot. There were no railings to guard her from plunging to the mosaic tiles below. She closed her eyes and breathed in the bite of the salt air and felt the wind sweep across her cheek. She squeezed as close as she could to the bell tower wall, shielding her camera, and crouched down. There was barely enough room for her, and the distance was making her feel like she would faint and pitch forward. Part of her knew this was ridiculous—that risking the fall wasn't worth whatever Mabel could offer her. But this was the thing that had brought Cora and her father together again—their minds, working a case, solving a puzzle. They needed something like this, to cross all the complicated lines that had sprung up between them. She wanted so much to make him proud.

A strong wind whipped around the tower, momentarily costing her balance. Cora's ankle gave out a little, and she caught herself just in time before the camera went tumbling out of her hands to smash on the tiles below.

She clutched the camera to her body like it was her lifeline—her very last shot at the life she wanted. She melted back into the shadows.

Then she brought the camera to her eye, her sheer determination blocking out any fear that was left.

*   *   *

"Hello, Truman," Clementine said.

She had summoned him there, to the Astral Suite, while everyone else was indulging in the hours-long six-course meal. And Truman had come, intrigued by what he would find. Clementine kept him guessing, in a torturous way he rather liked. He knew none of the guests would think anything of his absence. They were used to his disappearing for work at all hours of the day.

She was wearing a nightgown that he'd never seen before. White. Leaving just enough to the imagination. She had scattered vibrant crimson rose petals across the sheets. It was meant to be romantic, but it looked like the bed had been shot.

His throat tightened. He could have spent last night in a morgue.

"We ended on a bad note earlier," she said.

She turned. She had pulled her golden hair up to show the nape of her neck, and she was wearing a chain of violets that she took off, one by one, dropping them on the floor as she came toward him.

She was so lovely. So alive.

She slipped the strap off her nightgown. Down the curve of her shoulder.

He cleared his throat. A hunger stirring.

He saw the glint of the ocean shifting behind her and the white moon rising. The lights were amber and honey in the suite, and the teakwood carved window was open. It was never open. He started to object, and then she touched her finger to his lips.

"Everyone's at dinner," she said. She looked up at him with those large, yearning eyes. As though she really saw him. Not what Mabel saw now when she looked at him, what his father had seen. Not even what Truman saw in himself sometimes, when he looked in the mirror and remembered the terrible things he had done. "I thought we could play a daring little game tonight, just this once," she breathed, coming close enough for his hands to almost touch her. "There's nothing like the thrill of almost being caught."

Truman had been growing ever more paranoid, but perhaps it had been about all the wrong things. Distrusting all the wrong people. When he sat without protest, Clem climbed onto his lap and made a sound like purring in his ear. He traced his thumb down her throat and she shivered, as though he had set off a trail of fireworks across her skin. A new, urgent desire stirred in him. He smelled the hint of violets.

He tightened his grip on her.

He had come so close to dying last night.

Tonight, all he wanted to do was live.

*   *   *

Cora's heart pounded as she climbed back into the bell tower.

Three images, clear as day, were captured on the film in her camera.

A passionate embrace. Clem half-clothed. Byrd kissing her collarbone, her shoulder, her lips.

There was no denying it was them. Clem was almost looking at the camera.

Cora felt the excitement explode and fizz in her belly.

She had done it. After all those months of near-misses and hoping, she had done it.

But as she slipped back over the railing, her eye caught the slightest movement below. She abruptly dipped down and saw Jack, sneaking in the shadows of the bushes beneath her. He was holding a camera of his own.

The full force of the realization hit her in a wave.

Jack was going to try to steal her blackmail.

Of course. They were both getting desperate. They both needed that shot for their own purposes. She steadied herself against the railing and looked down to where he had been crouching. A grim satisfaction dawned over her. She had scouted that area before, and her shots were undoubtedly better. Unless the lighting hit with absolute perfection, he wouldn't have gotten much.

But there was still a chance.

She tucked her camera away. She had never known one person to make her feel every spectrum of feeling the way he did—from magnetic attraction to schoolgirl crush to a cold, vibrant fury. But she would handle him, just like she had handled this job.

She hurried down the bell tower stairs and over to the main house, nodding at the guard who let her in.

Then she shut herself inside the telephone booth and dialed the number for the Fairmont Hotel.

"Hello," a receptionist answered. "How may I help you?"

"I need to speak with a guest staying at your hotel," Cora said breathlessly. "It's urgent. Her name is Mrs. Mabel Byrd."

"I'll connect you," the receptionist said. But a moment later, she came back on the line and said that Mabel wasn't picking up.

"Do you want to leave a message?" she asked.

Cora hesitated.

"Yes. Please tell her that Ella Duluth called," Cora said, glancing at the birds on the patterned wallpaper, "and the eagle has landed."

CHAPTER THIRTY-ONE

Three hours later, Cora sat on the floor of the locked bathroom, squinting with giddiness at the developed photographs. She had intentionally left the contact sheet a bit overexposed. It would be just enough proof to show Mabel the goods, without giving up her bargaining power with the negatives needed for the newspapers.

Cora hid the evidence in her room, splitting it just in case by tucking the canister of negatives in her biscuit tin. She hugged the tin to herself and locked it away. Then she headed to the house, where the guests were streaming out from their raucous dinner to smoke cigars, play cards, and swim. It was half past eleven. It was clear that the week of parties was coming to a head, with only tomorrow night remaining. She felt the excitement swelling in the air like a heat wave. The sensation, the nerves, that something big was going to happen.

She could feel Jack watching her over the rim of his cocktail. There didn't appear to be a camera on him, and she felt a pinch of unease. The buzz of her initial triumph was fading. Even though her prints were better, she had to make sure that he didn't get to use his first.

She ducked into Macready's office and checked the latest schedule. The night would be tricky. The guards were moving with more frequency, and covering more ground. She committed the times to memory, then slipped across the esplanade to the guest cottages, determined to finally play things the way Jack did.

Dirty. And without remorse.

She picked the lock of his suite and slipped inside.

His room was just as it had been the last time she'd been inside it. She searched it, again. Checked the hidden drawers and his nightstand, and riffled through his clothes. She couldn't find his camera or, more importantly, the damning negatives. A troubling thought prodded at her. Where had he gotten the camera in the first place?

She looked everywhere she could imagine. Was it possible he had it on him? Or that he'd hidden it somewhere in the main house? Damn him. She scrawled a note for him and left it tucked into a book she put on his nightstand. He would notice immediately that it wasn't one of his own. *The Hound of the Baskervilles*, her favorite mystery. They had discussed it once at Pelican.

Meet me at 1:45 between guard shifts, she wrote. *I have something for you.*

She shut away every part of her that felt tender. She was all done with mercy. Tonight, she was only her father's daughter.

She returned home and stripped the boots off her aching feet. She put on a pair of warm socks, and checked that the negatives were still safely hidden away in the package of biscuits. Then she ate the biscuits alone, crunching in the silence, and tucked herself into bed.

∗   ∗   ∗

When Cora awoke, moonlight was cutting through the window onto the crumpled biscuit packet she had dropped on the floor. Daisy must have covered her with a quilt when she came in, and was now softly snoring in her own bed. Cora wiped her mouth with the back of her hand and checked the clock. Half an hour until her meeting with Jack.

She rose, washed her face as quietly as she could, and changed into something more strategic. She put on fresh underwear and black stockings. She pulled out Bobby's favorite dress: ink-black and satin, it clung to her body much more than the uniform did. She lined her eyes with kohl. To a security guard, she would look like one of the guests, and that would raise fewer questions.

She pulled her hair up into a chignon, so that it showed the long, aching curve of her back. Her eyes were more green than hazel tonight. She spritzed herself with perfume, rubbing it along her wrists and the backs of her knees. Her body was starting to buzz.

She stopped to examine herself in the bronze mirror. It had a small chip in the upper-right corner, and she could almost see the fifteen-year-old girl she used to be staring back at her, determinedly wiping the storm from her eyes. She was cheered by her indefatigable grit.

She had survived everything that came at her before now. And she would survive this night, too.

Cora threw on a coat, strapped her gun to her thigh, and locked the door behind her. Her heels faintly crunched on the gravel walk, so she moved off the gravel to the ground, the soil still moist from the storms. She paused once, her heart climbing into her throat when she heard the sound of Macready's voice, but she waited in the shadows and then crept on without being discovered.

The Roman Pools that had been built beneath the ballroom were dim, and she paused at the doorway to listen. The pools were kept unlocked, and she heard nothing but the gentle slap of water against tile.

She stepped into the temperate chamber and was hit with a wall of moist air. The water glowed an unearthly aquamarine, warmed by the lights buried within it. Cora walked around the lagoon-like pool to inspect the corridors and make sure that she was truly alone. Ten thousand glass tiles were inlaid into the walls; incandescent golds and blues, the walls rippling with mosaics. The moonlight shimmered across them, highlighting stars and mermaids and Roman goddesses, tridents and fruit trees and temples. Her steps echoed.

Wisps of steam rose from the heated water in delicate white mist. There were arched alcoves tucked on either side of the pool, where the rooms became more like private baths. The ceiling was a dome, covered with cobalt tiles. The clock on the wall read 1:43.

She checked her gun. The chamber was loaded with three bullets. The steam was making her begin to perspire. The clock hands shifted steadily to 1:55, and she wondered nervously if Jack had missed her message. Or, more likely, simply didn't care to come. She adjusted the neckline of her dress, her anger growing as the minutes ticked by. Then suddenly she froze as the door creaked open, letting in a bit of light. She could feel a curl of cold night cut through the humid air.

Jack entered cautiously, blinking as his eyes adjusted to the dimness. He was wearing a coat over a three-piece suit. His shadow fell over the lapis lazuli tiles, darkening them.

"You're late," Cora said flatly.

She stepped out into the moonlight.

"Good to see you too, Cora," he said. He closed the door and locked it behind him. She made her way toward him, her heels clicking with a delicate sharpness against the tiles.

She looked, and felt, dangerous.

Jack gave a low whistle when Cora stepped into the light. She stopped short.

"We've been playing a game, haven't we?" Cora said. "I want it to end, now."

"All right," Jack said. He smiled. "Although I happen to find that games can be—"

He cut off when she showed him a bit of leg, the hilt of her gun. She gestured to the pool chair tucked into the alcove, which she had positioned out of sight of the door. He didn't get to control this, for once.

"Sit," she directed.

He whistled under his breath again, but the light had gone out of his eyes.

And when he moved, she saw that he had something with him. Something that looked like a satchel. She froze.

"Put that on the floor," she said. "And push it toward me."

He complied, setting the pack on the tiles and giving it a gentle shove in her direction.

Then he gave her a bow, the humor gone from his face, and made a show of sitting.

"I don't know what you mean when you say we've been playing a game," he said carefully. "I haven't been playing one, Cora."

"But you haven't been completely honest, either. Have you?"

He was silent.

She was dying to have it out with Jack, once and for all. So she could finally leave him and this place behind on her own terms.

"I've noticed a pattern with you, Jack."

"And what's that?" he asked.

"That you've grifted everyone you've ever met. The Pelican guards, your contact in the underground. Florence. Me."

"Is that why you brought me here?" he asked. "We're back to that again? An interrogation?"

She turned on a flashlight and pointed it toward his face.

"I want to hear about the night of the Bastion heist. March 23rd, right?"

He squinted back at her. "All right."

"Start with that afternoon. What did you do?"

If nothing else, she was leaving with answers to the questions that had plagued her for half her life. The questions that had kept her awake at night through the years, as she stared up at the ceilings of her apartments in California and New York, wondering what the truth had been.

He inhaled warily. "All right. Fine. It was a Saturday. I . . . played some baseball in the neighborhood. Picked up some scraps of meat at the butcher for my ma."

"You remember that?"

"Of course. It was the last day of my life that was ever normal."

Cora had made honey bread with her mother the day before Jack escaped. It was one of the days that Cora felt itchy and irritable, and she had criticized the way her mother added the ingredients, the way the flour left a snowy print on her dress. But her mother refused to break that day, and eventually Cora had relented and apologized, and they had eaten the honey bread on chipped china and drunk tea, looking at catalogues. That was the last normal day of Cora's life. And it was seared like heated iron tongs in her memory.

She leaned forward.

"Now tell me. What were you and Leo doing on the evening you got caught inside the Bastion museum?"

*   *   *

Jack had kicked the can down the alley of that night so many times over the years. It was dark and painful, the stuff of nightmares. He didn't want to go back. But she was standing in front of him, shining that bloody light in his face.

"Can you turn that down a little?" he asked. "I know you're just being your charming detective self and all, but it's starting to give me a headache."

She acquiesced and shifted the light a little. He could see a bit of her leg and, despite the circumstances, it was driving him crazy.

"Start at the beginning," she ordered. There was a delicate, faint pulse showing at the base of her neck.

He closed his eyes. The light from the bulb was still hot on his corneas and he could see it, blazing like a halo.

"Leo and I had gone for dinner," he said slowly. "Leo was pretty dizzy with this dame he'd known from school. He wanted to ask her out on a proper date, but he chickened out, like I told you. So we walked the area of this flower shop where she worked while he tried to get up the courage."

"This girl. She never saw you?"

"No."

"So no one could verify your claims."

"Right." He shivered and looked away. Leo had never gotten over the shame of it. If only he'd had courage earlier that night, and not later. Their whole lives would have fallen differently.

"What was the flower shop called?" Cora asked.

"Forget-Me-Knots. Spelled like k-n-o-t-s—you know, like the kind you tie."

"And the girl?"

"The girl was called Lila O'Malley. Leo and I were walking around that area until nine o'clock while he tried to get up his courage. Ever been there? That grassy strip along the Fens?"

Cora shrugged. "It was dark by then, I'd imagine?" she asked instead.

"Pitch-black. Hardly any streetlamps. It had just started to rain." He could still remember the way the chill set in, seeping down to his bones.

"What did you talk about?" she asked. "Do you remember?"

"School. Architecture. Starlets. Stupid kid stuff."

"And then what happened?" she asked. He heard the sound of a waterfall pouring into the pools, felt the heat of the room in perspiration on his lip.

"We were crossing the street at the corner just outside the museum. We were going to grab the streetcar home."

"Leo had given up on talking with the girl at that point?"

"He knew he'd missed his shot. The flower store was closed and Lila walked right past us. He mumbled hello, but she didn't even hear it. He was kind of glum like that way he'd get sometimes, and I was trying to cheer him, doing this god-awful impression of Charlie Chaplin. We were waiting on the bench for the streetcar to come. And then we heard this horrific scream." He swallowed. He still remembered the sound of it; how it had instantly turned his blood to ice.

Cora tilted her head. "What did you do?"

"It was late. The museum was supposed to be closed and the street was empty. Leo said to me: 'Did that come from the museum?'"

It was as if Jack could see it playing out again on a screen in front of him. Him and Leo, standing there hesitantly, those moments crystallized forever in time. "You want to know the truth?" he asked ruefully. His chest felt hollow. "In that moment, I didn't want to help. I just wanted to run." He had never admitted that to anyone. He was used to being the one who jumped off the highest branch into the creek, climbed the fence posts and got his hands cut up into ribbons with barbed wire, dared Leo to talk to girls. Some nights, when Jack felt like being generous to himself, he wondered if maybe it had been less about cowardice and more of a premonition. If they hadn't gone—if they had just called for the police instead. . . .

"So, Leo was the one who went first?" Cora's eyebrow arched. "Sounds unlike him."

"Right. He always wanted to stop and think things over, weigh all the options before he made any big decisions." Jack shrugged and sighed. "He told me once on Pelican that he blamed himself for everything that happened to us. But he had been so sick and tired of feeling like a coward, after he chickened out on the thing with Lila."

"What happened next?" Cora asked.

"We found the museum door set ajar with a crowbar, and a woman screamed again from somewhere inside. The sound of this woman was awful. She was hysterical, screaming for help. Saying something about her children."

Cora's eyes narrowed. "Why wasn't she mentioned in anything I read about?"

"We told the cops and the jury, but somehow that part of the story never made it into the papers. Just another part of the slam job against us."

"What was she doing when you came upon her?"

"I actually never saw her," Jack admitted. "That was the thing. We followed the woman's voice deep into the museum, but the whole thing was a setup. To frame us. There was no woman, no children. Instead, all we found were the guards, tied up and bleeding."

Jack grimaced, his chest tightening. He still saw it sometimes in his nightmares, the way they had walked into the gallery room and seen the two guards, pale as anything. Tied with wires and sitting in chairs, their mouths bound, their blood spilling onto the floor like slicks of dark red oil. One of them was clearly already gone by the angle of the way his head was tilted, and it had made Leo retch.

Jack had reached the one whose head was still lolling and ripped off the cotton binding around his mouth. "It's going to be all right," Jack had told him. "We're going to get you help. Where is the woman who screamed?"

But the man was already fluttering in and out of consciousness.

"What do we do?" Jack had pleaded to Leo, but more to himself. He had been starting to back away. It had smelled like sweat and iron, a nightmare scene set amongst the silent, priceless art. Except for the pieces that had been cut clean from the walls.

"The guards were covered in blood, then," Cora said. "The same blood that was found all over your clothes and hands when the cops showed up."

"We tried to help stanch it." Jack had taken the razor blade he found next to the chair and tried to cut the ropes free. He still remembered the way the guards' blood had been slick and warm. How he'd slipped in it and tried to stay upright. "We weren't running when the police came. We were just in the wrong place at the wrong time."

"And the guards were dead by the time the police did arrive," she said. "So they couldn't tell what really happened. That might be seen as rather convenient."

"I'd say that was actually pretty damn *in*convenient for us," Jack snapped. He knew, like any good investigator, that she was hunting around and pushing his buttons. It was working.

"You were the only two people still alive they found in the whole place."

"And with none of the art. Don't you think that's pretty incredible, Cora? We were two poor Irish youths from Dorchester, and they pinned it on us. They never found the art. They convicted us without ever even finding it. Where would we have put it? Come on. We would have run. Why would we stick around with the guards' blood on our clothes? Why wouldn't we have fled with this supposed accomplice?"

"Your version makes sense. But the court's does, too." She swung the light away in reprieve.

"And then there were the photographs of us. Damning ones, coming out of the Bastion handcuffed and covered in blood. Someone who happened to be there at just the right moment to snap them."

"The person who paid Byrd off to frame you," she said. And then her face changed as she watched him. She had seen something in him that he hadn't meant to show. "There's something more, though," she said. She studied him, her eyes bright and ringed with gold. "Isn't there?"

There was. He'd had a growing suspicion that there was more to the story than he had guessed. Cora was an even better private investigator than he had realized. He tried not to notice the way the delicate chain around her neck slipped around her collarbone. The way her full mouth was turning with that calculating look on her face. It was surprising how fearsome she could be. And even more surprising how attractive Jack found it.

"Jack," she said. "Where are the photographs you took of Clem and Truman tonight?"

He raised his eyebrows. He hadn't known she was there. She was full of surprises.

But then again, so was he.

He gestured toward the satchel on the floor near her foot. Cora nodded, eyes narrowing. But her hand stayed near her gun, at the ready, just in case.

He reached into the satchel and handed something to her.

It was a camera.

"Where did you get this?" she asked. Her brow knit in confusion, near the small scar on her forehead. "And how did you know where to be tonight?"

"I had an accomplice."

Cora looked up sharply. "Daisy?"

"No," he said. "Clem."

In her eyes, he watched as the realization dawned. "These will cost Byrd the presidency," Cora said slowly. "And perhaps half of his fortune. Why would she do that?"

"It's self-preservation. She wants to be the new Mrs. Byrd."

"And this gets Mabel out of the way," Cora said.

"Right—as long as Clem doesn't get caught as the source of the leak. I offered to do the dirty work of getting it to the competing papers for her. She has no idea you're involved at all."

"That *I'm* involved?" Cora asked. Faltering.

Jack loosened his tie around his neck. "I was only there tonight as backup," he said simply. "In case you didn't get my message."

"Your message. . . ." She moved imperceptibly as the pieces clicked into place.

He felt a flush of warmth. Such a simple, stupid thing. To give someone a gift. To be the source of pleasure, rather than pain. "You didn't trust me—understandably," he said. "I didn't think you'd come if the message was from me."

"You're giving up your leverage to blackmail Byrd," she said, in disbelief. "For me."

He had been so single-minded for so long. So fixated on himself, his goal of justice and revenge. It was like a sweet breath of air, to think of someone else. He had realized, standing on that staircase with Clem, that if he betrayed Cora to get what he wanted, he would never truly be free. Leo and Rusty would still be dead. But Jack had been given another chance, to finally make one thing right.

Cora was giving him the opportunity to hold on to the better part of himself.

Just like she always had.

He rubbed the back of his neck and didn't meet her eyes. She took a step toward him, and he braced himself against the nearness of her. In that dress that made him almost forget his own name.

"Jack," she said, her lips a half-step from smiling, and he heard a thousand different things in her voice.

✳   ✳   ✳

A shock of warmth rushed through Cora's body. She was feeling lightheaded.

She didn't need his photographs, and anyway she knew undoubtedly that hers were better. But that wasn't the point.

"What if we could use these for both of our purposes?" she asked. "What if I give them to Mabel for the newspapers but you could confront Truman before they ran? We could play them against each other."

"I'm not so sure about that," Jack said slowly. She saw the twitch in his jaw again, the one she'd glimpsed earlier. The hint of something more, something that was making him wary. "I'm starting to wonder if Byrd was more involved than I thought."

She stopped short. "You think Truman Byrd was behind all of this?" she asked.

"At first I didn't," Jack said. "I knew he was broke back then. He didn't have the money at the time to make those payouts to the other witnesses. I thought someone was paying him off, too. But now I'm wondering if he was more involved. Deep enough that even blackmailing him wouldn't be enough to get him to come clean."

"How deep are we talking?" Cora asked.

"One of the paintings from the heist that night was never sold. The only reason someone would hold on to it rather than take the money is because it had value of a personal nature."

She searched his face. "What are you saying, Jack?"

"I think it's possible that that painting is here."

His eyes were blazing like coals, and she almost couldn't catch her breath. She was aware of how little space remained between them, how easy it would be to reach out and touch him. She hadn't missed the way he had looked at her when he came in the door and did a double-take at her dress. It had sent delicate sparks shooting straight through her.

He took off his tie. Then he knelt and began to unknot his shoes.

"What are you doing, Jack?" Cora asked. She followed the smooth curve of his back. She told herself she shouldn't.

"Someday," he said, stripping off his socks, "I want to tell my future children I swam in this ridiculous pool."

"Your future children?" Cora asked.

He grinned at her suggestively. She felt a zinging shock all the way through her body.

She saw the flex of his hands. Remembered the warm pressure of them on her waist, the way he had wrapped them around her rib cage.

This could not happen. There was too much history between them. And no possible future.

He stripped off his pants, down to his knickers, and she flushed as she saw the smooth definition of his chest. Traced down the hard lines to his stomach muscles. There was a bandage on his arm, covering the path the bullet must have left across his skin.

He eased himself into the water, his arms tightening, grimacing the slightest bit as the water reached the bandage. He took a deep breath and dove under the surface, reemerging a moment later. His hair was wet and dark across his forehead. Water dripped from his eyelashes. Cora's mouth went dry.

"Water's warmer than I thought," he said.

He cocked an eyebrow. Like he was extending an invitation.

Cora felt something awaken within her. She kept her eyes on him as she parted the dress's slit around her upper thigh and unstrapped her gun. She laid it next to the camera he had brought. It was healing an old, deep scar, that he had risked himself to help her, just as she had done for him all those years ago.

She reached down and, one by one, took off her heels.

He treaded water, hungrily watching her every move.

She rolled down her stockings, stripping them off her legs. She looked at him as she glided her dress off her shoulder and stepped out of it, down to her slip, never breaking eye contact. She could feel the satin clinging to her in the heat, and he made a sound like clearing his throat. She padded softly toward him, the tile warm and slick beneath her footsteps.

He looked as though he were barely breathing by the time she reached the edge of the pool.

"This is how it's supposed to go, isn't it?" she asked. "We fight," she began. She slipped into the warm water, feeling it slide up her leg like a caress, until it reached her thighs, her hip bones. "And then . . . ?"

Jack swallowed hard. She saw the handsome angles of his face. His cheekbones and jawline. His black hair, his eyes darkening with something else. She smelled the familiar, beckoning scent of him.

His lips parted, sending droplets of water down the curve of his mouth, and all she could think about was everything this man had given up for her.

Everything she needed to settle her own future and even destroy his, if she wanted.

The waves parted around her waist and she felt the satin of her slip grow slick against her body. He had an almost inscrutable look on his face.

"You are gorgeous," he said, and she flushed with pleasure because she sensed how deeply he meant it. Her breathing hitched as she came to a stop in front of him. He hesitated. Then he reached out to graze his fingertips across her face, as light as butterfly wings. She closed her eyes and tilted her face toward him. He swept his thumb over her cheekbone, her lips. Her heart was beating hard and frantic beneath her ribs.

"Jack," she said, faltering. She didn't know if she could handle this. She had both wanted him and hated him for so long that she felt like she could crack.

He took a small step back. "We don't have to do this," he said gently.

"I've felt so many things for you over the years," she said, trailing off.

His lips parted. "I believe you. You've confused the hell out of me this week," he said wryly. "I came here wanting one thing. And now everything has changed."

She could see his pulse beating furiously at the base of his throat.

"I'm sorry that I hurt you all those years ago," he said, his hand flexing in the water. "I've always wanted to make it up to you. I know this doesn't quite do that. But I hope you can forgive me someday."

He ran a frustrated hand through his hair, and he gave her a look that made her ache. She hadn't known until that moment how much she had needed him to say those words. She felt an old, corroded part of her heart coming loose. And beneath it, she could feel warmth pooling in her body.

"I forgive you, Jack," she said. "You're free from what happened between us." She moved through the water toward him. It was true—remembering Pelican was like touching an age-old bruise and finding the tenderness healed. She stood on her tiptoes and brought her lips to whisper in his ear. "And now I'm free too."

His hands tightened around her waist and her body ignited. He looked her in the eyes and smiled.

And then he kissed her.

His mouth was warm and soft, and she drank him in. Musk and mint, familiar and new. She felt the rough shadow of stubble on his face, the shock of heat that went through her. She couldn't believe this was happening.

"You can't even imagine," he said hoarsely, "how good you feel," and she felt dizzy as he sent glittering sparks across every nerve in her body. He kissed her collarbone, setting off a fresh burst of fire that made her draw a sharp breath and sent a drop of water caressing a delicate line down the front of her slip. Her thoughts were dissolving. All those years of tension and anger and want and confusion had built up and were now coming to a head.

She lost her footing in the water, accidentally pressing into him, and he made a dark sound that curled through her.

"I've wanted to do this since the night in the basement cellar," he whispered, shuddering as she kissed all along his ear. He slid his hand up the curve of her hip, yanking her slip back down to cover where it had ridden up her thigh, as though his desire to protect her and his want for her were warring inside him. She drew his mouth back to hers, delicious and desperate. Blissful and dizzy with want pulsing through her veins. The thrill of feeling it reflected in him.

Jack picked her up and carried her to the edge of the pool. The water lapped at the smooth skin of his stomach, the muscles that cut into them. Pushing her gently up onto the ledge, he growled and urgently kissed along her jaw. He stroked his fingertips along the tender skin at the back of her knees and set her alight.

Then he drew his hands back, where they weren't quite touching her, and it drove her wild.

"Why did you stop?" she asked breathlessly. Her whole body was on fire.

"I don't want to go too far," he said, gasping. "I can't be with you until I'm free."

She pulled him toward her. "Jack," she said in his ear.

"I love that," he said, making a noise as he kissed her throat. "When you say my real name."

She whispered it again and again. She wanted to stay there forever, knowing him and being known by him, glowing brighter and burning wherever he touched.

CHAPTER THIRTY-TWO

SATURDAY, MAY 3, 1930
~ Day Seven ~

The next morning, Cora's lips were pillowy and bruised from kissing Jack. She ran her fingertips over them, smiling with pleasure. A tingle shot down her spine every time she thought of him. The simmering anger she felt when she believed he had double-crossed her had given way to a hope-tinged fear that it was too good to be true. Until the way he had looked at her; the smile that had parted his mouth when he kissed her.

Feeling alive and on edge, Cora watched the sunlight cut through the wood beams of the Astral Suite in gold mist. There was no room to feel tired, even though she had barely slept. There was a rush pulsing through her veins, her lips buzzing as she delivered Clementine's tray the final time. She could still feel the way Jack's arms tightened hungrily around her waist. The undeniable thrill she had felt when she realized that he had chosen her future over his past.

Cora stole a glance at Clementine as she slept, curled up within her satin sheets. Her breaths were even and her hair spilled out across the pillow, a jewel-toned satin sleep mask secure across her face. She was lovely in the golden light.

Cora wanted to thank her. Clementine had set several things in motion that were going to change Cora's life, Truman's, Mabel's—and her own. But it was more than that, Cora realized. Clementine had set her free from something Cora didn't even realize she wanted.

It was the freedom from having to betray her.

"Any messages left for me?" Cora asked Daisy under her breath when she reached the kitchens.

Daisy shook her head.

She took one look at Cora's lips and raised her eyebrows.

Cora flushed.

"Get going, ladies," Macready barked. "This is the busiest day of the year." She set them to work on so many tasks that Cora wasn't able to steal away again for another hour.

As soon as she could, she settled into the telephone booth and closed the door behind her. She called the Fairmont. There was no answer.

With a slight note of alarm, she left another message for Mabel.

And then she realized, too late, that she had forgotten to call her father.

$$* \quad * \quad *$$

Truman ate a cherry iced pastry at his desk and examined the miniature train car. He touched the carriage gingerly, because the gold paint was starting to fall off in chips. He took a sip of black coffee. Today would have been Elias's fifty-ninth birthday.

It had felt like fate that Truman had been standing in front of *The Resurrection of Lazarus* at the Bastion when he was given the chance to resurrect what was already over. He had done the final math that very morning, counted out every last cent, and had forced himself to face reality. His tabloid had been running for two years, and it wasn't close to breaking even. He would have to return to his father and be humiliated by the man who had, as it turned out, been right about him. He would be emasculated in front of

Mabel. His dignity had been stripped off in patches like birch bark, exposing the soft, raw wood of himself beneath.

He had eyed the *Lazarus*. It had been his mother's obsession after Elias had died. Truman remembered visiting the Chicago museum when it was on loan, going almost every day. They went to look at it more than they visited Elias's grave site. So Truman had lingered there, that fateful day years later at the Bastion, where it had long since been returned from its loan. He had stared at the swirls of paint the same way he had done when he was a boy, standing next to his mother, taking her gloved hand in his when she had started to cry and he had felt the unbearable pinch of sadness in his belly. He had always turned it to anger. Just like he'd seen his father do.

"My mother and I used to look at this painting for hours," he had said softly to Mabel. Only she was no longer standing next to him. She had moved on to the next room, wearing that red dress, looking like a firecracker even despite the crowds. The museum had been Dolores Bastion's home once, and it was kept dim and shadowy, with the drapes drawn and flickering, low-lit sconces on the walls.

That was when Truman had seen the man saunter up to Mabel. He'd tried to cop a feel, bending to whisper something suggestive in her ear.

Truman had come up silently behind them.

"Come on, sugar," the man had said, his hot breath in Mabel's face. He had tried again, this time putting his hand up her dress. She had slapped his hand away, and the man had laughed and then leered at her.

When he turned, Truman had seen that the man was wearing a guard's uniform. He worked at the Dolores Bastion museum.

"Who's this?" the guard had asked, when he saw Truman's expression.

"Her husband," Truman answered. "And I'll kill you and drop your body in the Fens out there if you touch her again."

The guard had laughed at him. "Next time, why don't you pick someone who can pay his own way?" he'd asked Mabel.

Truman could hardly remember what had happened next. That old anger, the humiliation of eating beans and watching balances dwindle. Of Elias and his mother rotting away in their coffins while Truman knew his father would trade him for them in the span of half a blink. And worst of all—the flash of shame that had crossed Mabel's face before she could hide it.

He had blacked out with fury, lost control and started throwing wild punches, and he wasn't even sure whether they were meant for his father, the man from the printing press threatening to shut him down, or the guard who had tackled him and was now calling for backup. Truman completed his spiral of disgrace by being readily escorted out, a bruise already forming around his right eye. He was informed that he could never return to the Bastion again—paying guest or not. And then, while his buddies held Truman down, the lecherous guard had kicked him repeatedly in the ribs for good measure.

That had been the death of the old Truman.

Next would come the resurrection that would change everything.

✳   ✳   ✳

Cora's heart turned to a deep thudding as she picked up the telephone.

An image of Jack grabbing her thigh came into her mind. "Now everything has changed," he'd whispered.

She took a deep breath. She couldn't think about that now. Especially before she placed a call to her father.

She would think about it later.

She picked up the receiver and dialed the Bitterlake police department.

Chief Bellanger picked up on the second ring.

She gritted her teeth.

"Chief Bellanger," she said warmly. "It's Cora McCavanagh. Is my father there?"

"Miss McCavanagh," Bellanger drawled. "We need to keep this line open for emergencies. It isn't a private number for family chit-chats."

"Family emergency," she corrected him coolly. "And it's rather urgent. Is he there?"

"No."

She exhaled. She could practically hear Chief Bellanger adjusting his oversized belt buckle in the background.

"I just need him to know that I'm all right and that I'll be home on Sunday. Could you tell him that for me?"

"We'll see," he said. "I'm not the secretary."

"Thank you, you've been supremely helpful, as always," she said, and hung up on him.

*　　*　　*

Clem dressed in an emerald day dress with puffed sleeves that was cut low and tied around the waist—one of Truman's favorites—and drank the coffee Ella had left her. She was too nervous to eat any of the food beneath the domed trays, and instead left the house and wandered the grounds. The morning was warm, and she nodded at some of the groundskeepers as she passed them on the paths. She trailed a lone peacock, watching its feathers spread out behind it like a jeweled bridal train, and then plucked off a handful of rose petals, wondering what she had done. Truman could easily ruin her if he found out—and would he? Would her career be over? Would she be sent packing back to Florida, with her mother tsking and the neighbors shunning her at the grocery store? She had put away some of the money from her films, but it wasn't nearly enough to last for the rest of her life—especially at the lifestyle she hoped to live. Perhaps she would end up like the rest of them after all, working for pennies, the fine dresses and caviar a distant memory, turning to dust in her mouth.

Maybe she should have just been content with what she had.

She shredded the soft petals in her fingers and let them trail to the ground.

She would find out soon enough.

CHAPTER THIRTY-THREE

Truman's private theater was nestled deep in the west wing of the second floor. It was dark and windowless, and had lush crimson curtains hanging across the suspended screen. The walls were filigreed with twenty-four carats of paper-thin hammered gold that made them look like they were smoldering with fire when the sconces were lit.

Cora stole inside for a chance to think. She paced through the dim theater, examining the framed film posters on the golden walls.

A moment later, Jack slipped in after her. She was somehow aware of his presence before she even saw him, as if her body were attuned to him, and she felt the rush he caused within her everywhere.

She pushed him roughly against the wall and kissed him, his hands running like lightning over her body.

"I found some more of the pattern yesterday," she said, kissing down his throat.

"What is it?" he asked, his voice like dusk.

"The code, hidden all over the house." She slid off him and turned to examine the frames again.

He traced a finger down her neck, sending delightful shivers down her spine.

"This is distracting," she murmured as he lifted her hair and kissed the nape of her neck. "Do you want my help, or not?"

"I haven't decided," he said. "Right now, this is pretty much all I want."

"Look," she insisted, taking a step away. She smoothed her uniform, re-pinned her mussed hair, and tried to calm her racing pulse.

She pointed to the posters. "What do you see?"

He studied them, a frown drawing his brows together. *"Ben-Hur, Yasmina, Radio Magic, Dante's Inferno."*

"Yes," she said. "They fit the pattern." Her eyes traced along the wall. "But what about these?"

She pointed to a series of frames that held the posters *Berlin, Robin Hood, Destiny.*

"It's missing the Y," she murmured. "Isn't it?"

"There are only so many films that start with *Y*, I'd gather," Jack said.

"No," she said, coming closer. "There's something more." She stopped to examine it. "There's a hidden door here into the projector room, between *Berlin* and the *Robin Hood,*" she said. The gears of her mind were turning. "I think it's not knowing the pattern that's important—it's being able to tell when something *doesn't* fit."

"Riddles upon riddles," he murmured. He looked up at her.

"You helped me," she said. "Now I want to help you."

The youthful light in his eyes returned. He took her face in his hands, cradling it. "Have I mentioned before that you're brilliant?" he murmured. A beautiful smile crossed his face, breaking like the dawn.

Her stomach tipped.

"I'm glad I met you, Cora McCavanagh," he whispered in her ear. "Twice."

*　　*　　*

There were brass owls perched along the faucets in the pools' guest houses.

Doves embedded in the circular plaques of the ballroom's outer walls.

Carvings of herons in the bell tower. Blackberries, yucca, raspberries, and dahlias in the tiles in the bathhouses of the outdoor pools.

Jack strolled the path, eyes sharpened, as the gardeners brought in pots of white roses and golden-rayed lilies for the night's final event. Clementine ignored him as he approached the clay tennis courts. She was finishing a round of doubles with Simon Leit, William Morton, and Kitty.

"Coming to the picnic?" Simon called, wiping his face with a towel.

"In a bit," Jack said.

"Save me a card game tonight?" Kitty asked. She leaned against her racquet, her red lips curving into an inviting smile.

He smiled at Kitty, polite and non-committal, and kept moving. The water in the outdoor pool was turquoise and brilliant in the sun, and he could see the black tiled egret in the center. The water would be crisp and cold, unlike last night. He tipped his head back and smiled, feeling the sun warm his face. Cora had tasted like apples.

He was headed toward the catacombs Florence had mentioned, left beneath the West Terrace where builders had built over the old ruins, and he examined the tiles and the greenery. He felt a sense of gamesmanship, a quickening in his veins while he searched for an entrance.

Look for the thing that was off.

He saw the same set of mosaic tiles that he had followed to the hidden entrance of the bell tower. He examined them now. Blue, yellow, red, green. Blue, yellow, red, green. He followed the pattern until two of the tiles changed. Instead of green, they were white.

BYRW.

No, Jack thought.

Dutch white. Florence had said that Truman only used Dutch white.

The BYRD pattern completed—that's what Jack had to look for.

He pulled the greenery back and found an alcove hidden behind it. He stepped inside.

The catacombs were cool and stark. There wasn't much to be seen; just old staircases and dust. Jack stood inside for a moment, breathing. He thought of the missing painting of the *Lazarus*. He'd studied the art incessantly following his years at Pelican, learning everything he could about the paintings that had stolen his life. It had become almost an obsession. Because he knew they were the trail of breadcrumbs, leading both before and behind him. *The Raising of Lazarus* was a depiction of Jesus, dark and shadowy. Extending an outreached hand over a man sitting up in a tomb. It would be roughly three by two feet in size.

He made his way deeper into the tunnel. The path slanted downward.

He glanced up at a dripping sound. Water, and perhaps some other liquid, leaked through the joints above his head to create stalactites, and Jack knew that no priceless artifacts, no paintings would be hidden here. It was too damp.

He stopped. The rest of the catacombs had been concreted in. A dead end.

Unease prickled at him with each new find. The feeling that this wasn't an obsession of a well-ordered mind. Perhaps it was too strong to think of it as a sociopathic tendency. Perhaps it spoke of a deep wound that had gone wrong somewhere—something that, instead of healing properly, festered along the way.

He turned back for the entrance and stepped out through the greenery.

"Everett? Is that you?"

Jack's head turned, his heart rate spiking upon recognition of the voice. Truman was walking alone, toward him. He was dressed in white for the picnic and had a jaunty cane in his hand. It clicked methodically on the tile walkway.

"Where did you come from?" he asked. His voice was nonchalant but his eyes were sharp.

Jack smiled. "Just trying to soak up every last minute in this place," he said easily.

It was then that Jack noticed Dallas Winston stationed at a careful distance behind Truman, watching him as closely as Jack had ever been watched on Pelican.

Jack knew he had bought himself enough reprieve from Truman's suspicion when he saved him from the bullet. But even that would only stretch so far.

"Shall we?" he said, gesturing down the hill toward the picnic. "I've heard the deviled eggs are so divine that they need a new name."

But Truman made no attempt to move. He fixed his eyes on Jack.

"Do you like fireworks, Mr. Conner?"

Truman's eyes were bloodshot. Jack stared back at the thin threads of red that webbed through the white and tried not to look away. "I'm not sure," Jack said. "I suppose I still feel a little jumpy about the idea of sudden, loud booms."

"Yes. Well. We couldn't end your time on the Hill without some sort of grand finale, now, could we?"

"Didn't we already have that?" Jack asked carefully.

Truman laughed; but to Jack's ears, it sounded more and more unhinged. "Maybe so," he said.

His cane scraped along the path like the point of a nail, with Dallas Winston following behind.

*　　*　　*

From the fourth-floor balcony, Cora saw Truman leading Jack down the hill for the picnic. When he was a safe distance away, Cora moved soundlessly toward Byrd's room.

She paused over the photographs that hung in the hallway. At first glance, they were travel images. But upon closer inspection, she realized they were Barcelona,

Yosemite,

Rome,

and Damascus.

She shivered a little and felt for the presence of false walls, passages, or panels in the walls behind them.

But there was nothing false there.

For once, everything was just as it seemed.

Cora hesitated outside the closed door to Byrd's bedroom. She had never stepped inside it before. She pushed open the door. It smelled like him— expensive cologne and aftershave. There was an antlered chandelier hanging from the ceiling; dark paneled oak walls; and a coffered ceiling plated with gold leaf. She stepped inside, closing the door behind her, and made her way to the closet, where she rummaged through the shelves holding his leather shoes and silk ties. She examined a carved box with engraved flowers and a small silver duck sculpted on top. Inside were cigars, a pistol, and a deck of playing cards. It made her think of Jack. She knew that they were running out of time to find the files, and the truth about the Bastion—but perhaps he would gain some satisfaction knowing that he'd played a part in taking half of Byrd's fortune from him. Maybe that was the cost of the future Jack had lost.

Maybe it was the closest thing to justice Jack was ever going to see in this lifetime.

Cora suddenly heard the creak of a floorboard just outside the door.

She held her breath, dropped to her knees, and crouched behind the Italian writing desk. She forced herself to breathe quietly and, like a child, she slipped her hand into her pocket and let it close around the worry stone.

Dallas Winston poked his head into Truman's room and glanced around it. Cora stilled, waiting for what felt like an endless moment. Finally he closed the door again behind him and moved on down the hallway.

She rose, letting the worry stone drop back into her pocket. She pictured her father's worn, tired face. The lines downturning at his mouth. About what her mistake had cost him. And about what Jack had said.

The way he had looked at her, his eyes like deep wells, when he said: "Redemption is only possible with the truth."

That was out of the question. She would still rather live the rest of her life wearing a chain-mail jacket of guilt than ever let her father know the truth.

Which also meant that after tomorrow, she could never see Jack again.

The thought filled her with so much sadness that when she stood, she almost missed it. A tapestry, hanging on the wall next to Truman's bed. It was a giant oak tree, covered in all different kinds of fruit. Oranges, apples, lemons, and persimmons. All except for one branch.

She drew closer.

There was a finch on it.

The tapestry was caught behind the massive four-poster bed, and she had to use all her strength to move it even an inch. The tapestry was thickly woven and was attached to rings at the ceiling like all the other tapestries, but this one hung loose at the bottom edge.

She stepped beside the bed and gently pulled the tapestry's hem away from the wall.

Behind it, she found an enormous safe. A vault door. Large enough to possibly lead to an entire, secret room.

*　　*　　*

When the guests were beginning to drift away from the picnic, Cora waited in the shadows of a tree, hanging thirty paper lanterns at Macready's direction. She watched Jack make his way back up the hill. She tried to judge by the way his head was turned down, the slope of his body, and the length of his stride, whether he had found anything.

"Keep moving, Miss Duluth. We need a hundred of these up by tonight," Macready said, shoving another armful of paper lanterns at her.

Cora bit her lip and steadied her hands, using a pocketknife to cut the strands of ribbon and then tie the cream lanterns into the boughs of the trees. She had decided that tomorrow, when the parties were done and the guests had departed, she would buy a ticket to San Francisco. She would make arrangements to meet Mabel at her room in the Fairmont, and they could do the deal in person there. Mabel would have her negatives and Cora would have enough money to start the rest of her life.

She felt a twinge. Whatever that was going to be.

Finally, Macready stopped observing her and moved on to her next task. Cora glanced toward Jack's room, preparing to dump the rest of the lanterns somewhere. She was so engrossed that she almost didn't hear the clearing of a throat.

She stepped down from the ladder, peering through the boughs, to find Matias Rojas, the chauffeur. He had slicked-back hair that always smelled faintly of verbena, and Daisy thought he looked a little like the actor Ramon Novarro.

He gestured to her with an air of not wanting to be seen, and she followed him to the shadows that the main house threw onto the walkway.

He thrust a folded piece of paper toward her.

MESSAGE RECEIVED.

EN ROUTE.

MEET AT THE AIR STRIP, 5 P.M.

"I'll drive you," he said. He walked away, leaving her to stare after him wordlessly as his steps echoed on the tiles.

CHAPTER THIRTY-FOUR

J ack unlocked his door, opened it, and came face to face with Cora. A smile filled his mouth, his entire face.

He wouldn't think about what came after tomorrow.

He felt almost deliciously drunk.

In one motion, he pulled her into the safety of his room and closed the door behind them.

"Found anything yet?" she asked hazily, pulling at the collar of his shirt.

"No," he said. "You?"

She flashed him a delighted, mischievous smile.

"What is it?" he asked, his pulse taking off in a gallop.

"There's a safe," she said. "Big enough to be a vault, even."

"Where?"

"Behind a tapestry in Truman's bedroom."

His heart stopped. "How do you get into it?"

"There's a code. Four letters."

"Did you crack it?"

She shook her head. "I didn't have much time. I tried B-Y-R-D, of course. And B-I-R-D."

"Damn. I suppose he wouldn't make it that obvious."

"We should make a list of every four-lettered type of bird we can think of," Cora said. "And tonight you'll have to find a time to slip away, when everyone else is distracted."

"Truman said there would be fireworks," Jack said. He winced. "Though I do get the sense that Dallas Winston suspects something is up. It's going to be hard to shake him."

Cora inhaled deeply. "I have a feeling that a prime opportunity will present itself to us tonight."

He looked at her. "The fireworks?"

"Of a sort," she said. "Mabel Byrd is coming."

"Here?" Jack felt the blood drain from his face.

"Tonight. She's on her way right now. Truman has no idea."

Jack closed his eyes.

"What?" Cora whispered. She touched his face gingerly. "Jack, what is it?"

He shook his head. "Mabel is the one Truman sent to cover the trial," he said, opening his eyes. "The moment she sees me, I'm done for."

*   *   *

Mabel Byrd was flying over the swaths of green in Truman's biplane.

"I'd like to surprise him," she told the pilot. "I'll pay you triple to keep this one little flight a secret."

It was her plane, too, but not for much longer.

She looked out over the hills for what would likely be the last time. She remembered the first time she had flown to the Enchanted Hill with Truman. He had purchased the land and wanted to show it to her. Florence Abrams had met them there and they had hiked the hill together, the three of them standing at the crux of it, between old oak trees, and had looked out at the mountain range. Truman and Florence could see something she couldn't as they had dreamed up the house together. But she had breathed the salt air greedily, sucking it into her lungs after that climb.

"We own land as far as you can see," Truman had whispered in her ear.

After Florence had gone, they had eaten a picnic lunch under a grove of trees and made love out in the open, because there was no one else for miles.

"Mrs. Byrd," the pilot said now.

Mabel looked up. Just like the plane, that name wouldn't be hers for much longer, either. She felt the smallest prick at that. Names were such important, such personal things. She supposed she could keep it, but she would never wear it the same way again.

"We'll be arriving shortly," the pilot said, and she nodded brusquely. No use getting sentimental over something like a name—that was exactly the sort of ridiculous thing Truman had always indulged.

But Mabel had thought that any soft, fleshy part of her had hardened over like a shell long ago, and she was surprised to find that anything could get through anymore.

*　　*　　*

Matias was idling outside the zoo, parked where the road switchbacked and hid itself from the house. The car, a Bentley, had windows tinted like smoke, so that one could only see a faint outline of whoever might be inside.

Cora slid across the supple leather of the back seat.

The chauffeur turned the steering wheel and meandered out onto the road. He glanced at her in the rearview mirror. His brown eyes were unblinking.

"Is Mrs. Byrd paying you double, too, then?" he asked.

Cora stared at the monstrous castle disappearing behind them. The Mexican fan palms rose to heights even above the bell towers, swaying.

"No," she said simply. She crossed her legs at the ankle and felt the film canister nudge against her breast.

She had no idea what the night would bring. If Jack would flee before giving Mabel the chance to spot him. If he would leave her a note with some way for her to reach him—or if not, if they would ever meet again. She pictured herself waiting with her heart in her throat every time the telephone rang, or the postman came to the door. Always waiting, hoping, for something that might never come.

But she still had time. She would see this through to the end. It mattered less what the score was between her and Jack; they had helped and wounded each other in a hundred different ways. Now all she wanted to do was set him free.

The airstrip was little more than a mile down the road, a narrow stripe shorn into the emerald grass of a field. It was set back away from the sea, but Cora could see the foaming waves, the kind that would knit white lace and then pull it back apart, scattering sprays of bubbles like pearls. Waves in a temper, she used to think when she was a girl. Tantrumming.

Matias parked the car and, without another word, pushed open his door. He leaned against it and lit a cigarette, watching the speck of a small airplane grow larger as it approached the airfield. It seemed to wobble in the clear blue sky, but landed and rolled to a sputtering stop on the grass in front of them.

Cora shifted, her heart beating harder. When the engines stopped spinning, the door opened and stairs unfurled. Mabel appeared in the doorway, looking like an aging starlet, dressed meticulously and draped in a fur. She had been beautiful once, and still was from a distance. But as she neared, the illusion fell away. Her sunglasses barely concealed her hollow cheeks and pale, papery skin. Cora knew that the woman wasn't that old—perhaps only in her late forties—and that while money couldn't buy youth, it usually had the power to make it at least appear more elastic. But Mabel seemed aged even from their meeting six months ago, brittle and bitter, her perfume masking something that would make one recoil.

When Matias opened the door for her, Cora noticed she was still wearing her wedding ring.

Matias loaded Mabel's bags into the trunk and slammed it shut. Mabel raised a manicured eyebrow at Cora and slid off her sunglasses. Her eyes were slightly bloodshot, but the diamonds distracted from that, hanging heavily from her drooping earlobes.

"Miss McCavanagh," she said in greeting.

"Hello, Mrs. Byrd," Cora said.

"Matias," Mabel purred as the chauffeur returned to the car and started the engine. "Has anyone made Truman aware that I'm coming?"

"No, Ma'am," Matias said. "No one knows of your arrival but the people in this automobile."

"Good," Mabel said, settling back into her seat. She let the fur drop behind her. "I'm hoping for the element of surprise. And I'm not planning on staying long."

There was a nervous excitement to her that had been absent at their first meeting. A joyful anticipation, Cora would have said, except that nothing about it was joyful.

"I had my doubts about you," Mabel said, eyeing Cora.

"I know," Cora said.

"Well?" Mabel asked, practically trembling. She peeled off her gloves, watching Cora with glittering eyes.

Cora placed a manila envelope into her hand.

Mabel opened the envelope's clasp and removed the contact prints, unwrapping the sheet like a delicate present. Cora had expected revulsion or hurt at what the images contained, but perhaps that had shriveled and become something else a long time ago.

Now there was just delight.

Mabel examined the contact print with a magnifying glass. "Well done, Miss McCavanagh."

"Those are merely contact prints," Cora said. "Evidence to prove that I have what I promised. The quality isn't good enough to run large-scale in a newspaper. I have the negatives, which I will hold as collateral until we've exchanged payment."

Matias's eyes flicked to the mirror, then back to the road.

"Here's half of what we agreed upon," Mabel said. She dipped into her handbag for her billfold and counted out a thick wad of bills, which she placed into Cora's hand. Cora could have sighed at the weight of them. "I'll wire you the rest to an account of your choice upon receipt of the negatives." Mabel folded the contact sheet away in her pocketbook.

Cora wrote out a bank number and then handed over the film canister.

Mabel looked inside, sealed it shut, and breathed a sigh of relief. One single set of prints meant a fortune for both of them. The door to Cora's future swung open. And Jack had been behind it all.

"You'll be grateful to know that I've already secured you another opportunity," Mabel said. The car turned left onto the road that led to Enchanted Hill, and the house came into sight for the first time. Mabel glanced up at it, expressionless. Her breath was faintly stale with cigarettes. "My good friend Trudy will be in touch. You can expect a payday like no other. You just made your life."

"Mrs. Byrd," Matias said, glancing over his shoulder from the front seat, "were you expecting company?"

Cora turned, her stomach flipping a little. A strange car had turned left off the main road and was following them up the hill.

"I've arranged for a few members of the press to be my personal guests tonight." Mabel smiled down at her hands as she rolled her gloves back on.

"Truman's press?" Cora asked.

"No," she said. "His rivals."

Cora hesitated. "Are you certain you want to do this in person?" she asked. "You could run the images in the papers tomorrow. Catch Mr. Byrd off-guard from a . . . safer distance away."

The corners of Mabel's mouth creased downward. She opened up a compact and reapplied her lipstick, a deep wine red. "As I recall, he likes fireworks on the final night of his parties," she said. "But I'm guessing those will be nothing in comparison."

The automobiles were coming to a stop in front of the tinted glass of the guardhouse. Matias was rolling down the window, and the security guard leaned his head into the car. Cora tilted her face away, hoping he would merely assume that she was Mabel's personal maid.

"Mrs. Byrd," he said, with unmasked surprise. "I wasn't expecting you."

"No one was," she said, giving him a coy smile. "I do hope you'll keep my secret a little longer." She gestured behind her. "And for the guests coming up in the second car. We have a big surprise planned for Truman."

The security guard's smile was like plaster.

He hesitated. "I'm under strict instructions to clear any unexpected arrivals with Mr. Winston," he said.

She laughed. "Are you suggesting I need permission to enter my own house?" she asked. There was an unmistakable edge of warning to it.

He wavered, and then relented. "Of course not. Come right in, ma'am," he said.

He gestured the car forward.

"Aren't you at all concerned about how he will react?" Cora asked.

"His temper, you mean? No." Mabel snapped her compact shut. "He can't afford to get out of control in front of his esteemed guests." She spoke faster, her excitement revealing a Brooklyn accent that Cora guessed had taken years of practice to erase. "I know he's been on the lookout for an assassin, but I'm better armed with a camera than a gun. That's why tonight is perfect."

The butlers began to retrieve the luggage from the car's trunk, and Mabel glanced back at the men disembarking from the second car. "If you're going to sell the world a story, better make sure it's the version you want told."

Mabel smiled and picked up her handbag with the contact sheets and negatives inside. She replaced her sunglasses. "Be careful tonight," she said, throwing open the door. "It wouldn't be wise, Miss McCavanagh, to ever let him know you were part of this."

* * *

Jack stood in front of the mirror and dressed for dinner.

He pulled his white necktie tight.

Then he packed his suitcase, ready to make a quick exit that night. If it came to that.

He hoped it would.

He tugged on his pristine white jacket.

Then he opened the chamber of Cora's gun and looked at the bullets.

CHAPTER THIRTY-FIVE

Truman leaned against the stone railing on the esplanade, sipping a Gibson martini beneath the towering Mexican palm fronds. He had requested white tie for dinner. It was the final evening of parties, and he expected his guests to pull out all the stops in glamour. So far, they hadn't disappointed. Clementine was wearing a satin dress in siren red that tied around her waist and found every curve on the way down. Kitty had on some art-deco monstrosity that was likely the latest fashion, and Lola was dripping in silver sequins. Clementine caught his eye and smiled over the rim of her drink. A private, meaningful smile. He had a hard time not returning to the way she had been last night. More passionate, more desperate. More like she had been at the very beginning.

Perhaps almost being assassinated in his own home did have its advantages.

He watched with calculated attention as Dallas Winston made his way through the party. He stood out against the gentlemen's white suits, dressed in a black tuxedo and bow tie. The look on his face was pinched and urgent. Truman took a long, slow sip of his drink. That expression was never a good sign.

Truman swallowed and looked behind Dallas.

The first thing Truman noticed about his estranged wife were her gloves. They were black satin. She was wearing a long black gown gathered with some enormous bow that probably cost as much of his money as a museum antiquity.

The look on her face was triumphant. A knowing smirk that set his veins on fire.

Mabel. That bitch.

He tried for another sip of his drink, but he had already drained it.

He felt the last drop of it hit his tongue as Mabel strode toward him. She knew she had him trapped—that he would have to be both civil and welcoming. It would have to be the best acting job of his life, pretending to be happy to see her.

"Mabel," he said. He embraced her with a kiss on each cheek. She smelled of menthol cigarettes and her perfume, which made his stomach turn. Out of nowhere, he remembered the night in New York City when they had climbed into an abandoned construction project. They had gotten drunk and dared each other to use the wooden scaffolding as a balance beam. When they had both survived the feat, they had made love and then had coffee with chocolate pie at Lottie's Diner afterward.

"How unexpected," he said.

"Surprise," she whispered in his ear, as if it were the most delicious thing she'd ever said.

He took her gently by the arm and smiled at his guests. "My wife, ladies and gentlemen," he said, and they all clapped and raised their glasses to her.

Clementine was watching intently, a flush rising in her cheeks. Her eyes were bright aquamarine. Kitty leaned forward to whisper something in her ear, then tittered and looked away.

Mabel took a glass of champagne from one of the servants and raised it to acknowledge the guests. Ronald Rutherford stepped forward to greet her.

"Mabel," he said.

"Ronnie," she said, kissing him on the cheek.

"Are you going to behave tonight?" he asked grimly.

"Now, does that sound like me?" she asked. She pinched his cheek.

Truman guided her to a more private balcony on the esplanade, where they could pretend to be retiring for a smoke.

"You've brought additional guests." He looked beyond her to three men who were helping themselves to canapes. None of them looked familiar. He leaned down to whisper menacingly in her ear, "Who are they?"

"They're here for my own protection," she said. She took a sip of champagne, then lit a match to flare against the end of her cigarette.

"Your own security?" he scoffed. "Good God, woman, do you actually think I'd try to kill you?"

"I think in your wildest fantasies you already do."

He gave a nod of acknowledgment. "Perhaps. And now that you mention it, are you sure that you don't have anything to do with the hit that was ordered on me?"

She didn't pretend not to know of it, a fact that made Truman slightly uneasy. "Of course not, Truman. A quick death would be too good for you. I'd choose something more subtle." She took a long drag. "Like poison."

She shot him a wicked look, as if they were flirting. And strangely, Truman felt as though they almost were.

She had once told his father off when she was liquored up on Relsky and blazing mad as a cat. Truman had actually wondered if she would try to scratch out his father's eyes. Franklin Byrd had been so used to treading up and down on Truman's mother that for a moment, he'd actually been speechless. Once he'd recovered, he had sneered and told Truman he'd better let Mabel go or he'd end up on the wrong side of the leash. Perhaps his father had been prophetic after all. But at the moment that Mabel had taken on his father and made him briefly mortal, Truman had never wanted anyone more.

"No, they are here for my security in other ways," Mabel said. "They're from the newspapers that you don't own. Try to send them away and see what happens. I'll make a scene like you can't imagine in front of all your high-profile guests." She tapped the cigarette so that the ash fell like dirty snow on the floral tiles. "And your mistress."

"Why are you here, Mabel?"

"I missed you," she said. "Am I not welcome here in my own home?"

Truman snorted.

Ronald Rutherford and Dallas Winston were watching from the shadows. So Truman did the only thing he could do. He summoned Macready and said, briskly, "Set the extra places for dinner."

*   *   *

Cora stepped inside the magnificent dining room, wheeling a chest of silver. The long oak table had been set for thirteen. Roses spilled across it in bursts of tangerine and dusk pink between tall white candlesticks. There were coral tea roses that smelled of cloves; deep pink Apothecary's Roses that Jack said were bred in ancient Persia. She and Daisy set out damask chairs and added four more place settings to the table. Lights reflected in the water of fingerbowls, which held floating golden and peach Soleil d'Ors and scarlet camellias.

Cora used silver tongs to tuck freshly baked rolls inside the crimson napkins, but she was thinking of a grotesque with four plaques of monsters on one of the outer walls. One of them she recognized from the Welsh flag, *Y Ddraig Goch*. She was certain it formed the Y in BYRD.

Kitty wandered in, wearing a dress the deep color of blackberries. There were diamonds woven through her hair that almost looked like tears.

"Can I help you, miss?" Cora asked.

She ignored Cora and nonchalantly strode toward the table. Leaned over to smell the roses, and palmed a name card. She switched it so that she was sitting by Beaumont Remington.

She took a piece of shrimp from one of the waiting trays and then sauntered back out of the room.

Cora moved to the table and did a switch of her own. She took the name card for Everett Conner and placed it at the other end of the seating arrangements, so that Jack would be as far away from Mabel as possible.

She reached into her pocket and felt the smooth lines of the worry stone. She had given Jack her gun.

All she had left in case things went sideways were the small pocketknife and a shred of ribbon left over from the lanterns.

∗   ∗   ∗

Jack pulled a folded paper list from his pocket in the heart of the Gothic library. He had made the initial list with Cora, and now he had an encyclopedia of birds spread open in front of him on the heavy oak table, scribbling down as many four-lettered names as he could find. He could hear the distant sounds of the party beginning as the guests made their way from their rooms down to the foyer.

He started down the hallway, toward where Cora told him to find Truman's room. He paused just outside the heavy oak door until he could hear the booming sound of Truman's voice several floors below. Then he glanced over his shoulder to the left and right and let himself inside.

The room smelled of cedar wood and Truman's cologne. Jack eyed the tapestry, finding the finch just as Cora had described. He strode forward and wrenched back the massive bed, moving it half a foot. Then he moved the tapestry and inhaled at the sight of the vault door. His fingers shook as he examined the bronze keys of the lock. They were raised letters, almost like the strikers of a typewriter. Thirty-six letters to choose from. Four spaces to enter.

"Almost there, Leo," he whispered.

Jack placed his fingers on the bronze letter dial. He clicked through, trying first B-Y-R-D and then B-I-R-D. It hadn't worked, just like Cora said. He tried C-L-E-M next. Nothing.

He felt a rush of anger, tinged with homesickness. He wanted so badly to go home. To knock on the door, like he was just coming back from a long day away rather than almost half of his lifetime. He wanted to see his mother's face light up. He didn't want it to be full of fear or anxiety, shutting the door on him. Feeling like she had to call the cops to turn him in.

He gritted his teeth and fiddled with the knobs. He knew, even if he could force Truman into printing a retraction, it would never be possible for him to truly go back home, not after what had happened with Rusty. Not without Leo by his side.

He moved to the list in his pocket, watching the ticking second hand of the gold clock on the mantel. The first ones were C-H-A-T and C-R-O-W.

He went through it methodically. There were forty-five options. All the way down to W-R-E-N.

By the time he came to the end, he was sweating profusely and his hand was starting to cramp.

The lock hadn't budged.

$$* \quad * \quad *$$

Cora left the kitchens lit and steaming with dinner: vichyssoise cooking in an enormous copper pot on the stove. French bread, crispy and fresh from the oven. Lamb with mint sauce. Pâté de foie gras.

The sky was a glowing yellow, the golden color of a comice pear, when Florence Abrams strode in wearing a tuxedo with a white bow tie and a white pocket square. "I'll have a drink," she said to Cora, and began to look around the room. As if she were searching for Jack.

"Wine?" Cora asked. "Whiskey?"

"Get me a Last Word."

When Cora returned, sunset was filtering into the Assembly Room through the loggia. It made the room feel cozier and striated with colors. The crimson unfurling roses and peonies were enormous and bursting, about to fall apart, lending themselves to an atmosphere that already felt lush and unbalanced.

Clementine kept to the edges of the crowd, making her way along. She smiled widely, and laughed. She truly was a better actress than most of her critics gave her credit for. But Cora could sense the barest hint of nervous energy. That aura of teetering balance, of looking over the precipice at a great fall.

Mabel was smoking a cigarillo over a chat with Simon Leit about the tennis courts in Monte Carlo. She stared Clementine down without greeting her, and exhaled a stream of smoke into her face at the moment she passed. It was clear that Mabel was toying with Truman. Making him pretend to be glad to see her, parading in front of his guests in his own home. A vein in Truman's neck subtly throbbed.

For the first time that night, Cora felt afraid.

*　　*　　*

Jack stood in front of the safe in the fading light. He had taken off his necktie and sweated through his shirt.

He cracked his knuckles and thought.

What was important to Truman? He had his newspaper, *The Post-Courant*. That miniature train car that he sometimes played with. He had hated his father, and now, possibly, his own wife.

Jack wracked his brain. Truman had bested him years ago as a teenage kid.

But Jack had fought back. Beaten Truman first in cards and then by infiltrating his house.

Now there was one last battle between them.

"You remind me of someone," Truman had once said to him. "My brother."

What had his brother's name been? Elijah? Elliot?

ELIAS. It was too many letters. Jack ran his fingers over the rim of the safe. He blew out his breath in frustration.

He had paid half of his life as a debt for stolen art that meant nothing to him. The only art that had ever moved him at all was the stained-glass window at his home parish. He'd thought of it often, and it had taken on new significance to him over the years. The Return of the Prodigal Son. The son who left and came home again.

The son.

He imagined standing next to Truman in the Billiards room. Looking at the photograph on the wall.

THE ROWS, it was called. An art school, for his mother.

R-O-W-S, Jack tried.

The lock didn't budge.

He swallowed. Closed his eyes. The clock was a faint ticking.

A play on words, Truman had said. On his mother's name.

R-O-S-E, he tried.

And he heard a distinct click.

He broke out into a sweat.

Pulled the lever.

And it opened.

CHAPTER THIRTY-SIX

J ack stepped inside the vault. It was a small room, roughly the size of Truman's formal closet, made entirely of stone.

One wall was covered with walnut cabinets. Jack began to open the drawers one by one. He quickly took stock of what he was seeing: velvet pouches of diamonds. Gold bars. Bank bonds.

He opened the closets, looking for the mob's incriminating files. But even more than that, he was looking for the painting. Growing more and more convinced that it was somewhere nearby. He parted a collection of rare fur coats, concealing another filing cabinet. He bent to look inside.

The drawers were full of statements. Insurance payments. Records of sale. Blueprints for the house. Invoices. Jack skimmed through them quickly, his heart pounding in his ears. Nothing stood out to him. Nothing seemed overtly damning. His heart sank. If only he had more time, he could probably make some sort of sense out of it.

The files were organized by date, and he forced himself to go back through and look at anything from around the time of the Bastion murders. There wasn't anything of interest prior to then. But he paused over an invoice from Massachusetts General Hospital.

"Paid in full," it said at the top. The patient treated was Truman Reginald Byrd. Jack looked at the date listed. Truman had been hospitalized as an inpatient during several days of Jack and Leo's trial.

But Truman had always said that the reason for missing the trial of the decade was that he was busy traveling and overseeing the management of his paper. Jack narrowed his eyes. Why would Byrd lie about that?

He turned around in the vault, looking at it from every angle. Hoping to see some additional crack that would suggest more hidden doors.

But there were no more birds or puzzles that he could see. He fought back the feeling of desperation in his throat. Would the mob come for him, now that he'd failed to find those files for Virgil? They might, if they found out who had saved Truman from their bullet.

Maybe he was only meant to have come here for Cora all along. To redeem some part of himself that he thought had been buried with Leo in the Bay. Could he leave now and finally move on? Had he done what he came for? Even if it wasn't what he was expecting, or what he had even thought he wanted?

He put his hand on the doorknob, knowing that he had found the edge of the road, and it was a dead end.

✻　　✻　　✻

"I'd like to begin this last soirée with a toast!" Truman said. "To all of you."

Mabel ate her olive. It had been soaked in vinegar. Truman looked older to her. Flabbier. More tired. His white vest strained at his belly. Mabel remembered the day they had married, back when things were simpler and wilder. She had worn a white camellia in her hair, and she never in a million years would have imagined that this was how her marriage would end.

Mabel gave the slightest nod to the newspaperman on her right.

Slowly, he reached into his bag for his camera. The others were like echoes, unfolding less than seconds behind.

Truman raised his glass in the air. "And to my wife," he said.

Mabel came to stand next to him, and felt him almost imperceptibly stiffen. After all that she had done for him, and after all the years he had humiliated her. Every time he put Clementine on the front page of his newspaper, that shrew Trudy would purposefully bring out a copy while they were out having brunch, open it wide to read while sipping her café au lait and pretend that she wasn't watching for Mabel's reaction. Mabel never gave her the satisfaction. Twenty years ago, she would have lacerated her with a devastatingly placed barb. Now she was cool and opaque, a one-way mirror glass.

Truman must have sensed something hiding behind her smile this time. The corners of his mouth tightened. He gripped his glass, but kept the look of fake pleasure plastered on his face. He knew her well enough to know that something was coming.

And she knew him well enough to understand just where to twist the knife.

She relished it all.

"We'll end the evening with dessert and port on the esplanade under a sky full of—"

She saw the moment he noticed, too late, that one of Mabel's newspapermen was brandishing a camera. For the first time, he tripped over his words.

Mabel took a step closer to Truman.

"What is this, Mabel?" he asked her through gritted teeth.

She drew out a sheet of photographs with a flourish.

She smiled broadly, her deep-red lips showing teeth.

"Excuse me, everyone," Mabel said, cutting him off. "I have a present for Truman. It's a surprise. I'm so glad you will all be here to witness it."

"What are you doing?" he asked. He looked desperately around the room for Winston. For Rutherford. For anyone who could possibly come to his aid.

"A parting gift," she said, handing the sheet of photographs to Truman. "The first look at tomorrow's news. You're seeing it before anyone else does." She smiled wickedly. "I know how much you love that."

The blood drained from his face.

He flinched at the first flash of a bulb.

It captured the look on Truman's face as Mabel asked coolly, and one final time, for a divorce.

*　　*　　*

Cora entered the room just as a smattering of flashbulbs went off.

She raised her hand to shield her eyes from the brightness. Some of the starlets had gasped in surprise. Daisy was standing frozen in place, as though she didn't know what to do. Everyone else was watching the spectacle, either in delight or horror. Ronald Rutherford moved toward Mabel, grabbing her by the arm to usher her out.

"Time to go, Mabel," he said.

Clementine's face was pale. She stood back, clutching Kitty. She had just the right look of concern, of curiosity. As if she couldn't possibly imagine what was pictured on that contact paper.

Dallas Winston picked up the telephone to call for backup. And at that moment, Jack slipped into the Assembly Room.

Her heart leaped at the sight of him.

She would still get a chance to tell him goodbye. To find out if he'd discovered something in the vault. She could hardly believe that a mere handful of days ago, she had surprised him by coming through the secret passageway. Certain that he had come to steal something, when she caught him standing in front of those four paintings.

The four paintings.

Cora turned.

"You're being escorted out of here," Dallas Winston was saying to the nearest newspaperman. "And you'll leave all your film behind."

"I'm afraid that's not how the free press works," the newspaperman said.

Mabel was standing just beneath the looming portrait of Truman, looking pleased at what she had unleashed. Her face was flushed. She lit a cigarette. She was enjoying her victory.

"Stop them," Truman thundered. "Do not let them leave the grounds. Escort them upstairs to my office. Now."

Cora watched him still trying desperately to regain control. The man was almost unrecognizable, compared to the portrait of him on the wall. The one painted by Celeste Lourd. It was embarrassing now, how different he looked in the flesh. Sweating and purple. Straining. Veins bulging at his temples.

Her eyes sought out the pattern almost without thinking about it.

Blake, Jack had told her that night. *Yeats. Lourd. Degas.*

Four paintings.

Her heart began to thud dull and heavy in her chest. It didn't fit the pattern.

Almost. But not quite.

She moved as if through water, watching as Dallas Winston and the other guards began to wrestle the rival newspapermen toward the door. She had seen for herself how many people Truman kept in his pocket, managing every story the way he wanted it to be told. His network of newspapers, magazines, media; the police down the Hill. Who knew how vast his web was, or how far it reached now?

The only people who had no loyalty to him, who were for certain not in his pocket, were the rival newspapermen that Mabel had brought in.

And Cora suddenly knew what she had to do.

She walked toward Byrd's portrait while everyone else was watching the struggle with the newspapermen. She waited until she was right beneath it—the painting that didn't fit in the pattern. She took a deep breath, summoning her courage. And then with one sharp movement, she knocked the massive frame from the wall.

It fell with a crash that made the rest of the room jump. Kitty let out a small shriek. For a moment, the struggle stopped as everyone turned to look at her.

Cora didn't want to know what would happen if her hunch was wrong.

"What the hell is going on?" Truman shouted.

Daisy rushed over to help Cora as she struggled to right the painting.

She was the only one who saw the flash of the pocketknife in Cora's hand.

"We need more security in here!" Truman boomed. "Now!"

"Can you help me?" Cora asked. She gave Daisy a meaningful look.

Daisy met her eyes. She held the frame steady, shielding Cora with her body. It was enough for Cora to strip off the back corner of the portrait.

Her fingers were shaking as she peeled it back.

For a moment, she thought she had made a mistake. Her heart sank.

But then she looked closer and saw something dark and shadowy, hiding in a layer beneath.

The guards were striding toward her. She used the knife as leverage to pop off the heavy, gilded frame. The guards were almost to her now.

"What is this?" she cried. "There's something hidden here."

She stepped back to see the rest of the room staring, aghast, at her. At the portrait of Byrd that was sliding forward, like the skin of a peeled fruit, to reveal something else secreted behind it.

Another painting.

She was counting on someone there to recognize it.

The guards reached her at the moment when she knew someone had. A glass suddenly dropped and shattered.

She closed her eyes.

"That's a Rembrandt!" Governor Gilham cried.

"Is that—?"

"The missing—*stolen*—"

"The Bastion—"

The bulbs turned toward Cora, and she shielded her face as they started flashing. The guards seized her and pulled her away, wrenching her arms behind her back.

She looked over at Jack. His face was stunned as he looked back at her, his eyes burning with every possible emotion.

Governor Gilham strode toward Truman. "What is the meaning of this?" he barked.

"I have no idea where that came from," Truman said. He was gripping his glass, stuttering to get the words out. "I've never seen that before in my life."

Mabel stood next to him. Her face, Cora noticed, had gone deathly white.

"I'll get the police here," Dallas said, making a move toward the telephone.

"That's not necessary," Truman said, stopping him. "This is all a prank, some practical joke of some kind. A different sort of assassination attempt, just on my character—"

Dallas hesitated. But Truman watched as Jack parted the crowd and moved to the panel in the wall with the secret telephone. He raised the receiver to his ear.

"Hello?" he said, his eyes meeting Truman's. "I'd like to report a robbery here at Byrd Castle."

Jack watched as the newspaper cameras turned to find a new source, the bulbs beginning to flash again in a cacophony. They lit up Truman's face like the fireworks that had just started to explode in bursts of color and sound outside.

Jack was too busy watching Truman to notice the man who had slipped in through the doorway. The way that Cora suddenly froze, turning toward him in sheer panic.

When Jack finally looked up, he locked eyes with a policeman dressed in uniform. Former Pelican Island Head Guard Patrick McCavanagh, number 2667.

The fireworks outside went *boom*.

CHAPTER THIRTY-SEVEN

I t took Cora's father less than half a glance to recognize the man who had ripped a hole through the seams of his life.

Jack hung up the telephone. He tightened, taking a step backward, as if the shadows could hide him.

Cora shook free from the guards holding her and made her way through the crowd toward her father. He was staring in shock at Jack.

"Da—" she said.

Cora's father looked at her, his face flooding with a thousand different emotions. "You know who that is," he said quietly. "Don't you?"

Of course it would always come down to this. The two of them, with Cora standing in between. Jack hadn't moved since he first locked eyes with her father. He wasn't running away. He was looking at them both, straight on, head held high. She watched him touch his pocket, concealing the pearl handle of the gun she had given to him.

The gun her father had given to her.

"Get out of the way, Cora," her father said. He made a meaningful gesture toward his own gun.

Jack's mouth twitched. He couldn't escape this time. She could see the realization on his face. He clenched his jaw, resignation dimming in his eyes.

It was like watching him die.

She wondered if this was what Leo had felt when he had reached down and picked up the rock.

"Wait," she said. "Da. Please."

She could see it written on his face in that moment. A flash of confusion. And then all the worst fears he'd ever had about her, confirmed.

Cora tried to keep herself in front of Jack, but he stepped out from behind her. Made a motion to shelter her instead.

Cora's father shook his head in disbelief. "I grew concerned when I didn't hear back from you," he said. "Thought you were caught up in something dangerous here. So I paid a visit to my friend Johnny down at the station, trying to decide if I should come up here and check on you."

His eyes settled on her, the disappointment in them searing. "I can tell you that this is the very last thing I expected to find."

The security guards were flooding into the room, cordoning people off. Surrounding the painting. The tension in the room was palpable, and even thicker between Cora, her father, and Jack. They stared one another down, hardly breathing.

One of the security guards came up behind them.

"Patrick McCavanagh? Is that you?" he asked. "What are you doing here?"

Cora's da didn't take his eyes off Jack.

"Serving as backup," he said.

The guard looked between them, sensing the strain.

"Everything good here, Patrick?" he asked. His hand came to rest on his gun.

Cora's father licked his lips. For a moment, Cora didn't know what he was going to do.

She held her breath, watching the pulse quicken in Jack's neck.

"Just accompanying Miss Duluth here for questioning," Cora's father finally said.

"All right," the other guard said uncertainly. Cora's father waited until he had moved on before taking a menacing step toward Jack.

"Listen very carefully," he said in a low, gritty voice. "You don't exist. You died. And if you don't want that to become your reality, I better never see you again."

Cora flinched at the animosity in his voice. The look of revulsion on his face. It didn't change when he turned to look at her.

"Sir—" Jack said, taking a protective step toward Cora. "I—"

"Go." She said it curtly and turned away from him. To make sure that he did, before her father had a chance to change his mind.

Jack hesitated, searching her face.

"Go," she repeated softly.

She felt her father stiffen beside her at the intimacy of her tone.

Jack clenched his jaw. He ducked his head into a terse acknowledgment to former Head Guard McCavanagh, then melted into the crowd as the police began to swarm Enchanted Hill.

"Da—" Cora said, but her father cut her off.

"I don't know what you've gotten caught up in here," he said, stepping forward to block her from Truman's line of sight. He brandished his weapon subtly as a warning, until Truman looked away. "But just get through this mess tonight and we'll talk in the morning."

Her heart rose tentatively at his use of the word "we."

But she noticed that even so, he never quite looked at her.

CHAPTER THIRTY-EIGHT

MARCH 21, 1915

"I have an idea," Mabel said.

She held a piece of meat to Truman's face where the Bastion guards had taken their boots and batons to him, and Mabel's eyes were lit with a look Truman recognized. The one she often had right before she suggested something outlandish. Like the time they hit every bar on the strip, and Truman dropped down on one knee and proposed to guarantee them a round of free drinks at each one.

"I'll go back and find that guard who copped a feel again," she said. "Wear the same red dress." She would bat her eyelashes. Say that she had given it some thought and had changed her mind. Would he show her parts of the museum after hours? A private place where they could be alone?

"Only I'll carry a rope and a pair of razors in my handbag," she said, as she found a tender spot on Truman's temple and he winced.

"And the two of you will be watching," she said, examining the bruises forming on Truman's face. "So you can slip in after me."

"The two of us?"

Ronald Rutherford leaned forward, playing with a Swiss army knife. Swinging it open and shut. Narrowing his eyes at her. "That's quite an assumption, Mabel."

"You'll knock out the guards, tie them up, and use the razors to cut out a few paintings. Do you know how much even one of those is worth?"

She had knelt down, cupped Truman's face in her hands. "No more free days at the museums," she'd said, looking him in the eyes. "Instead of begging for invitations, we'll have to start turning them down."

And then she'd twisted the knife enough that he'd rather die than pull it out again. "We'll have the life we always wanted. And you'll never have to crawl back to your father," she said. "Not ever again."

Truman had felt the cold, wet meat on the raw places of his face. It was the most insane and the most desperate scheme Mabel had ever had. But what else did he have to lose? And if it worked—he could pay back the entire loan. With interest, even. He leaned forward, the pain in his face receding a little. Perhaps at one time he had believed that integrity and dignity were things that went hand in hand.

But the older and more desperate he got, the more willing he was to trade in one for a chance at the other.

Rutherford chuffed and stood, tucking his knife in his pocket. "She's kidding, right?"

But Truman knew Mabel. He felt a bitter surge of vengeance rise up like acid. A chance to avenge himself against that little bastard guard and his father, all in one go.

"She's not," he said. "You in? What could you do with three hundred thousand dollars, Rutherford?"

Only the problem was, things had gone wrong when they decided to infiltrate the Bastion. They went sideways. And maybe so had he.

CHAPTER THIRTY-NINE

SUNDAY, MAY 4, 1930
~ Day Eight ~

Cora's father had barely said a word to her all morning.

But at least he was there, idling in the parking lot of the police station, waiting for her when she emerged into the foggy morning after a night of questioning.

She shielded her eyes from the weak sun and gave him a small wave. He didn't acknowledge it.

"Where are you headed?" he asked roughly when she climbed into the front seat next to him. He stared straight ahead.

She faltered. Wondering if she had enough courage to ask if she could stay with him.

"I was thinking I'd set up my business," she said carefully. "I don't think I'll be seeing the rest of Mabel's payout, but even so, what she gave me is enough to get me started. . . ."

She trailed off as he turned right at the intersection and began to drive toward the train station. The opposite way to his home in Bitterlake.

She swallowed, disappointment sinking in. But he was there, wasn't he? He cared enough about her to stay and make sure she was all right. But something had changed between them. He was, without saying it in so many words, rescinding his offer for her to come live with him. She stared at the purse in her hands, loaded with Mabel's cash. Or maybe she hadn't been clear enough? Maybe he didn't understand that she had been thinking of coming to Bitterlake with him?

She watched the police station recede in the rearview mirror, growing smaller and smaller. Cora pulled out her cigarette case, wondering if she should say something. She offered her father a cigarette, and reluctantly he took it.

"Did you tell them about Jack Yates?" her father finally asked.

Cora cleared her throat. "No," she said lightly. It had been tricky work, making sure she didn't mention Everett Conner's involvement at all. She lit her own cigarette.

"You knew it was him. For how long?"

Cora took a drag, letting the paper catch and flicker. She didn't answer.

Her father had been so proud once, standing at attention in his gray Pelican uniform. She remembered her mother tying his crimson tie. Polishing the badge on his hat. How much he had wanted someday to be Warden.

"I let him go," her father said, as if he still couldn't believe it. "When I could have had him captured. I could have told the police everything. Redeemed myself."

She exhaled smoke from her cigarette. Hardly breathing. "Why didn't you?"

"Because you were caught up in all this somehow," he said. For the first time, he cut her a glance. "Weren't you?"

She swallowed hard. Her heart beat fiercely in her chest. She saw herself standing on the Brooklyn Bridge, getting ready to throw her dog tag in the water. She saw Bobby looking at her. Asking her for her darkest secret. She reached into her pocket and, as her fingers closed around her worry stone, she thought of her mother, standing alone on her island of grace.

She pictured Jack in his suit, walking toward her with a smirk on his face, a drink in his hand.

Redemption isn't possible without the truth, Jack had told her.

What she wanted now, more than anything else, was to finally be free.

"I was the one who helped him escape," she said. "When I was a girl."

Her father's neck flushed red. His hands gripped the steering wheel. As if he wanted to break it.

"I'm sorry, Da. I'm so sorry. I've wanted to tell you for years."

Would she go back and change things if she could? For so long, the answer would have been an instant yes. Now she didn't know.

Her father's mouth tightened in a line. "Those boys killed someone that night."

"I know," she said quietly.

"Rusty. My friend."

"I've lived with the guilt of that for years."

"And I let that bastard go."

"It was more complicated than that, Da, I promise. It always has been."

"No, Cora. Not to me."

He pulled into the train station. She turned to him, feeling the tightness in her chest threatening. "Da—" she said.

He reached toward her and for a split second, she thought he was going to embrace her. To tell her that he still loved her, no matter what. That he forgave her.

Instead, he reached across her and opened her door.

She waited there in the in-between. Wanting to find the right words. Wanting to give him time to change his mind.

He stared straight ahead as if she were already gone. As if she had already been gone to him for years. Perhaps not saying a word to the police about Jack was the most he could do for her.

It all hurt so much, she could hardly breathe.

She climbed out of the car and retrieved her trunk. By the time she turned back and opened her mouth, he was already reversing. She stood in the shadow of the train station, feeling her heart fissure like lightning as he drove away without another word.

*　　*　　*

Clementine smoked a cigarette while she pored over the morning papers from a room in the San Luis Obispo motel. She had sent Rita out to buy them all that morning, her face shielded with a pair of Clementine's oversized sunglasses. The papers were scattered in sections over the rumpled sheets. Clementine hadn't bothered to take off the makeup from last night's party. She picked her way to the bathroom, examining her skin under the garish light. Her face was puffy, shadows gathering beneath her eyes. The curtains were drawn, and cigarette butts littered the motel-room ashtrays. The bathroom smelled faintly of mold. Last night, she had wanted to drink an entire bottle of Contratto to numb the shock.

She had picked up the telephone to call for room service. But at the last moment, she had remembered that outside of the Hill, alcohol wasn't supposed to exist. Slowly, she had set the telephone back down.

She was supposed to have woken up in the Astral Bedroom that morning with a clear path to becoming the next Mrs. Byrd. After the scandalous photos ran, Truman's presidential dreams would be dashed, and Mabel would be a strangling cord finally cut free for good. Clementine had planned to give Truman a few days to mend his ruffled feathers and then propose that they go skiing at a chalet in Switzerland, or perhaps ride on a gondola in Venice. She had wanted to visit art museums and operas and taste gelato. Send frivolous postcards to Rita and Kitty, and maybe even her mother. Buy gowns of Italian silk and exchange cheek kisses with the king of Italy's wife.

Instead, Truman's contorted face looked at her from the front page. In the last shot, his expression was so hateful that he looked nothing short of a monster. Clementine shuddered.

She pictured Truman in bed next to her, laughing at the way he'd persuaded the prime minister to dress up like a clown at last year's costume party. Feeding Clem's dog out of the palm of his hand. Crying at a private screening of *Children of Eve*.

Rita rolled over in the bed. "What are you going to do now?" she asked softly.

Last night, Clementine had gathered her things in a dazed panic while two policemen looked on. Stuffed her old life in a bag as if it were something that had died. Her jewels. Her gowns. She touched them now, running her fingertips over them like shells she had collected from a short, shimmering afternoon at the beach.

"You can come stay with me," Rita offered. "Until you get your feet back under you."

"Thanks," Clementine said. She opened the curtains and winced at the sunlight, looking out at the mirror of the sea, her sightline now almost equal to it. Her coffee cup sat full on the side table. It tasted burned compared to what Ella would have brought her.

She went into the bathroom and closed the door behind her. She took out all of her makeup and surveyed it. Clem slowly and carefully selected each piece, covering each flaw, taking her time. She wondered if her association with Truman had brought her so high to the sun that her wings had melted, and now she would be untouchable. She would let the dust settle; and then, in a few weeks' time, she would summon her courage and ring Berty to find out.

In the mirror she saw a girl, lying in the grass with mud caked beneath her fingernails. Making herself a bracelet out of violets.

Clem brought a trembling cigarette to her mouth. "Rita?" she called through the door. "Do you have a telephone number for Beau Remington?"

She put on her perfume.

$$*\quad*\quad*$$

Cora walked into the train station, her chest tight. She stood in front of the departures board for a long time, looking at the list of destinations. She wiped the silent tears that snaked down her face until they were done falling. Then she bought a one-way ticket to New York City.

As she turned, she saw Daisy, sitting on a bench, her worn trunk at her feet.

"Daisy!" Cora called. She crossed the platform and slid into the seat next to her, grateful for the chance to say goodbye. "Where are you off to?"

Daisy squinted up at the board. "Going home to Bismarck. I'll stay with Anette for a while and see if I can get a job at the Biltmore." Cora nodded, feeling a fresh stab of guilt. Because of what she had done, Daisy and a lot of other hardworking people were out of a job.

"I'm sorry," she said. There was always collateral damage when she got involved, and it seemed to hit the people she loved the most.

"Macready said she'd put in a word for me," Daisy said. She nudged Cora's foot with her boot. "What about you?"

Cora cleared her throat. "I was hoping to go home with my father. But we don't see eye to eye about some things. So . . . I guess I'll go back to New York."

That dream of returning to New York City triumphantly with Mabel's money in her pocket had been like a glittering jewel that, now in her hand, looked dull and deadened. No one would be waiting for her there when she stepped off the train. Maybe she would call Theresa and see if she wanted to have dinner. Or maybe she'd start all over. Become a brand-new person. Again.

Cora asked Daisy to watch her trunk while she went to the lavatories. Then she hid a wad of Mabel's cash in her jacks bag. She scribbled something on a piece of paper and stuck it inside, cinching the purse strings tight.

For Anette and baby Esther, the note said.

When the train whistle rang, she hugged Daisy tight, smelling her familiar smell.

"My real name," she whispered, slipping the jacks bag into Daisy's purse, "is Cora."

CHAPTER FORTY

SATURDAY, MAY 24, 1930
Cambridge, Massachusetts

At a corner market on the way to Mount Auburn cemetery, Jack Yates stopped to examine the buckets of flowers. He bent casually to pick out a bouquet of Alba Maxima roses, knowing everything that their white petals symbolized: innocence; remembrance; and new beginnings.

He paid for the bouquet and walked down the cracked sidewalk toward the cemetery. The day was warm and mild with wisps of clouds, and he pushed through the rusted front gate, eyeing the vines of ivy that were creeping up along the stone walls. He inhaled the scent of green grass and freshly tilled earth, and wound through the grave markers until he came to a stop by a large pond flanked with weeping willows and a majestic white granite colonnade.

He was on his way to his own memorial service.

New commemorative plaques and headstones for Jack and Leo were being dedicated near the gravesite where their father had once been laid to rest. Jack stayed at the far edges of the cemetery, keeping his distance from the crowd of black-clad mourners—a mix of friends and family, reporters, and a large congregation of curious onlookers. As he passed by fifty yards away, they sang a hymn led by a priest dressed in a white alb.

He was letting them bury him.

He had waited anxiously for the papers to come out in the days after the Byrd scandal, scouring them for any mention of himself or his alias. He had caught the first train out of San Luis Obispo, praying he could get as far east as possible before the news of his survival broke. He sat in the express train's first-class compartment, dressed in a sharp day suit, surrounded by damask. The train had hurtled through the Sierra Nevada tunnels like a bullet passing through a chamber.

He had ordered a cup of coffee. And a second one. Full of sugar, just the way Leo would have liked it. He left it on the glass-topped table, as if Leo could walk through the door at any moment. Lift it to his lips and cheers.

Jack had closed his eyes, tilting his head back.

And then he waited for the explosion that never came.

In fact, the rival papers had never discovered his existence. They had been too busy turning on Truman. They ran photographs of the Yates boys as children. The storyline became much more sympathetic, a tale of two brothers who had been wrongfully convicted only to commit a crime when they were trying to get back their freedom. They had paid the price for it by drowning. It was an angle that the rival papers were leaning in to—so many deaths that never would have happened if the brothers hadn't been framed in the first place. The story was lurid and fantastical, stirring up public resentment just before Truman's trial.

And even more importantly, it meant that neither Cora—nor her father—had talked. They had protected him by deciding to keep his secret.

He shifted in the shadows of the cemetery. Someone had mounted a bright wreath in the colors of red, white, and blue beside Leo's plaque. Their mother was there, standing at the graves. Her eyes were red-rimmed, and she clutched a handkerchief below her nose. He had sent her a letter days ago so that she would finally know for sure that he was still alive, but that Leo was gone. And that he would never be Jack Yates again.

He waited to approach the gravesite until the crowd dissipated and only a few errant programs from the service lay strewn in the grass. Jack waited until he was completely alone before he came to stand in front of the headstone plaques, still clutching the bouquet of white roses.

JACK TURNER YATES.
LEONARD RORY YATES.

He closed his eyes. He remembered pulling himself from the purpleblack Bay without Leo. Aching, he had lain in the cold sand for a moment. He hadn't seen Leo go under, but he had swum back with the last of his strength to try to find him. Then finally he had retched into the sand, turned, and let out a silent scream toward the heavens.

Free at least, but at the cost of his brother.

He bent to place the roses on Leo's grave. And then he left one for himself. The boy he used to be.

A dragonfly sailed past and snagged his attention, its translucent wings like stained glass. It made a thwicking sound and landed on a large bouquet of black-eyed Susans someone had left on Leo's grave.

He bent to look at the card.

It was signed from Ella Duluth.

Jack smiled, shaking his head. He palmed the card and left the cemetery, hailed a cab to Dorchester, and ate dinner at a dingy restaurant that he remembered. He ordered lasagna and garlic bread dripping with butter that was as good as anything he'd had at Byrd Castle. Then he paid the bill and walked by memory down the old familiar streets of his childhood. He saw the place where he once had fallen from a tree. Where Leo had kissed Suzy Donnelly and dreamed of being a violinist. Jack followed the split sidewalks of his neighborhood with dusk setting and climbed the creaking wooden stairs of his mother's front porch, feeling the soft rot of the boards give beneath his feet.

He was starting to shake. It surprised him, how nervous he felt.

He had left all those years ago, so young—a completely different boy, just out for any other night with his brother. But he never came back.

His mother's voice was muffled through the wooden door. He could smell the grease of her hash fry left over from dinner, as if he were just coming home from an hour at the park.

All along, he had thought Leo would be there, tall and lanky, standing next to him.

He knocked and heard the radio inside being turned down. He pictured lying awake in Cell Block D on Pelican Island, staring at the cement ceiling with his elbow crooked under his head, still practically a kid himself. Cora must have been sleeping just down the hill in the guardhouses, with the fog horns sounding and the boats slipping soundlessly past. He had dreamed of this moment a thousand times, the vision of it as smooth and worn as the banister beneath his palm. A prayer he had planted while the locusts still swarmed and all he could see was a barren rock.

He hadn't known yet what things came out of the dark and secret places. That flowers could take root on a desolate island, while rot spread through a gilded mansion above the sea.

The patter of his mother's footsteps approached.

"Jack?" he heard her whisper tentatively on the other side of the door. As if she could sense him, had always sensed him, as he made his way back to her.

Jack's heart climbed into his throat, and the moment stretched out, piercing him forever. It hurt more than he'd expected. It felt better than he'd ever imagined it would.

His heart swelled with love.

He steadied himself and looked up as the final lock turned.

* * *

Cora stood in front of the door to her small rented office with a newspaper tucked beneath her elbow.

She jiggled the lock. She still couldn't believe it was hers. The office was barely larger than a closet. It still smelled like fresh paint. And the mail slot was overflowing.

Cora stepped inside and flicked on the lights. She had paid for the office and a telephone line using the cash that Mabel had handed her in the car. It was only half of what Mabel had promised her, but Cora didn't expect to ever see the rest of it. And that was all right.

She had officially adopted Ella Duluth as her alias, and her profile had skyrocketed. She'd given interviews to the reporters who wanted to know how she'd figured out the painting was there. She gave them the same story she'd fed the police, and told them she was just getting started. If they wanted more, they could publicize her name and burgeoning business career, but absolutely no photographs that showed her face—or she would never give them another scoop or interview again.

She poured herself a cup of coffee and drank it black, slipping off her shoes beneath her desk, and began to open her letters. They were in a pile half a palm thick. She couldn't help herself—she quickly scanned the back of each one, looking for male handwriting. Either her father's, or Jack's.

Every day, Cora put on her makeup and did her hair, even when she was just planning to put a kettle on and sit and read a book at her rented apartment. She told herself it wasn't because her heart secretly leaped every time the telephone rang or there was a knock on the door. Her father's silence made it clear where he stood. Her stomach clenched whenever she thought of him.

As for Jack—he had escaped one final time and hadn't looked back. She had kept his identity as secret as her own. He would know how to find her if he wanted to, and she hadn't heard from him.

She swallowed down her disappointment as she made her way through the stack of envelopes and then turned to her notepad.

She spent the next two hours making phone calls, taking down notes for a new job and jotting an address to speak with someone for a lead she was following. When it was time for lunch, she opened the final letter.

It was typed, and postmarked from Massachusetts.

Her heart skipped a beat.

Tucked inside was an article from the *Boston Herald*.

LONG-LOST REMBRANDT FROM INFAMOUS
HEIST RETURNS TO THE BASTION IN
HOMECOMING CEREMONY

The note was unsigned. But there was a date written in the margins, and four words faintly underlined on the newspaper.

Bastion. Yates. Rembrandt. Dolores.

Abruptly, she sat up in her chair.

*   *   *

Florence Abrams climbed from the back seat of the car and shut the door. The bell towers of Byrd Castle rose up before her, and her heart clenched a little more with each step toward them. What would become of it now that her child was the site of an infamous disgrace?

Florence clasped her handbag as she crossed the red tiles she had set into the clay herself. She paused at the esplanade overlooking the ocean, and listened to the wind sing through the palm fronds, carrying the salt of the sea to her. She had come to say goodbye. She watched the zebras grazing. She wondered what would happen to the house, the animals, once the police were finally gone.

She walked through the open-air loggias. The house teemed with special agents from the FBI. Tracking mud onto the floors. Taking down priceless works of art to check behind their frames. They needed her to make sure they had found all of the last secret passageways.

She consulted with them on the blueprints, the catacombs, all the secret areas that she could name. She told them about the codes Truman liked so much, so that they could look for any more hidden places even she didn't know about. And then she climbed the stairs to his office one last time. Accompanied by an agent, she went to his desk and pulled out the one thing he had asked her to get. The train car, flaked with gold paint.

She was standing there, holding it, when she heard a shout.

She walked over to the banister, and watched as they began to dig. Eventually, they raised a large wooden crate that had been buried beneath the aviary.

Florence closed her eyes. *Oh, Truman,* she thought. She knew whatever she was looking at would likely be the nail in his coffin.

They cracked open the crate and found hundreds of damning files. Cover-ups, thefts, murders, and frame-ups by the mob and complicit public servants on half of the east and west coasts.

Apparently, Truman Byrd was just the first domino whose fall was going to bring down many others.

*　　*　　*

Truman woke on a cot that creaked with rust. The mattress was thin and lumpy, as though he were lying on a pile of teeth. The prison tunic felt like burlap, and the lights flickered as the guard came to rouse him for his morning meeting. His defense attorney, Melville Clayton, was waiting in the conference room. Mel was the best that money could buy, and, walking down the hallway toward him, Truman was paying by the footstep.

Mel stood when Truman entered. For a moment, they sized each other up.

"Coffee?" Mel asked. Truman nodded, and Mel arranged for it to be brought. Then he settled back into his seat and templed his fingers.

"This conversation is off the record, of course," Truman's attorney said, his voice brimming with assurance. "No one here but us. So I'd like you to tell me the whole truth, Truman. What is the story with the Bastion?"

Truman inhaled deeply and sat back in his chair. "There's nothing to tell," he insisted. He took a sip of sludgy coffee. "I'm being framed."

Mel raised an expensive eyebrow.

Truman still remembered the way he and Ronald had sweated beneath their masks, a bit of whiskey on their breaths for added courage. And even more than a decade later, Truman still relished the look of surprise that had flashed across the Bastion guard's face when they sneaked up behind him and Mabel.

"Remember me?" Truman had whispered. And then had cracked him over the head with a crowbar.

"You can trust me, Truman," Melville said now. He leaned forward, the wire frames of his eyeglasses catching the light. "Or at least, trust in the fortune you're paying me."

But there was no one Truman trusted anymore, save for possibly his old friend Ronald Rutherford. Mabel had been the one to make the introduction to the black market, by way of a close cousin she had grown up with in Brooklyn. Ronald had done the meeting and brought the goods. And Truman had spun the tale in his paper.

Except he had kept one thing for himself.

Truman had handed Mabel the razor and pointed to the *Lazarus* that night. "I want that one," he said. "For me." And Mabel had planted a kiss on his lips and gotten it for him.

But the guard Ronald was tying up hadn't been completely subdued.

Without warning, he grabbed Truman's knife and caught him in the side with it. Truman had cried out. Felt the warmth of the blood as it began seeping through his clothes. There'd been a brief struggle. And then he heard the sick puncture sound Ronald's razor had made when it met flesh.

The guard had lain, choking in his own blood, while they came up with a new plan in a matter of ten terrifying minutes. It had been thin as spider silk, and just as strong. It was a miracle that it had held past that night.

They had decided to dispatch the other guard to keep him quiet. It had been unfortunate but necessary. And then, while he and Ronald sneaked out the back with the paintings, Mabel had waited in the shadows until she saw two men outside. When they were close enough to hear her, she started screaming. She had always been a master of tricking men into doing what she wanted, using herself as bait.

And then she had set the hook.

"Truman?" Melville prodded.

No one had ever guessed how a fledgling, maudlin tabloid had gotten such an inside scoop. The infamy of that story was the match that launched Truman's publishing empire. Mabel's cousin had vouched for her, and

Ronald had sold four of the five paintings for almost a million dollars to black-market buyers. And along the way, Truman swayed public opinion of guilt toward the Yates brothers.

But he'd kept the *Lazarus* for himself.

He'd waited to seek treatment for the wound in his side until enough time had passed that no one would draw any connection to the robbery. In the meantime, the wound festered, and he ended up in the hospital with an infection the week the trial commenced. He'd had to send Mabel to cover the trial in his stead.

Now Truman pulled the tunic away from his neck. He itched to edit the stories about himself with his own pen.

Everything irritated him. He hadn't heard a word from Clementine since his arrest. Or any of the many guests he'd hosted with extravagant generosity over the years.

In fact, the only letter he had received was from the nurse he'd paid off in Illinois to take care of his father.

She had sent word that his father had died peacefully, and just as the man had wanted: listening to Haydn quartets, talking about the young son he had once lost, with the nurse holding his dry, papery hand.

He had never once told Truman that he was proud of him.

Truman took out the train car from his pocket. He ran his fingers over the old peeling paint.

"You're going to get me out of here," Truman told his lawyer. It was an order. "Whatever it takes."

"I will," Melville assured him.

But Truman had seen that look before. He had been that man himself, too many times. The cool assurance that was merely a mask for detached indifference.

And for the first time, he felt fear. He cradled the train car in his hands. There had always been a way out; and if there wasn't, he made one.

He couldn't accept what would happen to him if the trial didn't go his way. That after everything he had built, his own end would come without fanfare or comfort; without deference to his will or all of his careful orchestrations.

He would die worse off than his father had.

Alone, wings clipped. In a cage.

CHAPTER FORTY-ONE

FRIDAY, JUNE 13, 1930
Boston, Massachusetts

Cora stood in front of the stone mansion façade of the Dolores Bastion museum. Banners unfurled in the wind, heralding the return of the lost Rembrandt. She took a deep breath. She was dressed in a new navy suit that was almost black. She wore white gloves, a cloche hat, and red lipstick in a shade that reminded her of Dina, always staining her lips on the Pelican ferry. Cora clutched a smart purse in her gloved hands and walked confidently in pumps she had purchased with Mabel's money, sidestepping a piece of gum.

The museum inside was cool stone, and her heels echoed across the tile floor. She purchased a ticket and wandered through the small pockets of crowds toward the open-air courtyard. Sunlight filtered from the third-story glass atrium to fall on violet lacecap hydrangea and golden oncidium orchids. She leaned against one of the stonework arches and closed her eyes. She knew hope always played the long game, but she hadn't realized how much it could hurt.

Most of the letters she had written to her father had gone unanswered. She had gotten one card in the mail for her birthday. Short, perfunctory: *Happy birthday*. He didn't use her name—much less her nickname—but at least he had signed it *Da*.

Cora dipped into her pocket for her worry stone out of habit before remembering that it was no longer there. She had posted it in her last letter to him, worn down from years of all her worries and wounds. But this time, she had planted it like a seed—hoping that someday, if she waited long enough, she might open the mailbox and find the hint of something new growing there. She was learning herself how much forgiveness could be a gift. A method of release, in the same way that tears were.

Cora opened her eyes just as Jack stepped out into the mottled sunlight. He wasn't dressed in a hundred-dollar tuxedo, his hands cascading a waterfall of cards as he sipped a martini on Enchanted Hill. He wasn't in the chambray uniform of Pelican, sifting the dirt and pebbles with his calloused fingers. He was all the iterations of himself she had ever known, and yet more. Today he looked relaxed. Handsome. He strolled toward her, hands in his pockets. He had grown a beard in the weeks since she had last seen him.

She could still faintly see the scar he once had gotten from the Gasper.

Her throat closed. She felt a simple, golden joy well up inside her at the sight of him. And she realized why he looked so different.

It was the first time she had ever seen him free.

"Jack," she said.

She smiled at him. Her truest friend, on what often felt like little more than a giant, turning rock.

"In a lot of ways, my story started here," he said quietly. "I came back because I want to rewrite it."

He hesitated. And then he offered her his hand.

She could look back and see how the relationships in her life either broke like a bone or breathed like a pair of lungs. The ones that survived had mirrored the symmetry of blood vessels and tree branches—places of exhale, where failings were breathed in and turned into mercy. Like alchemy, her father might say.

Like a miracle, her mother would say.

Cora followed Jack to the third floor, where they stood side by side in a dimly-lit room in front of the Rembrandt. Like they had unknowingly done so many weeks before.

"I want to rewrite it with you," Cora said. Jack brought her hand to his lips.

She turned to the *Lazarus* and felt a glimpse of what it must have been like to cross back over the threshold; how the world around him must have sung with new life. So she would hold out hope that some stories could be remade, even as the mailbox stayed empty and the locusts swarmed. She had seen for herself what could sometimes still be.

And so she would never stop looking.

ACKNOWLEDGMENTS

Thank you to Greg, James, Cecilia, and Liv. I'm surrounded by so much love and beauty in you, and I'm grateful you're mine.

To Sarah and Kevin Bain, Hannah Bain, Andrew and Angie Bain and family: thank you for your endless love and encouragement—and for always making me laugh like no one else.

To Mark and Barbara Murphy: thank you for loving me so well. My books would not exist without your help and support. (And I would never have known the proper way to describe Moxie.)

Janlyn Murphy: thank you for being such a wonderful sister-in-law to me.

Thank you to the Bains, Goldmans, Nelsons, Shanes, and Westwaters. Beth, thank you for your early read, much encouragement, and for bringing me Donut Bank.

Pete Knapp: I'll never forget you calling me in the Botanical Gardens to tell me this book sold. Thank you for your thoughtful, insightful edits and for always believing in me. I am grateful for the gift that you are in my life.

Laura Schreiber: working with you has been a dream! Thank you for your vision and care for this story and for the ways you helped it to become the best version of itself. You are such a gifted editor.

ACKNOWLEDGMENTS

Kayla Olson: I never would have made it this far without you. We have laughed and cried together on this wild, winding road—I'm so grateful to have someone to walk it with.

April Welch: Thank you for our life-giving conversations and your beautiful presence.

Catherine Bakewell: I'm so grateful for your friendship and kindred spirit.

Thank you to Autumn Krause, Gabby Nickel, Anna Priemaza, Sarah Dill, my NBO crew, Britteny Hess, Jenna Worrell Stewart, Becky Mecredy, Renee Worcester, Jen Wolford and the rest of the RI, Alexandra Nesbeda, Caitlin Dalton, Wendy Huang, Anna Delia, Sarah Hoover, Anne McKim, Addie Peyronnin, Katie Allen Nelson, Tara Goedjen, Kristin Gray, Rebecca Ross, Misa Sugiura, Jennifer Carter, and Chris Iafolla.

An enormous thank you to Stuti Telidevara, Abigail Koons, and the entire team at Park & Fine Literary and Media.

Thank you to the amazing team at Union Square and Co., including Stefanie Chin, Jenny Lu, Phil Gaskill, Lisa Geller, Rich Hazelton, and Jo Obarowski.

Thank you to the book people: librarians and booksellers, the bloggers, Instagrammers, BookTokers, and readers that I have connected with along the way. A special thank you to Emily Hall Schroen and Main Street Books, and my friends at the Novel Neighbor and the SLCPL.

Oh, I want to name you all! Thank you to the special people I have known and loved in Evansville, Indianapolis, West Hartford, Massachusetts, San Francisco, Hong Kong, Tokyo, and Missouri. Thank you for sharing your lives with me.

Thank you to the employees of the Hearst Castle, Alcatraz, and Isabella Stewart Gardner properties who gave my imagination the ability to take flight. Thank you to Jolene Babyak for her book *Eyewitnesses on Alcatraz*, which helped me better understand what it might be like to grow up on Pelican.

Finally, I am thankful for every part of our stories that isn't wasted. I've never known love like this. Isaiah 61:3.

Thank you for reading.